THE FAR SIDE OF THE SEA

The Story of Kino and Manje in the Pimería

A Novel By

Ben Clevenger

Published by

JESUIT FATHERS OF SOUTHERN ARIZONA

TUCSON, ARIZONA

Published by
Jesuit Fathers of Southern Arizona
Tucson, Arizona

ISBN 0-9661562-2-6

Library of Congress
Control Number: 2003108684

Typesetting by Types
Text set in 11 pt. Californian, chapter heads Carlton.
Cover and art by Raymond Harden
Printed in the United States of America

DEDICATION

To my father, Cruce P. Clevenger, a devoted parent and faithful Christian, a man who would have understood Kino's pioneering spirit and would've been, I believe, his biggest fan.

A NOTE TO THE READER:

"Pimería Alta" was the name given by Padre Kino to the lands we now know as northern Sonora and southern Arizona. An area of more than 32,000 square miles, it is bounded on the south by the Río Magdalena, on the east by the San Pedro river, on the north by the Gila River, and on the west by the Gulf of California. Kino chose this term—the Pimería Alta—because these were the homelands of the native Americans known in his day as the Upper Pimas.

In modern times this area is known to those interested in the history of the Southwest as, simply, the Pimería.

ACKNOWLEDGMENTS

Many thanks, first, to Charlie Polzer, S.J., ethnohistorian and Kino scholar, who cheerfully and patiently answered all my questions. To Jorge Olvera, archaeologist and architectural historian, who taught me much through the pages of his delightful book, *Finding Father Kino*, and who kindly shared with me the story of his journey to Alicante on the coast of Spain. To John Kessell, David Laird, Kendra Gaines and all the others who offered valuable advice and encouragement when I needed them most. To Ray Harden, who designed the elegant cover and drew the fine maps and other works of art, and to Sharon Nicks, who in enduring good spirits did the layout work and brought together all the pieces for a book as handsome and readable as any writer could desire.

And extra-special thanks to my wife, Gene, who never wavered in her support.

* * * * *

It is with special sadness that we report the recent death of Jorge Olvera. Dr. Olvera passed away on January 11, 2003, seven weeks shy of his 88th birthday, in Mexico City. A modest man of many talents and interests, Dr. Olvera lived a long life filled with good humor, high adventure, love of family, and extraordinary professional achievement. He is greatly missed by all who knew him.

Most of the small sketches appearing on the opening pages of the Olvera chapters of this work came from scenes and objects imagined by the artist, Ray Harden. There are two exceptions. For Chapter 4, he made the drawing from Frances O'Brien's famous pencil sketch of Father Kino, and for Chapter 50, from photos of the bust of the padre recently done by the noted sculptor, John Sherrill Houser, and cast in bronze at Desert Crucible, Tucson, Arizona.

AUTHOR'S FOREWORD

In 1687 A.D., Eusebio Francisco Kino, a Jesuit missionary, came north on horseback to the borderlands we now call northern Sonora and southern Arizona, in what are now Mexico and the U.S.A. His assignment: spread the gospel to the native peoples—the Pimas and Papagos—and represent the Church and Spanish Crown in matters of faith in this perilous country far out on the "Rim of Christendom." For twenty-four years he did so with astounding vigor, resilience, and charity.

Father Kino introduced the Indians to horses. He taught them cattle ranching. He brought them other domestic livestock and a variety of new crops, including citrus and winter wheat. He exposed them to European culture and showed them more efficient methods of irrigation. He called this land the "Pimería Alta"—Land of the Upper Pimas. Most of this vast area—more than thirty-two thousand square miles of desert thickened by stubby dark mountains and cut by steep canyons and burbling rivers—he explored, sometimes with a few friendly Pimas or Spanish soldiers, but as often alone. In the process, he drew the first accurate maps of this part of the country. He established some twenty-five missions and visitas and brought thousands of Pimas and Papagos—the O'odham, as they are known today—to the Christian faith.

And he did all this in the face of unrelenting attacks by Apaches and constant bureaucratic hassles from the Church hierarchy.

To be sure, there were other notable priests in northern Sonora in those years—Gilg, González, Campos, Aguilar, Iturmendi, Kappus, to name a few—but none so capable and innovative as Kino. None whose vision so influenced the development of these lands.

By some measures, Eusebio Kino was a simple man. He drew no salary from the Church; he had few possessions and seemed to need few. He saw his duties clearly and met them head on. But if he was a simple man, his accomplishments were manifold and sweeping. In his time, in one way or another, he touched the life of virtually every person in the Pimería—through his ministry, his farming and ranching, his extensive travels. Even today he touches us with his spirit. Visit one of his old missions—San Ignacio, Tubutama, Caborca, San Xavier del Bac; many have survived the centuries—and you'll feel his presence. And in the quiet faith of the Mexican people, in the piety of the O'odham, in the innocent play of children in the dusty churchyards, you'll see the results of his labors.

So how does an author tackle a subject like Kino? With trepidation, I assure you. I knew I didn't want to write his story as a historian might. That's already been done by others far more capable than I (try Charles Polzer's *Kino, A Legacy*, or Herbert Bolton's *Rim of Christendom*). No, I needed a different approach. And I soon realized that I couldn't, without help, tell this man's amazing story with the depth and scope it deserved.

Fortunately, I found just the people who could help me: Juan Mateo Manje and Jorge Olvera.

Manje was born in Spain in 1670 and came to Nueva España in 1692 as an alférez, an ensign, in the Spanish Army. He was assigned to a cavalry unit based at San Juan Bautista, a three-day ride from Kino's home mission, Nuestra Señora de los Dolores. When the young officer wasn't chasing Apaches, he often rode as military escort to the padre on his long journeys across the Pimería. Manje came to know Father Kino well and, luckily for us, kept a detailed record of their travels together. Some years later he collected his writings in book form, calling it *Luz de Tierra Incógnita.* Manje's original manuscript ended up in the National Library in Madrid, Spain, but a hand-written copy eventually found its way to the Archivo General in Mexico City. In 1954, Harry Karns, of Nogales, Arizona, published his English translation of *Luz*.

Jorge Olvera, unlike Manje, is a man of our time, a modern archaeologist and historian, the kind of man who thrives on a challenge. And he got one—in 1965, when he became part of a team of scientists charged with finding the burial site of Father Kino. The good priest, it seems, had been misplaced. At least no one knew where his bones lay, and the Mexican government wanted him unearthed so they could build a monument to him. So Olvera left Mexico City for the Sonoran desert. In the months that followed he learned a lot about Kino, hot winds, frontier villages, and desert dirt, and wrote entertainingly of his search for the padre's bones in *Finding Father Kino*, published in 1998.

So I have asked Juan Mateo Manje to tell Kino's story as he lived it at his side. He has graciously agreed (in my mind, anyway) to do so. And we will follow Jorge Olvera as he searches modern Sonora for the lost grave of the famous padre. If I haven't recorded their accounts precisely as they might have dictated them, I pray they'll be generous in their forgiveness.

One final point. The historian Charles Polzer tells me that in the Pimería Father Kino would have used and taught from a Spanish translation of the

Vulgate Bible, itself a translation to Latin. Where I have used quotations from Scripture, I've taken the liberty of using the English-language Bible with the wording that seemed best suited to the circumstances of the scene.

This, then, is the story of Father Eusebio Kino. It is a work of fiction, but one that I have tried to keep as faithful to the relevant facts as possible. Any errors, blunders, or bloopers in the narrative are mine alone; I make no attempt to foist the blame onto my new friends, Manje and Olvera.

Ben Clevenger

Pencil sketch of Padre Kino by Frances O'Brien, 1964.

PROLOGUE

Northern Sonora. Año D. 1693. September.

adre de Dios, I thought, and tried not to vomit.

The bodies lay in muted disarray near the wagon at the bottom of the arroyo, blood everywhere—blood seeping into the sandy grit of the wash, blood smeared grotesquely over the faces of the dead, blood pooled on the pine-planked seat of the still-smoldering lumber wagon like excrement from some hellish demon. A tall alamo, a cottonwood tree, its gnarled roots arcing into the wash, gave meager shade to the dead. Under the baking sun, its leaves seemed as pale and juiceless as the bodies.

"Campesinos," Father Kino whispered. He made the sign of the cross. "Settlers, Ensign Manje," he added. "Very poor. I count four."

The padre and I were sprawled on our bellies in the dirt on a ridge above the wash. Prickly pear and creosote bushes grew in abundance around us. Along the wash, trees and green shrubs I did not know by name formed thickets with small plants the padre had called brittlebush. The desert was strangely quiet. Above us, black vultures circled on currents of furnace-hot air, but I heard no birdcalls, or even the rustle of wind in the trees.

I wiped sweat from my neck. The acrid odor of smoke filled my nostrils even as bile filled my uneasy stomach. "Where are the animals?" I said. "I see only the wagon...and the dead men."

"They would take the mules to eat," Kino whispered. "If there were horses, they would take them, too. Later, they would slice the neck veins of the horses, so the children can drink the blood."

Mother of God, I thought again. I had been in the Pimería only a few months and had met the padre just a week before. We had been scouting near Imuris, looking for fresh grazing lands for cattle he had recently moved to the mission at San Ignacio, when we saw smoke in the distance. We had spurred our mounts, left them in a gully at the foot of the ridge, and crept cautiously up to where we now lay. Two days before, Kino had prefaced our ride with these words: "Sometimes, Ensign Manje, there are unpleasant surprises in the desert. You have to be prepared for them."

Unpleasant surprises. Not exactly the words I would have chosen for the fate of the dead settlers, but they would suffice.

"Come," Kino said softly. "We will go down and see if anyone is still alive." He stared down on the carnage, sweat glistening on his sun-weathered face. "May God bless their humble souls."

Peasants. Hauling timber, probably from the slopes of the Pajaritos, Kino had said. Hoping to sneak their load past the Apaches. Taking it to one of the silver mines near San Juan Bautista, or to the visita at Cabúrica—which the padre affectionately called San Ignacio and seemed to love almost as much as his own mission, Dolores. Trying to earn a few pesos, the loggers, and who could blame them?

But they had not slipped past the Apaches.

Beyond the hills to the east, a column of gray smoke trailed lazily into a sky so intensely blue it looked as if the color had been layered on with a trowel.

"They have stopped to eat the mule meat," Kino said. "They let the world see their smoke. That means they believe they are safe from Spanish troops."

"Do they know we are here?"

"I doubt it," he said.

"Will they come back?"

"Probably not, but anything is possible."

"Why," I asked, "would they have their children drink the blood of horses?"

"They believe it makes the children brave."

"...And does it?"

He shrugged and wiped sweat from his upper lip. "They are surely brave."

In the wash we confirmed the four dead. Two with arrows through their chests, one with an arrow embedded in his neck and another deep in his eye socket. The fourth man lay gutted, his entrails spilled upon the earth, black buzzing insects already working at his curdling blood. As we stood over him, a cob of liver floated up from his belly and slid slowly down the side of his blood-soaked camisa. In hours, I knew, this arroyo would crawl with the stench of death.

A sourness had risen into my throat; nausea. I tasted again the wheat tortillas and hot chiltepine peppers from our small noon meal. I tried to choke them back. This I had vowed: I would not vomit.

Kino found a fifth man beyond a tumble of boulders near the wash. The man had been staked to the ground, spread-eagled, facing the relentless burning sun, his eyelids sliced off so he could not blink. His wrist and ankle tendons had been severed. The shaft of an arrow protruded from his thin chest. Perhaps the Apaches had grown impatient with hunger, Kino told me, and wanted the man dead before they rode out.

"I knew these men," he added grimly. "They have done work for me at the Dolores mission. Good and decent men, all of them."

We knelt in the sand and recited the Pater Noster. While the priest said more prayers, I inspected my flintlock pistols and fought the sickness that tried again to climb up from my stomach.

"Why did they cut the man's tendons, Father?" I asked when he finished his prayers.

Muscles clenched in his jaw. "The Apaches believe that men can come back from the dead to seek revenge. With their tendons severed, the dead can do them little harm."

The dead can do them little harm. I could think of no adequate response to that, so I gave none. We unloaded the burned timber, made what repairs we could to the wagon, and adjusted the harness to our horses. We lifted the bodies of the campesinos into the wagon. When we rested in the shade of a tree at the edge of the wash I polished the blade of my espada, my sword. Kino watched as I worked the brightness of the steel.

"Ensign Manje," he said, "Are you a Christian?"

"Yes, sir."

"So you know the Bible's Book of Isaiah?"

"Some of it."

"I'm thinking of chapter thirty-five, the fourth verse. *'Say to those with fearful hearts, Be strong, do not fear, your God will come, He will come with vengeance, He will come to save you.'* " Kino probed the sand with a twig and drew two lines that formed a small cross. " 'Do not fear,' the Scriptures tell us. Are you afraid, Ensign?"

"No," I said, perhaps a little too quickly.

He stared at me, his blue eyes unblinking. Behind him the hot sky seemed to vibrate with color, like candles flickering behind pale stained glass. At that moment I had a feeling the padre knew every thought in my head.

"Yes, I am afraid, Father," I admitted finally. "But I am not paralyzed by my fear."

He seemed to weigh my words. Then he smiled, the dark skin crinkling at the corners of his eyes. "You will do fine in this country, young man."

We were sharing water from a calabaza, a gourd, when a sound caught our attention—a soft rustling of dry leaves. It came from a stand of willow trees no more than ten varas from where we stood. A cottony dryness filled my mouth and I felt again the stirrings of nausea. I pulled one of my pistols from the red sash around my waist and handed it to Kino; I took the other in my left hand and drew my sword. Sweat ran into my eyes and dripped from my chin. I stood in the torpid heat of the afternoon, my heart thumping in my chest, and studied the trees along the edge of the wash.

To my surprise, a little Indian boy, perhaps a year old, toddled into a clearing. He was playing, plucking at straws of grass, but he froze, wide-eyed, when he saw us. He wore tiny deerskin moccasins and a taparrabo, a loincloth made of undyed cotton.

"Pima?" I whispered. "Ópata?"

"More likely Apache or Jocome," Kino said softly. "The parents are somewhere nearby. They will come for the child. Soon, I think."

They did. The mother, wearing only moccasins and a deerskin skirt, darted into the clearing, grabbed the child, and ran back into the trees.

"There," Kino whispered, motioning toward a tree near the clearing. I saw nothing, but an instant later an Indio stepped into view. He was tall compared to the Pimas and Ópatas I had seen, and solidly built; I guessed him to be about my age. He wore nothing but a loincloth and moccasins that came up and tied under his knees with a leather thong. He had his dark hair pulled back and held in place with a headband made from a black bandanna. Stripes of red and yellow paint emblazoned his face. His eyes reminded me of dark stones, and even as he stood motionless before us he seemed to swagger.

"Jocome," Kino said.

Hair prickled on the backs of my arms. Blood thrummed in my temples and I felt a surge of revulsion and alarm like nothing I had ever experienced. The Indian seemed to me, in that first startling moment, a demon straight from the fires of Hades.

In this desert heat, it was easy enough to believe.

When the horses caught the Indian's scent, they shied, frightened, in their harness. The priest gentled them, then turned back to the Indio. Kino spoke in Spanish, his voice firm, his words short and simple. "You are Black Skull. You are a Jocome. Your wife is Runs-Like-A-Rabbit."

"I am pleased, Santo-Jesus-hay, that you know of me and my wife.

Perhaps that means you know enough to fear us." The Indian's Spanish was surprisingly good. In his left hand he held a bow with an arrow fitted into the string. A knife with a white bone handle hung in a beaded scabbard at his waist.

"You and your warrior friends killed five innocent men here," Kino said. "And tortured one of them. So you have come back to ask God's forgiveness?"

"Your God is nothing, priest. I came back so Ish-kay-nay, my son, could have the pleasure of seeing vultures feed on the flesh of dead mestizos."

The varied song of a mockingbird, muted but insistent, reached us from the trees.

"His wife," the padre whispered. "Telling him she has the child hidden safely away."

I cannot say what I was thinking at that moment; perhaps I was not thinking at all. In my fear and excitement I said this to Black Skull: "Tell your wife her bird imitations are stupid and pitiful."

The warrior's gaze settled back on me. "Tell *your* wife she is a stinking puta, Spaniard."

"I have no wife," I said as calmly as I could. "I am Alférez Juan Mateo Manje of the Compañía Volante, Army of Spain." The long blade of my sword gleamed in the sunlight. "If you surrender now, I will see that no harm comes to you or your family."

"To-dah, Spaniard. Anah-zon-tee. You talk like a crazy man. And who is this Santo-Jesus-hay in the strange black shirt that looks like a woman's dress? Is this the famous Kino who speaks of a Spanish God to the cowardly Pimas? Is he your wet nurse, soldier? You are big and wear a colorful officer's uniform, but I doubt you are yet weaned from your mother's breast."

"Get back, Father," I said to Kino. "Behind the wagon. This is soldier's work now."

"Whatever happens," Kino said, "God is with you, my son. Remember the words of Isaiah. Do not be afraid. God will not abandon you; nor will I."

I have to admit, I could have been a little smarter about it. The Indio surprised me when he dropped and rolled to his right, came up on one knee, and put an arrow through the sleeve of my camisa, furrowing the skin of my arm. Aaaiiii, it burned like a hot coal! I hurried a shot with my flintlock but he ducked aside and the ball kicked up dirt behind him. I threw the weapon and missed with that too, but caught him in the chest with my shoulder before he could fit another arrow and we went down hard in the sand. I grabbed his bow, tried to wrest if from his grip. He yanked it away. As I pushed myself up he reached for another arrow. I felt a rush of warm air on the skin of my neck as the arrow thunked into the wagon behind me.

I charged him, swinging my sword wildly, hoping to keep him off balance. He ducked my swings, feinted, and came in low. His fist caught the side of my head, jarring me. He punched me in the stomach, knocking the air out of me, then got his arms around me, squeezing, crushing my chest. I tried to pound his kidneys, tried to swing the steel blade at his legs, his head, anywhere, but I had bad angles for it and I had no strength; I could get no air into my lungs. He tightened his grip. I tried to push him away, but I could find no leverage. Pain jabbed at my sides and I wondered if he had snapped my ribs. Strange lights flashed in my eyes.

I could smell him now: a rancid, damp beast that stank of pale meat carved from the flank of a mule. I could taste his dirty hair in my mouth as I struggled, could see the oily pores under the streaks of vermilion and ochre on his sweating face. In his effort to crush the life out of me, the muscles in his neck corded like steel cables.

Somehow I managed to get my forearm under his chin. I pushed upward, then used every last particle of my strength to bring my knee up hard into his groin. I must have landed a solid hit; he grunted and stumbled backwards.

I dropped to my knees, struggling to catch my breath, to shake the dizziness that clouded my mind. The Jocome stood a few yards away, his dark face twisted in pain.

"You will pay for this, Spaniard," he mumbled.

I retrieved my sword and slowly pushed myself up from the sand. I barely had strength to raise the sword. Black Skull stepped closer and knocked it from my grasp. It clanged loudly against a granite boulder near the edge of the wash. Out of the corner of my eye I saw Runs-Like-A-Rabbit dash from the shadows, grab the sword, and run back. I was still panting, sucking air; sweat formed a rime on my face. My sleeve was bloodied where the arrow had pierced it. My arm ached. My entire body ached.

"I have a crippled old grandmother," Black Skull said, "who is stronger than you. And now you have no sword, Spaniard."

Kino's tranquil voice drifted to us from across the wash, startling us: "And now you have no bow, Jocome." The padre was perched on a boulder, Black Skull's sturdy bow in his hand—when and how he had gotten it I had no idea. As we watched he put the bow under his boot heel, bent it, forced it again, and broke it. I could see my flintlock tucked into the loose folds of his black robe.

Black Skull was reaching for his knife when I swung at him, my fist grazing his jaw. It did him little damage. He landed a solid blow to my shoulder that sent a jolt of pain into my neck. I swung again and caught him with a glancing blow to his chin that took a patch of skin off my knuckles. I shook off the pain, dove at him, and we went down again. I got a boot back and kicked him in the face. Blood spurted from his nose. We pushed ourselves up. Before he could set himself, I kicked him hard in the thigh. He got his knife out and swiped at me in a wide arc. I got a hand on his wrist, slid behind him, and twisted his arm high behind his back. He dropped the knife.

I shoved him; he stumbled forward. As he recovered his balance and turned to face me, I picked up his knife.

"Your choice," I said, easing out a long-held breath. "You can stay and fight or you can run and pray I am too poor a marksman to put this blade into your back."

Blood streaked the Indian's face and flowed briskly from his nose. He pulled another knife from the calf of his moccasin. "Stupid Spaniard. Did you think I carry only one?"

So, I thought, we are not finished. I dropped into a crouch and readied myself, as well as I could, for Black Skull's next asalto. I was not worried. I was exhausted and my arm burned with pain, but his nose was broken and he was losing blood. I believed I had the advantage of him now.

Well, perhaps I was a *little* worried.

At that moment, the trill of a mockingbird, loud and melodic, floated out from the trees. The Indian hesitated, his attention drawn to the birdcall. Then he relaxed. His dark eyes roamed over me.

"Ussen has smiled on you, Alférez Mon-hay," he said. "I would have killed you." He slipped the knife back into his moccasin, turned, and loped toward the trees. I raised my arm, intending to hurl the big knife after him. I had a good angle for it and plenty of time to make the throw, but my arm seemed almost paralyzed. I could not do it. A moment later I saw a flash of paint ponies through the underbrush and heard unshod hooves scrabbling up the rocky slope of the draw.

I stared at the alien knife in my hand, wondering why I had been unable to throw it, and in that instant saw something that made my pulse race: on the skin of my palm, the unmistakable imprint of a cross. "Heavenly Father," I said softly.

Then I saw the cause of it, a small cross made of stone, affixed to a leather thong wrapped around the white bone handle of the knife. My grip had been so tight on the handle that it had pitted my skin. The cross was a deep vibrant blue, maybe an inch in length and half that in width. Flecks of yellow in it made me wonder if the stone was lapis lazuli.

"They are gone, Ensign. We are safe now." Kino stood in the grassy clearing where we had first seen the Jocome child. His blue eyes glinted in the brightness of the afternoon. In his big hand my flintlock pistol was silvery and luminous against the faded blackness of his robe.

"Your first enemy warrior?" he said.

"My first, yes." I sat in the shade of a willow tree and wiped sweat from my face with a cotton cloth. To the west the sky was layered with ribbons of orange and pink. White clouds skittered on the jagged edge of the horizon.

"I thought so," he said. "Did you enjoy fighting him?"

"...Yes," I admitted.

He nodded and stared thoughtfully at me.

"I am not surprised," he said finally. "You fought him well."

"Gracias."

"But you must learn, my young friend, not to give away your sword."

I sighed. "True enough, sir."

"Come," he said, "we will give thanks. Then we will carry the campesinos to Imuris for a decent burial."

After we prayed silently and Kino sang the Pater, he brought me sweet grapes and a gourd of water for my thirst and dressed the arrow wound of my arm with a poultice of mallow root and wheat flour. We watered the horses. When we were ready for our journey, I said, "Father, why did Black Skull abandon the fight when his wife called?"

He shrugged. "Perhaps she was telling him that their son, Ish-kay-nay, was in some kind of danger. Perhaps she saw—or thought she saw—soldiers coming. Or maybe this is simply God's way of affirming the prophecies of Isaiah, that He will save us from our enemies." The padre shrugged again. "On the other hand, they are Jocomes. They are like Apaches. Who knows why they do what they do."

He climbed onto the wagon seat. "You made no attempt to chase him down, Ensign, or to throw the knife into his back." From his tone I believed he was not judging me; he was simply stating a fact.

"I have never killed a man before," I said. "It is not easy, is it?"

His gaze moved to the mountains, where smoke from the Jocome cookfires still seeped into the sky. "Some day," he said, "you will have to kill him, you know. Or he will kill you. He will not forget your meeting today, and his anger will grow."

"Why, Father? I did him little real damage and he did me little. No one won; no one lost. We fought to a draw. Why would he be angry?"

Kino glanced back at me. "Pride. Hatred for the Spanish. Embarrassment. But mostly pride. He knew you were new in this country, and he will believe he should have easily taken you. His pride will not let him forget."

I thought about the padre's words for a moment, and decided not to worry about the Indio. I had fought him once and survived; I could do it again. Besides, as vast as this country was, it seemed unlikely I would ever see him again. I took another drink from the gourd of water and asked the padre this: "If he had bested me in our fight, would you have shot him...to save me?"

"I would have fought him, certainly."

"But would you have killed him?"

The smile lines deepened in Kino's weathered face. "When Black Skull knocked your sword away, I asked God for permission to do exactly that. So far He has given me no clear reply. Until I hear from Him, I will keep your pistol at my side."

I laughed as I climbed onto the wagon seat beside him. I showed him the blue cross.

"Lapis," he said.

I glanced at my palm and was surprised to see the mark of the cross still visible.

"From my grip on the knife handle," I explained. "The cross was tied to it."

Kino's eyes glowed. I wondered if he would mention Isaiah again.

He did. "Sometimes," he said, smiling, "we forget that God is watching over us. Protecting us, always. Perhaps this is His way of reminding you of that." He flicked the reins. The horses struggled against their harness and the wagon with its load of dead creaked slowly up from the wash.

"Perhaps, Father," I said.

Perhaps. But where, I wondered, had the little cross come from, and why did the Indio have it?

The Pimería Alta of Padre Kino 1696

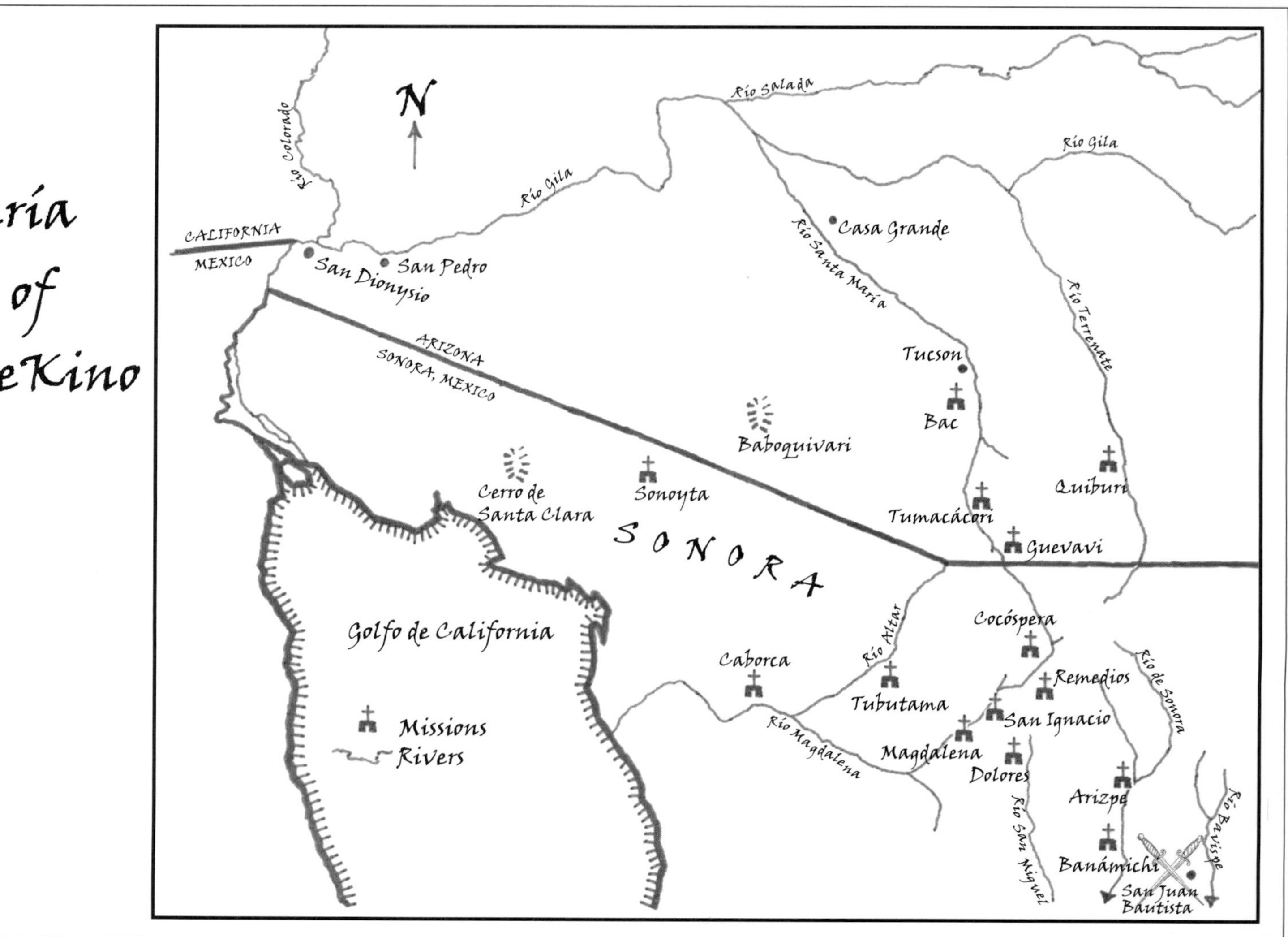

CHAPTER 1

Mexico City. 1965.

In the kitchen of his small apartment Jorge Olvera leaned closer to the mud-stained map of Chiapas that lay open on the breakfast table, as if proximity and the mildewed odor of it would sharpen the memories. He drank deeply from a cup of water, then replaced it on the table. On the map his finger found the mountains and, nearby, the rain forests. He touched the steaming jungles where Zoquen women with ink-black hair wove huipils, their brightly colored blouses, on looms made of saplings, and lean dark men tended rows of corn and cotton in smoky clearings near their villages. In his mind Olvera saw flowers of vivid reds and yellows, and glistening blue insects, and colonial ruins half-hidden by vines so stout they could strangle a horse. He heard the raucous calls of macaws in the trees and smelled the rich dark humus of the jungle and felt on his shoulders the warmth of the sunlight as it slanted through leafy foliage bordering the swollen Río Usumacinta that even now would be hurrying its brown waters northward toward the mosquito-ridden Gulf.

Olvera remembered the x's he had inked onto the map to mark the Zoquen villages, and he saw the dots marking the locations of Ixhuatan, Copanaguastla, and Palenque. Ah, Palenque, the Mayan ruin where his friend, Lhuillier, had found the Tomb of the Temple of The Inscriptions. And Palenque had made his friend a famous man, at least in the strange, mud-caked corner of the world inhabited by field archaeologists.

But he, Jorge Olvera, had done all right, too. Especially at Copanaguastla. There he had used his shovel and pick to expose a fine sixteenth century Spanish colonial ruin, had written it up, published his findings in the usual journals, and drawn the praise of scientists and historians he respected. Yes, in Chiapas he'd done very well indeed.

But that was then; this was now.

And now he had a decision to make.

In his closet Olvera pushed aside journals on archaeology and art history and retrieved his machete. He hefted it and took comfort in the weight of the massive blade. He found his poncho and sweat-stained fedora and the canvas rucksack that held his compass and binoculars. The boots with bits of mud still clinging to the spurs; his Remington bolt-action rifle; the ointments and salves and dressings—all the alien-smelling things that made up his snake-bite kit; the saddlebags that still gave off the strong odors of horse sweat and rich Mayan earth. All these he pulled from the closet and arranged neatly on the yellow linoleum floor of the kitchen.

He found his dog-eared book on Japanese history, opened it, and thought about the job offer he had recently received. In Tokyo, representing Mexico's Ministry of Commerce. The position offered a good salary for doing what would probably be easy and routine work, giving him time to explore the Orient, maybe study some architectural history and do some archaeology.

Olvera coughed, aware again of the stench of traffic smog in his room, of the din and clamor of autos and buses crowding the street below. He closed the window against the intrusions and removed the spurs from his boots. With a wet cotton cloth he cleaned the dried mud from the spurs. In a drawer he found a tin of polishing cream. As he worked the cream into the boot leather, he allowed his conversation with Jiménez to percolate again through his mind...

Jiménez Moreno—probably Mexico's best anthropologist and ethnohistorian, head of Historical Research at the Instituto Nacional Anthropologia y Historia. Two days before, the professor had telephoned and asked Olvera to come to his office. No explanation. He had said only that he had a project that might be of interest. So Olvera had gone, a bit annoyed with himself, frankly, for so hastily biting at such flimsy bait. And bait it had surely been, dangled before him by this master dangler, Jiménez. Still, you never knew what might come of such a thing. So he'd gone.

Jiménez was tall, with smooth dark skin and short white hair already going thin. This day, as always, he had had an appearance of dignity about him, an air of quiet competence. His gray suit, though inexpensive, fit him well.

"Thanks for coming," Jiménez had said, pulling a chair closer to his desk for Olvera. "It's good to see you again, my friend. Please, have a seat. I'll get right to the point. Have you ever heard of a Jesuit named Kino? Eusebio Kino? He was a priest in northern Sonora."

"I might've heard the name," Olvera said. From the street below he could hear the angry blasts of car horns, the profane shouts of impatient drivers. Again he wondered why he was here.

Jiménez cleaned his reading glasses with a handkerchief. Finally he looked up. "You have plans for the near future, Jorge? For the next few months?"

Olvera hesitated. "Nothing besides school, no, not yet."

"I'd heard you were taking graduate courses, and I know of the job offer in Tokyo." Jiménez's white hair glistened with sweat in the afternoon heat. "I also hear that you might go back to Chiapas."

"I've thought about it, yes."

"Jorge, I'm very interested in this dead man, Kino. We have to find him, and we have little time to do it. By 'we,' I mean our country, Mexico. Our Minister of Education has assigned this responsibility directly to me, and I hope to influence you to join me in this project."

"What do you mean, *find* Kino? If he's indeed dead—"

"He's definitely dead," Jiménez said. "He's been dead for over two hundred and fifty years. We have to locate his grave. We have to dig up his bones."

Olvera sat a little straighter in his chair. "Why? What happened? Where is he buried?"

"Somewhere in Sonora. In a village called Magdalena, we *think*. But no one knows for sure."

"Why do you have to find him?"

"Tell me something, por favor. Are you a man of faith?"

Olvera thought about it. "Not really, sir."

"But you're Catholic?"

"I was born a Catholic, yes, so I suppose I still am."

Jiménez tapped a pencil on his desktop and stared at Olvera. "Are you familiar with a monument in Washington, D.C., called Statuary Hall?"

"I don't know of it, sir."

"Truthfully, neither did I," Jiménez said, "until a few weeks ago, when our Minister of Education came to my office. He told me that Statuary Hall is a place in which each of the states in the Estados Unidos is allowed to honor its most prominent citizens with fine statues of bronze. Since each state can have only *two* such statues, the authorities there are quite vigilant in selecting only those individuals whose contributions they consider very great indeed. Arizona made its first such designation in 1930. They chose a man named John Greenway. I'm told he was a mining engineer who was largely responsible for founding Arizona's copper industry. Most people agree that Señor Greenway was an excellent first choice for Arizona."

"Who was their second choice?"

"Take a guess."

Olvera laughed. "Now you'll tell me it was Father Kino."

"It was. Amazing, isn't it? Father Eusebio Francisco Kino, a man who lived, died, and was buried in what is now Mexico. He traveled extensively in Arizona, but he never actually *lived* there. That was no problem for the Arizonans. They unveiled his new statue in Washington at a big ceremony this past February. Our Ambassador to the U.S. was in attendance."

Jiménez grew serious as he tapped his pencil. "It shows that the Arizonans recognize the contributions he made to the lives of the people who settled those borderlands. They believe he was a very important part of their early history, as he was of our own, in Sonora. Our Presidente Díaz says the statue in the hall in Washington honors all of Mexico. But it's very embarrassing to our government that we do not even know where this priest is buried. We have to find him so *our* government, too, can build a monument to him. The Presidente feels very strongly about this."

At the window Olvera stared out over the campus and down to the busy street. "I understand the need to find him, sir," he said finally, "but why *me*?"

"Because you can do the job. I've followed your career with interest, and I know you. You've proven yourself capable."

"But, sir— "

"Over here, Jorge, have a look." Jiménez rose from his desk and walked to a map spread open on a table. "These days," he said, circling a portion of the map with his slender finger, "we know this area as northern Sonora in our country and southern Arizona in the United States. Kino called it the 'Pimería Alta,' after the Pima Indians who lived there. The map shows the early settlements, some native, some Spanish. Here, this is the town they called San Juan Bautista. It no longer exists. There's nothing there now but cactus and rattlesnakes. I've read that in Kino's time it was a silver mining town and the capital of Sonora, headquarters for the Spanish cavalry and for civil authorities under the control of the viceroy."

"They still mine silver there?" Olvera said. Well, he was an archaeologist, wasn't he? An archaeologist couldn't help such thoughts.

Jiménez smiled. "As far as we know, the silver is gone. But look, here is San Ignacio de Cabúrica," he continued, pointing, "and Guevavi and San Cayetano del Tumacácori. Here are Tubutama and Imuris. Before Father Kino came, these were simple Pima villages. They grew corn and beans and squash, but not much else. Kino taught them about horses and livestock and brought them new crops. But most importantly, he saved their souls.

He made Christians of them. Those who would listen, anyway." Jiménez tapped a spot on the map. "Here is Nuestra Señora de los Dolores, Kino's home mission. It sat on a high bluff overlooking the Rio San Miguel. A beautiful place, they say. It was a working cattle ranch, but it also had vegetable gardens, fields of wheat and cotton, vineyards, a winery, citrus groves. It's gone now. The mission, the Indian village—all of it, disappeared. The buildings were made of adobe. Over the years they simply crumbled back to dust. Now nothing remains there but wind and dust and memories."

Jiménez turned back to him. "I know you have concerns about your credentials for such a project. Truthfully, what we're doing won't require a doctoral-level archaeologist. We'll do the stratigraphic and horizontal record-keeping required, but no more, and we'll keep the string grids and sifting-screens to a minimum. We'll be looking for only one thing and that's the grave of this priest, Kino. No, my friend, what this project requires is a man with knowledge of architectural history, like you, and a man who loves a good mystery. This job needs a *detective*, and I believe you have the makings of a very good detective."

"I'm flattered by your words, Professor. Still, I—"

"Now," Jiménez went on, "I have to be honest with you. You weren't my first choice. There are others in Mexico more experienced than you, and I've tried to interest several of them in this project. All have refused to join me."

"Refused? Why?"

"They don't believe we can succeed." Jiménez sighed. "They don't want to risk failure, especially hunting for a man who was 'only a priest,' as one of them said. One actually told me he would've joined me—if the gravesite I sought had belonged instead to a general in one of our glorious revolutions."

Olvera stared at him.

"So, Jorge," Jiménez had said that morning, smiling again, looking him straight in the eye. "Will you help me find the gentleman's bones?"

In his kitchen Olvera refilled his cup with cold water and took a long drink. He glanced again at the map of Chiapas and the little book on Japan.

There would be little to gain in going to Sonora, of course. That northern state and its history, interesting as they might be, were simply too far removed from the academic centers of Mexico. And, in spite of Jiménez's optimism, Olvera could see little chance of finding the padre's grave after all these years. And of course if he joined Jiménez he would lose the job in Japan and he would have to postpone any return to Chiapas.

On the other hand, he suspected, a successful excavation of the padre's remains could bring him a degree of professional satisfaction that he might not find in Japan. It would bring glory to his profession, and even more importantly, to his country, Mexico. It might even be, well...*fun*.

He had to face the truth, though: the Sonoran project would be risky for his career. What if they devoted a year, two years, who could guess how long—and came up with nothing? The other archaeologists, whoever they were, had been skeptical enough that they had refused to be a part of it. Maybe they were right. After all, these were seasoned scientists who knew the likelihood of failure when they saw it.

Another thing. He knew almost nothing about this man, Kino. Who *was* he, anyway? If Jiménez had asked him to find the grave of, say, Cabeza de Vaca, or Vásquez de Coronado, now that would've been something. But a Jesuit who'd lived and died in Sonora? Maybe the archaeologists had been right about that, too.

On the other hand, he was tired of sitting in libraries. Tired of writing papers and memorizing facts and figures. Tired, to be honest about it, of graduate school. He felt a need to get outdoors again, to breathe fresh air and do something physical.

Olvera sat in a chair at the breakfast table and stared at his rifle and boots on the yellow kitchen floor. He drank more water from his cup. He ran his finger over the smooth gray steel of the machete blade and thought about his need for a regular and adequate paycheck; about field work and his career and his future.

After a time he returned his things to the closet and straightened the kitchen. He had decided this: he wouldn't rush a decision. He would drink a little wine and have some cheese and bread, and think more about these important matters.

Three days later Olvera went to the office of the apartment manager and told him he would be leaving soon.

The manager said, "We'll miss you, Señor."

"And I will miss you, my friend." Even in the office the air was thick with the smell of traffic smog.

The manager, stooped and old and always curious, said, "If I may ask, por favor, where are you going?"

"To the desert," Olvera said. "Up north, near the Estados Unidos. I'm going to Sonora."

"Whatever for?"

"To dig up a dead priest."

"*What*?"

"I'm going to find a man called Eusebio Kino," Olvera told him solemnly. "To honor my country and my profession."

"You don't sound very excited about it."

"It will be difficult. Maybe I won't even find him."

The manager arched a bushy white eyebrow. "Then why are you going?"

Olvera shrugged. "Because a lot of experts have said I will fail."

"And you have to prove these experts wrong?"

"Something like that, yes."

"Maybe God will bless you in your work."

Olvera laughed. "Maybe."

The manager pulled two bottled soft drinks from a small refrigerator in the corner. He popped the lids off and handed one of the drinks to Olvera. "So," he said amiably, "tell me about this man, Kino."

CHAPTER 2

Sonora, Nueva España. Año D. 1693. December.

"So, Ensign Manje," Father Campos said, spurring his horse to catch up to me, "tell me about this man, Kino."

I turned in my saddle to look at him.

"He will be my supervisor in the Pimería," Campos explained when his mount had pulled even with mine, "and I know little about him."

We jumped our horses over a gully bordered with creosote and prickly pear, then slowed to a comfortable pace and turned upstream along the bank of the Río de Sonora, now wide and brimming from the winter rains. "Father Kino? I know little about him, myself," I said.

I glanced behind us, to Private DeJulio and the Pimas tending the rope line of pack mules. DeJulio waved, letting me know that everything was all right. I took a moment to study the mountains around us, but saw nothing out of the ordinary.

"But you have met Kino?" Campos said.

"A few months ago." I thought about Campos' questions, then shrugged. "Well, I suppose I know a *few* things about him. I know he carries an astrolabe everywhere he goes and he uses it to draw maps. He seems to have no fear of the Apaches. As to his appearance, he is taller than you and old enough to have some gray in his hair. As to his character, I can only witness that he takes good care of his horse."

Campos chuckled but said no more and we rode on in silence.

Agustín de Campos was not a large man, but he was broad across the shoulders and he had a look of strength in the set of his clean-shaven jaw. I knew him to be in his early thirties, though he looked younger, his wide face now pink and radiant in the spangled morning light. He rode his horse, a gelding palomino with a white blaze, as if he had been born on it.

After a time I told him about the butchered settlers Kino and I had found near Imuris and my fight with Black Skull, the Jocome, and about Father Kino's gentle ministrations to the arrow wound I had sustained. I rolled up my sleeve and showed Campos the scar, still red and raw, on my arm. His eye twitched; he looked away.

Oh, Madre. In those early days I was never quite sure how deferential I should be toward priests, or how official, or even how personal I might be without offending them. I was young, after all; just twenty-three years of age, only an ensign. And already I knew that not everyone viewed the Spanish Army with fondness and adoration—especially outside the borders of the mother country. And now, *aaaiiii*, I had opened my stupid mouth and needlessly frightened the padre.

"Please accept my apologies, Father," I said. "Perhaps I should have kept these things to myself."

Campos was silent for a time, and I saw him finger the bronze crucifix he wore on a leather cord around his neck. Finally he smiled, and when he spoke his voice was low but clear. "No, it is good that you told me. I have to know what to expect in this new country. New to *me*, anyway."

"I suppose so, Father." We worked our horses up a slope that brought us onto a promontory of sandstone and soft gray silt. Ahead, the mountains were almost violet in the early morning light. I heard the call of ravens, and in the wind I could smell the mustiness of the marsh grasses that grew along the riverbanks.

"How long have you been in Sonora, Ensign?"

"Half a year or so," I said.

"I understand that Kino plans to assign me to the mission called Cabúrica. In Ures they said it is a pleasant place. Have you seen it?"

"I have," I said. "It is beautiful. Kino calls it San Ignacio de Cabúrica."

His black robe billowed in the cold breeze. His dark eyes were sparkling again and I had a sense that whatever fears he might have felt earlier had now eased. "How far is it from here?" he asked.

"Not far," I said. "Corporal Escalante tells me if we keep a steady pace we will reach Dolores in four to five days. San Ignacio is an easy day's ride from there."

Over his shoulder I could see a lone cloud the color of pewter riding the top of a saw-toothed mountain that seemed marbled in a moist blue haze. Scrub cactus and leafless mesquite trees with dark twisted trunks dotted the low basin of desert that stretched from the river to the foothills on both sides of us. Along the river, hackberry, cottonwood, and thick stands of bunch grass glowed in the cool brightness of the morning sun. I saw egrets and a blue heron rise into the wind above the water, and tiny fish drifting in the silvery shadows of sycamores that towered over the bank. But I saw no one other than Private DeJulio and the Pimas, and no movement in the desert or on the mountainsides. Earlier, I had sent Escalante out to scout the trail ahead and to keep an eye on our flanks. Where he was now, I had no idea.

"This is beautiful country," I heard Campos say. "But it seems nothing at all like Spain."

"Especially the summers," I said.

"What are the summers like?"

"*Madre de Dios*, you do not want to know."

He laughed. "I hear it gets warm here."

"Like the inside of a burning barrel, Father. Personally, I much prefer this winter weather. It is cold, yes, but the sun shines, and the midday hours can be very pleasant."

"I think I will like it here, whatever the weather."

"I believe you will, sir," I said.

Campos had traveled far in the last half year. He had arrived in New Spain at Veracruz, like everyone who came from Europe, and had traveled on horseback in a caravan of tradesmen and fortune seekers on the same route I had taken the year before: into the mountains to Ciudad de Mexico, across to Guadalajara, then north to Durango and Conicari. There, officials had dispatched a rider to the presidio at Real San Juan Bautista with news of the new priest's arrival. General Domingo Jironza, commander of the Compañía Volante and all military forces in Sonora, had assigned to me the task of fetching Father Campos at Ures, thirty leagues south of San Juan, and safely delivering him and a pack train of building supplies to Father Kino at Kino's home mission, Dolores.

General Domingo Jironza, I should tell you, was my uncle. Over the years this would prove as much a curse as a blessing, but that is a story for another day.

Don Domingo had picked two trusted soldados—DeJulio and Escalante—and a few Pima servants to go with me, and at Ures we had found Father Campos waiting for us at the mission. He had greeted us warmly, even helped us load the mules with the lumber and carpentry tools we would deliver to Kino. On the ride south we had had no problems, had seen no sign of Apaches. In spite of our good fortune so far, though, I was uneasy. I was still new to the difficult task of leading troops in the field, and I was not quite as confident in my abilities as Don Domingo seemed to be. I had not forgotten how easily Black Skull had taken my sword from me in that bloody wash near Imuris.

Nor had I forgotten Don Domingo's warnings: "Watch your back, Juan Mateo," he had said. "They slip over the mountains, usually in groups of five or six. Usually the younger ones, the hotheads, looking for plunder or hoping to pull off a revenge raid against some settlers or Pimas. Be aware of everything around you, and if trouble comes, look to Corporal Escalante for advice. He has been in Sonora most of his life."

Again I glanced back at DeJulio and the others and scanned the mountains around us. I saw nothing that alarmed me, but I saw no sign of Escalante either, and that worried me some. He had been gone more than two hours.

I excused myself from the padre, reined my horse around, and rode back to DeJulio. He saluted when I came alongside him.

"Any problems, Private?" I said. We had put a white mare with a bell around her neck at the front of the towline, and the other mules seemed contented enough to follow her without making trouble. Too much trouble, anyway. These were mules, after all.

"All quiet, sir," DeJulio said. He was a small man, dark-skinned and swarthy. Like most of the soldiers and many of the settlers in Sonora, he was mestizo, a person of mixed Indian and Spanish ancestry. Don Domingo had said he was a good man to have along when there were Apaches around.

I hoped there were none around now.

"Keep a sharp eye out," I told him.

"I will, sir."

At midmorning we stopped to rest the animals where a pebbled creek joined the river in a small forest of hackberry and squawbush. We took a light meal of goat's milk and pinole—a paste of toasted ground corn, sugar, beans, and bits of squash—and watched deer drink at the water's edge. After filling our water gourds we rode steadily northward over a rolling plain of sacaton and grama that rippled in the breeze like fields of ripe brown wheat. Down the slope from us the river twisted and plummeted its way from the plain that stretched out before us. In all directions the mountains formed rough brown ridges on the horizon and rose sharply into the vivid blue sky.

Still I saw no sign of Corporal Escalante.

I was wondering what to do about that when my thoughts were interrupted by shouts from the rear. I turned in my saddle and saw Escalante coming up fast on his sorrel mare, past the pack mules and the Pimas and

Private DeJulio. He reined his horse in a cloud of dust, his blue uniform coat flapping in the breeze, his horse wheezing, its back lathered with foamy sweat.

"Riders," he said, giving me a hurried salute. "Probably four miles behind us."

"How many?" I said.

"Five, sir. And something else." He pointed to a mountain that formed a looming hulk to the southeast. "Smoke, sir."

I scanned the area with my telescope. Finally I saw them: against the cloudless blue of the sky, faint black bubbles drifting lazily with the wind. "They know we are here," I said, "and they are informing all their friends?"

"That would be my guess, sir," he said. Corporal Escalante was tall, with fair skin, a neatly-trimmed mustache, and a narrow, pleasant face. He had come from Durango and owed his height and fair skin, he had told me, to his father, a gunsmith from Spain. His mother, I had learned, was a native Mexican with Aztec blood.

"Corporal," I said, tucking my telescope back into my saddlebag.

"Sir?"

"I am glad you are back safely."

"Thank you, sir."

We kept moving north, sometimes near the river, often closer to the foothills—whatever route seemed to promise the faster passage. We rested the horses and mules no more than we had to, but watered them often and took small meals in the saddle. Late in the day we skirted the little Opata village of Baviácora on the river—in Ures we had heard rumors of smallpox. From a rise we could see the mud-and-twig huts the Pimas called kihs, but we saw no one outside. No one tending the acéquias, the irrigation canals that fed out from the river. No one with the cattle that grazed the hillsides. No one working the fallow fields that would soon be planted in winter wheat. Father Campos wanted to ride down and tend the sick and offer sacraments to the dying. "No," I said firmly, "we stay away from there," and reminded him that I was responsible for the safety of everyone in the group.

He tried to persuade me, invoking the moral authorities of Jesus, the Apostles, Moses, Abraham, even the Jesuit General in Rome, but I held my ground.

Not long before sundown my horse surprised a skunk and the whole lot of us caught a good spraying. We scrubbed ourselves in the cold water of the river and washed our outer garments with amole soap that the Pimas had made from yucca roots, but still we could not rid ourselves of the stench.

Since it was almost dark, we made camp in a stand of sycamores and started a small fire. Two of the Pima servants—a young girl whose name I did not know, and Lupita, an elderly woman—served us boiled beef and stewed tepary beans wrapped in warm flour tortillas. We huddled at the campfire and silently ate our fill. Through the canopy of branches, stars glowed with a faint light and I could see a crescent of moon drifting in a darkened arc of sky. Around us the smell of damp wool mingled with the clinging odors of horse sweat and skunk spray. In the distance a coyote yipped, and then another.

"Probably complaining about the smell around here," Father Campos said, and we all had a good laugh.

When our clothes had dried, we spread our bedrolls near the glowing coals; I placed my sword and arquebus, my flintlock musket, within easy reach. For warmth we would sleep in our uniforms. As for the boots, I would sleep in mine. An officer's boots, I had learned, were too tall and heavy to pull on quickly if trouble came.

"Escalante," I said, "will take the first watch, DeJulio, the second. I will take the last. Try to get some sleep. We are safe. No one can see us here."

"No one but the scorpions and snakes," Escalante said. I knew he was making a joke, but I noticed he kept his boots on and his arquebus close by.

Me, I was not worried about scorpions or snakes. I was worried about the smoke and the riders the corporal had seen. I touched the little lapis cross I had taken from Black Skull and now wore under my shirt on a cord around my neck. In the cold night air the stone felt warm to my touch and I drew comfort from it.

That night I dreamed.

I rarely dream. Even in those early youthful years I was usually so tired by nightfall that I crawled between my blankets and slept like a dead man. I always credited this to the fact that soldiering is hard work, and that sheer exhaustion led me to sleep soundly. There could have been more to it than that, I do not know. But it seemed to me that my mind rarely found enough time for both resting itself and entertaining itself, and that was fine with me. But this night I dreamed.

None of it made much sense. My father and mother were in the dream, and horses, and a café that seemed to be in Real San Juan. General Domingo Jironza, my uncle, was in it, and a beautiful black-haired woman. Even Father Kino, whom I had only recently met and barely knew, made an appearance. In the dream nobody got hurt and no one died, and it lasted only a short time, but I suppose it told me a few things about some of the people who had been important in my life, or one day would be.

Otherwise the night passed without incident.

After mass the next morning, before sunrise, we drank chocolate and had quince jam on warm tortillas and readied the horses and pack mules in the cold air of the early dawn.

Campos wrinkled his nose. "I still smell of skunk," he said.

"We all do, Father," I said. To the east the sky was liquid blue over the mountains, edged with pewter gray and powdery streaks of gold, and on the grasses that grew along the riverbank, moisture glistened like small silver coins.

He stared out at the mountains. "Have the heathens forgotten us?"

"They remember," I said.

But it was not Apaches or Jocomes, I soon learned, that would ruin our day.

When we broke camp I gave Escalante orders to take the group on northward and make the best time they could. My intent was to climb the nearest mountain and look for the riders he had seen, and catch up to the group before they reached Guepaca, a little Opata village on the route to Opodepe.

On the mountain the manzanita was so thick I had to hack my way through much of it. When the slope became too steep for my horse, I tied it to the trunk of a juniper tree with bark like the hide of an alligator, and on foot I scrabbled higher over boulders and rough outcroppings of granite. Finally, my legs aching and lungs burning, I reached the top. In all directions I saw mountains cut by dark canyons; foothills cut by shallow washes. The desert between them was spotted with scrub cactus and brown grasses and the tall stalks of a plant I had heard Father Kino call sotol. Below, from the foot of the mountain, the river climbed into a series of hills crowned with boulders of sandstone. In the distance I saw snow on mountaintops and a dust devil spinning across the desert floor.

But I saw no riders. Except for the odd little windstorm, I saw no movement. No smoke or columns of dust in the air; nothing to tell me Apaches or anyone else were in the area.

I caught up with the others near the riverbank, where they had stopped and tied the animals. Escalante and DeJulio stood with their muskets near the rim of an arroyo with old Lupita and the girl and the Pima men. The girl, her dark eyes alert, her black hair bright in the sunlight, held a leather bag filled with arrows.

"Where is Father Campos?" I asked.

"In the arroyo, sir," Escalante whispered, pointing. "He went to relieve himself. I think he picked a very bad place for it."

Finally I saw the priest—at the bottom of the draw, almost hidden by a large boulder. He was sitting in the sand, his black robe gathered around his knees. On the boulder not two feet from his face lay a cascabel—a rattlesnake—its thick body drawn into a coil. Its squat dark head was up, its tail, marked by rings of black and white, rising out of the coil. The grayish-brown of its back blended smoothly with the rocky terrain, and even from here I could see that the snake's belly was white as goat's milk.

No one moved. Even the air was still, the leaves motionless on the creosote bushes that grew along the top of the draw. Overhead, the sky was a blanket of blue. "*Stay still, padre, por favor*," I said under my breath, "*stay very still.*" I could smell the river now, the musty scents of dead fish and brown leaves moldering in shallow pools, and from the arroyo I could hear the muffled *ch-ch-ch* of the diamondback's rattles.

CHAPTER 3

Madre de Dios, I should have remembered to warn the priest. Father Campos was new to Sonora and I was the officer in charge and I should have thought to tell him about the cascabels—the thick-bodied snakes with sharp fangs full of poison and dark pods that rattled and pranced on their tails. I had known they doze in the sun on warm winter days and that their bite can kill. Father Kino had told me there were green ones in the deserts to the west, and he had heard there were even pink ones in the mountains that bordered a vast, mighty canyon in the despoblado, the alien, dangerous lands that lay far to the north of the Pimería.

But this was a big brown one with patterns of diamonds on its dark back and I had forgotten to warn the padre—and my lapse had put him in grave danger.

"Alférez," Corporal Escalante whispered, "with your permission, sir, I could cross to the other side of the arroyo. If you stay on this side, perhaps one of us can get off a good shot at the snake."

"First, we pray for Father Campos," I mumbled, "then we shoot the snake, and when all that is done, I will try to learn something from this experience."

He started to laugh, but stopped himself. "Sir, we have to be careful here. If we fire and miss, the snake will strike the padre for sure."

"Then we have to kill it," I said, "with our first shot."

"The only way to do that is to blow its head off."

"Then that, Corporal, is precisely what we will do."

"A fine plan, sir," he said, "excellent."

Escalante was a good soldier and I liked him, even if he did have an annoying tendency to patronize me on occasion. The truth was, though, there had been times when I deserved it. This, sadly, was another of them.

I closed my eyes and said a quick Pater Noster, then sent the corporal across the arroyo, as he had suggested. I sent Private DeJulio and the Pimas to look after the horses and mules. I had not forgotten the riders and the smoke signals, but they would just have to wait their turns for my attentions.

The sandstone boulders on this side of the draw were worn and crumbly and covered with a dusting of fine sand. I worked my way along the rim, my boots making muffled careful sounds on the rocks, my eyes on Father Campos and the rattler in the sandy bottom. Here, the sides of the draw were steep, covered with loose rock and pale gray brittlebush that had died back in the cold of winter. Finally I found a flat ledge not far above Campos and the snake. I lay on my belly and turned my arquebus down at the serpent.

But the snake moved just enough that I could not find a good shot.

I crept a little closer to the edge.

The snake's black tongue probed the air. Sweat shimmered on the padre's forehead and collected in shiny drops on his chin. A fly buzzed in the air before his face. I could almost smell the fear that radiated from him. Still, he held himself motionless before the snake.

The sun grew warm on my back. I became aware of small beetles trundling over rocks, of scurrying lizards; of birds calling softly from tall trees near the river. Muscles cramped in my shoulders, and I smelled again the stench of skunk in my clothes. Across the arroyo, Escalante lay in a wallow of dirt, his attention fixed, his hands steady, his musket trained on the scene below. Grime and sand stained his blue trousers and coat, but the red swatches on his collar and on the thick cuffs of his coat sleeves seemed bright and vivid in the clear desert air.

I crept out still farther on the ledge, thinking if I could get a few inches closer to the snake, or maybe even a few feet—

And that, of course, is when the sandstone crumbled under me and I went sliding and tumbling down the slope toward the priest and the waiting rattlesnake. I shouted at the padre; I grabbed frantically for the stalk of a brittlebush and tried to dig my boot heels in, tried desperately to stop my clumsy spill into the ditch. But I couldn't halt my fall. I landed on my belly at the bottom in a cloud of dust, and immediately heard the *ch-ch-ch* of the rattler. It was less than four feet away, its attention on me now, its dark tongue testing the dust-choked air between us. Where the padre was and what he was doing at that moment, I had no idea. The world around me had gone soundless, the arroyo suddenly tinted in ghostly tones of gray. In the next instant I saw the snake's head coming at me, mouth gaping, venom shimmering on its fang tips like tiny drops of dew. I rolled and kicked at the serpent as I tried to scrabble out of its reach. I felt its strike hit my boot. Musket balls thunked into the sand and the odor of burnt powder drifted down to me with the deafening echo of gunfire along the rim, but I had no time to look for the soldiers.

Fighting for air, I tried to push myself up. The snake came at me again and I scooted backwards in the sand, trying to put space between us. Its dark slatted eyes studied me, its tongue darting and probing. It pulled itself into a coil and I could hear its rattles now, thrumming in my ears. But I couldn't move. I couldn't take my eyes from the thing. I could not even pray. I felt paralyzed, as if the horrid reptile had somehow taken control of my will.

But *someone* must have been praying.

Out of the corner of my vision I saw a flash of movement at the top of the draw, then saw an arrow slice into the snake's neck, pinning it to the ground. I caught a glimpse of the Pima girl, a bow in her hand. I watched the snake as it writhed and twisted, finally pulling the arrow from the soil. Then it came at me again, tracking over the sand, the arrow still fixed eerily through the flesh of its neck.

Frankly I have never been much of a sprinter. Oh, I had plenty of stamina in those early years in the Pimería; I could run long distances. I just was not very fast. Especially with these heavy boots. I was not what anyone would call fleet of foot.

But this day I sprinted out of that draw. I *boiled* out of it.

Back at the top, winded and sweaty, I found Father Campos staring down at the snake's undulating body as it tried vainly to free itself from the arrow. A moment later it shook itself in a brief violent convulsion, then ceased moving. I saw nausea rise into the padre's pink face. He dropped to his knees and emptied his stomach onto the rocks.

I managed not to vomit, but at the river I drank cold water and took deep breaths of cool moist air and rinsed the sourness from my mouth with goat's milk and corn meal. I brushed the dirt from my red tunic. It would take more than a brushing to get my boots and white trousers clean, but I did what I could.

When I found the girl, she was tending the pack animals.

"Thank you," I said to her, "for killing the cascabel."

"De nada," she said, smiling.

"¿Como se llama usted?" I said.

"Rosenda Delgadilla María de Jesús de Tuczani'ubi." She laughed—a high, tinkling sound full of girlishness and spirit. "My friends call me White Leaf. It is much easier to say."

"Then I will call you White Leaf, too."

"If you wish, sir." Her Spanish was good. Like all Pimas I had seen, she had smooth dark skin and shiny black hair cut straight across her forehead. Her deerskin skirt and cotton camisa were clean and well-made and her dark eyes glowed with confidence. I guessed her at about sixteen years old.

"Tell me," I said, "how did you get so good with your bow?"

"You are new here, Ensign, so you did not know my father."

"No, I did not know him," I said.

"He was killed in battle three years ago, near El Tupo. Stabbed in the neck by Oso Azul. Have you heard of him? He and his band are Ohb-Apaches from the Sierra Madres. The heathens cut the sinews in my father's arms and legs so his soul could not come back and take revenge, and they cut open his belly so vultures could feast on his entrails." She picked my horse out of the herd and walked it to me. "Soon I will be a warrior," she said vehemently, "like my father. I will kill Ohbs and make them pay for his death. That is why I practice so much with my arrows."

"How old are you?"

Her eyes moved away. "Eighteen."

"...*How* old?"

She flushed. "Thirteen. But I will be fourteen in a month."

I filled some gourds with water and hung them from my saddle. "Whatever your age, White Leaf," I told her, "I am proud to have you with us." I climbed onto my horse and touched the brim of my blue bicorn. "Tell Lupita and the others, por favor," I added, "to get the pack animals ready. We leave in five minutes."

She gave me a mock salute and an impish grin. "Yes, sir, Señor Skunk, sir."

I laughed, pulled Campos' palomino out of the herd, reined my mount around, and rode back to fetch the padre.

We rode northward along the river, making good time, and reached Guepaca in less than an hour. There we turned west along a faint trail that would take us over a mountain pass and back down to the desert and the Pima village of Opodepe on the San Miguel River. Near the top of the pass I sought out Corporal Escalante and pulled my horse alongside his big sorrel mare.

"Thanks for your help today," I said.

"I did very little, sir."

"You did plenty. And you are all right now?"

"Fine, sir," he said.

We ran our mounts up the last of the inclines and stopped at the top of the pass. Brown mountains filled the landscape to the north and south, and ahead, on the plain below, I could see the mud huts of a Pima ranchería and a blue cord of river twisting down from the north and the pale hard desert that stretched to the west in a glinting yellow haze of afternoon sun. I turned in my saddle and watched the little white mare, the bell jingling under her neck as she led the other mules clopping and braying up the hill. Almost by chance I saw a cloud of dust, faint against the darker slopes of the hills near Guepaca. Then I saw the riders. Four? Five? They were coming in our direction.

I was sure Escalante had seen them, too. "Apaches, Corporal?"

He checked the powder load in his musket. "Possibly, sir. I think we need to get to Opodepe as soon as we can. We will be safe there for the night."

"Keep the animals moving," I said, and spurred my horse back down the line. I found Father Campos riding with the Pimas at the back of the mule train.

"I admire your courage, Padre," I said when I came alongside him. "All that time with the snake and you never moved a muscle. How did you do it?"

Campos smiled. "I asked myself how Eusebio Kino would have handled such a situation."

"And how would he?" I asked him. He had torn his black robe getting out of the arroyo and had sewn the edges together with twine. Now the twine had worked loose and the thick wool cloth flapped in the chill breeze of the early evening.

"Well," he said, "it occurred to me that there were two issues involved. First, Padre Kino, being a good Jesuit, would probably have offered a very earnest, very long, and very motionless prayer to God and Francisco Xavier and Ignacio Loyola and all the other saints in heaven. So I did that. One at a time, every saint I could remember. It took a while."

I chuckled. "And the other issue?"

He looked off at the mountains in the distance, but I could see the grin on his face. "Kino, I believe," he said, "would have been more circumspect in his choice of a place to take his relief."

"Next time," he added, laughing aloud, "so will I."

We rode steadily westward, talking little. We saw no smoke and no further sign of riders. At Opodepe the Pimas had heard of our coming. They had swept the trail with brooms made of sage and they welcomed us to their village carrying crosses fashioned from mesquite branches. Father Campos said a mass for them at their vah'kih, a ramada with corner poles cut from mesquite, its roof made from tree branches, twigs, and agave leaves. That evening we enjoyed a meal of grilled beef, peppers, and tortillas and drank a toast of wine with the village chiefs, who were gracious hosts.

The next morning we rose before sunrise and headed north up the valley of the San Miguel. Once we saw puffs of smoke above the Santa Teresas to the east, but we saw no more of the riders.

That afternoon near the river a raven spooked Private DeJulio's horse, throwing the soldier onto some rocks and bruising his shoulder. We fashioned a sling for his arm from a strip of cotton cloth and got him back in the saddle. Otherwise not a lot happened, and two days later we reached the Pima village of Cosari, the home of Father Kino's mission, Dolores.

Hundreds of Pimas met us on the trail bearing gifts of food and small crosses made of mesquite. They gathered around us, singing and chanting, and escorted us through the village to the church. The children, in loincloths and coats made of deerskin, ran alongside us, giggling and pulling the tails of the mules. We must have made a grand and comical sight.

Around us were orchards and vineyards, and on the hillsides that sloped down from the church I saw the mud-and-twig huts of the Indios, and oxen and horses; sheep and goats and grazing cattle. On the flatlands below, irrigation canals cut through vegetable gardens and wheat fields, the waters shimmering like bands of silver under the December sun. Behind the church, the paddle of a water-powered mill turned lazily under an aqueduct, and beyond these I could see a small blacksmith's shop and carpenter's shop and covered ramadas for the cooks.

Padre Kino met us at the door of the church. He wore frayed gray trousers and a rough shirt of undyed cotton. Apparently he had just finished his bath, as his gray-flecked hair was wet and plastered in ringlets on his narrow forehead. He smiled widely from the doorway and made the sign of the cross. "Praise God," he said.

Campos and I dismounted and I introduced the two padres. Kino gave the new priest a warm embrace. "Welcome to the Pimería, Agustín."

Campos smiled. "I am pleased to be here, sir."

"How was your journey?"

"Enjoyable, Father, and quite routine."

I stifled a laugh. Campos and I had secretly agreed to shade the truth in a minor, ecclesiastically-acceptable way, on the theory that if we did not tell Kino *all* the dumb things we had done, perhaps he would assume we were clever and apt enough to actually survive in this land. Mistakes aside, I liked my new life here and I wanted to stay.

"And Ensign Manje," Kino said, turning to me, "it is good to see you again. Thanks for bringing the padre."

"My pleasure, Father."

"And your journey, like the padre's, was routine?"

"Totally uneventful," I said. Behind us the mules came to a stop, the white mare's bell jingling in the cool evening air.

Kino looked us over again, his blue eyes moving from my soiled uniform to Campos and his torn, dirty robe, then lingering on Private DeJulio and the grit-smudged sling that supported his swollen arm. Kino's brow was furrowed now, and he studied us intently.

"You said everyone made it back safely, Ensign?"

"No problems," I said.

"You are certain there were no serious injuries?"

"Everyone is fine, Father," I said.

Smile lines deepened at the corners of his eyes. "Come, we will get the animals fed and watered. Then I want to hear all about your trip."

He wrinkled his nose and laughed softly.

"And all about the skunk," he added.

CHAPTER 4 Mexico City. 1965.

With the help of a librarian at the university, Olvera found a biography of Eusebio Kino: *Rim of Christendom*, by a Norte Americano historian named Herbert Bolton. What he hoped to learn about the priest, Olvera wasn't quite sure. A few basics about his family and early education, he supposed. How he got to the New World. A little about his missions. But he doubted he would find much on Kino's last days, or anything at all on the location of his burial site. Otherwise, someone would've uncovered his remains before now. Frankly, the book would probably be something of a bore. Jesuits lived lives of quiet contemplation, didn't they? Filled with teaching and devotion, but little excitement?

Still, he thought, it couldn't hurt to rummage a bit in the life of this priest who had roamed Mexico's northern desert almost three centuries before. He took the book to a quiet corner of the library. A meticulous man, he made careful notes as he read...

- ***Born Eusebio Chino (pronounced Keen-o) August 10, 1645—only son of Francisco and Donna Margherita Chino, on a farm near the village of Segno in the Province of Trent in the Tyrol of northern Italy. Three sisters, Caterina, Margherita, and Ana María. Family owned home, farm, livestock, vineyards. Known to be moderately well-off.***
- ***Young Chino had normal childhood, filled with school work and farm chores and tending of cattle and other livestock. Religious, even as a child; drawn early to teachings of San Francisco Xavier.***
- ***Father, Francisco, died when Eusebio was 15 years old. Much of family property sold to pay debts and finance Eusebio's education.***
- ***In mid-teens, left family to attend a Jesuit gymnasio, a high school, in Trent, a few miles south of Segno. Graduated from Trent. Went to Germany, University of Halle, near Innsbruck, to study logic & rhetoric. Known to be a very good student.***
- ***At Halle, eighteen years old, he fell ill with a mortal disease that very***

nearly took his life; doctors believed he would die. At suggestion of a wise and friendly priest, Chino prayed to San Xavier, his personal patron saint. Promised San Xavier if he would intercede on his behalf with God and he survived, he would enter priesthood, join Jesuits, and volunteer for missionary work in the Orient, no matter the hardships.

- ***Survived. Kept promise.***

Olvera closed the book and spent a while thinking about what he'd learned. He had been surprised by some of it, frankly. Maybe even a little amazed.

From an encyclopedia he learned that the Italian village of Segno sat in the rugged Val di Non, the Valley Anaunia of Roman times, high in the Dolomite Alps, a region known for its hardy farmers and prosperous cattle ranches. It was, he guessed, a land of incredible beauty, with tall green peaks, clean air, and cool summer breezes. He preferred not to even *think* about the winters. Maybe it was those *winters*, he thought, that had given the young Kino his backbone.

Olvera went back to the biography, making deliberate notes as he read. After another hour of study he returned the book to the desk and thanked the librarian, a young woman with pleasant eyes and soft brown hair. He asked if they had any books on the history of missionaries in the Americas.

"A few," the librarian said. "Would you like the names and authors?"

"Yes, gracias," he said. Almost as an afterthought, he asked if they had anything on the Pima Indians of northern Sonora and Arizona.

"Of course," she said. "Histories, mostly."

"Anything on the Apaches?"

The librarian smiled. "Sure."

"Maybe I should take a look at them, too," Olvera said. "Anything else I should see?"

"On the Indians of northern Sonora? Well, there were other tribes, but some of them have disappeared. They're extinct now. You'll read about them in *Rim* if you keep going with it. The Ópata, the Jocomes. The Mansos. There were others, but those are the ones I remember."

"Extinct? What happened to them?"

"Some," she said, "were killed off by the Spaniards. Some intermarried with other tribes and eventually just lost their identity." She shrugged. "In that part of the country, who knows, maybe the others died from snakebite."

Olvera chuckled. "How do you know all these things?"

"I know about the Indians," she said, "because I've taken courses in anthropology. I know about the rattlesnakes because I have a cousin who lives in Sonora."

"Maybe I should take my snakebite kit with me."

"You're going to Sonora?"

"Soon," he said.

"Well," she said, "watch where you step."

The next day at his apartment Olvera telephoned Jiménez Moreno at the Instituto Nacional and told him what he'd learned.

"Excellent work, Jorge," Jiménez said. "Kino almost died, he prayed to his favorite saint, and when he survived, he actually did what he'd promised. I find that amazing. What did he have, smallpox, plague? Typhus?"

Olvera sipped water from a cup at his breakfast table and said, "I haven't been able to find that information, sir."

"I suppose the nature of his illness doesn't matter much now, Jorge. But the incident tells us something about him, doesn't it?"

"It tells us he had a strong will."

"And faith."

Olvera thought about that. "Probably. And discipline."

"And his family was supportive?"

"I'm sure of it, sir. After his father died, his mother sold the family vineyards for money to put him through school."

"And the family name was actually Chino, spelled with a C-h."

"They often spelled it that way, but sometimes they spelled it C-h-i-n-i, or even Q-u-i-n-u-s, depending on the circumstances. During his early years in Italy and Germany, he apparently preferred Chino. But when he wrote in Latin, as the educated often did in those times, he used Eusebius Quinus."

"Why did he change it to Kino with a K?"

"Even in those days," Olvera said, "Chino was the Spanish word for Chinaman. And when he reached the New World he discovered Chino was also used as a contemptuous term for mixed-race people of low caste. Apparently he chose to keep the pronunciation he preferred—*Keen-o*—but not the spelling. Maybe he did it simply to avoid confusion. No one really knows."

"This is all very interesting." Jiménez paused on the other end of the line. "But what we *really* need to know," he added, "is when and how, and especially *where*, he died. We need to know where they *buried* him."

"Right, sir," Olvera said into the telephone. "I'm working on that."

CHAPTER 5

In the busy week following Olvera's decision to join Jiménez in his search for Kino's burial site, he found little time to study the priest's life. From the last chapters of the Bolton biography, though, he did manage to pick up a few facts on the circumstances surrounding his death. On March 15th, 1711, he learned, Kino rode from his home mission, Dolores, to the Pima settlement he called Santa María Magdalena, a distance of some ten or twelve miles. He went at the request of Father Agustín de Campos, a fellow Jesuit and part-time minister to the visita at Magdalena.

The occasion was a special one. For months Kino and Campos had been supervising Pima laborers in the construction of a small adobe chapel near the main mission church. Now the chapel was finished and ready for use. It was to be named in honor of San Francisco Xavier, Kino's patron saint, and Campos had invited Kino to sing the Mass of Dedication. It would be a fine celebration. They would have festivities and food and probably a baile, a dance, that would last into the night. Soldiers would've been there, Olvera supposed, and merchants and Indians and ranchers.

Olvera knew the Sonoran desert to be a dry, rough land strewn with cactuses, but he had little understanding of it beyond that. Nor could he picture the priest's face—the face was still unformed in his mind—though he could see the lone figure on horseback, desert around him, maybe a few mountains in the distance. Still, this was a beginning, a finite place and moment from which he could begin his search into Kino's last day.

From *Rim* he learned that Kino probably arrived in Magdalena sometime during the late morning hours on that 15th day of March, 1711. After greeting his friend, Campos, at the mission church, he probably took a short siesta. He was, after all, sixty-five years old.

He would've prayed. Olvera had no doubt that he would've sought the advice of Francisco Xavier and the Virgin Mother; he would have thanked God for this fine new chapel he would dedicate. He would glance again at his breviary to remind himself of the proper ritual of the dedication service, and he would have reviewed his notes for his sermon. But he was old, and if he was like most people that age, Olvera guessed, he would've rested.

In the professor's office at the Instituto Nacional, Olvera reported to Jiménez on what he'd learned about Kino's final day.

"Excellent, Jorge." As always, the professor looked very dignified in his pale suit and crisp white shirt. "I've made arrangements for your transportation to Sonora and for your lodging. And I've contacted a physical anthropologist here in Mexico City. He's young, but highly qualified. When we find the priest's bones, he will be able to identify them. I mailed him some notes explaining our project. I hope he'll join us."

"That's good to hear, sir."

"But we're running out of time for research in the national archives. The Minister of Education wants us in Sonora within days. He wants *you* there, anyway. I'll be a few days finishing up some projects here before I can leave."

"I'll be ready," Olvera said.

"Will you have time to learn how the priest died, and where?"

"I think so, sir," Olvera said. "If I were a betting man, I'd say they buried him under the floor of that chapel he went to dedicate. That was a common practice in those days."

"I agree, Jorge. Have you finished the biography?"

"It's a big book, sir."

Jiménez smiled. "Good luck, my friend."

In the Archivo Nacional, Olvera found lots of monographs and historical pieces on Sonora and stacks of yellowed documents on the old missions of the Pimería. These were interesting, but they told him little about Kino. His luck changed when he came across a book called *Luz de Tierra Incognita*—a surprisingly detailed diary kept by a Spanish cavalry officer named Manje, who rode for years with Kino. Then Olvera made the most incredible find of all: another diary in book form, *Favores Celestiales*, kept by the padre himself.

With what he'd learned from *Rim*, he began putting the pieces together: near the end of the Mass of Dedication in the new chapel, Kino complained of feeling ill. He told Campos he couldn't continue. Campos helped him to the guestroom, where Kino rested, probably sleeping a bit. He remained there through the evening and died quietly around midnight.

In none of the references could Olvera find mention of Kino's symptoms. No indication of any treatment he received; no name of anyone besides Campos who might have had some knowledge of Kino's illness or of his burial. Still, this was important information and Olvera made careful notes in his journal. But again he wondered: Where had Father Campos *buried* the man?

Finally, in a dusty document called *Las Misiónes de Sonora y Arizona*, he found what he needed: a copy of Kino's obituary. It had been filed by Padre Campos in the chapel's libro de entierros, the burial register. It included this statement: "*And Resting in the Lord, he is Buried in this chapel of San Xavier on the Side of the Gospel where fall the second and third sillas, in a Coffin...*"

Olvera felt his heart thumping. As he and Jiménez had suspected, their man was buried under the chapel he had gone to Magdalena to dedicate. The obituary said, too, that he was buried *on the Side of the Gospel.* Olvera knew enough about religious terminology to know the meaning of that: the left side of the church as you enter from the front. The right is the Side of the Epistle. So now he had the key to the puzzle, the rest would be easy, right? Go to Magdalena, find the chapel, dig under the left side, and find the padre's bones. Like hacking away vines from a Mayan ruin, layer by layer, and finding inside a chest filled with gold or the tomb of an ancient child-king. No, Olvera had no illusions that it would be *that* easy. In field archaeology, nothing ever was.

Too, there was this small problem: What could he make of this word, *sillas*? Chairs. A silla was a chair or a seat, and to Olvera this made no sense— "*...Where fall the second and third sillas, in a Coffin...*" Why would Campos write of chairs in a frontier church in Sonora? Such places in the seventeenth and early eighteenth centuries had no chairs or seats. They had no pews, either. Worshipers stood in the nave, occasionally kneeling on the floor. Most frontier churches in the Jesuit era had walls of adobe and roofs of pine or mesquite logs and saguaro ribs caulked with mud and twigs. Most had floors of packed dirt; a lucky few had pine planks for flooring. Some had altars carved from mesquite, and behind the altar some would have had a retablo built of wood with niches that held painted statues of saints. But none had chairs, Olvera was certain of it.

Still, for the first time since his decision to join Jiménez's project, he felt the first faint twinges of optimism.

Silla. He found the word in a dictionary: chair; seat. He searched a second dictionary, then another. Chair. Just chair. Well, there was a silla de montar, but that was a saddle. Campos wouldn't have been writing about saddles.

But these were modern dictionaries, defining modern words. Could this be an *old* Spanish word known in Campos' time but lost to the twentieth century? In his younger years Olvera had worked briefly in the field of paleography, the study of ancient writings and inscriptions. He went back to the books he trusted. Again, he found no alternate meaning for the word.

Well, maybe Campos hadn't meant chairs. That's what he *wrote*, yes, but maybe it wasn't what he'd *meant*. Maybe he'd intended to use some other word that just looked—or sounded—like sillas.

Maybe, Olvera thought, I'm using the wrong dictionaries.

CHAPTER 6

The Pimeria. Año D. 1694. February.

n the first day of February, I rode northwest out of San Juan Bautista with Father Kino and six of my soldiers, through Arizpe and over a mountain pass to Dolores at the Pima village of Cosari on the Río San Miguel.

At Dolores we were met by Father Kappus from a mission to the south, and Wigberto Bustamente. Wigberto was a mayordomo de recua, a pack train master. Because he was good at his work, the army often rented his mules and his services, even as he regularly overcharged us and tended generally toward a cantankerous and irreverent view of things. Much like his mules, from what I had seen of him. He had brought sixteen of his mules, plus his pet macaw, a talking bird named Teodora that knew more profanities than I, and in Dolores we loaded the pack animals with food, gifts, and farming utensils.

Coxi had joined us there, too. Coxi was chief of the Pimas who lived at Cosari and along the San Miguel. He had brought twenty of his people, mostly men, and on our journey they would serve as teamsters, cooks, and—if trouble came—fighters. Kino and Kappus would represent the Church, of course. I was there as Ensign of the Compañía and as Lieutenant Alcalde Mayor. As such, I represented the army but also the civil authorities of Sonora and Carlos Segundo of Spain. We made a large and colorful party, and in this brisk cold month of February we were bound for the western deserts of the Soba Pimas and the Golfo de California.

In the years to come, I would travel with Kino on many such expeditions—some far to the northwest, others to the north as far as the Río Gila—but this was my first such extended journey, and I rode eagerly and with great anticipation.

We made stops at Magdalena on the Río San Ignacio, and at Pitiquito, small settlements of Pima Indians. Father Kino pointed out the fields of winter wheat and the flatlands that in springtime would be sewn in beans, squash, and corn. On the hillsides I saw the kihs, the mud-and-twig homes, of the Pimas, and cattle growing fat on the winter grasses. At each village along the way, Kino and Kappus celebrated mass, baptized infants and sick adults, and taught catechism. As representative of the government, I gave speeches and handed out ceremonial canes to the chiefs. The canes were decorated with colorful ribbons and had shiny brass knobs on the handles. We gave the villagers trinkets and farming tools such as hoes and shovels, and they thanked us with baskets of mesquite flour and corn, which we gave in turn to the villagers in the next settlement along our route.

Frankly, I felt a little strange about my part in all this. I knew exactly what the viceroy and the king would have me say to the villagers, and I had no problem standing before them and talking about the many blessings and responsibilities of citizenship in their new country, Nueva España, and about their obligations to the king. No, it wasn't a lack of information or even a youthful lack of confidence that bothered me. It was another problem altogether: I still could not speak Piman. In school, I had studied Latin and Italian as well as my native Spanish, and had always found languages easy enough to master. But the Pimas spoke with a wide range of odd grunting sounds that seemed to echo out from the backs of their throats and I was having trouble learning their language. Thank God, once again, for Father Kino. When I mangled things too badly, he kindly translated for me, and with good humor he kept me from making too much of a fool of myself.

The desert in February amazed me.

The air seemed crisp and freshly scrubbed, and melting snows from the mountains had given new moisture to the creeks and lowlands along our route. I saw woodpeckers with red caps, butterflies with white wings, and oddly-colored little hummingbirds that zipped and popped and ricocheted through the warming air.

"Spring comes early in the desert, Juan Mateo," Kino told me. "This is your first in the Pimería, I believe."

"My first, yes," I said.

"The weather can change this time of year. It can surprise. But even that is a blessing, I suppose."

I told him I had seen some deer earlier, very small, with white tails and smooth gray coats.

"Uhwalig Mashath," he said.

"That is what you call them?"

He chuckled. "No. That is a Piman term that means 'Moon of the Deer-Mating Odor,' which is what the Pimas call our month of February. We just call the deer 'white-tails.' This time of year many of them are out foraging and mating."

As we rode Kino pointed out bladderpod and groundsel already showing vivid yellow flowers, and pink fleabane and purple verbena and shrubs with delicate white blossoms that gave off a sweet smell almost like citrus. Mock-orange, Kino called it.

Very pleasant, this section of the desert in February.

But the farther west we got, the flatter, drier, and more desolate was the land.

In the western desert I saw lizards, rabbits, and gallinazos—turkey vultures—but little plant life except creosote bush, which Kino called hediondilla, and white-barked shrubs he called bursage. Wigberto called them burroweed and happily grazed his animals on them at every opportunity. We dug holes in the sand of dry washes to find water for our horses and mules, and to fill our gourds for drinking. It seemed strange to me, and sometimes frightening, that the western desert had so few rivers to quench our thirst. Only flat dry earth that stretched all the way to the gulf. I could hardly imagine how bad it must be in the heat of summer.

"Do not worry," Kino told me west of Pitiquito. "This is February. We will see rain soon. We will have plenty of water."

Truthfully, I did not believe him. I saw no clouds anywhere.

"Be patient, Juan Mateo," he said. "It will rain."

It rained the next day.

Baskets full. All day long, the water working down from the distant foothills to rise and surge in the washes and run in silvery rivulets across the lowlands.

We bogged down in the mud. We made a temporary camp in the lee of some boulders, and when we had the animals settled, I shared a tarp with Father Kino. Someone had started a fire and made chocolate, and we drank ours, steaming and warm, snug under the canvas, the rain coming steadily but not hard. In the distance I could see a lone saguaro and shrubs with bare branches rising out of a sea of dark mud, and once I thought I saw deer moving ghostlike in the gray haze of rain.

"So, Juan Mateo," Kino said, sipping his chocolate, "how is General Jironza?"

"Fine, sir. He sends his regards."

"Thank him for me, please. He is a good man. Do the soldiers resent you because you are his nephew?"

I shrugged. "A few say I have had some advantage from it, but most accept me as I am. They *seem* to, anyway."

"Good. And how are the others in your family? I have hardly heard you speak of them." In the faint light the padre's narrow face was shadowed, his gray-streaked hair damp and curly over his forehead.

"My father died a few years ago," I said, "and my mother still frets that I came to the New World." I laughed. "She thinks death lurks behind every rock here. You know how mothers are."

Kino was quiet for a time. When he spoke his voice was distant, subdued. "Do not think badly of your mother, Juan Mateo. She just wants you to be safe. And, yes, I know how mothers are. My father died when I, too, was young. I was fifteen. It was a hard time for my family."

My comment about my mother had sounded flippant and uncaring, I realized, and I found myself embarrassed by my own words. I changed the subject. "Was your mother pleased that you became a priest?"

"She was, yes," the padre said, "but like yours, she fretted about my coming here. She hated the distance it put between us. But finally she accepted it. She made her peace with it. And with my father's untimely death."

"Do you mind if I ask a personal question, Padre?" Rain pelted the canvas in huge drops now and I could hear Wigberto's mules braying and complaining on their picket behind us.

"Go ahead," Kino said, "ask."

"I have heard that you almost died, when you were a student in Germany. They say you were saved by prayer, and that is why you became a priest and came here as a missionary. Is this true?"

He stared at me, then took another sip of chocolate. "Where did you hear that?"

"From the soldiers, sir."

He sighed. "They gossip like old crones."

"Some of them," I admitted.

For a while he said nothing. The rain continued, and in the closeness I could smell horse sweat and the damp wool of his black robe and the rich dark scent of the chocolate. I decided he was not going to answer my question.

But he did, finally. In his own way.

"Juan Mateo," he said, "do you know chapter thirty-one of Psalms?

David's book? Yes, of course you do. Verses seven and eight? '*I will be glad and rejoice in your love, for you saw my affliction and knew the anguish of my soul. You have not handed me over to the enemy, but have set my feet in a spacious place.*' "

I laughed. "The Sonoran Desert? He set your feet in a spacious place, all right."

"Yes." Kino's blue eyes glowed. He sipped again at his chocolate and smiled. "Amazing, is it not?"

The rains slowed to a drizzle that looked like it might continue for a while, so we loaded the animals and continued westward, my sergeant and I at the head of the column. Behind us were my other soldiers, then Wigberto and his pack mules and Teodora, the macaw, and the priests. Guarding the rear were Chief Coxi and his Pimas. The mules were sure-footed and steady in the loose rock and mud and we made good time over the faint trail to Caborca.

Coxi.

I should tell you about him, because to understand Coxi is to understand much about the eastern Pimas. Physically, he was imposing. He was about my height, tall for a Pima, with dark skin and thick, coal-black hair. On his wide face he had tattoos of dots and odd curved lines from charcoal rubbed into puncture wounds made with cactus spines. Like many Pimas, he had similar markings on his chest. He wore pants of dusky gray cotton, a shirt of antelope hide, and moccasins made from deerskin. He had narrow shoulders, a deep chest, long, powerful arms, and he walked with a rolling bowlegged gait, like an old sea pirate. He was about Kino's age, I guessed, his late forties, though with Indios in those early days I was never quite sure.

It was his long arms, I think, and his quickness, that had made him such a formidable warrior. When Kino had first come to Cosari, Coxi had quickly picked up the Spanish language, and Kino had taught him history, geography, even some mathematics. But it was warfare that had earned him his fame. Kino once told me that the villagers in Cosari claimed Coxi had killed more than thirty Apaches, twelve in hand-to-hand combat.

"I am glad he is on *our* side," I told Kino on the first day of that journey.

"Praise the Lord," he replied, and made the sign of the cross.

But it was not only Apaches that Coxi had fought. He had also fought the western Pimas. For a lot of years, I had learned, the eastern and western Pimas had been at war. Even though they were closely related and spoke the same language, they had little in common. The eastern group—the Akimel O'odham, as they called themselves—lived along the rivers in permanent communities and farmed the land. In most years they enjoyed an abundance of water, wild game, and crops, and lived reasonably comfortable lives. But because they were closer to the Apacheria, they fought the heathens more often and lived in constant fear of attack.

There were other famous chiefs among the eastern Pimas, I had learned. The most notable was Coro, who lived at Quiburi on the Río Terrenate. Father Kino tended to lump together all the Piman groups that lived along the northern rivers; he called them Sobaipuris. In time, I came to call them that, too.

Then there was Soba. Soba was chief of the Pimas who lived in the western desert near the gulf, the flat, arid country where we were now headed. They had no rivers and little opportunity to farm, and survived primarily by fishing, hunting, and foraging. They had few permanent settlements and were basically nomads. They called themselves the Hia C'ed, I think, but Kino called them, simply, Sobas.

Between the River Pimas and the Sobas were other groups that shared the sloping, cactus-studded bajadas that lay between the verdant mountains and the western desert. These groups, too, had little access to water, but they had some: the washes that flooded after heavy rains. They had devised some clever ways of growing tepary beans and corn along them, and of damming the shallower ones, but in spite of it they, too, led a harsh, hungry existence. These groups called themselves Tohono O'odham, or Desert People. Kino, like almost everyone else, called them Papagos. I eventually came to call them Pababotas, though I have no recollection of how that got started. Since we were the first Europeans to give them names, I suppose we believed we were free to give them whatever names we wished.

And they had been fighting among themselves for years.

This, I suspected, could be a serious problem for us. As it turned out, I was not the only one who had been worrying about it. We had been underway less than an hour when Kino rode up the column of mules and pulled his horse alongside mine. "Be watchful," he said. "Where we are going, there could be trouble."

"Because Chief Coxi is with us?"

He nodded. "The Papagos and Sobas have long memories."

"I have already warned my sergeant," I told him.

"Good. One reason we are here—and the main reason I brought Coxi—is to show them that all the groups need to band together against the Apache. If they will unite, we will all be a lot safer. I pray I can make them see it."

"I agree, sir," I said.

The next day we reached Caborca on the Río del Altar, where Kino gave talks on Jesus and Moses and said a mass for the villagers. We stayed the night, and left early the next morning after a breakfast of tortillas, wild roots, and dried beef, which we shared with the local chief. The people seemed amiable enough, but I will tell you, I didn't relax until we had that settlement far behind us.

West of Caborca we came to a large mountain range. While the others made camp, Kino and I climbed the highest peak. On his first visit to this area, he told me, he had named the peak El Nazareno, after a merchant ship that sank in Cádiz Harbor and left him stranded a second year in Europe when he was trying to get from Italy to New Spain. I asked him about the ship and how it sank and if he had almost drowned, but he had no interest in talking about it. "It was not my favorite part of the journey," was the most he would say. Anyway, from the summit we saw the Golfo, and with our telescopes we saw four tall peaks rising into the sky across the water. He had named them, he said, the Four Evangelists: Matthew, Mark, Anthony, and John.

"...Antonio?" I said, laughing. "Why not Lucas?"

Lucas, he explained, was already taken. Early Spanish mariners had given that name to the southern cape of California. Cabo San Lucas, they had called it.

"We are running out of acceptable names," I said, teasing him a little.

A few Papagos from Tubutama and a number of Sobas from the sandy western desert joined our procession toward the coast. Many of the Sobas had never seen horses, or even men with light skin and steel swords, and they ran away, afraid for their lives. Kino went after them, and in almost every case was able to gentle their fears and bring them back. They talked little with Coxi and his people, but seemed happy to be with Father Kino and he was delighted to have them with us. The Sobas and Papabotas looked much like the Pimas from the San Miguel Valley: dark, slender, their thick black hair cut straight above their brows. They had the same strange charcoal tattoos on their faces and chests, but they seemed leaner and more than a few looked poorly nourished. The women wore rabbit skin skirts and coats of antelope hide; few of the men had much more than simple loincloths to protect them from the weather. All the Sobas, even women and older children, carried bows and deerskin bags filled with arrows. From their strong smell I knew they bathed rarely, and many had lice teeming in their hair. They seemed, at least to me, very poor and very primitive.

I can hardly imagine what they thought of *us*—my soldiers in their warm wool uniforms of crisp dark blue, the long coats trimmed in red at the sleeve cuffs and collars; their boots and leggings and, across their chests, leather bandoleros filled with lead balls and powder supplies. Our horses must have amazed them, too, with their long tails and big eyes and their saddles and tack and the leather armor that covered their rumps. And what could they have thought of Teodora, with her bright red and blue feathers and her squawky voice that reeled off curses in surprisingly fluent Spanish? Probably about the same thing they thought of my white pants and red officer's coat with its gold epaulets and the fluffy ostrich-feather plume that rode atop the wide-brimmed hat I often wore.

General Jironza, frankly, preferred that his officers wear the bicorn hats. They looked more professional, he said. But the plumed hat did a better job of keeping the sun out of my eyes, and, truthfully, I just liked the look of it. Dashing; stylish. Jaunty, but still properly official.

"Dashing? Jaunty?" the general had said the first time he saw me in my feathered hat. "You look like a French dandy, Juan Mateo. A *poseur*." The general, like most of us, cared little for the French.

But both hats had been approved by Carlos Segundo for cavalry officers, and in those callow youthful years I wore mine much of the time.

In fact I was wearing it when we reached the gulf shore, on the fifteenth day of February. The rains had passed. The day was sunny, the afternoon air warm and sticky and thick with fat buzzing insects. From his saddle Kino pointed across the gulf. "California, Juan Mateo."

The water sparkled. It was blue as indigo, gilded like hammered gold, placid now in the breezeless, humid air. Gulls with gray wings wheeled and dipped over the beach, their *hiyah-yuk-yuk* cries mingling with the throaty shrieks of terns and the gurgles of small waves that lapped at the sand. Sandpipers scurried after the retreating waves and pecked at invisible things in the white sand, and I could see plump gray clouds riding the horizon as if they were too weighted with moisture to lift into the fading sky.

"I hope to go back to California, Juan Mateo."

I slapped at a mosquito. "You liked it?"

Kino nodded. "Admiral Atondo and I tried to start a mission at La Paz, near the southern tip, and another, farther north at a place we called San Bruno. The Indians wanted us there...some of them, anyway. At least in the beginning." His robe seemed faded and pale in the dying afternoon light.

He shrugged. "We had little rain. Our crops dried up. We couldn't feed ourselves, much less the Indians, and the viceroy had few pesos to spare us. And at La Paz, there was that horrible time when the Admiral and his men turned a cannon on some peaceful Indios. It was loaded with grapeshot and killed several of them and injured even more. The others turned against us, of course, and made our lives difficult. I cannot say I blame them, Juan Mateo. But we had no fresh water and no food and we were trapped on the beach. We had to abandon the mission." He sighed. "There was much I wanted to do there, but we failed miserably."

"That is when you came to the Pimería?"

"Right after that, yes," he said. "Manuel González is the visitor at Oposura. He had the responsibility for making my assignment. He decided I could do more good here."

"I hear you have done lots of good here, Father."

"Some, yes. We have brought a love of God to many of the Indians. But much remains to be done." He aimed his telescope out over the gulf, then back around to the mountains north of us. "And more of this world to see, Juan Mateo." He brushed a strand of graying hair from his forehead, and in his eyes I saw a look of...what? Wistfulness? For an instant, though, I saw something more. Determination? Resolve? Maybe I was seeing, simply, his refusal to acknowledge defeat—from lack of rain, or hostile forces, or anything at all.

But my attention soon wandered from his words. Flies and mosquitoes buzzed in my ears; gnats ate at my skin.

"California is a big island, Father," I said. "Maybe there are other places that would be more fertile and welcoming." More welcoming than this infernal beach, I thought, and whapped another zancudo.

"A big *island*?" The padre smiled mischievously. "Are you sure California is an island?"

"The maps say it is," I said.

"Maps," he declared, "can be wrong."

A stingray glided silently over the sandy bottom near the water's edge, and a few yards out I saw a gleaming silver fish rise from the depths and take an insect that flitted above the shimmering surface. The padre and I climbed down from our horses and walked along the beach.

"Maybe some day," I said, "we can follow the gulf northward and find out for ourselves if the maps are wrong."

He turned and studied me, his eyes bright. "I have thought of building a small barco," he said, stretching the words out, as if he were testing the sound of them.

"I have always wanted to sail one," I said. In later years—when I knew

Kino better and had some insight into the strength of his intellect and the depth of his determination—I would remember this moment. But in those early years in the Pimería I was young and impetuous, full of spirit and curiosity. Boating up the gulf for a look around just seemed like a fine way to spend some time.

"Are you serious?" he said. "You would help me?"

"I would like that, Father." I picked up a seashell and skimmed it across the water. "When I came through Mexico City on my way to Sonora, I had to file a report on my journey with a General of Cavalry there. He had a large, plush office, and right in the center of it he had a Coronelli globe. I had heard of them, but never seen one. It was amazing, probably five feet in diameter. You had to walk around it to get to his desk."

"I have heard they are very accurate," he said. "With all the continents beautifully drawn, and all the coastlines and mountain ranges and major rivers."

We watched gulls and terns circling out over the water. After a time I said, "My soldiers tell me you enjoy cartography, Father. They say you have made maps of the Pimería."

"Well, I have mapped everything I have seen, but there is still much I haven't seen."

I swatted a gnat. "When I saw that globe in Mexico City, I think it was the first time I really understood how big the world is." I turned to him. "Would you teach me to make maps?"

I think my question surprised him, because he smiled and something changed in his eyes. "I would be pleased to teach you, Juan Mateo."

"Maybe we could make our own globes," I said, grinning, "and we could be rich and famous like Father Coronelli in Venice."

He chuckled, then turned his attention back to the pack animals and men waiting patiently behind us. I saw him talking with Chief Coxi and my sergeant; and with Wigberto and Father Kappus. I picked up more seashells and skimmed them across the water. I watched the ripples spread, and threw more shells, and wondered if Kino had already forgotten California and the boat and his promise to teach me how he made his maps.

But of course he had not. After a time, satisfied that the animals were all right and that the men were ready to make camp, he found me again.

"Then we shall do it, my young friend," he said happily. "We will build our boat at Caborca, then dismantle it and transport the components to the shore on mules. The Indios of Caborca and Tubutama respect us and want Jesus in their lives. They have told me so, and we have seen evidence of it just this week. I am certain they will help us. So that is what we shall do—build ourselves a boat and go exploring and draw some new maps!"

"That sounds good, Father," I said, " but I have to be honest with you, I know nothing about boat building."

He smiled. "God will help us, Juan Mateo. We will find a way."

On our trek back to Dolores we stopped in Caborca and Father Kino talked to the Indians again. He told them how God had created the heavens and earth and made all the animals and plants, the mountains, the oceans, the birds and horses and cattle and fish. How He created night and day and made man from the earth, called him Adam, and gave him a soul; how He made woman from Adam's rib and called her Eve. Kino told them of God's Commandments and taught them the Ave María and the Credo. He reminded them to make the sign of the cross and to pray every day, and told them how good people are rewarded with eternity in heaven. And he talked to them about the wisdom of joining the eastern Pimas for defense against the Apaches. The Indians seemed to find comfort in his words and I found myself worrying less about trouble between the Pima groups. I looked forward to our next visit, when we would cut some trees and lay the keel of our boat.

And the following month we did return. That was when I learned about the ma'makai, and when I fell forty feet from the top of a cottonwood tree.

CHAPTER 7

The Pimería. Año D. 1694. March.

Imagine a grassy hill in the Sonoran Desert, the hill dotted with scrub cactus and ocotillo, its brown rocks seared by centuries of sun and wind, its dirt surface scored by the looping tracks of sidewinders and pocked with burrows of pack rats and tarantulas, and in the middle of it all: a boat.

Well, not a complete boat.

Not even a large boat. What we had, and what we loaded plank-by-plank onto lumber wagons and oxen at the Dolores mission, were the barracanetas and istamanales—the top-timbers and futtocks—of a shallow-draft sailing vessel. Our plan: transport them to Caborca. There, Father Kino and I would search out the right trees and cut the keel and ribs. After all the wood had dried in the sun for a few months, we would return with wood-working tools and Pima and Ópata carpenters from Ures and Banámichi, and we would lay the keel, attach the ribs, build the rudder, and piece together the hull and deck and spars. When we were confident that all the parts fit, we would dismantle the boat, carry the components to the gulf, and reassemble them at the shore. And pray for a tide that was high enough to float the crazy thing.

That was our plan. What did I know about boats? Well, from my voyage from Europe two years before, I knew a little something about Atlantic storms and seasickness remedies that did not work and wool uniforms that refused to dry in the damp salty air. I knew a few useless facts about barnacles, and the symptoms of scurvy, and even how to make rumfustian from eggs and gin and spiced sherry like the pirates do. But about building boats I knew absolutely nothing.

"But you are still willing to sail it with me, Juan Mateo?" Padre Kino asked as we loaded the wagons. His eyes glowed.

"Definitely," I said, and wondered how he always seemed to know what I was thinking. "I am looking forward to it."

As he worked he hummed an old Andalusian melody that Corporal Escalante sometimes played on his guitar. Gypsy music. I had always liked the rhythm of it, the energy and vigor.

"*Vlaminco*," Kino said, smiling widely. "In Seville they wear black and dance it on tables."

I had never seen him so excited.

We left Dolores in the early morning of the sixteenth day of March, a long and gangly column of men, wagons, and animals. Counting Wigberto's teamsters, the Pima servants, Father Kino, my soldiers, and me, there were more than forty of us. The day was warm and bright. I had learned that March in the Pimería can be unpredictable: weeks that are cold and damp, or sunny and pleasant with the lowlands and hills paved in wildflowers that dazzle the eye. This was one of the good ones.

We reached the Pima village of Magdalena that afternoon. The villagers welcomed us, and we made camp and settled in for the evening. Magdalena had no church as yet, but Father Kino said a mass in a ramada roofed with twigs and branches. We had just finished our prayers when a Pima runner came in. "A rider," he said in rough Spanish. "Coming fast." He pointed north, towards San Ignacio. I took my arquebus and two soldiers and we walked to the edge of the village with Kino to await the new arrival. Minutes later Father Campos rode up in a cloud of dust and reined in his horse. The palomino was breathing hard and Campos' wide brow was furrowed, his youthful face flushed even pinker than normal.

"Agustín!" Kino said. "What happened?"

"Apaches." Campos dismounted and hurriedly greeted us. "Yesterday they attacked the settlement at Imuris. The Pimas fought them off, but they managed to kill some cattle and steal a few horses. Worse, they got away with some Pima children. Three of them, stole them right out of the church yard."

Kino's face changed, and he made the sign of the cross. "Did you go there?"

"Last night, as soon as I heard about it." The young padre wiped dust from his face with a bandanna. "There was little I could do but say prayers with the Indios and help them clean up the mess. When I got back to San Ignacio this morning, I sent a rider to Dolores to tell you about it. But later I learned from a runner that you were coming this way with a pack train, and I thought I should ride down here myself."

"I am glad you did, my friend," Kino said. "And you handled the situation well. But you say no Pimas were killed? Or even injured?"

Campos nodded. "They fought hard, and God blessed them. Except for the children they lost, of course. They managed to kill one attacker."

"The Apaches will be angry at losing one of their own. They will try to take revenge on anyone they come across."

"What direction did they go?" I said. "How many were there?"

"North," Campos said, turning to me. "Toward the Santa Ritas. Eight of them, not counting the one the Pimas killed."

"Maybe I should take a few of my men," I said, "and go after them."

"No," Campos said. "By now they would be too far away. Besides, last night I sent a rider to notify the soldiers at Real San Juan. He returned today and said he had met a unit from your Compañía near Arizpe. General Jironza was with them. He sent Lieutenant Solís and twelve men after the Apaches. I think the general would want you to stay with Father Kino and the pack train. He said it is not likely the Apaches will turn south again, but they could."

He was right, I suspected, so I did not argue it. "Do you know," I asked him, "who their leader was?"

"At Imuris they said it was Black Skull's band."

Kino closed his eyes and whispered a quick prayer.

"What will they do with the children they stole?" I asked, and realized the answer before Kino could give it.

He sighed. "They will probably kill them."

We left Magdalena the next morning and headed west for Caborca.

At each village along the way Kino celebrated mass and taught the catechism and talked to the Indios about God and Jesus and the Commandments. At Tubutama we were met by Father Daniel Januske, the priest there. He welcomed us; we stayed the night, enjoying good food and Januske's pleasant company, and left early the next morning.

At the major settlements—Tubutama, Atil, Santa Teresa, Vacpia, and others—I gave talks about King Carlos and our duties to him and I gave canes of justice decorated with ribbons to the local chiefs so they could use them to prove their authority in local civil matters. I still had not mastered their language, but we had good translators with us and I did all right. On a cloudy day the last week of March we reached the Río Concepción and the mission Kino had founded the year before and named La Purísima Concepción de Nuestra Señora de Caborca. Quite a grandiose name for a little flat-roofed adobe chapel and one-room house of mud and straw in a small Pima farming village.

Still, it was a pleasant-looking place, and I saw much in it to like, as I had on our visit the previous month.

We stopped our horses on a hill overlooking the river, wide and fast-flowing now from the spring rains. A breeze that seemed to be growing colder stirred the grasses that grew along the trail. Behind us, the men and pack animals slowed, and the wagons loaded with lumber and tools creaked to a halt. From the trail we could see cottonwoods forming a leafy canopy over the marshy banks of the river; cane and willows nestled in the flood plain. Cattle grazed on grasses that grew in clumps between the mud-and-twig kihs dotting the hills. In every direction there were farmlands cut by irrigation canals and we saw Indios working steadily in the fields.

The chief and many of the villagers welcomed us with crosses of mesquite they had placed along the trail and with woven baskets of dried corn. At the adobe capilla, Kino gave thanks for our safe passage from Dolores and prayed for the stolen children of Imuris and for the safety of all peaceful Indios.

That evening, after a meal of roasted rabbit and bread made from the flour of mesquite bean pods, the padre and I took mugs of chocolate and walked down to the river. The moon was hazy over the trees and I could hear insects buzzing in the sacaton that grew along the banks.

"Do you think it will rain, Father?"

He shrugged. "Possibly."

"So what do we do tomorrow?" I said.

He took a sip of chocolate and smiled. "Tomorrow," he said, "we cut a tree for our keel."

The next day began normally enough, though it was unseasonably cold and damp for March, shrouded in fog and swirling mists.

After an early meal of hot corn mush and fresh oranges, we began our search for the proper trees. For the keel we needed a tall stout tree, and not far from the mission we found one—a cottonwood. This was not the best kind of tree for boat building, but we quickly learned that it was the only tree in the area tall enough for our purposes. When the fog briefly cleared, we estimated its height at thirty-eight to forty feet. Kino wanted to take it with the root ball intact, as we needed the added length so we could cut the keel in one piece.

We had three Indios with us. Ernesto and Lorenzo Otuca'tuot were Papagos from Tubutama. Brothers. About my age, I guessed. They seemed quiet, and maybe poco perezoso—a little lazy—but pleasant enough. The third was White Leaf, the Pima girl from Dolores who had killed the snake that still occasionally slithered and rattled through my night dreams. When we had the big tree's roots seemingly freed, we pushed on the thick trunk. Nothing happened. We pushed harder. Still the tree remained upright. We discovered that the central taproot was stout and deep and we had not reached it with our axes and picks. We worked at it some more. Still we had no success.

"All right," Kino said. "We will get a rope from Wigberto. I will climb the tree and tie the rope to the top branch. We can use the mules to pull the tree down."

I stared up at the few lower branches I could see through the dense fog. A lump of queasiness formed in my stomach; my pulse throbbed in my temples.

Frankly, I do not like high places. Ledges and edges, I stay away from them and always have. I have had this problem since early childhood. Why, I do not know, but I can tell you this: I had no desire to climb to the top of that big tree.

On the other hand, Kino was a priest twice my age and I was a soldier. Which meant it was time for me to stop making excuses and do my job.

I took a deep breath. "No," I said, "this is a job for a soldier, Father. You stay down here, por favor, and pray for me."

Finally he agreed. I looped one end of Wigberto's rope around my waist, and Kino and the Pimas boosted me high enough that I could reach the lowest branch. I pulled myself up. Taking care not to look down, I cautiously worked my way up the trunk, branch by branch. Damp fog surrounded me. I could see no more than five feet in any direction. The only sounds I heard were the strained raspings of my own breath. Cold seeped through my coat and stung my skin. I had an eerie sense of aloneness, an uneasy feeling that the world had abandoned me in that high frightening place. At the top I quickly tied the rope to the trunk and started back down. I had descended only three or four feet when I felt the tree tilt a few degrees. I heard the rhythmic thunking of axes and felt sharp jolts coming up through the tree's trunk, but I couldn't see what was happening through the thick branches below and the fog that seemed to be worsening by the minute. Were the Indios hacking again at the taproot? I yelled at them. I heard Kino shout, but I couldn't make out his words. The tree began to sway, and now the top whipped through a widening arc that left me dizzy. I clutched the tree with all my strength, fighting the nausea that tried to rise in my stomach. The padre's shouts echoed up through the damp air as the tree—with me still lodged at the top—began to fall, slowly at first, then picking up speed. I squeezed my eyes closed and felt cold air whistling faster and faster past my face until the tree, in a deafening crunch of grinding, splintering branches, crashed to the ground.

For a time—I could not say how long—I was aware only of a silent darkness, as if someone had thrown a heavy cloak over me. I felt no pain. Of course not. No doubt I had been mortally injured—perhaps a broken neck or crushed skull; no one could have survived such a fall. Or perhaps I had just died of fright from being so high in that tree. When I dared to open my eyes, wondering beforehand whether I would find myself peering into heaven or into a darkened anteroom of hell, I found myself looking instead into the worried face of Father Kino and the dark pretty eyes of White Leaf.

I drew in a breath of air. I eased it out, and drew in another.

"Look, Father, he has opened his eyes." The girl's words were faint but clear. "And he is breathing."

"White Leaf," the padre's distant voice said, "do you remember the large statue of San Francisco Xavier that I brought from Europe, the one in the church at Dolores?"

She nodded. "Carved from the wood of an acacia tree."

"Yes, that one," Kino said.

Now she was smiling mischievously. "I see what you mean, Father," she said. "Ensign Manje looks a lot like that statue. He does not move; he makes no sounds. His face even has that same strange gray color like old acacia wood."

"Still," the padre said solemnly, "I find no broken bones and I see no blood."

I could see no humor, if that is what it was supposed to be, in any of this, but at least I was gaining the faintest hope. Perhaps I was still alive and—no, that was impossible, I was surely dead, I was surely in he

"You are in neither heaven nor hell, Juan Mateo," the padre said, smiling widely now. "You are still in the Pimería and seemingly unharmed. Perhaps you would kindly release your grip on this poor tree before you crush it to pulp."

I released my grip. I blinked and wiggled my toes.

"God obviously wants you alive," Kino said. "I believe He must have important plans for you."

"You think so, Father?" My words sounded like the croaking of a frog.

"Yes, I am sure of it."

"...I pray His plans do not include my climbing any more trees."

Kino laughed and pulled me from the tangled branches. He brushed leaves and twigs from my uniform and said a prayer of thanks to God for my survival. The girl gave me warm chocolate and put a wool sarape around my shoulders to ward off the cold. I retrieved the lapis cross that hung from my neck and kissed it. If I had thought of it, I probably would have kissed the girl, too, and maybe even the padre.

I rested for a time, and when I felt better I said, "White Leaf, once again I owe you my thanks."

She was hacking limbs from the fallen tree with an axe. She smiled. "I am pleased you are all right, Ensign Manje."

At least she had not called me Señor Skunk, as she had before, or made any more comments about my looking like a wooden statue. I had no time to think about this, though, because I saw Kino staring curiously at Ernesto and Lorenzo, the brothers from Tubutama. They had coiled Wigberto's rope and loaded it onto one of the mules. They were watching us through the fog, their dark faces as blank as slates of stone.

"Is something wrong?" I asked.

Kino turned to me. "White Leaf," he whispered, "has just told me that Ernesto is an apprentice to a ma'makai. If I had known, I would not have brought him today."

"A ma'makai? What is that?"

"A type of shaman. A medicine man. Many Pimas and Papagos believe they have power to control the weather, and that they can cause disease or even death for anyone who disobeys them or anyone who says their magic is weak."

"So it was Ernesto," I said, grinning, "who gave us this horrible fog."

Kino shook his head. "Por favor, do not make light of this, Juan Mateo. The ma'makai have a lot of influence over many innocent Indians."

"What are you saying, Father? That Ernesto *wanted* to kill me? That he *meant* to bring the tree down with me still in it? Why would he do that?"

He stared at me for a time, his blue eyes troubled. Finally he said, "White Leaf and I tried to stop him from chopping the roots while you were at the top. I took the axe away from him, but it was too late. When the tree started to go, he turned to us and apologized. He said he had not known you were still up there. He claimed he did not hear our warnings."

"And you do not believe him?"

"I was shouting in his ear."

"...So what do we do?"

He thought about it for a moment, then said, "For now, nothing."

By the end of the next day we had the trees cut for the boat and the lumber sawed and everything laid out to dry on the side of a hill. Father Kino wanted to stay in Caborca a few days to talk to the Indians again about Jesus and God and the mysteries of the rosary. I decided to go exploring. Kino reminded me about the ma'makai and warned me not to go alone. Truthfully, I was not worried about the shamans. My own inclination was to believe the falling tree had been nothing more than an unfortunate accident. I probably would have continued in that belief if something quite odd had not happened just a few days later. Before that, though, I almost got myself killed—again.

Maybe I had better explain.

The day started about like any other: cool, clear; seemingly safe. On Kino's advice, I took Private Díaz and two Indio guides with me on my ride of exploration. Half a dozen leagues south of Caborca we came to the village of Unuicat, home of Chief Soba. The chief, like his villagers, was thin, almost scrawny. Many of the Indians went about almost naked for lack of clothes, and I saw that many of them were dirty and infested with lice. Still, they seemed happy, and they welcomed us with what little they had to offer. I gave them a bag of corn and a sack of wheat flour, and talked to them about the King of Spain and our duties to him, and told them God wanted them to cast aside their grievances and join with the eastern Pimas in defense against the Apaches. They seemed to understand, and thanked me for my visit.

The next morning we continued our ride.

It was one of those perfect spring mornings that over the years I would come to associate with March in the Pimería. The air was crisp and cool and dry, the sky cloudless and intensely blue. By now I knew many of the desert plants, and they painted the lands around us in flamboyant color; the scent of wildflowers filled the spring air. Goldpoppy and owlclover formed surging carpets of orange and purple between clumps of bursage, with mariposa and bladderpod adding their splashes of gold and white. Brittlebush with flowers of brilliant yellow speckled the dusky earth between stands of prickly pear and cholla. At the base of a hill just ahead I could see the glossy red blooms of chuparosa and penstemon, and hummingbirds with crimson throats darted among them. We rode in silence toward the hill, taken by the grace and beauty of the March desert.

They hit us at the foot of the hill.

The first Apache arrow caught Private Díaz between the shoulder blades, soaking his blue coat with blood before he finally fell from his mount. The second glanced off my saddle and just missed the chin of Juan José, one of my Papago guides. At first I didn't see the attackers, but from their war whoops and shrieks I guessed there were plenty of them. I got a pistol out and caught one on his paint pony as he came screaming at me full gallop down the hill. I shot him square in the face. Another came at me on foot and I wheeled my horse around and got a musket ball into the thick of his leg. I had no sense of what the guides were doing, I was just trying to stay alive. I jumped off my horse and went after the leg-shot Apache on foot. I caught him behind a tumble of boulders. He tried to gut me with his knife but I got out of his reach and swung my arquebus at him hard. The barrel caught the side of his head and he went down in a lump. When I looked up, the fight was over, the Apaches gone. They had vanished like smoke into the rocks and hills. My two guides were shaken but unharmed.

The entire skirmish had taken less than a minute.

I took longer than that to catch my breath.

"Good work," I told the Papagos.

"You, too," Juan José said.

My heart was thumping so hard I could hardly talk. "What happened to ... the others?"

"I got one," Juan José said. "In the chest. The others picked him up and got him back on his horse, but he will die soon."

"Was it Black Skull's gang?" I asked him.

He shrugged.

"Tall," I said. "Wears a black headband."

He shrugged again, and I knew he had been too busy to take notice.

The ball had passed through the Apache's thigh, exiting on the backside. He was still unconscious. I tied a strip of cloth around his leg to slow the bleeding and tied his ankles together. With a stout rope I bound his wrists behind his back; I threw him on his belly over the saddle of my horse. Private Díaz was dead. We got him over his own horse, the arrow still sticking from his back, and tethered the animals together. We made Caborca by nightfall.

Father Kino said prayers for Private Díaz and I said a few words at his service. We buried him on a hill above the river with a small cross of mesquite to mark his grave.

After the service, Kino asked if it was Black Skull's band that had attacked us. I told him I did not know.

"Watch your back, my friend," he warned.

I promised I would. Was I worried? Not really. I remembered what the padre had said about Black Skull's pride, though, and his comment that the Jocome's anger would grow until he found a way to kill me. I vowed to be more careful in the future, even when the wildflowers were in bloom and everything seemed quiet and peaceful. *Especially*, I was learning, when everything seemed quiet and peaceful.

With the oxen and mules we would be slow getting back to Dolores, so I ordered the wounded Apache bound tightly and sent on ahead. Two Pimas and Private DeJulio would escort him to the presidio at San Juan. I did not trust the Pimas alone with him. Frankly, I had begun to suspect they would kill him at the first opportunity.

"Take him to General Jironza," I told DeJulio. "As fast as you can travel. Maybe Don Domingo can trade him for the children the Apaches stole at Imuris. If they are still alive."

"I will hurry, sir."

To Wigberto, the mayordomo, I said, "Will you loan the Army one of your wagons to transport the prisoner?"

He shook his big head. As always, he had about a four-day stubble of beard and breath that reeked of onions. "But I will rent it to you, Señor," he said, "for a very good price. Two pesos. And for that price I will even give you the use of one of my very valuable teamsters."

"But the Army is already paying you for the wagons and teamsters."

"This is a special circumstance, Señor."

"Not *that* special," I said.

He shrugged. "Some would say yes, some no."

I stared at him.

Over his shoulder I could see Teodora, his red-and-blue macaw, perched on the seat of a wagon. "*Two pesos, two pesos,*" she squawked. "*Get going, you lazy stupid lop-eared mules.*"

Wigberto belched and wiped his mouth with the back of his hairy hand. "Two pesos. It is a very good price, Señor."

But the strange incident that brought back memories of Ernesto, the ma'makai apprentice, and the falling tree happened the next day, near Oquitoa. Clouds had come in again, and the day was thick with a moist gray fog. Father Kino and I had ridden ahead of the others and stopped in a copse of sycamores near the river for a meal of pinole and goat's milk. We were sitting on the riverbank taking our food when we heard something coming through the brush. I retrieved my arquebus and we stood to see who or what it was.

"*Hello, priest. Hello, soldier.*" The voice was thin and shrill, and came to us from a distance. Through the fog I saw a strange dark object moving slowly in our direction. When the apparition reached us, I saw it was a bony and stooped old woman on a huge mouse-gray stallion. Her hair was matted and dirty. She had sunken cheeks and dark wrinkled skin that reminded me of old harness leather. Piercing eyes, the same odd shade of gray as her stallion, gave her the look of a madwoman. Over her colorless dress she wore a gamuza, a coat of antelope hide, and on her fingers and wrists she wore rings and bracelets of silver.

"Señora," the padre said in greeting.

Her gray eyes grew wide as she looked down at us from her horse. "Hear me, priest; and you, soldado. Soon they will fill the arrow with arrows...I have read it in the tracks of the black bear and seen it in the droppings of the pantera. And you, soldier," she added, stabbing a bony finger in my direction, "beware of those who speak in strange tongues." Before Kino or I could reply, she reined her stallion around and rode slowly back into the mist, her bracelets jangling in the damp still air.

I stared after her. "Madre de Dios, who was *that*?"

Kino smiled wryly. "Now you have met Gonzala Hurtado. 'Old Gonzala,' they call her. She's a curandera."

"What did she mean, 'Soon they will fill the arrow with arrows'? And what did she mean when she told me to beware of those who speak in strange tongues?"

Kino shrugged. "She keeps the settlers stirred up with her crazy riddles and impossible tales. They say she knows a lot about herbs and simple treatments, though, so no one runs her off. She rides the country alone on that big horse. People say the Apaches are afraid of her and robbers refuse to harm her. The vaqueros at Dolores say the grulla stallion is her lover, that it kills anyone who denies or betrays her. She worries me, Juan Mateo. I wish the people were not so superstitious. It cannot be good for them to hear such stories."

I agreed. But the incident with Ernesto and the tree—and now the old crone's riddles about arrows and people who speak in strange tongues—had left me full of questions. And perhaps a little unnerved. Something was happening in the Pimería, or *about* to happen, and I had no idea what it was.

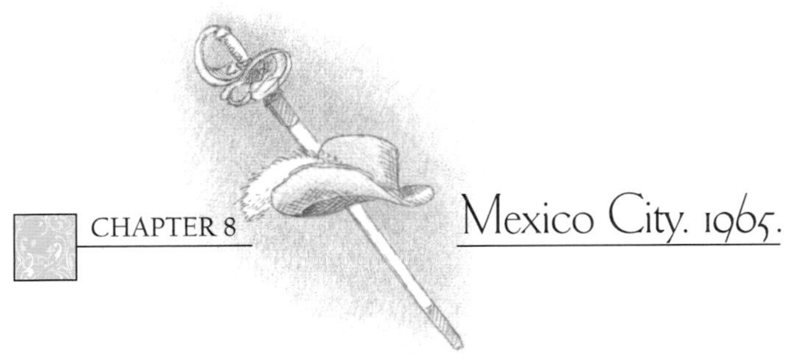

CHAPTER 8 Mexico City. 1965.

"I have some good news," Jiménez said to Olvera when they met again in the professor's office. Jiménez placed his reading glasses on his cluttered desk and massaged the bridge of his nose.

"And bad news," he added. "Which do you want first?"

"The good, por favor," Olvera said.

"I've spoken with an historian in Hermosillo. He tells me there's good reason to believe the town called Magdalena on our modern maps is at the same site as the Pima village Kino knew as Magdalena. He says the Sonoran state archives show no record of any other place by that name, or any similar name, that could be confused with it."

"Excellent," Olvera said, thinking, too, of his own good news.

"The historian reminded me that Magdalena is still a small town. He also reminded me that most of its citizens now are Mexicans rather than Indians. Over the centuries some of the Indians moved away and most of the others were assimilated into the Mexican culture through marriage."

Olvera wrote careful notes of this information. When he finished, he told Jiménez of his good fortune in learning a few things about Agustín Campos, the priest at Magdalena, and of the obituary Campos had filed on Kino's death. He quoted the line that had caught his attention: "*...And Resting in the Lord, he is buried in this chapel of Saint Francis Xavier on the Side of the Gospel where fall the second and third sillas, in a Coffin...*"

After a time Jiménez said, "On the side of the Gospel—that part I understand. That would be the left side. But *sillas*, Jorge? It makes no sense. They wouldn't have had *chairs* in a frontier church."

"I believe I've solved that riddle, sir."

"Good. What have you found?"

"It occurred to me that there might be a similar word that Campos could've confused with sillas. I found such a word in a dictionary for architects. The word is *sillares*. It's an old architectural term for ashlars.

These are the large stones cut square on each face that were used in construction of masonry foundations. Now we would call them 'stone footings.' I suspect this is what he was referring to."

Jiménez smiled. "Good work, my friend. Now we're making progress."

"I think so, sir. Now we know we have the right village, and we know where Kino was buried *in* that village." Olvera hesitated. "So, what's the bad news you have?"

"Two things. The first concerns this Chapel of San Francisco Xavier, the one under which Kino was supposedly buried." Jiménez retrieved his reading glasses from the desk and slipped them on again. "My contact in Hermosillo knew of it. He says it no longer exists. There is no trace of it, and no one knows where it was located. So, if your Father Campos in fact buried our man under it, we have much work to do, because now we have no chapel under which to look."

Olvera glanced up from his notes. "Well, we knew it wouldn't be easy. What's the other bad news?"

Jiménez leaned back in his chair. "You remember the physical anthropologist I told you about? He, too, refuses to be a part of our project. He said he has no interest in searching for the bones of a priest that no one ever heard of, under a church that no longer exists, in a town of no possible importance."

For the first time in days, Olvera laughed. "We'll find the bones," he said. "And we'll find a way to identify them." He thought about this new information, this double dose of bad news. "But now in Magdalena," he said, "they have a church?"

"Oh, yes, a large one. I'm told it dates to the early 1830's. Built by the Franciscans. Possibly on the site where Campos built his main church, but no one is certain of that. There's a small chapel, too, but it's some distance from the church. The Proctor Chapel, they call it. Or the Chapel of San Miguel. Many of the local citizens think it's the chapel where Kino was buried. Others doubt it, like my friends in Hermosillo, as I told you. Of course we'll have to take a close look at it when we get there." Jiménez unfolded a map of Sonora and smoothed it flat on his desk. He touched a circle that marked the site of Magdalena. "Problems, Jorge, always problems. But we won't give up. We'll go there and dig our trenches and find these ashlars, these footings."

Jiménez rose from his desk, stepped over to a window, and stared out at the trees that lined the street. "This man, Campos, the priest who buried Kino—what more do we know about him?"

"A few things, sir." Olvera thumbed through his notes, found the page, and began to read. "Agustín de Campos...probably a Spaniard...he was just out of his Jesuit training when he came to the Pimería. That would've been in December, 1693. He was assigned to the mission at San Ignacio, a Pima village a few miles north of Magdalena. Kino had already introduced cattle to the Indians there and taught them the basics of ranching, and planted wheat and established orchards and vegetable gardens, but when Campos came, he had only a makeshift adobe chapel for his worship services. It didn't take him long to build a larger church, though." Olvera flipped to the next page of his notes. "His new church burned to the ground in 1695. The Pimas revolted that year and destroyed a lot of church property. Campos and Kino immediately rebuilt the church. Campos remained as minister at San Ignacio for forty-three years." Olvera looked up from his notes. "I would guess he was well over seventy when he died. And for a lot of those years, he also served as visiting priest for smaller villages nearby, like Magdalena."

"He must've been quite a resilient man. Much like Kino, I suspect." Jiménez turned from the window. "You've been to Sonora, Jorge?"

"Never, sir." He told Jiménez of the diaries—Kino's and Juan Mateo Manje's—that he'd found in the archives.

"Juan Mateo Manje?" Jiménez said. "Who was he?"

"A friend of Kino's," Olvera said. "A Spanish officer."

"Let me know if this soldier can tell us anything useful."

"I will, sir."

"The Minister tells me you have to leave for Sonora by the weekend."

"I'll be ready," Olvera said.

"When you get to Sonora," Jiménez said, "I want you to go first to Hermosillo. See if the state archives have anything that might be of use to us. Then I want you to talk to the owner of the Cervecería de Sonora."

Olvera stared at him. "You want me to go to a *brewery*, sir?"

CHAPTER 9

Hermosillo, Sonora. 1965.

"In order to understand what happened at my husband's brewery," Señora Genoveva said to Jorge Olvera, "first you have to understand what happened to the churches of Sonora in the 1920's and '30's. And to understand that," she added, "you have to know something about Presidente Calles."

"And Presidente Cárdenas," Olvera said.

"Yes. I suppose he was just as bad."

"I remember," Olvera said. "I was young, but I remember."

Olvera and the woman sat in comfortable chairs in the airy sala, the living room, of the widow's home in Hermosillo. The walls, finished in white stucco, gave a look of shiny dark earth to the saltillo tiles of the floor. The furniture was made of sturdy woods and looked to Olvera as if it'd come from Spain. On a burled walnut table before them were cups and saucers of fine china, spoons and napkins, a pot of coffee on a silver tray, and silver bowls of sugar and cream. In the bright morning light the Señora's hair, too, was the color of silver, and very clean, and she wore it pulled back from her narrow forehead and pinned in a bun on the back of her slender neck. To Olvera everything here looked expensive, even the woman herself.

A maid in a white cotton dress poured coffee for them, then quietly left the room.

"Perhaps, sir, you would prefer a beer?" the widow said.

"Oh, no," Olvera said. "Coffee is fine. Gracias."

She laughed softly. "Me, I don't care much for beer. I prefer strong coffee with double cream, even in this summer heat; even though my late husband was in the brewery business. Does that surprise you?"

"These days," he said, "nothing surprises me." Well, that wasn't quite true, he knew. This visit with the widow of the brewery owner had certainly surprised him. Even now he still wasn't sure why Jiménez had wanted him here. On his arrival in Hermosillo, Olvera had telephoned and learned from the woman that her husband had died. He explained that he was in Sonora to search for the gravesite of Padre Kino and had been advised to speak with her husband. Without hesitation she had said, "Yes, of course. Please, come by tomorrow at ten o'clock." As if everyone who looked for Kino always paid her husband—or her—a visit.

So he'd come, still wondering.

"I know you're here," she said, "to ask about the bulto."

A bulto? Now he was even more puzzled. A bulto was a statue. What did a statue have to do with Kino?

The widow didn't wait for Olvera's response. "The stories you've heard," she said, "are true. Kino brought with him from Europe a large and valuable statue of San Francisco Xavier. The rumors say he kept it at his Dolores mission for a time, but eventually it ended up in the church at Magdalena."

"...With Father Campos?" Olvera sipped his coffee.

"I don't know when it was moved, or by whom, but I know it remained in the church at Magdalena until the early 1930's. Which brings us to the brewery—"

"Por favor," Olvera interrupted, "yes, the brewery."

The widow stirred cream into her coffee and stared at him. "I suppose," she said finally, "you have a working knowledge of our country's Constitution?"

Olvera did. The current version went back to 1917, composed after one of Mexico's bloodier revolutions. It was a complex document of many parts, but its major themes had been socialistic and anticlerical: more rights for the poor, fewer rights for the Church.

"I have to ask," the woman said. "Are you a Christian?"

Olvera shrugged. "Not much of one, Señora."

"Still, you would know that since 1917 the churches in Mexico have not been allowed to own property. Not legally, anyway. You know the government actually owned all the churches."

"I knew that, yes."

"For a time after 1917," she said, taking a sip of her coffee, "our leaders wisely ignored the provisions concerning churches and religion."

Olvera nodded. "Until Plutarco Calles came along in the 'twenties. And then Lázaro Cárdenas in the 'thirties. It's common knowledge, Señora. These men created an atmosphere where persecution of Christians was not only tolerated, it was openly encouraged."

"Sadly, that was especially true in Sonora," the widow said. "The first place the soldiers went was Magdalena. They confiscated all the religious symbols—all the Bibles, the statues of saints, the paintings and religious images—and literally tossed the worshipers into the street. They converted the church into a meeting hall for labor unions. Many of the Christians resisted, of course, and more than a few went to jail for it. Some died."

"*¡Viva Cristo Rey!*" Olvera said. Not because he was a believer, really, but because he knew his country's history.

The Señora smiled. "Yes, that was their slogan, 'Long Live Christ the King.' And of course in Magdalena the soldiers took the bulto of Saint Xavier from the church. My husband said it was beautifully carved of wood from an acacia tree. He said the soldiers brought it here, to his brewery, and burned it."

"Burned it?"

"Yes. There was nothing left but black soot."

"...I see," Olvera said.

"Are you all right, Señor? You have such a strange look on your face."

"...I'm fine, yes, I'm okay."

A new thought had come to Olvera, a new possibility. He would need time to think about it, to visualize the implications of it more clearly. But he no longer wondered why Professor Jiménez had wanted him to hear the widow's story. He rose from his chair. "Thank you, Señora, for your time, and for the coffee. You've been most kind."

That night, Olvera telephoned Jiménez in Mexico City.

"So, Jorge," Jiménez said, "what do you make of the widow's tale?"

"Interesting. A statue that once belonged to Kino, burned in a brewery."

"Yes," Jiménez said, "but there's more to the story. In Magdalena now there's an elderly woman named Dolores Vásquez who says the statue was *not* destroyed by the soldiers. She says someone, at great personal risk, stuffed a sack with heavy papers made up to feel as if the sack held a statue, and that's what the soldiers burned. Vásquez says she later saw the real statue in the workshop of a local painter, a man by the name of Ortiz, who was secretly making repairs to it. She says no one knows what happened to it after that."

"So now," Olvera said, "I've heard *two* stories on this statue. I have no idea which is true. Maybe neither. Maybe it doesn't matter."

"But the story *itself* is important, is it not?"

"Oh, yes," Olvera said. "The story is important. At first I couldn't understand why you wanted me to talk to the widow. Then I learned that in the 'twenties and 'thirties, the Christians of Sonora, and particularly Magdalena, did everything in their power to hide their favorite religious articles from the government."

"And the significance of this is...*what*?"

"Well, to me, it raises the possibility that those same Christians may also have felt compelled to protect their favorite priest, Father Kino. They could've dug him up—if anyone actually knew where he was buried—and spirited him away. Out of town, probably. Out of Sonora, possibly."

"My thinking, exactly," Jiménez said. "I prefer to believe this didn't happen, because if it did, it makes our task a lot more difficult. But, yes, we have to accept the possibility of it."

Olvera shrugged. "If it happened, we'll learn of it. We'll find the bones."

"See, Jorge?" Jiménez said, "I knew you'd make a splendid detective."

CHAPTER 10

San Juan Bautista, Sonora. Año D. 1694. April.

On a warm morning in early April, over a meal of tortillas and boiled corn with onions, Father Kino told me about Juan María Salvatierra. I had never heard of the man, but Kino seemed intent on talking about him, so I listened. On a fine spring day like this, I could think of many things worse than having breakfast with the padre in the courtyard of a pleasant little café near the plaza.

"Salvatierra," Kino said, "is a Jesuit."

And, like himself, Kino told me, he was an Italian. He had come to New Spain as a young priest and had served for years as minister of a successful mission in Chínipas, in the mountains east of Alamos, far south of the Pimería. But by 1690 Salvatierra had been promoted to Father Visitor for the young territories of Sinaloa and Sonora and it was in this capacity and in that year that he came to Dolores on the banks of the Río San Miguel. He arrived on horseback, alone, on Nochebuena—Christmas Eve.

Juan María Salvatierra had not come to deliver glad tidings and joy.

He was a large man, Kino told me, of naturally gruff countenance, with a hawk nose, a gaunt, hatchet face, and brooding eyes. Kino had welcomed him, of course, and assured him he would do everything in his power to make the Visitor's stay an enjoyable and comfortable one.

"Why was he there?" I asked Kino.

He shrugged. "Rumors. Stories going around. It is the Visitor's job to keep an eye on things, as you know."

Rumors? Stories? What was he talking about? I waited for him to continue. At the tables around us, people I took to be government employees, settlers from outlying areas, and officials from the silver mines talked in low voices over tortillas and oranges and grilled meats and drank chocolate from mugs of pewter. We drew a few curious glances. I made little of it, assuming simply that the busybodies had never seen a priest having a meal with a cavalry officer.

The padre still had not explained, so I tried nudging him. "Rumors?"

He sipped his chocolate. "In my years here...I have made a few enemies."

He would say no more than that, so I waited again for him to continue. When he had finished his corn, finally, he did. "Father Salvatierra wanted to meet the other priests in the Pimería," he said. "And he wanted to see the missions and visitas I had started."

"All of them?" I said.

"Every one, Juan Mateo. But remember, in 1690 I had been in the Pimería only three years, and I had only a few priests to help me, so there were fewer missions to see...and most of those were still quite small and modest."

Naturally, Kino had first shown the Visitor his own mission, Dolores; gave him a tour of the fields and vineyards, showed him the winter wheat growing green and strong in the flatlands, the irrigation systems and mill and carpenter's shop; the vegetable gardens and winery and large adobe church with its heavy doors to keep the Apaches out. They rode into the hills and Kino showed him the cattle he had brought up from Ures and introduced him to the Pimas he had taught to tend them. He showed him the goats and sheep, the blacksmith shop, and the good, strong horses grazing on grama and sacaton that grew in thick spills along the river. And of course he invited the Visitor to take part in the Christmas Mass, where he could see for himself the Pimas crowding into the church for worship and hear the newly-formed choir of Pima women who sang the Christmas songs in Spanish and even a few in Latin. The padre spoke to me of these things with modesty, but with a touch of pride, too, and I found myself, for no reason I could justify, sharing in his pride.

Of course in 1690, Kino told me, the church wasn't completely finished and the vineyards needed a few years yet, but altogether the village of Cosari and its people and the Dolores mission looked pretty good.

"And Salvatierra was impressed?" I said.

"If he was," the padre said, smiling faintly, "he kept it a closely-held secret."

I chuckled. "So you took him to see the other missions?"

"Yes, even before the New Year arrived. We were gone a month. And I was worried, Juan Mateo. Because he had the authority to shut down my missions. He knew it, and I knew it, and he knew that I knew it. On our journey we took pack animals and extra horses and several servants and cooks. I wanted the Visitor as comfortable as possible."

"No soldiers?"

Kino shook his head. "Juan María Salvatierra is a bear of a man, and he had faced down the Tarahumara in the Sierra Madres. He has no fear of the Apaches."

So they had ridden out of Dolores, their pack train behind them. In Magdalena and Remedios, Kino showed him the brush shelters that served as visitas for the visiting priests, and introduced him to the local chiefs. He showed him the fields that in springtime would be planted in corn, beans, squash, and cotton. In San Ignacio de Cabúrica he showed him the one-room adobe building that served as chapel and priest's quarters; he took him to see the cattle he had driven up from Dolores and introduced him to the Pima vaqueros who already were making plans for the next roundup.

The padres rode to Imuris and El Tupo and on northwest to Tubutama, and in all these places hundreds of peaceful Indios welcomed them. In that first week Kino introduced his guest to the local chiefs as well as to the other priests who labored in Kino's rectorate: Fathers Pineli, Arias, and Sandoval. They saw the small adobe churches, and the Indian lands under cultivation, most of them fallow in the winter season. They saw the wheat coming along and orderly rows of citrus and quinces and apples and the fields that would be planted in melons and beans and chickpeas and sweet cane. Near the rivers they saw cattle and other livestock Kino had introduced to the area, and in the desert they met Papagos who proudly showed Salvatierra their methods of flood-farming along the washes during the summer months. *Ak chin* farming, they call it, Kino told me.

"What was the weather like?" I asked him.

"The weather?" He seemed puzzled by my question. "I cannot say that I remember."

I had to laugh. This confirmed something about the padre that I had suspected for some time. When he rode out of Dolores to visit his old converts or to find new ones—anytime, actually, that he was doing God's work—he was single-minded in the extreme. He didn't *remember* the cold because he never *felt* the cold.

From Tubutama, he told me, they rode north up the Río Altar to Sáric and Tucubavia, where hundreds of Indios welcomed them. In all these places, he and the Father Visitor taught catechism, baptized sick infants, talked to the Indians about God and His laws and Jesus and His parables, and told them stories from the Bible.

"By this time in your journey," I said, "Father Salvatierra must have seen the success of your missions, right? Now he was satisfied?"

Kino laughed. "We had been in the saddle two weeks before I saw his first smile, and even that did not happen until we had gone even farther north."

They had planned, he said, to turn southeast from Tucubavia, and return home by way of Cocóspera. But in Tucubavia they were met by Indians from far north of there. They carried crosses of mesquite and begged the missionaries to go with them and baptize their infants and preach to their families where they lived near a great river that ran wide and deep.

"And you went with them?"

"A new village of innocent souls, and a great river," Kino said, smiling. "How could we resist?"

So they had ridden north out of Tucubavia, the Indians leading the way on foot. They crossed a mountain range and descended into the valley of a wide river whose waters ran northward. On an earlier visit Kino had seen the river in its smaller, southern part, and knew that it came from mountains to the east; it was called, he told me, the Río Santa María.

They had ridden on northward, Kino and the Visitor, along the Santa María. At the Indio village—Kino said they called it Tumacácori, a Piman word that meant "place of the flat rock" —they had prepared brush-roofed ramadas for the priests and their servants and welcomed them with singing and dancing. But there was more, Kino said. While they were preaching to the Indians at Tumacácori, Indians from even *farther* north arrived in the village. They came from a village called Bac—a much larger settlement, they said, than Tumacácori. It was near another place called Tuk'shon, on the same north-flowing river. They wished the priests to come with them and preach to their families at the villages.

"So," I said, "Bac and Tuk'shon, two more villages of innocent souls."

"And that," Kino said, "is when I saw the first smile from Salvatierra."

"It took a while," I said.

"Yes. But unfortunately, we had run out of time. Salvatierra had to get back and make his report, so we were unable to ride any farther north."

"But he smiled, finally."

"Oh, yes. In the end, he was very happy with what he had seen. He returned to Ciudad de Mexico and filed his report. In it he asked that *more*, not fewer, priests be assigned to the Pimería. But on the ride back we talked about the possibilities in the Californias, too. He agreed with me that the bounty of the Pimería could be used to feed the natives there. He even liked my idea of building a boat to explore the gulf. Now we exchange letters regularly. We have become good friends."

"Amazing," I said. I still had no idea why he was telling me all this.

"I am telling you all this," he said, apparently reading my mind again, "because I want you to know we have allies in the Church hierarchy when we set sail—which could be soon, if God wills it. Can you go to Caborca and help me finish the boat?"

I grinned. "I have to see the general this morning. I will ask him."

"I am seeing him, too," he said. "I hope to sell the army a hundred head of cattle from the mission at Dolores, and I have to negotiate a fair price with your uncle."

"Good luck," I said, and chuckled.

"Don Domingo," I added, "is worse than Wigberto."

Before we rose from our tables he whispered, "One more thing, Juan Mateo. Have you heard anything more about the ma'makai, or about the old crone, Gonzala?"

"No, nothing." I shrugged. "Perhaps it was all our imagination."

He crossed himself and said, "I pray you are right, my friend."

To pass the time until I could see the general, I wandered over to the presidio corrals. My favorite mount, a blue roan gelding, had caught a leg in a gopher hole the day before, and I wanted a look at him. I found him in the covered shed where they tended the sick and injured animals. The air reeked of leg poultice and liniment, and near the stalls I could smell gall soap and balm and purgatives. My roan's leg was better. I brushed out his coat and gave him a bit of sugar.

When I got in to see the general, he was in fine spirits. I supposed he had made a deal for the padre's cattle that favored, shall we say, the government's view of a cow's general worth. At any rate, he was glad to see me and motioned me into a chair across from his desk. On the whitewashed walls around us were shelves of books, and crossed steel swords that represented his cavalry unit, the Compañía Volante, and portraits of old men I guessed were earlier governors. His office was actually the sala of his living quarters and was, even in the crush and clatter of the presidio, an airy and private place, fitting for a man of his rank.

"Thank you for coming by, Nephew," he said. "There are several things I wanted to talk with you about. First, I have arranged for Lieutenant Solís to give you another lesson with the sword. He will meet you at the barracks when you leave here."

"Thank you, sir," I said. We had done this before, and already I had learned a lot from Antonio de Solís. I had found little to admire in his manner and attitude, but he was good with his sword and he had seemed willing enough to teach me.

Don Domingo gestured at the sabers that hung on the wall behind him. "The arquebus and pistol are excellent weapons, Juan Mateo. But it is your sword that will keep you alive in close combat with the enemy."

"Yes, sir." I believed him. He had been in enough battles in his years in Sonora. He had killed his share of Apaches and Jocomes.

Domingo Jironza Petris de Cruzat was of average size, but he wore his gold-trimmed red and white general's uniform like a much larger man. He had sun-roughened skin, large brown eyes, and a neatly-kept mustache; he wore his long hair—still as black as coal after all his years in Sonora—brushed back and curled at the top of his collar. He had come from Spain as a young military officer, as I myself had. I liked him, and would have liked him even if he hadn't given me a Barb pony when I was a youngster in Aragón and he was still at the university. I named the horse Domingo and rode it daily until I, myself, left for the New World. Don Domingo, actually, was the reason I had come. He had written my family with the request that I come west and help him bring civilization, manners, and good breeding to Nueva España.

It was the good-breeding part, I always suspected, that had finally tempered my mother's objections. Had my uncle's petition gone ungranted, I might have spent my life in Spain, serving the army somewhere along the rough and tangled border we shared with our old enemy, France. There would have been pressure to marry, of course, and to sire a stable full of children. In truth, it would have been more than just *pressure* to marry. In Spain, my relatives would have picked a mate for me and I would have had no choice in the matter. Though I had a bit more freedom here on the frontier of Sonora, more than once the general had reminded me it was time for me to find a wife. I could find no fault with that. Such feelings ran strong in our bloodlines, and it was no easy task for a young man of good family to avoid weddings, wives, and midwifery. But I was happy with my life in the Pimería, even without bride and heirs, and thankful still that Don Domingo had posted his letter home to Aragón.

He tossed something small and dark at me. I caught it in mid-air.

"Do you know what that is?" he said.

I rolled it in my palm and held it up to the morning light. It was a lump of dried mud about the diameter of a peso coin. Embedded in the surface were grains of something that looked like sand, except for their colors: black and red.

"Do you have a magnet, sir?"

Don Domingo, his eyes never leaving mine, pulled a small rectangular magnet from a drawer of his desk and handed it across to me. His face gave away nothing, and I could see he was working hard to keep it that way.

I removed the red sash from my waist and wrapped it around the magnet, then held the magnet near the cake of mud. Black grains jumped across. I pulled the cloth away, let the grains drop from the cloth onto the general's desk, and handed the clean magnet back to him.

I grinned. "The grains that look like red sand are fragments of crushed garnet. The black granules are iron oxide. Magnetite."

"...And that is important because...*why*?"

"Because where you find garnet and magnetite sands together, that is often a place you can find gold."

"Gold." Don Domingo smiled widely. "They taught you well at the university."

"Thank you, sir. Where did the mud come from?"

"One of my captains found it last week on patrol. Near Baviácora. He did not stay long in the area. The Indios there have had smallpox in recent months, and the captain wished to keep his men away from the danger."

I knew about the smallpox, but that did little to curb my excitement.

"When are you going out?" I asked him.

"Soon, Juan Mateo. Would you like to go?"

"Yes, sir," I said. "Absolutely."

But I had other things on my mind, too, and wanted to voice them while I had the general's ear. "Sir, do you know of a Jesuit official named Salvatierra who visited Kino at Dolores four years ago?"

He nodded, so I went on. "Father Kino told me the Visitor came because of rumors and stories going around. Kino said he had made enemies. What was he talking about?"

Don Domingo leaned forward in his chair and put his elbows on the desk. "At that time, yes, there were plenty of stories going around. There still are, though the padre has managed to scuttle at least a few of them. And it is true, he did have enemies. He still does. Some of the miners and ranchers do not like him because he enforces the King's cédula against taking Indians as slaves. Some say it is none of his business, and start rumors about his honesty. Some say he is greedy and just wants the silver and gold for himself."

That made no sense to me and I said so. "Are you serious?"

"Very serious. And they complained that he refused to administer sacraments to the settlers—he gave them only to the Indios. In fairness I have to say there is truth in that, though it is not the fault of the priests. The law, as it is currently written, forbids the Jesuits from ministering to anyone but the Indios." He shrugged, then went on. "But there have been other complaints against him, too. Some of the church officials themselves—high-placed people in Durango and Ciudad de Mexico, I am told—are jealous of him. Some begrudge his accomplishments. Some dislike his German accent. Remember, most of these priests were born in New Spain. They have a different culture, and more than a few of them view all Europeans as rude and arrogant. They probably see *us* that way, too, Juan Mateo. Some have started rumors that there are not many Pimas in the Pimería, implying that Kino needs no more priests. Some have even started rumors that the Pimas are as bad as the Apaches in attacking settlers."

"Is any of this true?" I asked him.

Don Domingo shook his head. "No, but the rumors and stories have been a continuing problem for the padre. For the army, too."

I changed the subject again and asked him about the Apache prisoner I had sent back from Caborca in hopes of trading him for the Pima children that Black Skull had taken at Imuris.

"We still have him in the stockade, Juan Mateo. I have sent Francisco Acuña out to see if he can make contact with the Apaches. He has not reported back yet."

I knew Ensign Acuña. He was fluent in the Piman and Apache languages as well as his native Spanish. The general and other senior officers often used him when they needed a good translator.

"And if the children are already dead, sir?"

Don Domingo shrugged. "We will turn the prisoner over to the civil authorities for trial."

Turn the prisoner over to the civil authorities for trial. I had been in the Pimería almost a year now, and by this time I should have known what that meant for the prisoner, or for *any* Apache warrior the army took captive. To be truthful, I had my suspicions, even then. But such thoughts were not pleasant ones for me in that first year and I chose not to pursue the subject with the general, as I had chosen not to pursue it with others. What was I thinking? Maybe if I refused to openly acknowledge certain aspects of life in Sonora, they simply would not exist. Or maybe they would exist only as rumors, invisible wisps of iniquity and outrage that had nothing to do with me.

Sometimes, I have to admit, I was incredibly naïve.

The general and I talked about a few other things, most of little consequence, until he rose from his desk. This was his signal that I was dismissed—I may have been kin, but he was still the general—so I stood, too, and snapped a salute that would have made Carlos Segundo proud. The general smiled and walked around and put his hand on my shoulder.

I knew what he was going to say.

And he said it, his brown eyes shining. "I do not want you to think all the miners and ranchers are bad people. There are plenty of good families in Sonora. In fact I have arranged for you to stay a few days with friends who ranch near Ures. They are hosting a dinner and dance this weekend, quite formal, I understand." He handed me an envelope that I knew would be a letter of introduction. "Take a few servants and ride down, Juan Mateo. Give some thought," he added, "to finding a wife."

When I walked out of the general's quarters, I saw a man sitting on a bench under a sycamore tree near the parade ground. He wore dark pants and a white shirt and he carried a knife and pistol in a leather belt across his chest. He had the light skin and soft features of a Spaniard, or maybe a Frenchman. His eyes were an odd shade of gray, and he had a beard and mustache that almost hid the cleft deformity of his upper lip. He looked familiar, and I remembered when and where I had seen him: that morning, at the little café near the plaza where I had breakfast with Father Kino. I felt the man's eyes on my back as I hurried off for the officer's barracks and my sword lesson with Lieutenant Solís, but at the time I did not make much of it.

I should have.

CHAPTER 11

The Pimería. Año D. 1694. June.

In the sixth month of this year, Father Kino lost his boat, Corporal Escalante lost a finger, and I lost any naïvete I might still have had about the summer heat in Sonora.

Oh, and I lost my hair, too. Every sweat-encrusted strand of it.

Actually the month had started off well enough. On June 6, a warm though pleasant day, Kino and I left Dolores for Caborca with Pima and Ópata servants and carpenters and a pack train of boat-building supplies.

After a journey of three days we reached the mission at Tubutama where we enjoyed the hospitality of Daniel Januske, who was priest there. The next morning after mass I told Kino of my curiosity about the lands north of Tubutama, and told him I had heard tales of a great mountain there and wanted to see it. He gave me his blessings and prayers. He would continue on to Caborca with the pack train, he told me, and I could meet him there in time to help with the boat.

"Baboquivari," he said.

"Por favor?"

"That is the name of the big mountain, Baboquivari."

"I had wondered," I said, "if it had a name."

"Take a couple of men with you, Juan Mateo," Kino said. "And be watchful."

"I will, Father," I assured him.

That first day, all went well. With two Christian Indians from Ures I rode north up the Río Altar to the Pima villages of Gutubur and Sáric and then to Busanic and Tucubavia. As the hours passed, the heat grew, but we had plenty of water and suffered no problems. The river valley was rich with vegetation, and along the banks we saw deer and javelina and coyotes; even a ringtail cat and a few bighorn sheep. As I had suspected, this was fine country, the river flanked by rolling hills veneered with ironwood and saguaros, and on the horizon, by mountains that rose gray and rough against the pale blue sky. In the thickets I heard cicadas thrumming their staccato songs and I saw white-winged doves darting among the saguaros, feasting on ripe pitahayas, the crimson fruits that grew at the top of the tall green arms.

In each village we talked to the people of God's love and I told them of their obligations to King Carlos and his designated representatives, the viceroy and the army. One of the men with me was a young Pima known by his Spanish name of Francisco Xavier. He was one of our most reliable translators. Like Ensign Acuña, he spoke fluent Spanish, Apache, and Pima. Francisco helped me greatly in my talks with the villagers, who seemed pleased to have us.

We followed the Altar to its end, then turned northwest in the afternoon heat and rode into dry brown desert that supported little plant life but creosote, prickly pear, and the occasional bursage. We saw mountains in the distance in every direction, but the largest loomed directly ahead as a dark jagged mass against the glaring azure sky: Baboquivari. I asked Francisco about the name.

"The Papagos call it Waw Kiwulk," he told me. "Which means

Constricted Mountain. The early settlers had trouble with the Papago words. For the Spaniards, it ended up as Baboquivari."

"Well," I said, chuckling, "that is close."

We jumped our horses over a ditch lined with brittlebush that looked dry and dead in the summer heat. "Close enough," he said.

Seen from the west, Francisco said, the mountain looks as if it has been squeezed in the middle, giving it a peculiar bulge at the top, thus explaining the Papago name, Constricted Mountain. From our angle it was beginning to look like a massive boulder with a castle on top. As we came closer, it began to resemble a dark knob with a huge boat stranded on its slope. I considered naming it Noah's Ark, though I had no illusions that anyone would prefer that to Baboquivari. According to Francisco, the Papagos believed Waw Kiwulk was the home of I'itoi, the Creator. I'itoi and Buzzard and Coyote, he told me, were the first creatures created. I'itoi then created man.

"And the troubles began," I joked.

"They certainly began for the Papagos," he said.

I had not forgotten Kino's advice. As we rode I kept a watchful eye on the mountains and desert around us. Once, as we neared Baboquivari, I thought I saw riders in the foothills, but I lost them in the glare of the sun and was unable to find them again. The Apaches and their allies had renewed their depredations on the eastern villages, but I had heard no reports of recent atrocities in this part of the Pimería. I spurred my mount to the top of a rise and studied the foothills with my telescope. Nothing.

"Our traditions say I'itoi lives in a cave," Francisco said when I returned, "high on the west side of the mountain. Maybe it was I'itoi you saw up there."

"Do you believe all that, Francisco?"

He was a small man, slender but wiry; I suspected he was very strong for his size. He had dark skin, big eyes, and the same odd charcoal tattoos on his face and chin that I had seen on most of the Pima men. His horse was a small paint. I had heard he had taken it from an Apache war chief.

"No, Señor," he said solemnly. "I no longer believe in I'itoi. Now I am a good Christian, like you."

"Father Kino is happy for that," I said.

"Gracias," he said.

Francisco and men like him were what Kino called *temastianes*: Christianized Indians, mostly Ópatas and Pimas from farther south, who offered their skills to the frontier missions. Most taught rudimentary Spanish to the newly-converted Pimas and instructed them in the catechism. Some worked as blacksmiths or carpenters or as overseers on the mission farms, and taught these skills, as well. But a few had very special abilities, and Kino found much use for them, too. Men like Francisco, the translator, and his brother, who would become a famous artist. Father Kino had told me more than once that he could not have built his mission at Dolores—or any of the others, for that matter—without the help of his Pima and Ópata temastianes.

Not that the Pimas and Ópatas actually *liked* each other. I had heard rumors of trouble between them, and I asked Francisco about it.

"Yes, there is trouble," he said. "But it is not new. The Ópata lands are south of the Pimería, which means the Ópatas were Christianized a number of years before many of the Pimas were."

"That is a problem for the Pimas?" I asked him.

"A big problem, Señor. Because the Ópatas have been around the Spanish longer, they generally have a better command of their language, they understand Spanish culture better, and are more assimilated into the Church. Which means, usually, that Ópatas who go to the frontier as temastianes are usually placed in charge of the 'less-enlightened' Pimas."

"In other words," I said, "they look down on them."

"Often, yes," he said.

"And I suppose these Ópatas have authority to punish the Pimas who work under them?"

He smiled wryly. "Now I think you see the problem."

We rode on, rounding the southern foothills of Baboquivari, and found a small settlement of Papagos who had good fields of corn and excellent pasture lands. They had a small spring that produced green water, and I named the place Pozo Verde. We gave the natives trinkets and talked to them of God and His Laws. From there we turned due north and rode to the little village of Cupo, where we talked to the Indios and stayed the night. Most had not seen horses before and a few ran from us. Francisco got them back, though, and we enjoyed showing them our saddles and harness and taking them for short rides. I showed the chief my musket and sword and he showed me how he carved his bows from the branches of wild mulberry trees. He showed me the yerba de flecha plant and how he made poison from its resin and applied it to his arrow points. And he showed me how he cut his arrows from the stalks of bushes that grew, he said, along the banks of a big river far to the north—

"Whoa—" I said. A *big river*? "North of here?" I asked him through the translator. "What river is this?"

The chief shrugged. "A river. Large. Wide and deep." He pointed. "It flows from east to west."

"Where does it come from and where does it go?"

The chief said something and shrugged again.

"He has no knowledge of that, sir," Francisco said.

"Have you heard of this river, Francisco? What can you tell me about it?"

"I have heard rumors, yes. People say there are large houses near the river. They are called the Casas Grandes and have been there for years, since before the Spanish came, even. The houses are tall, maybe thirty or forty feet in height. The river and the houses would be several days' ride north of here."

"Who built these...houses?" I said.

"No one knows, sir."

"Several days' ride?" I sighed. "All right. But we shall see them, Francisco. Some day."

He smiled. "I hope so, sir."

We left for Caborca early the next day, hoping to put as many miles as possible behind us during the cool morning hours. At midmorning we stopped at a wash. Cottonwoods, willows, and ironwoods bordered the wash, and recent rains had left pools of water in the sandy bottom. While our horses drank and rested, we sat in the shade on boulders of brown sandstone and shared a meal of pinole and chiltepine peppers.

That is when things began to go bad.

Not because of the peppers, though they were very hot, but because of the man who stepped from behind a cottonwood with an arquebus aimed squarely at my chest.

"If you reach for your weapons, Señor," he said, "I will shoot you." He was dark-skinned and large, probably mestizo, with thick hands and scarred knuckles. I saw a pistol tucked into his bandolera, the handle black as coal against the soiled white of his shirt. He jabbed the musket barrel toward the Indians, then turned it back on me. "The same goes for them, amigo," he said.

"What do you want?" I said. "We have no money."

The two Indios were standing now, their pinole forgotten.

"Toss it here, Señor," the stranger said.

"Toss *what*?" I said.

"*The lapis cross, Ensign. Toss it to him, but do not stand up.*" This voice, louder, came from behind me, and I turned to see a second man with a musket. He had light skin, a full beard, and a cleft lip. "*S'il vous plait, monsieur*, raise your hands so I can see them."

I raised my hands. "What lapis cross?"

"The one you wear on a cord around your neck. The one you took from an Apache named Black Skull." I had seen the man before, and remembered where: at the presidio near the parade ground, outside Don Domingo's quarters. His words were crisp and sharply spoken, as if he were accustomed to giving orders; to French soldiers, I had no doubt.

"Ah, *that* lapis cross," I said over my shoulder. "Are you common thieves, sir? What is your business with us?"

"Do not turn around, monsieur, but keep your hands up, oui, that is right, no weapons, please. I do not want to have to kill you. Now, slowly remove the cord from your neck."

I glanced at Francisco. "On kah-yay," I whispered. His dark eyes glowed; he nodded slightly. With my eyes on the mestizo, I removed the cord.

"What is your name, sir? Tash-ay-ay?" I said over my shoulder. I could feel the cross, warm and wet with sweat in my hand. "Nah-kee?"

"No," the Frenchman said from behind me, "my name is neither Tash-whatever-you-said, or Nakee. I am Henri. That is all you need to know. Now, slowly," he added, "give the cross to Diego."

"Diego," the mestizo said, smiling. "That is me, Señor." He stepped closer and held out his big hand.

Which is exactly what I had hoped for. I shouted "Kah-yay!" and came off the rock and put my shoulder hard into the belly of the dark-skinned man just as the Pimas hit the Frenchman behind me. I heard the air spill from Diego's lungs; he grunted in surprise, but stayed upright. I stepped back and chopped him hard in the face, and then a second time. Neither punch fazed him. He slugged me with a beefy fist that rattled my teeth. Before I could clear my pistol from my sash he got off a musket round that grazed my cheek, drawing blood and stinging my skin.

From behind me I heard another shot and the sounds of a violent scuffle, but I had no time to investigate; Diego pounded me in the face again. Pain exploded behind my eyes. I ducked his next swing and threw one that caught him in the side of his neck; he groaned, but the punch did little to slow him. Finally I got my pistol out and squeezed off a shot, but I was off-balance and the ball thunked into a tree behind him. Before I could step back he swung his musket in a wide arc that caught my shoulder and sent pain ricocheting into my neck and knocked me tumbling into the wash.

Somewhere in the fracas I had lost my feathered hat and the little blue cross; luckily, I still had my sword. I saw no sign of Diego, so I scrambled out of the wash, angled away from the clearing, and ducked into a copse of willows. My shoulder ached and I could feel swollen flesh beneath my shirt. Blood ran from my nose. A couple of teeth wobbled in my mouth, but I could find no broken bones and the pain seemed bearable. I worked my way through the trees toward the clearing.

Through the foliage I saw the Pimas on the ground. Francisco had a bloody cut of his forehead and the other Indian had a swollen eye that had already started to go purple. Still, both Pimas were alive and I was happy for that. Diego stood nearby, his musket trained on them. Henri was on his hands and knees, sifting through twigs and dead leaves at the edge of the clearing—looking, no doubt, for the little cross he wanted to steal from me. I slipped from the shadows and stepped behind the Frenchman and placed the tip of my sword's blade on the back of his neck.

"Señor," I said firmly, "if Diego has not dropped his arquebus and stepped away from the Indians by the time I count three, I will run this steel through your ugly French throat. *Uno...*"

Diego turned from the Pimas, raised the arquebus to his shoulder, and sighted down the barrel at me. "Shall I shoot him, Señor Pitot?" he said.

So. The Frenchman's name was Henri Pitot. I would try to remember that.

I pushed gently on the sword and drew blood from the skin of the Frenchman's neck. His foot twitched; his hands clutched at the dry brown earth. Sweat beaded on his forehead and I watched blood trickle down his hairy neck and spatter like red paint on the ground. I tweaked the blade. The trickle turned to a steady flow.

"*Dos...*" I said, and smiled at Diego.

My smile, truthfully, was about as authentic as pyrite gold. With Diego's musket not twelve feet from my head, he could not miss me. Still, I thought I had the advantage of him, for this reason: his jefe had no wish to die. And die he would if I pushed harder on my sword. I preferred not to think beyond that simple fact.

"So, Henri," I said, "your choice."

"*Monsieur*," Henri mumbled, "*s'il vous plait*, he will drop the weapon, please. Diego...put down the musket...now."

Diego hesitated. He looked at the Frenchman, then back at me. Finally he shrugged, dropped his arquebus to the ground, and stepped away. I pulled the flintlock pistol from his belt and took another from Henri.

With the Frenchman still on his hands and knees, I stood before him and put his own pistol to his forehead. "Why," I said, "did you try to take my cross?"

Henri stared up at me.

"How," I asked him, "is it so valuable that you would risk your lives for it?"

He started to speak, then stopped.

"Well?" I said, and nudged him with the pistola. I wiped sweat from my lip.

He blinked. "Really, you do not know, monsieur?"

"If I knew," I said, "I wouldn't be asking."

"But you just came from Baboquivari."

"Yes. So?" In that moment I remembered that earlier I had seen, or *thought* I had seen, riders in the foothills near Baboquivari. Had it been these two?

The Frenchman laughed, a strange, cackling sound that came from deep in his belly.

"This is all very humorous, Señor," I said, poking him again with the pistol, "but now you will tell me why you want the cross. And what it has to do with Baboquivari."

He laughed again. "No, monsieur. I do not think I will tell you."

I grabbed his arm and yanked him up. His face and neck were smeared with blood. I put the pistol to his temple. He stared straight ahead. We stood like this for a time. Occasionally I prodded him with the pistol, but he would say no more. Finally I lowered the weapon. "Madre de Dios," I sighed. "I assume you have horses. Find them. Go. Leave us, por favor, before I change my mind and put a lead ball through your useless French brain."

Without a word the would-be thieves plodded through the trees and down into the wash and out of sight. We followed the crunching of their boots on the gravel until the sounds faded from our hearing.

I found my hat in the wash and Francisco found the blue cross at the edge of the clearing. I held the cross in my palm and studied it. It looked like it always had: quite ordinary. Oh, it was nice lapis, certainly, but I could not imagine it was worth risking one's life for. Why had these miscreants wanted it?

As we were climbing onto our horses Francisco said, "You surprised me back there, Ensign. I did not know you spoke Apache."

"I know about ten words of it," I said. "Fortunately I know tash-ay-ay, nah-kee, and kah-yay."

"Apache words for *one, two,* and *three,*" he said, smiling. "And you did very well, Señor, although I suggest that your accent needs some minor improvement."

I donned my feathered hat and adjusted the brim to a rakish angle. "I shall work on that," I said, and grinned widely.

We mounted up and rode steadily southward towards Caborca in the growing heat of a clear, cloudless summer day. We found little water for our horses and grew thirstier as the desert stretched out before us, the land seemingly drier and flatter and more desolate with each passing mile. We rested our mounts in what little shade we found, but we encountered no creeks or even any pools of stagnant water. As the sun rose in the sky, our thirsts became barely tolerable. We slowed our horses and finally climbed off and walked them, as their need for water was as great as ours. Heat rose from the ground in waves, shimmering before us, and in the distance I saw mirages that looked like lakes of blue water. At every wash we came to, we dug in the soft bottoms, but got nothing but handfuls of dry sand. The swelling had worsened in my shoulder, and I knew the Pimas were suffering with their injuries. Still, we kept moving, urging the horses on, our throats more parched with each step.

But late in the afternoon, by the grace of God, we stumbled onto a Papago settlement where the villagers offered us water from earthen jugs. We drank and celebrated and drank some more and splashed in the water like children.

We shouldn't have. I suppose I drank too much; or maybe the water was tainted. Whatever the problem, by the time we reached Caborca I could barely stay in my saddle. My mouth was sore and cracked, my head ached; my stomach roiled as if I had swallowed a loop of rawhide rope. My face felt hot, the skin of my arms, cold and clammy. I vomited many times.

The heat in Caborca was unbearable, the sun almost blinding.

I remember little of the week that followed. Later I learned that Father Kino had done what he could for me. He tried to get nourishing soups into me, and a few simple herbal remedies. But my condition worsened; I became feverish and, according to those who saw me, sometimes delirious. I became vaguely aware of being strapped in a litter made from branches and horse blankets; I was aware of voices around me, but I drifted in and out of consciousness and understood little of my circumstances. I dreamed of a giant monster that looked like a gray whale and was called a nehbig; it lay in the hot desert sucking up everything that came near, sucking up Indios and settlers and animals and even entire villages, and I dreamed of a giant woman named Ho'ok who had claws like an eagle and tricked Papagos into coming near so she could catch their children and eat them. When I thought I could tolerate these monsters no more, I'itoi came—Elder Brother, they called him; the Creator. He looked like an old man, stooped and white-haired and pale, but he killed the nehbig by cutting out its evil heart and he slayed Ho'ok the crone by burning her alive in a cave on the side of Baboquivari Mountain.

With the monsters gone, after a time I came partly awake. I was slick with sweat and so thirsty I feared I would faint again. I was on a wool blanket on the dirt floor of a room with walls of adobe, and in the night-darkness I heard loud snoring. It had to be a priest, nobody snores like priests, but I had no idea what priest this might be or where I was. Propelled by my thirst I stood, unsteady on my feet, and took a few tentative steps. I found a doorway and wobbled somehow into the adjoining room. In the moonlight I saw an olla high on a shelf. I knew the jug held water. I could *smell* the water; I could *feel* it.

With a long pole I pushed at the jug, jiggled it around on its shelf. I saw the jug falling, remember it hitting me, soaking me; then I lost consciousness again.

When I finally awoke enough to have any semblance of reasoning, it was daylight and I saw that I was in the guest quarters of the mission church of Father Campos at San Ignacio. I learned that Indios had carried me in a litter on their bare shoulders for the six days it had taken to walk the hundred-and-thirty miles from Caborca. I learned that I had been feverish and delirious throughout, and that Father Kino had been so concerned about me that he had given me the Sacrament of Extreme Unction—last rites.

I learned I had not actually dreamed about the nehbig and Ho'ok, but that on the long journey from Caborca, Francisco had walked at my side and passed the time by telling me folk stories and legends of the Papago people.

I learned that I had overturned a water olla in Father Campos' living quarters and soaked everything in the room as well as myself, and that the water had helped to break my fever. I also learned that the fever had caused all my hair to fall out.

Sunblistered skin...cracked lips...sunken, bloodshot eyes...thin as a worm. And now I was bald, too.

Actually I looked kind of comical.

Father Kino certainly thought so; he had a good laugh out of it.

From my sickbed I told him about the robbers who had tried to take the lapis cross from me. He had already heard the story, of course, from Francisco.

"Henri Pitot and a big, dark-skinned man named Diego. Do you know of them?" I asked the padre.

He shook his head. "And they wanted nothing but the cross? They were not after money?"

"Only the cross," I said. "But why? And how did they even know I had such a thing? Or that I took it from an Apache and wear it on a cord around my neck? And the Frenchman mentioned Baboquivari, as if that explained everything. What could he have meant?"

"I have no idea," the padre said. "It all sounds very strange. But I am pleased that you chose not to kill them." His face changed and I knew what was coming.

"There is something I have to say," he said.

"I should not have fought them," I admitted.

Kino nodded. Light from the doorway flooded the room and flared on his face. The smell of grilled onions and chilies drifted in from the cooking ramadas, and I could hear Pima children playing in the yard. "You are smart and capable, Juan Mateo," Kino said, "but you are also young, and in your youthfulness you are often impetuous and naïve. You should have just given the cross to the bandits. I hate to think that you or the Pimas might have been killed for a little cross, even if it is a symbol of our Lord's crucifixion."

He was right and there was little I could say in my own defense, so I did not try. Instead I told him about my visit to the Pima village of Cupo, and about the chief's story of a large west-flowing river north of there, and I told him of the large houses said to be near the river. "Big houses," I added, "*huge* houses. And the chief said the water runs wide and deep in the river. *Very* wide. *Very* deep. And he said the houses are enormous, Father, really, really enormous."

Kino chuckled and rolled his eyes, and I realized he had seen my chattering for what it was: an amateurish attempt to change the subject. I grinned sheepishly.

But my story about the river and the houses must have surprised him, at least a little, as he was silent for a time. Finally he said, "You are certain of this river, Juan Mateo?"

"No, sir," I said, "but the chief at Cupo was sure of it."

"And there are Pimas living along it?"

"The chief said so. And other tribes, too."

"So," he said, "I suppose you want to go and see this place?"

"I would like that, Father. But first we should finish the boat and explore the gulf, should we not?"

"That *was* our plan, yes. You have not seen the letter, have you?"

"What letter, Father?"

Kino left my sickroom and came back shortly with a letter. The letter was from Juan Muñoz de Burgos, the Father Visitor. Burgos wrote in no uncertain terms that Kino was to immediately cease work on this impossible boat project because he had more important ecclesiastical duties right here in the Pimería and ought to be attending to them forthwith, and besides, was this not a *desert*, after all, and what in heaven's name was he doing with a *boat* in the *desert*? There was more, but the rest of it made the same point: Kino was to stop work on his boat.

I arched what little remained of my eyebrows. "He means it?"

"Oh, yes," Kino said. "He means it."

"Madre de Dios," I groaned. "There goes our sail on the gulf."

Kino smiled. "It is not the end of the world, Juan Mateo."

For an instant I wondered why he was smiling, because I knew how much he wanted the boat. Then I realized he was simply doing what he always did when someone placed an obstacle in his path: he went over it or around it, or he found another path. I wasn't certain which route he had decided to take in this instance, but I had a pretty good idea. In the short time I had known him, I had come to understand that as long as he could find new lands to explore and more innocent souls to save, he needed little else to make him happy. But there was another thing I had learned about the padre: even in the obstacles themselves he usually managed to find a relevant Scripture, a moral lesson. I wondered if he would do it again this time.

He did. "You know the book of Romans, Juan Mateo," he said, "Paul's writings to the Christian churches of Rome. In his letter, chapter five, he wrote, '*We also rejoice in our sufferings because we know that suffering produces perseverance; perseverance, character; and character, hope. And hope does not disappoint us.*' "

"I hope you will persevere and bring me a big cup of water," I told him. "Or, better, a stiff drink of mescal."

He laughed, and when he returned with my water he looked again at the letter from Burgos. "He is very clear about the boat," he said.

"But he says *nothing*," he added, grinning, "about not exploring a large river north of Cupo."

See what I mean?

After a few weeks of rest I was back with my horse soldiers, and for most of the remainder of the year I chased Apaches and Jocomes and Mansos. We killed a few and captured a few and those we caught we sent to the civil authorities in San Juan for trial. Private DeJulio took an arrow in his thigh and Corporal Escalante lost a finger to an Apache's knife, but the post surgeon did his business and soon had them both back in the saddle. Lieutenant Solís worked his usual tricks on the battlefield, personally taking off the heads of four Jocomes who strayed a little too close to his sword.

In September I rode to Baviácora with Don Domingo, Corporal Escalante, and two Pima servants; we were looking for the red and black sands that could lead us to gold. We found no garnet or magnetite, no gold and no silver, but we managed to ambush three Apaches in the hills near Guepaca. We killed them and left their bodies to rot in the sun.

Forgive me, por favor, I have no wish to boast—or to hide the truth of our own regrettable losses in this difficult year. One of our captains died of smallpox, and two men, of rabies caught from coyotes. One of our Papago guides perished from measles. Six of our brave soldiers died from Apache arrows; three were captured by the enemy and presumably tortured to death.

Still, we stood firm; we stayed in the saddle and did our jobs.

Once, later, in San Juan Bautista, I saw the Frenchman, Pitot. He was alone, unarmed, and I was in the company of other soldiers. I ignored him; he pretended to ignore me. Nothing came of it.

I saw nothing more this year of Old Gonzala, the curandera, or of Ernesto, the Pima ma'makai. Or even of Diego, the hombre with the big fists. I did not see Black Skull, the Jocome, though we chased him into the mountains a few times after he led raids against Nacosari and Cocóspera. I did not see White Leaf, either, though I heard she had grown taller and prettier.

Nor did I find a wife among the daughters of the ranchers and miners, as Don Domingo would have had me do. Many of the women were comely—fair-skinned and elegant—but at this stage of my career I found little time for the rigors of a proper courtship.

And what of Father Kino? Unable to work on his boat, he used most of the remainder of the year to oversee the harvests at his missions, tend the livestock, and minister to his beloved Pimas and Papagos. In October we heard rumors that miners were using Pimas as slaves, and in that month I rode with Kino and Ensign Acuña to inspect the silver mines near Real San Juan.

At the mines we were not warmly received. Kino forced the release of three innocent Indians from servitude and gave a stern rebuke to the owners of the mines. Acuña and I gave them yet another copy of the king's proclamation against enslaving Christianized Indios and reminded them that they were not immune from prosecution under Spanish law if they persisted in such practices.

But the padre's year was not all toil and moil.

In November he rode out of Dolores with a handful of Pima servants—I was otherwise occupied or I would have been with him—and traveled north to the villages of Tumacácori and Bac on the Río Santa María, and even farther, to the banks of the large west-flowing river of which we had spoken. The Río Gila, he called it. He did many baptisms there, I later heard, and gave away presents and trinkets and gifts of wheat flour, and found the Pimas along the river to be friendly and docile. The large houses, the Casas Grandes, I heard, were made of adobe. The largest was four stories in height. All were empty. No one seemed to know why they were there, or even who had built them. Of course all this I heard from others. Until I could see them myself or hear the padre's account of them, I doubted I would know quite what to believe.

Certainly 1694 had been a full year.

And certainly in this year we in the Compañía, and the padre, too, had our good fortunes. But we had our sufferings, as well. I cannot say that we rejoiced in them, as Paul advised in his writings to the Roman churches; but we accepted them.

Yet we would soon have even more. The last months of this year would see the arrival in Sonora of two more young Jesuits, Francisco Mora and Francisco Saeta.

The Two Franciscos, as I would come to think of them. One would be a persistent thorn in Kino's side; the other would soon claim the martyr's crown. Both would arrive on the wings of war, and Kino and I would quickly find ourselves squarely in the middle of the whole bloody mess.

CHAPTER 12 Hermosillo, Sonora. 1965.

"A splendid detective," Jiménez had called him. But Olvera didn't feel like a splendid detective. At the moment he didn't feel like any kind of detective at all. He felt like an aging librarian covered with dust, cobwebs, and the musty odor of ancient manuscripts.

Olvera was weary of yellowed, worm-eaten documents. He was tired of searching through stale, fusty archives, tired of sitting in dimly lighted libraries. Tired of sitting, period. Tired of reading, making notes, then reaching for yet another dusty tome. His eyes were bleary. His back ached; his fingers cramped. Since his arrival he'd worn out three pencils. Sharpening, writing, sharpening yet again. He wanted to get outdoors, to swing a machete at something, to hack away the frustration he felt from being cooped up in this place with its old books and old papers and old moldy smells.

Still, he had to admit: Much of what he'd learned about this priest, Eusebio Kino, had been interesting, even incredible.

Now, in his hotel room the evening before he would leave Hermosillo for the northern desert and Magdalena, he took his hand-written notes from his briefcase. He slipped on his glasses and began to read...

- ***At Halle, eighteen years old, he fell ill with a mortal disease that very nearly took his life; doctors believed he would die. At suggestion of a wise and friendly priest, Chino prayed to San Xavier, his personal patron saint. Promised Xavier if he would intercede on his behalf with God and he survived, he would enter priesthood, join Jesuits, and volunteer for missionary work in the Orient no matter the hardships.***
- ***Survived. Kept promise.***

Olvera filled a glass with water from a pitcher on the bedside table. He took a drink, sat on the edge of the bed, and began reading again...

· Two years later, age twenty, completed studies in logic and rhetoric at Halle. Joined Jesuit Order and began novitiate in autumn 1665. Attended universities in Ingolstadt, Munich, Freiburg, Oettingen, concentrating on mathematics and astronomy while simultaneously pursuing Jesuit curriculum. Known to be an enthusiastic student.

· one of his professors: Adam Aigenler, world-famous mathematician and cartographer.

· interesting incident: Towards end of his schooling, Chino back at Ingolstadt, teaching grammar and math to undergrad students. Classroom visited by Duke of Bavaria (Duke's son was in Chino's class)—Duke so taken by Chino's teaching he offered him a permanent job as math instructor. Chino turned down the offer, citing other interests, ie desire to preach Gospel in the Orient.

· Ordained June 12, 1677, two months before 32nd birthday.

· Intensely desirous of assignment to Orient.

· Interesting incident: Chino and Antonio Kerschpamer, another young Jesuit from the Tyrol, received assignments; one would go to Orient, other to New Spain. But they weren't told who got which. Finally, they agreed to draw lots. On one piece of paper they wrote, "Oriente," on other, "Nueva España." Chino drew Nueva España. (Note to myself: He must've been incredibly disappointed !).

· Sailed from Genoa, Italy, for Cádiz, Spain in June, 1678, with eighteen other young priests (including Kerschpamer) bound for the New World, hoping to arrive Cádiz in time to make the Flota—the flotilla of warships and merchantmen that sailed each summer to Veracruz, Nueva España.

· En route to Cádiz, the ship called briefly at Alicante on the Spanish coast. At the church at Alicante, the young Jesuits saw the famed Veil of Santa Veronica, the cloth believed to have been used by the compassionate woman to wipe Christ's brow on His way to Calvary. At night, Chino saw veil carried in the dark streets by a solemn procession of monks with lanterns; monks keeping vigil in hopes that the veil would ward off plague, which was then prevalent in nearby villages.

· Storms in the Mediterranean, much mal de mer; constant threat of Algerine pirates—so-called Barbary corsairs. Fortunately, no serious problems, but with calms & contrary winds, arrived Cádiz half a day late to catch the Flota. Severe disappointment for priests. Extra year in Spain looming.

Half a day late. Kino had missed his ship to the Americas because they were half a day late to the port at Cádiz. Olvera sat for a time, thinking about history, thinking about how it's altered by such seemingly minor events. It was amazing when you really thought about it, how things happened, or *didn't* happen, because of some small incident like this.

Finally he set his notes on the rumpled bed, straightened his tie, and slipped into his suit coat. He thought about buying a newspaper, but decided against it. He knew he wouldn't like what he'd find: reports of more murders, more scandals in Mexico City, more corruption in the government, and now yet another war, this one in Viet Nam, pity the poor Norte Americanos. It seemed to Olvera there was always a war going on somewhere. Even in Kino's time, he'd learned. Even in the Pimería: war between the Apache and Spanish, war between the River Pimas and Desert Pimas, war between the Pima shamans and the Spanish. And on the east coast of New Spain in Kino's time, fights between the Spanish and the English; in Europe, an even larger war pitting the Spanish and French against the Austrians and English. And now Viet Nam all over the newspapers.

No, Olvera thought, no paper; not today. He walked a few blocks to a café where he had a dinner of eggs, chorizo, and coffee, and watched shiny new cars rush by in the street. After a second cup of coffee he returned to the hotel. He retrieved his notes and took up his reading again...

- ***Because they knew it would likely be at least a year before they could sail again, Chino, other Jesuits traveled upriver to Seville, Province of Andalusia (apparently Spanish church hierarchy didn't know what to do with 19 stranded energetic young priests). Used time wisely. Studied Spanish language, customs; worked with local priests; learned skills considered useful for frontier priests—ie, wine-making, vegetable farming, brandy-distilling. In addition, Chino found other activities: taught mathematics at Jesuit college, built scientific instruments such as astrolabes & compasses for use in map-making; probably traveled extensively in southern Spain. (Note to myself: I would guess he was intensely curious about Spanish culture and would want to see the country).***
- ***The following summer, 1679, had opportunity to sail for Americas, but learned ship would call en route on African coast to take on cargo of slaves. Chino, others, condemning the institution of slavery, refused to embark. Huge disappointment for them. A second year in Spain looming. Back to Seville.***
- ***July, 1680, another opportunity to sail with summer flota. Chino, others, excited to be underway at last. Cádiz Harbor windy, crowded with square-riggers, much maneuvering for favorable positions in the fleet. The Nazareno, Chino's ship, trying to avoid larger vessel, struck El Diamante, a shallow sandbar in the Bay of Cádiz. Battered by high waves and wind,***

Nazareno soon broke apart. Passengers saved by heroic efforts of crew, rowed to shore, but all baggage was lost; all books, cartography instruments, clothes, everything lost.

...All baggage lost; all books, cartography instruments, clothes, everything lost.

Olvera could see it: the ship breaking up in rough seas, her sails ripped and flapping, wind whistling eerily through her rigging as she slipped slowly under the rising waves. And he saw a lifeboat bobbing on the gray swells, saw sailors bent over their oars, saw the ropy sinews of their sun-darkened backs as they strained against the thickening waters that threatened to swamp the boat and dump them all to the sharks.

All baggage lost...everything lost...

...Now in the boat he saw the young priest, seasick from the sloshing, jostling water, his face pale and desperate, nothing left of his possessions but the sopping black robe he wore. All the training, the preparation, the two long years of waiting in Spain—and now *this*.

Olvera refilled his glass with water. He added two antacid tablets. When the fizzing stopped, he drank it, and as his own queasiness receded, he picked up his notes and continued reading.

CHAPTER 13

The morning he was to leave for Magdalena, Olvera had a breakfast of toast and coffee at a small diner and went back to his hotel to await the bus that would take him north. While he waited, he returned to his notes.

- ***Back in Seville after losing all belongings on sunken Nazareno, Chino, friends, prepared for a third cold Andalusian winter. Much plague & deadly contagious disease in Seville. Jesuits disheartened by wait, impatient; tried to stay busy.***
- ***Interesting incident: Chino, others marveled at bright comet that streaked over skies of southern Spain; studied it with home-made telescopes. Chino made notes on trajectory, speed, etc; Jesuits speculated on religious & earthly significance.***
- ***Early winter, 1680, Chino and group hurried south to Cádiz on coast on learning King Carlos II assembling armada to take new Viceroy of Peru to post in Nueva España. All excited. Another chance to sail.***
- ***Interesting incident: Chino was aware that many Spanish cargo agents***

and ship captains had strict quotas on number of non-Spanish persons & goods they would carry (probably due to growing nationalism among Spaniards, and maybe a general distrust of foreigners). Fearing he might not be allowed to sail with the obviously Italian name of Chino or Chini, the young padre used a phony name to get aboard. Name he chose: Eusebio Chavez. With his dark skin and recently-acquired fluency in the Spanish language, he managed to fool the ships' officers & agents. He found berth on small packet, a mail ship, that would split off from main group of warships in northern Caribbean to call at Veracruz, coast of Nueva España.

· At long last, January, 1681, the young Jesuits sailed for the New World !!

Chavez. Olvera smiled to himself, remembering his surprise when he'd first read of this. The young priest, it seemed, wasn't above a bit of chicanery when the occasion demanded.

At noon, the driver stopped the bus for lunch in the old ranching town of Santa Ana Viejo, on the Río Magdalena. Not much about the café or the food or the snug little town surprised Olvera, but the countryside did. He'd expected, he supposed, a flat, arid place with nothing to break the bleakness but an occasional sun-baked cow skull half-buried in the dirt or a lone vulture high in a simmering sky. Especially now, in the heat of August.

He found a place entirely unlike anything he'd imagined.

Northern Sonora, he saw, was a land of fertile valleys and undulating foothills cupped between narrow cordilleras, mountain ranges, that seemed almost purple in the distance. The river and its tributaries gave rise to a vast riparian area with a richness of vegetation like nothing he'd seen since Chiapas: cottonwoods, oak, willow, hackberry, walnut—and beyond the riverine country, saguaros and prickly pear; barrel cactus, cholla. He saw the wispy green plants called creosote bush and broad plains of bunch grass dotted with trees he knew to be mesquite and paloverde and ironwood. From all directions came the vibrant smells of green growing things and clean desert air. To Olvera, everything seemed colorful and aromatic, a pleasing tapestry of hill and canyon.

Pleasing, except, of course, for the August temperatures: already ninety-six degrees at noon. Back outside after his lunch, he scanned the sky, studying the clouds that looked like tufts of cotton on a plate of burnished turquoise, and wondered if it would rain.

Probably not, he thought.

· Chino, others, arrived Veracruz in New World first week of May, 1681, after three months at sea. Rode mules from coast up into mountains to Ciudad de Mexico. There, awaiting assignment, Kino (by now had changed spelling of name) wrote scientific treatise, Exposición Astronómica de el Cometa, on comet he witnessed in Spain, suggesting that some comets, but not necessarily this one, were possible causes of pestilence, wars, earthquakes, plague, etc. on earth. Stirred up much talk and debate in the New World & Europe; caused local astronomer, Don Carlos Sigüenza, to pen a strong rebuttal to Kino's outdated medieval view on villainy of comets. Kino already making a name for himself (though, in this case, we now know that Sigüenza was far closer to the truth).

· In Ciudad de Mexico, young Jesuits split up, went separate ways. Time of sadness & nostalgia, as they had been through much together. Still, it was a time of great excitement; new worlds opening to them, new challenges.

· Kino received first official missionary assignment from civil authorities and Church: to accompany Admiral Isidro Atondo as Priest and Royal Cartographer on military and colonizing expedition to lands known as the Californias across Golfo de California (in 17th century, Baja California still generally believed to be an island; all official maps were so drawn).

· Kino rode west to Nio on Río Sinaloa on gulf, joined Atondo's naval forces with three new ships.

While he waited to re-board the bus, Olvera studied the mountains with his binoculars and thought about the padre's journey from Veracruz. He retrieved his map and spanned the distances with his fingers, measuring: at least three hundred miles from Veracruz to Mexico City, probably closer to four hundred with all the switchbacks on those mountain trails. And another, what, seven or eight hundred to the Sinaloa River? Maybe closer to a thousand, and the entire journey on a mule. Amazing, Olvera thought.

Back on the bus again, he returned to his notes.

· Over next four years, Kino sailed Golfo with Atondo, establishing missions among Indios, first at La Paz, then at San Bruno, on east coast of what is now called Baja California. Planted corn, squash, beans etc. Some initial success, but in time, situation in missions grew bad. As water and food supplies ran low, storms kept supply ships away. Constant trouble from some Guaicuros, the Indians at LaPaz. Hostile, resented presence of soldiers. A few suspected of stealing, mischief-making.

· *Unfortunate incident: at La Paz, Spanish believed Guaicuros had killed young mulatto drummer boy from ship (not true, they later learned). Admiral Atondo, in uncharacteristic act of stupidity, turned two pedreros, small cannons, loaded with grape-shot, on a group of Indians peacefully eating pozole in small clearing. Three Indians killed, others burned, wounded. Kino exceedingly angry at Atondo and soldiers, but not much he could do.*

· *Finally, all colonizing efforts on Baja failed, due in part to poor crops (if they couldn't feed the natives, Kino & Atondo learned, they couldn't hope to convince them of value of Christianity and Spanish citizenship), due in turn to deficient rain. Killing of Indians hadn't helped, either. Hard lessons for all. Kino and Atondo much discouraged.*

· *When civil & Church authorities discontinued failed entrada in Baja, Kino asked permission to establish a chain of missions among the Seri peoples on the Sinaloa coast. This, too, was not to be. Father Visitor Manuel González, at Oposura, gave Kino his new assignment: explore lands and convert heathen Pimas in territories north and west of Cucurpe, out on far northern rim of Christendom.*

· *Before traveling to new assignment, Kino rode to Guadalajara, then headquarters for civil authorities in that region. Had heard rumors that Pimas were being used as slaves in Spanish-owned silver mines of Sonora, and hoped to find a solution before he rode north to the land of the Pimas. This practice of taking Indians for involuntary servitude, called repartimiento, was threatening stability of frontier. In Guadalajara, Kino given copy of a new, recently-received cédula, an official proclamation from King Carlos II, affirming no peaceful Indios in Nueva España could be used as slaves for the next 20 years (note to myself: this was essentially an emancipation proclamation; it must've been very good news indeed for Kino!).*

· *In March, 1687, Father Eusebio Francisco Kino, now 41 years of age, rode north towards Cucurpe and the unknown lands beyond (note to myself: I've found no documented description of his mood on that long journey, but I suspect he was excited and optimistic. Fate—some would say God—had granted him a second chance; this time, he wouldn't fail).*

· *At last, the Pimería.*

CHAPTER 14

Northern Sonora. 1965.

At last, Magdalena.

A fine little town, Jorge Olvera thought. Santa María Magdalena, Father Kino had called it; in a fertile valley facing the boundless baking desert that stretched to the west as far as Olvera's binoculars could reach. But no longer a Pima town, Jiménez had told him.

A quiet town. The morning after Olvera's arrival, he had a quick breakfast of huevos, toast, and coffee, then gave himself a walking tour. The stores and cafes seemed clean and well-tended. The morning air smelled of roasting corn and fried meat, and he could hear the faint chinging of wind chimes from a corner store that sold mainly to tourists in spring and fall. The streets were edged with cottonwood trees; bougainvilleas with garish red blossoms grew in profusion around the plaza. Of the homes he saw, most were small and modest with pale exteriors of painted plaster; most had tiled porches that glowed with color from flowers in bulging pots of brown clay. The homes had chimneys and terra cotta roofs and most of the yards contained bicycles and children's toys and dogs that didn't bark at him much. Olvera liked that, the dogs not barking. He'd been in villages in Chiapas where the dogs—no, forget that. Chiapas was a world away, and he had matters enough to think about right here in this world.

Matters like meeting the alcalde, the mayor.

Gerardo Nava Garcia, his name was. Jiménez had arranged for Olvera's appointment with Mayor Nava. It would be a social call, certainly, but its primary purpose was to pay respect to a local official who could open important doors for them. Still, there was much Olvera needed to do this day. With any kind of luck, he thought, this wouldn't take long.

By midmorning the outside temperature had reached ninety-two degrees. It wasn't much cooler inside. In the mayor's office in the Palacio Municipal, Olvera wiped sweat from his neck with a bandanna and said, "Thank you for seeing me, Alcalde. You're most gracious. Professor Jiménez Moreno looks forward to meeting you, also."

The mayor was younger than Olvera had expected; stocky, about Olvera's height, well-dressed in slacks, white shirt, and tie. He had short dark hair and wore glasses with heavy black rims. "I'm pleased you're here, Señor Olvera," he said. "Our trip will be delayed briefly, if you have no objections. I've asked my secretary to notify Gabriel Sánchez de la Vega that you're here. De la Vega is a pharmacist here. Like many of our citizens, he's also an amateur archaeologist. He, too, has sought the grave of Padre Kino and he, too, wishes to welcome you to Magdalena."

"Our *trip*, sir?"

"We thought we'd take you for a short drive in the desert."

"I see. I'm honored by your attentions, sir," Olvera said, "and those of Señor de la Vega." Jiménez had mentioned nothing about a drive in the desert. What was going on here?

Within minutes, de la Vega arrived. The mayor made the introductions.

"We're ready to go, then?" the mayor said.

De la Vega, a pleasant man with bright brown eyes, smiled. "Ready."

In the mayor's car Olvera said, "I'd hoped to see the Proctor Chapel today, and the parish church."

"You'll have plenty of time for that," the mayor said. At the edge of town, he turned northeast on Highway 15.

"Where are we going, Alcalde?" Olvera said.

"To Cocóspera."

"I've read about it," Olvera said, surprised. "One of Kino's missions, in ruins now. But why are you taking me there this morning?"

"So you can see the work of Kino," de la Vega said.

"So you can witness," the mayor said, "the Hand of God."

The Cocóspera ruins rested atop a high bluff that banked steeply down to the floodplains of the Río Babasac, a tributary, Olvera knew from his new map, of the Río Magdalena. He saw the great Cocóspera Valley spread widely before them, and to the south and east, the vastness and greenery of the Sierra Azul, the Blue Mountains, reaching into the heart of the Pimería. Along the river's edge Olvera saw cottonwoods and willows and a few tall trees that might've been walnuts, and out on the sandy plain below the hills he saw shrubs and bushes and scrub cactus in abundance. But he saw no crops, no animals; no sign of human activity. No movement but the rhythmic surging of the bunch grass in the wind that riffled the valley and blew dust into the air in clouds that seemed almost orange in the hot afternoon light. In Kino's time, Olvera had learned, cattle would've been grazing lazily on the slopes and he would have seen Pimas tending stands of beans and squash, and citrus groves, and vast fields of corn and wheat. He would've heard sounds of laughter and conversation from the Indio village nearby and from the casa cural, the priest's quarters, adjacent to the church. He might've seen a few Spanish soldiers, or a few settlers who had come in from the silver mines to buy food or woven cotton cloth. From the river he would've heard

Pima youngsters at play. From the bell towers of the church he might've heard the crisp gongs of the morning Angelus.

But not now. To Olvera the place seemed desolate. Stark. Almost eery in its muteness.

And the old church itself seemed large. Oversized, somehow, for the mesquite trees on the windy hilltop and the weathered white crosses that marked the graves in the camposanto, the cemetery, behind the church. He guessed the height of the ruins at twenty-five feet. Had the façade and bell towers been intact, it would have seemed massive, indeed.

He couldn't imagine the Hand of God in it, as the mayor obviously did, but still the old church and its setting were intriguing—the kind of place that would warm the heart of any archaeologist or architectural historian.

At the doorway, Olvera saw that the entirety of the roof had fallen, the towers and domes that'd been there in earlier times, now gone, the upper portions of the walls jagged and crumbled. The walls still standing were several feet thick, built of sun-dried adobe veneered on the interior and exterior with fired brick, these in turn coated with cracked and crumbling plaster that still claimed, on the inner walls, a few traces of whitewash and colored paint. Thick buttresses of mortared river rock supported portions of the walls; in other areas, the outer brick façade had peeled away from the adobe core and seemed on the verge of collapse. The windows, the sculptured niches, the inner walls of the nave, the elaborate plaster retablo—all were in advanced stages of deterioration, in some places missing large slabs of brick, leaving the worn adobe exposed. Birds flitted among the ruins and yellow wasps made buzzing sounds near nests located in crevices high on the walls.

"The adobe core," de la Vega said, "dates from the Jesuit era—from Kino's time. We believe he began construction of it in 1702 and finished it two or three years later. The Mass of Dedication was sung in the Piman language by Father Adamo Gilg. But that was in the adobe church, as it stood in its original form."

"The inner and outer layers of fired brick and painted plaster," Olvera said, "came much later, I presume. These were Franciscan?"

"Correct, Señor."

Olvera knew the history. The Jesuits, with González and Kino and Campos leading the way, had built the first missions in the Pimería, had done the initial work of teaching and catechizing the Indians. They'd been very successful at it. The priests who followed them were equally successful. Too much so, it turned out. Over the years the civil authorities in Durango and Mexico City and Madrid had grown increasingly suspicious of the power and influence of the Jesuits, not just in the Pimería, but in all of the New World. Finally, in 1767, the Spanish King, Carlos III, could no longer ignore the clatter and clamor of his advisors. He ordered that all Jesuits everywhere be arrested, no matter their circumstances or the nature of their work. The Black Robes were shackled in chains and brought back to Spain as prisoners in the musty, stinking bilges of ships normally used for carrying frightened slaves to the New World or fine silks from the Orient. Many priests died en route. Malaria, scurvy. Cholera. Malnutrition and pneumonia. Brutality from the guards. Those who survived the long voyage succumbed to the harsh realities of Spanish prisons. For the next century, the Society of Jesus was all but dead.

But in 1768, one year after the arrest of the Jesuits, this same king, Carlos III, sent the Order of Friars Minor—the Franciscans—into New Spain to continue the work he had forced the Jesuits to abandon. Friar-priests in blue-gray robes came with new materials and better building methods. They created beauty and style where the pioneering Jesuits had, by force of circumstance, been satisfied with functionality.

Olvera touched the wall near the doorway. He ran his finger gently over the worn surface of a brick. "But later," he said, "the Franciscans, too, abandoned Cocóspera. Because of the Apaches?"

The mayor nodded. "They were a huge problem. They made it impossible to live around here without constant vigilance."

Olvera stared out over the grassy slope that led down to the river, letting his mind run, thinking about all he'd learned from his books on Jesuits and Apaches and Pima Indians, and he tried to imagine what it must've been like here in those early years.

"Some of the damage is from weather," the mayor said, intruding on Olvera's thoughts. "But most has been from vandals."

"...Vandals?" Olvera needed a moment to bring himself back. "Ah, yes. You mean treasure hunters."

The mayor nodded. "There've always been rumors of hidden gold and silver in the old ruins. Even diamonds and other gems and precious stones."

Olvera glanced at him. "Could these rumors be true?"

"I don't think so." The mayor shrugged. "Of course in Sonora one is never sure of such things."

With his finger Olvera probed the outer wall near its bottom, then probed the soil. He scooped away a bit of dirt and studied it. "Señor Nava," he said, "do you believe the Kino chapel in Magdalena no longer exists?"

"I believe so, yes."

"And you, Señor de la Vega?"

"Yes, it's gone. Torn down years ago. Maybe two centuries ago, who knows."

Olvera stared at the ruins, at the broken bricks and crumbling plaster, at the fractured adobe walls. He could no longer hear the buzzing of the wasps, as the wind was strong now, pulling at his shirt and bending the branches of mesquites that grew near the church. "So you believe the Proctor Chapel," he said to the chemist, "isn't Kino's chapel? You believe all our clues are now underground?"

"All underground, that's correct," de la Vega said.

"If this is true," the alcalde said, "that's bad news for you, I fear."

"...Yes," Olvera agreed. "Such news would be bad, certainly, but not entirely unexpected."

Something was tickling his mind now, teasing him. Nagging. A fresh idea, maybe, or a new way of looking at something. Whatever it was, it lay just under the surface of his conscious thought. It had something to do with Cocóspera, he knew. With the ruins. As if the secret to finding Kino's bones in Magdalena lay somehow in the tumbled brick and broken plaster of this proud old church on this hot gusty hilltop.

He stared at the ruins and wondered, but no answer came.

CHAPTER 15

Sonora. Año D. 1694. December.

Lieutenant Solís had hanged three Pimas from a sycamore tree.

The next time I saw him, in the officers' barracks at the presidio in Real San Juan, I questioned him about it.

"I had no choice," he claimed. He was sitting on a wooden bench, polishing the stock of his musket and adjusting the tiny steel jaws that held the flint in the lock.

"I have heard," I said casually, "that the Pimas had done nothing wrong."

He smiled slightly, continuing his work, not looking up. "Perhaps, Ensign, but at the time I had no way of being sure of it." He spoke softly, but his words seemed to echo through the wardroom, empty now except for a few young officers in various states of dress, talking among themselves as they tended their weapons and polished their boots, preparing for another expedition against the Apaches. In the stone fireplace, burning logs warmed the room and threw off sparks that sputtered noisily in the dry air. The other men gave no indication that they heard our conversation, but I knew they were listening.

"There was a raid," Solís said, now looking up at me, "on a little Pima village on the Río Terrenate, not far from Quiburi. Horses were taken. General Jironza himself, your own uncle, sent me to find and punish the offenders." He leaned his gleaming musket against the wall and stood and faced me. He pulled on his white gloves, then shrugged, his dark eyes giving away nothing. "I took a sergeant and five men and we did our job. Maybe I executed the wrong Indians, and maybe they happened to be Pimas. So what? They were just Indians."

Was he challenging me? I had little doubt of it. Solís was not a tall man, but he was solidly built. He had small ears, bold steady eyes, and black hair that he wore short and brushed forward. His skin was dark enough that I suspect he had some Indian blood, though I never knew this for sure. He looked very official and very fierce in his red and white officer's uniform with his sword hanging smartly at his side. I suppose I looked as official myself, but in those early years I was too young of countenance to seem half as fierce. Solís was older than I by only a few years, but he was far more experienced—with Sonora, with war, with women, and especially with the sword. For his success against the Apaches he had become something of a hero to the miners and settlers. Still, for reasons I was only now coming to understand, I had never really liked him.

"They were just Indians," I said, "but they were *innocent* Indians."

"I will say it again," he said. "I had no choice. We had looked in every dirty, lice-infested Pima village along the Terrenate, and found nothing. So we turned west. Near Bac we came to another settlement. When we rode in, the Indians ran. They tried to hide. They had big racks of meat drying in the sun. What was I to believe? That this was rabbit meat? *Snake* meat? And they *ran* from us."

"Your own soldiers," I argued, "reported that it was deer meat—venison—not horse meat. And the Pimas ran because some of them had never seen horses or soldiers and you frightened them. The horses were stolen from that Pima village near Quiburi by *Apaches*, not by other Pimas."

"The horses were stolen by *Indios*," he said, "and that is all we know for sure. My decision to hang a few will prevent others from even *thinking* about stealing horses, no matter what their tribe."

From an open window I heard the shouts of sergeants working the soldiers on the parade ground. Sunlight filtered into the room and spilled onto the floor near Solís' gleaming black boots. I was vaguely aware of the other officers around us, but they were silent now, no longer milling about.

"I doubt that hanging even a *thousand* Pimas, Lieutenant," I said softly, "will have much influence on the social graces of the average Apache."

Still his eyes gave away nothing. "If you have a problem with my command decisions, Alférez, I suggest you take it up with the captain. Unless you wish to pursue it...in some personal way...with me..."

He let the threat linger in the air between us. I ignored it. I had no wish to fight him, though truthfully I did not fear him. Without his sword he was just another soldier, no stronger or quicker than I. *With* his sword, well, yes, that was a different matter. But he surely knew that if he used his sword, I would defend myself. He would know, too, that if he took my life, Don Domingo's justice would be swift and certain.

"No, Lieutenant," I said finally, "I have no wish to pursue it. You are the one who has to live with yourself."

"I have never found that particularly hard to do." He stared at me for a long moment, his dark eyes unblinking, his white-gloved hand hovering near the handle of his sword. No one moved. The presidio seemed strangely silent, the wardroom dark and hushed.

Then Solís surprised me: he slowly lowered his hands and smiled. Had I not known him, I might have believed the smile was genuine. Still, I was glad to see it.

"So, mi amigo," he said lightly, "perhaps we disagree on a few minor issues. Does that mean we cannot be friends? I hope not. When we return from our expedition we will drink together at the Red Coyote. Do you know of it, on the plaza?"

"I have been there, yes," I said cautiously.

"They have lots of good mescal and agreeable women. We will drink a toast to Carlos Segundo and to the Compañía Volante and even to all the Apaches we have dispatched to hell. So how about it, my friend? When we return?"

"When we return," I said, "I have to escort Francisco Saeta to Magdalena with a pack train and some livestock."

Still smiling, he said, "Saeta? The new priest?"

"Yes. The Father Visitor assigned him to the new mission at Caborca."

Solís laughed. "Another black-robed shepherd to watch over the hapless flock, eh? All right, then, when you return from Magdalena we will share a drink."

"I doubt I—"

Something changed in his eyes and then his sword was out and flashing through the air. He whipped it down sharply to the side of my neck. *Aaaiii*, it had happened so fast I had been unable to counter his move! Suddenly I could feel the steel against my skin, the blade harsh and knife-edged and hot as fire.

"Remove the blade," I whispered.

"Why should I? I have the advantage of you."

I prayed silently and tried to hold myself perfectly still. I became aware of a rhythmic pounding in my temples; wood smoke from the fireplace seemed to smolder and seethe in my nostrils like burning sulfur.

"*Remove the blade, Lieutenant.*"

"And if I do not?"

This time I said nothing. His eyes were wide, his mouth pinched, and

I knew he was thinking about killing me. Or perhaps not. With Solís, it was always hard to know. His blade bit into my skin. My heart was thumping; my mouth felt as if someone had stuffed it with cotton.

Finally, slowly, he lifted the blade away.

"You failed to parry my weapon, Ensign," he said softly. Mocking me.

I breathed in and out. Deeply, slowly. Fighting to control my temper.

"You need faster reflexes," he added. "If you wish to kill the Apache, you have to be quicker than he is. Today we will work on that."

I touched my neck, but found no blood. "What do you mean, '*work on that*'?"

"General Jironza," he said, "instructed me to give you another sword lesson today. So you have saved me from having to go out and find you. Today we will work on your reflexes. We will make you faster. Not fast enough to take me, of course, but much quicker than you are now."

"Roast in hell, Lieutenant," I mumbled.

He laughed and motioned me toward the doorway. "Come along, Ensign. I will teach you how to kill Apaches."

On our expedition we killed no Apaches. We didn't even *see* any. We were out three weeks, a force of five officers and thirty soldados and sixteen Indios—mostly Pimas, but with a few Ópatas, too—scouring the Guachucas and the ranges east of the Terrenate. Oh, the Apaches were out there. We knew so from their tracks and sign. At our approach they moved higher on the mountains, into the snowpack and pines and freezing nights, as aware of our presence as we were of theirs. But we never saw them. Black Skull's band in the Guachucas, Oso Azul and Mofeta to the east. According to our scouts, they probably had a total of sixty warriors, plus a ragtag assortment of women and children. About half were Apaches, the rest, Jocomes and Mansos from the Sierra Madres. Their numbers worried us. If the groups ever joined up, they could mount a deadly assault on any settlement they chose.

But we saw no Apaches and fought no one. We returned to San Juan Bautista cold, hungry, and tired, but with no injuries or illnesses suffered.

In mid-January, a few days after our return and after a breakfast of bean tamales and boiled corn, Father Francisco Saeta and I rode out of San Juan with Corporal Escalante, five well-armed soldiers, and Wigberto—with Teodora perched on his shoulder—all of us headed for the western desert and Caborca. We had twenty Pima servants and vaqueros with us, a herd of brood mares, seventy head of cattle, and mules loaded with corn, dried beef, and the vegetable seeds Saeta would use in his new gardens at Caborca. On wagons pulled by oxen we had two piedras de molino, the heavy round flat stones the padre would use with mules for grinding the fresh grains when his fields came into production.

Saeta had first come to the Pimería in October, and Father Kino had taken him to Caborca and introduced him to the priests along the way. He had returned to visit Kino at Dolores and to settle some business matters with civil authorities in San Juan. Now he was going back with more supplies and livestock, all donated by Kino and other priests in Sonora.

His Spanish was rough and he spoke softly, but he was understandable—and even a little humorous in his grammatical errors. From his accent and name I supposed he was Italian, though I did not know this with certainty.

"Gracias, Ensign, for your escort," he said, riding beside me at the head of the column our first morning out. "I suppose you could have find many things to do in this January weather that would be more pleasantful than taking another priest to his mission home."

"I am honored to do it, sir. The Church and the Compañía are glad to have you in the Pimería." In the chill morning air, our breath made clouds of white vapor as we spoke.

"And you will be backturning at Magdalena? Someone said this, I think."

I nodded. "From Magdalena, Corporal Escalante will take you on to Caborca. I have to return to Real San Juan. General Jironza has ordered another expedition against Oso Azul and Mofeta."

"The Apache leaders, yes, I have heard of them. I do not envy you your work. But I am respectful of you for it."

I chuckled. Behind us I could hear the cattle and the steady complaints of the mules and the occasional screechy profanity from Teodora. "Thank you, Father," I said. "I enjoy my work. Most of the time, anyway."

Saeta smiled. "I enjoy, too. I believe I will be very happy at Caborca."

We crossed the river in shallows and brought the cattle and pack train onto a shelf of sandy soil that supported a few saguaros and ironwood trees. Mountains, dark and gray, rose in the distance in every direction, but around us the desert was flat and open. We turned to the north again. I excused myself to Saeta and rode back down the column to check on the animals and men. I found Wigberto working the mules, Teodora perched behind him on the rump of his horse. She was a large bird, more than two feet long including her colorful tail. Her red and blue feathers glowed brightly in the morning sunlight.

"*Teodora*?" I said to Wigberto. "How do you know she's a female?" As usual, he had several day's growth of beard and smelled of raw onions and sweat.

He grinned. "She is from Brazil, of course. A bird this beautiful, she could only be a female."

I started to ride on.

"For one peso a week, amigo," he shouted after me, "I would proudly rent you this delightful bird."

I turned my mount back. "Why would I want to rent your bird?"

"To impress the pretty muchachas, Señor."

"I have no muchachas."

He shrugged. "Maybe so, maybe no."

Teodora flapped her red wings, then settled back on the horse's rump. "*All right, you lop-eared, dirt-licking mules,*" she squawked, "*get your fat asses moving!*"

Wigberto grinned. "See? Your ladies will be entertained. And they will reward you as only pretty ladies can."

Wigberto. What can I say about Wigberto.

When I found Father Saeta again, I asked him if he was seeing many Indios at his masses each week in Caborca.

"Oh, yes," he said eagerly. "Before me no full-time priests have been there. I am the first. So there is much to do."

Saeta was tall and slender, with a long narrow face and dark shining eyes. He wore wool gloves, a red sarape over his black robe, and a wide-brimmed hat like most Jesuits seemed to wear. There was something almost beatific about him—in the brightness of his eyes, in his youthful enthusiasm, in the gentleness of his voice. He looked about like I had always imagined Francis of Assisi had looked, but without the strange haircut and the birds on his shoulder.

"The Pimas," he continued, "have made an adobe chapel for me, and they are making now a small room for my living quarters. We have wheat growing niceful in the field, and we have corn and beans and squash and cattle." He turned in his saddle and surveyed the pack train behind us. He smiled. "Plus the animals and goods we have with us now. God has been generous, has He not? The cattle look healthy and strong, and the brood mares will help us build for the mission a good remuda. I believe my Pimas will be happy."

"I am sure they will, Father."

His dark eyes grew troubled, and for a while he said nothing. Finally I asked him if there was a problem.

"Please accept my apologies," he said, "I meant no rudity. I was thinking about my Pimas. Most are good, God-fearing Indians. But I hear stories, I do not know if they are true."

"What stories?" I asked him.

"Stories of medicine men who do not want priests there, and stories of unrest among the Indios. Some say that some of the Ópata overseers at Tubutama are difficult and punish the Pimas for minor infractions...how do you say it, harshful? And that some of the Pimas blame the priests for this. And of course I worry that such problems could spread to my own mission at Caborca."

I thought about Ernesto Otuca'tuot, the apprentice ma'makai from Tubutama who had cut down the tree with me still clinging to the top of it, and I remembered Father Kino's warnings about the medicine men. "I hear such stories, too," I said. "Whether they are true or not, I do not know. But I believe Father Januske can take care of any difficulties at Tubutama."

"Probably," he said, after a time, "it is not as bad as I think."

"Probably not," I said.

At mid-day we stopped at a small creek, overflowing its banks now from recent rains. We had a meal of pinole and warm frijoles and drank cold water from the creek. When we had rested the animals we resumed our journey. The day remained sunny but cold; bulbous silvery clouds pressed on the horizon. On the wind I could smell the oily pungence of creosote bush and the wet earthy odors of marsh grass and mud.

"It is beautiful country, this desert," Saeta told me. "Where I come from, it is very pretty, too, but here it is much flat and you can see for miles and miles." He smiled again, his eyes shining. "I like it. And these strange, tall plants with arms that point up to the heavens? You call them *saguaros*? And all the strange animals that live here. Everything, it is all wonderful."

"You seem to be adjusting very well," I said, "to the Pimería."

"There is one thing," the padre said after a time, "that I am not adjusting to so well."

"What is that, Father?" I asked him. Ahead, the mountains were blue-gray in the early afternoon light, and clouds with pink edges lay like crumpled blankets on the horizon.

"Beans," Saeta said.

"*What?*"

"At every meal, beans. Everywhere I look, beans. Pinto beans, tepary beans, chick beans. Black beans, red beans, white beans, every color and kind of beans known to mankind."

I laughed. "We eat a lot of beans here."

"I know they are nutritious, but I fear they make me very, well, —"

"*Gaseoso*?" I prompted.

He flushed. "Thank you. I find it most embarrassing."

"You will get used to it, sir."

"I certainly pray for that."

We camped for the night at the base of a small mesa topped with mesquite and cardón. If the wind blew during the night, I hoped the hill and the vegetation would afford us some protection. When we had the animals settled in, we started a small fire. In the growing cold and darkness we drank chocolate and had a meal of warm tortillas and stew made from onions and wild root potatoes. Afterwards I asked Saeta about his name. "Latin, is it not? I studied the language in school but I cannot remember what the word means."

"Yes, saeta is a Latin word," he said. "It means spear, or lance."

"Ah, yes. So you are Italian? Like Padre Kino?"

No, he told me, he was Sicilian, born in 1664 in the little town of Piazza Armerina. At the age of fifteen he had entered the Jesuit novitiate at Palermo, and for the next fifteen years studied humanities, physics, and theology at various universities in Sicily. "Until the Jesuit General in Rome finally decided I was old enough and allowed me to come here." He laughed softly. "Or maybe he just got wearyful of reading all my letters begging him to send me here. Anyway, I sailed from Cádiz to Veracruz, then spent a year in Ciudad de Mexico. I finished my studies at the Jesuit college there. And now here I am. In the Pimería."

"Doing God's work," I said.

Light from the campfire glowed in his dark eyes. "Yes, that is my job now," he said. "Saving innocent souls in this new land."

"Well," I said, "we are very glad you are here."

I spent a while staring into the flickering fire, enjoying the warmth of it, and thinking about missionary priests. I did not know many, but I knew Eusebio Kino and Agustín de Campos and Daniel Januske, and now I also knew Francisco Saeta. What I was struck by, I suppose, was how very different they were, each man with his own distinctive personality. And yet I was aware of how very much alike they were, too. All of them generous and curious and gentle, but strong, too, in all the ways that mattered. All good servants of the Lord. I thought about how incredibly fortunate I was to know them. It was, as Saeta would probably say, very niceful.

After a time, I made assignments for guard duty through the night and we slept under heavy blankets near the fire's embers. The night passed in peace.

The next morning Father Saeta said a mass for us and we got underway early. We had several miles behind us before the sun rose through gauzy reddish clouds to give us another cold but clear day. That morning on the flatlands we saw white-tailed deer, antelope, and javelinas, and in the foothills, coyotes and coatimundis. With the telescope we saw kit foxes on the side of a mountain and, later, a mother oso plateado—a grizzly bear—with two cubs.

Father Saeta never stopped beaming.

The afternoon of our third day we reached the San Miguel, flowing briskly now from earlier rains and runoff from snow in the mountains. We watered the animals and had a meal of pinole and roasted chiles. Around us in the trees, lark sparrows and warblers foraged for bugs, and mockingbirds and thrashers serenaded us with song. The cottonwoods were already putting out tiny green shoots and we found new blooms on some of them.

Saeta commented on the new growth in weather still so cold.

"Auppa Heosig Masheth," I said.

"*What*?"

I chuckled. "That is the Piman term for what we call the month of January. It means, 'Moon of the Cottonwoods Blooming.' January is when the cottonwoods usually put out their first new growth of the season."

"How do you know all these things?"

I shrugged. "Father Kino taught me."

We reached Cosari and the Dolores mission a few hours later. Unfortunately for us, Father Kino was away. He had gone north to Remedios and Cocóspera to supervise construction of some adobe buildings at the missions and to tend cattle he had recently moved to grazing lands nearby. We stayed the night, and slept well. The next morning Kino's cooks served us a meal of roasted corn and stewed teparies.

"Oh, Madre," Saeta said. "More beans."

"They are everywhere," I said.

He laughed. "Whole beans, mashed beans, dried beans."

"Hot beans, cold beans, stewed beans."

"Beans in tortillas," he said, "beans in tamales. Beans in soups."

"Beans in everything, Father."

"Again today," he said, "I will make a joyful noise."

We reached Magdalena that afternoon, and found someone waiting for us: Father Agustín Campos. He had heard of our coming and had made the ride down from San Ignacio to visit. Campos and Saeta, I learned, were old friends; they had sailed together from Spain in the summer flota of '93. Father Campos was in good spirits. His mission was growing and he was finding more Indians at his services each day. We spent the evening visiting with the local Pimas, eating and talking, enjoying the warmth of a good and hearty campfire.

The next morning I said my farewells to the group going on to Caborca, filled my water gourds, and prepared for my ride back to San Juan. Father Saeta gave me a fine present—a biography of Ignacio Loyola written in Spanish. I gave him a bag of beans.

No, por favor, I am making a joke. Actually I gave him a nugget of gold I had found in a creek in the Guachucas a few weeks before. At any rate, it was a sad parting because I liked him and had enjoyed his company.

Two of the Pima vaqueros accompanied me on the ride back to San Juan and we made good time to Dolores and on south from there. That first day we saw no Apaches and no fresh sign, and I had plenty of time to think.

I thought a lot about Father Saeta and Caborca. I knew that Kino had argued against sending him there. Saeta was, Kino had said, too inexperienced, and the dangers in the western desert were too great: vengeful Apaches, hostile ma'makai, disgruntled Piman laborers. And there was this: Caborca was simply too far away. If anything happened, it would take too long to get help to him.

But the Visitor, Father Burgos, had insisted. So Saeta, for better or worse, had gone to Caborca.

I remembered my words to him, "We are very glad you are here."

I hoped I could say the same in a year.

We rode on in silence, the Pimas and I, saying little, wasting no time. Before it was over, though, our journey back to San Juan would become a bloody and oddly discordant one. The first incident happened in the mountains east of Cucurpe. It was mid-morning and we had stopped to water our mounts at a creek. I heard her—the jangling bracelets, the heavy hooves of her big horse—before I saw her coming up the trail, Old Gonzala. By the time we were mounted up, she had drawn close. The Pimas, I noticed, had backed away, keeping a dozen yards between them and the old crone and her grulla stallion. I knew enough about the Indios to know they mistrusted her: they believed she could put curses on them. I worried little about curses, but I suspected her utterings would be as bizarre and unsettling as they had been at our earlier encounter. They were.

"I know you, soldado, oh, yes." Her voice, as I remembered it, was shrill and raspy. She wore a sleeveless coat the same shade of gray as her strange piercing eyes. Her wrinkled face seemed shrunken, almost hidden under a black shawl.

"Buenos dias, Señora," I said.

"I warn you, hombre," she said. "I have heard ravens call from the mountains, and I have seen hawks with white tails circle in the sky as the north wind blows its evil through the trees."

"And what does this evil wind say, Señora?" Her bare arms, thin and bony, were covered with spots that looked like mud-coated coins.

"You ridicule me, but I know the troubles that will soon pour down on you. I know that an arrow will soon fall from other arrows."

I remembered her words from before: *Hear me, priest, and you, soldado. Soon they will fill the arrow with arrows...I have read it in the tracks of the black bear and seen it in the droppings of the mountain lion. And you, soldier,* she had gone on, stabbing her bony finger at me, *beware of those who speak in strange tongues.*

Now she was at it again.

"I suppose," I said, "you are going to warn me again about those who speak in strange tongues."

"I have already warned you about them, soldado."

"I am not worried," I said.

"Then you are a fool," she rasped.

When she had gone, we turned our horses again towards San Juan. I spent a lot of time thinking about the crone's words, but in the end I could find no believable explanation for her warning about those who speak in strange tongues. The only strange tongue I had heard recently was French—from Henri Pitot, who had tried to take the lapis cross from me. But why should I beware of Pitot? Frankly I doubted I would ever see him again. I still did not know what the hag had meant by her warning, but I was sure it had nothing to do with Pitot.

After a time, though, I stumbled onto the answer to her other prophecy:

Soon they will fill the arrow with arrows...

An arrow will soon fall from other arrows...

I found it when I remembered the padre's comment on the Latin origins of his family name, Saeta. It meant spear, yes, or lance. But now I remembered its other meaning: *arrow.*

Is *that* what she was telling us? That Father Saeta was about to die? *Murdered* by *arrows*?

Whatever she had meant, who could believe it? What was she but an old madwoman? A crazy old thing that whispered odd tales and rode a strange gray stallion with eyes as malevolent as its master's? I decided to do the only logical, reasonable thing: forget the curandera and all her impossible riddles.

That, it turned out, would be a big mistake.

But my visit with Gonzala was not the only disquieting encounter I would have this day. The other happened on a narrow rocky trail in the mountains a few miles west of Arizpe. That is where they jumped us.

Four of them. Apaches, or maybe Jocomes.

They came at us with their screams and war whoops in a cloud of dust that thickened the air and choked our lungs. One of the Pimas, Antonio, went down with an arrow through his throat, blood erupting in shiny spurts from his neck. Another arrow ripped through my tunic and took a layer of skin off my shoulder. I got off a pistol shot that caught one of the heathens in the chest and knocked him out of his saddle. Through the dust I saw the other Pima lean from his horse and swing his war club at an attacker on the ground, shattering his skull. That made two down. I reined my mount around, looking for the other two. At that instant an arrow thunked into my saddle—not an inch from my cojónes. I saw the Indio who had fired it on a ridge high above us, his face as dark and grim as the granite boulders that partially shielded him. Even at this distance I could see the streaks of ochre and vermilion that arced across his forehead and nose. He reached for another arrow. I shouted a warning to the Pima and we jumped from our horses and darted into a stand of mesquite trees. I checked the powder in my arquebus. I counted to ten, poked my head out, and squeezed off a shot at the spot where the Indio had been.

But he was gone. Seconds later we heard the clatter of horses' hooves higher on the mountain. We stayed low for a time, watching, alert, but we saw no more of them. I said a prayer of thanks to God for keeping me safe and asked Him to take into His kingdom the soul of Antonio, the Pima who had died in the attack.

We got Antonio's body slung over his horse and lashed it in place with strong ropes. I pried the arrow out of my saddle and slipped it into my saddlebag. The arrow would be my souvenir, a wicked and lethal thing that had almost nailed my testicles to my horse's withers. That was not, I tell you, a pleasant thought.

There is a peculiar thing about skirmishes like this. They come on so fast and they are over so quickly that you hardly have time to be frightened. *Afterward*, yes, but not *during*. It hit me now as I was putting a dressing on the small wound of my shoulder. I had to give myself a few minutes of rest to get my stomach out of my throat and to stop the trembling in my hands.

But we wasted no time. The Apaches, I suspected, would be back. To gather their dead, if for no other reason. So we got out of there, pushing the horses hard for the rest of the day, and made San Juan late the next morning.

That evening in the officers' barracks I told Ensign Acuña, the translator, about the attack. Acuña probably knew more about Indians than anyone in San Juan, and in my short time in Sonora I had learned a lot from him.

He chuckled at my story. "So the arrow almost snagged your cojónes, huh?"

By now I could laugh a little, too.

"Apache or Jocome?" he said.

I shrugged. "I had no time to notice."

"You kept the arrow? Could I see it?"

I showed it to him. It was about two feet long, made of hardwood, as straight and firm as a fireplace poker. The arrowhead was a thin sliver of something that looked like slate. At its tail end, the arrow had a fletching of three equally-spaced black feathers tightly bound to the shaft with dried sinew and piñon gum.

"See the dried layer of gum at the base of the feathers?" he said. "Apaches and Jocomes both use it, but the Apaches use it more often. So, if you did not see the gum, it *might* indicate Jocome. But here we see it, so that hardly helps. Sometimes you see arrows where the makers have painted little symbols on the shaft to identify their rancheria or family group. As if they are proud of the arrow and want their enemies to know who they were. Sometimes they even paint a symbol that represents their actual *name*, like a signature..."

He went on, talking about Apache arrows and bows and how they sometimes made poison for their arrowheads from rotted deer liver and cascabel venom, but I was hardly listening. I was thinking about Old Gonzala, and Father Saeta out there alone at Caborca, and the painted face of the Indio who had almost killed me.

"But I see something else here," Acuña said, breaking into my thoughts.

I shook off images of the Indio on the ridge. "What?" I said. "The arrow?"

"The feathers," he said. "The Jocomes usually use gray or white ones. From hawks or eagles. Apaches use them, too. But these are black."

I nodded. "Which means...what?"

He looked up at me and shrugged.

"Maybe this is Black Skull's arrow," he said. "Maybe the black feathers are *his* signature."

My heart thumped in my chest. "The Indio on the ridge? You mean *that* was Black Skull?"

"If it was," Acuña said, laughing a little, "you are damned lucky to be alive."

Aaaiiii caramba, I thought. *Oh, Madre.*

CHAPTER 16

The Pimería. Año D. 1695. Early Spring.

They killed him the second day of April.

During Oam Mashath, the Moon of the Yellow Colors, as the Pimas reckoned time. In the first warm breezes of the new spring, when the mesquite trees had pushed out their first crop of straw-yellow buds, when prickly pear and paloverde glowed with blooms of saffron and gold.

The day before Easter, as we Spaniards reckoned time.

Father Francisco Saeta.

According to the first account to reach us in San Juan, they put more than two dozen arrows through his chest and belly and left him to die on the dirt floor of the adobe room that served as his living quarters near the chapel in Caborca. Father Saeta, thirty years old, still fresh from Palermo and the Jesuit college in Ciudad de Mexico, still in the first months of his mission to the innocents of the New World. Saeta, named for the Latin arrow, shot dead with arrows.

Outside the church they had butchered others, too, including a vaquero named José and a temastian visiting from Cumpas. They plundered the chapel, ravaged Saeta's room, and slaughtered all the cattle and horses they could find. A few hours later we heard from another runner that they had also sacked and burned the churches at Oquitoa and Tubutama, slaying everyone who resisted.

How many of these murderers were there? Where had they come from?

Where had they gone after their vicious attacks? And who, in fact, *were* they? Apaches? Jocomes? Disgruntled Papagos stirred into a frenzy by resentful ma'makai hoping to eliminate the influence of the priests? Everyone knew of the recent uprising in the Sierra Madres, where the Tarahumaras had burned churches and massacred Spaniards and other outsiders, including two Franciscans. Was Sonora sliding into the same inferno?

General Domingo Jironza quickly assembled a force to inspect the western missions and find the perpetrators. Don Domingo himself would lead the group, which would include Father Agustín Campos from San Ignacio as chaplain, a new priest named Bayerca who had been assigned to the mission at Cocóspera, Antonio Solís and me as junior officers, Corporal Escalante, a large company of soldados, a dozen Pima warriors, and another dozen Tepocas and Seris who had fought with us against the Apaches and seemed reasonably reliable.

"We have to get this stopped before they push the entire territory into revolt against us," Don Domingo said as we prepared our mounts for the long ride. "We must preserve Spanish rule. And we must punish the offenders severely."

"If we can find them out there," I said. "In thirty-two thousand square miles of desert and mountains."

"We will find them, Ensign," Solís said grimly, "if we have to look under every rock and cactus and grain of sand in the New World."

In truth, it turned out to be much easier than that, though it took a while and many people died in the process.

In Dolores Father Kino seemed safe enough. He wanted desperately to go with us, as I had suspected, but the general insisted that he remain in Dolores and keep the eastern Pimas pacified and quiet. After much spirited argument, the padre finally admitted to the wisdom of Don Domingo's view. Kino said a prayer for us and we continued west to Magdalena and El Tupo and on across flat, open desert to Tubutama. Though Father Saeta had been martyred in Concepción de Caborca, the general chose to go first to Tubutama because it was closer and we could get there sooner. We rode hard, always alert, searching constantly for enemy forces, but in all that vast, yellow-flowered desert, we saw no hostile Indians. Nor even a friendly one.

We found Tubutama deserted, the chapel burned, the outbuildings and log corrals still smoldering. No wind blew, and blue smoke hung in the warm spring air and clung to our clothes and irritated our eyes. We found several dead Indians, but the bodies had been mutilated beyond recognition and we had no idea who they were. In a few days, I knew, the stench would be overwhelming, and already I had to hold a bandanna against my face to breathe the foul, smoke-clogged air.

We knew that Father Januske, the priest, had escaped to safety, but nothing of value remained in his church. In one of the mud huts Corporal Escalante found an old woman who had apparently been too sick to flee. We questioned her about the attackers and asked her where the other villagers had gone. We learned nothing useful.

A few minutes later Escalante and I were talking near the old woman's hut when we heard a muffled cry. We rushed back to the hut and, inside, found a Tepoca warrior standing over her, a bloody knife in his hand; he had slit her throat. Before he could turn his knife on me, I grabbed him from behind and threw him out of the hut and slung him roughly into the dirt. He tried to get up. I kicked him in the head. When he tried to grab my leg, I put the tip of my sword on the dark skin of his throat. I sent Escalante to tell the general of the Tepoca's treachery, and I told the Tepoca if he moved so much as a finger I would run him through and feed his worthless head to the coyotes.

"She was a helpless old woman," I muttered.

He cursed me.

I tweaked the sword against his throat. "The general," I told him, "will have swift justice for you."

But the general, for reasons he never shared with us, chose not to punish the Indian. From that day on I kept an eye on the man, but I never learned why he had done what he did. Perhaps he had always wanted to kill a Papago and just took the first opportunity that presented itself. Perhaps it was part of a ritual, some aspect of Tepoca warrior tradition that I knew nothing of. Or perhaps he had no reason at all except as a reflection of some fundamental evil in his soul. At that point there was little, of course, that I could do about it. But the incident unsettled me, and memories of it disturbed my sleep many times during that year of 1695.

We found Pitquin and Oquitoa, like Tubutama, deserted and burned almost to the ground, with dead, putrefying cattle littering the fields. Near Pitquin we picked up an Indian woman named María and her children. They had nothing to eat and would not have been safe there, anyway, so we put them on horses and took them with us. We followed the Río Altar downstream under warm and sunny skies. Around us we saw hummingbirds and thrashers and orioles, and on the hillsides, marigold and penstemon still flaunting their yellow and red flowers of springtime. We saw quail and doves and, out on the desert, banana yuccas pushing up their stalks of creamy-white flowers. After the villages we had seen, the Altar Valley seemed a comfortingly serene and beautiful place.

A few miles out of Caborca, we stopped on the river and had a small meal of pinole, frijoles, and oranges. Because I was the only one in the group who had been to Caborca, Don Domingo sent me ahead to reconnoiter. I took a Pima and a Seri with me: I no longer trusted the Tepocas.

As it turned out, I should not have trusted the Seri, either.

In Caborca we found Father Saeta's chapel burned, and much damage done to the other buildings and huts. In a mesquite grove we found an Indian man hiding with two boys—his sons, I guessed. One boy looked to be about ten years old; the other, perhaps eight. They wore nothing but dirty loincloths and I could see sores on their skin and lice infesting their hair. In Piman I told them who we were and that we meant them no harm. The Seri seemed very curious about the Papagos, walking around them, touching them, even. He raised his bow and, before I could stop him, shot the smaller boy through the abdomen with an arrow. The boy cried out, his little face twisted in pain. I yanked the two pistols from my sash. The Seri was smiling.

"*Madre de Dios!*" I shouted at him. "Why did you do that? Are you *crazy*? Drop your weapon or I will shoot you!"

He dropped his bow. The injured boy, crying, tried to run. His father rushed to comfort him, but the boy squirmed away, ran a few feet, then stopped to stare tearfully at the arrow that protruded from his belly. Blood oozed from the wound. The boy touched the arrow, gently, his eyes wide, as if he could hardly believe the presence of it. He cried out again and fell to the ground, screaming in pain.

The older boy rushed to my side and clung fiercely to my leg.

"¿Como se llama usted?" I asked him.

"...Antonio." Tears streaked his face.

I took a deep breath; eased it out. I stepped over to the Seri and held both pistols within inches of his dark face. "If you harm Antonio or his father, now or ever," I whispered through clenched teeth, "I will track you down and kill you and every member of your family. Do you understand? In fact, if you move *now*, I will kill you *now*. Do you understand me, you son of a whore?"

I stood there, my breath rasping in my mouth, my pulse pounding, hoping he would try something. *Praying* he would try something. I would have liked nothing more than to put two lead balls through his brain. But he made no move against me or Antonio.

I climbed onto my horse with the gut-shot boy in my arms and rode to the place where Don Domingo and the others were camped. Of course we could not save the boy, but he survived long enough that Father Bayerca could give him the proper sacraments.

To get away from my anger for a while, I rode out to the hill where Father Kino and I had laid out the timbers for our boat. The wood was still there, well-dried and seemingly all right, but I had no illusions about our chances of finishing the boat. Not as long as Father Burgos was Visitor, anyway. Still, I had to check, because I knew Kino would ask.

That afternoon in camp, General Jironza questioned the Papago. I served as translator. By then some of my inner turmoil had dissipated and I was able to do my job, though I knew I would not soon forget what I had seen these past days.

"The people who attacked and burned your village," Don Domingo said to the man. "Were they Apache? Jocome?" We were standing near the river in a grove of willows and sycamore. I could hear the burble of eddies in the shallows and around us I could see butterflies with blue wings flitting among the purple blossoms of hedgehog cactuses that grew in the sand.

The man shook his head. He was still grief-stricken about his son and barely able to speak.

"Pi'a," he said. *No.*

"They killed the new priest. You are certain they were not Apache?"

"Ho'ni'juh." *Yes, I am certain.*

"Sobas from the coast to the west? Mestizo settlers?" Don Domingo's coal-black hair glistened in the sunlight. His uniform was, as always, immaculate, and his tall black boots gleamed with polish.

"Pi'a," the man said. *No.*

"Papagos, then, or Pimas from far to the east?" The General pointed in the direction of San Ignacio and Dolores.

The man wiped tears from his eyes. "Tohono O'odham," he said. "What you call Papago."

"Your *own people* did this?"

"Pi'a. O'odham, but not from my village."

I glanced at the general. He was frowning, his eyes dark and serious.

"So where were these O'odham from? What village?"

"...Tubutama."

"And where else?"

"...Some were from Oquitoa and Pitquin."

"Anywhere else?"

"No."

"Do you know their names?"

He shrugged. "...No."

"Are you a baptized Christian, sir?"

He turned to me, and tears welled again in his eyes. "Ho'ni'juh, Señor. Yes."

"And you swear to God you are telling the truth?"

"Yes."

"Why?" the general said. "Why did they do these things?"

"I have heard it was because of the Ópata." The Papago told us about the overseer at Tubutama, an Ópata. A brutal man. Cold-blooded and vicious. He beat the Papagos who worked for him in the priest's gardens, and groped and spit on their women. The Papagos grew to hate him, of course. When they caught him beating another of their people, they rushed back to their kihs for their arrows and bows. They killed the man, and in their frenzy burned the church and killed all the other outsiders. Emboldened then, they gathered more warriors to their cause and attacked the missions at Oquitoa and Caborca.

"I do not know if all this is true," he added. "But I have heard it."

"But if their anger was for the Ópata," the general said, "why did they attack the churches?"

"Because the overseer worked for the priest," the Papago said. "And the priest works for the Church. By the time the murderers reached my village," he added, "they feared no one, not even God."

"...Were the ma'makai involved in this?"

"I have been told so, Señor. Spreading false rumors about the priests intended to inflame the murderers even more, I have heard. But I do not know this for sure."

The general glanced at me, then turned and stared into the hills across the river. I knew what he was thinking: if the shamans were in fact involved, we could expect the situation to worsen quickly; we could expect full-scale revolt.

After a time I asked the man where all the villagers had gone, the ones who had had no part in the killings.

He pointed around. "Into the hills and mountains. They are afraid. They will not return until all the soldiers and outsiders are gone."

"And the insurrectos, where did they go?"

"Into the mountains." He shrugged. "Or home."

The general rubbed the bridge of his nose. He sighed. "Juan Mateo, tell him we will find the O'odham devils who burned his village and we will punish them severely for it."

I translated Don Domingo's words. Afterward in the silence I heard a warbler trilling from a cottonwood, and bees humming in a field of goldpoppies.

The Indio looked up at us, his dark face streaked again with tears. "That is good to know, Señor. And when are you going to punish the Seri devil who killed my son?"

The next morning at dawn Don Domingo summoned Solís and me to the bank of the river and said these things:

"Gentlemen, as subjects of the King of Spain and officers in his Army, we have certain duties and responsibilities. Among the most important of these is our obligation to maintain law and order in this land. Here is my decision: We will let everyone know that all adults from the traitorous villages—Tubutama, Pitquin, and Oquitoa—will be treated as traitors to the reign of Carlos Segundo. All are to be considered as guilty under Spanish law as the murderers themselves. If any of the villagers are willing to give us the names of the actual instigators and leaders, perhaps these citizens will be spared the pain of death. But perhaps not; I will decide each case as it arises. And when we identify the perpetrators of these heinous crimes against the king and the Church, we will show them no mercy. We will kill them. Because the villagers of Caborca chose to flee rather than fight to the death the murderers of Father Saeta, they, too, must be punished. I will make an exception in the case of the Papago man who lost his young son. There will be no other exceptions. Do you have any questions, gentlemen?"

I had no questions. Neither, apparently, did Lieutenant Solís, judging from the smile on his dark face.

That morning we destroyed the crops in the fields around Caborca and killed the few cattle and sheep we could find. And María, the woman we had found near Pitquin? General Jironza had Father Bayerca baptize her and hear her confession, then ordered her hanged from a sycamore tree.

Punish and kill. We had our orders.

The next few weeks saw us in the saddle almost constantly. We scoured the desert and mountains around Caborca and Tubutama, but saw no one. We found fresh tracks and sign, of course, but the Indians, whoever they were, managed to remain just beyond our reach. We heard of other atrocities in settlements to the north and west, but there was little we could do as we soon had to return to San Juan to re-supply our men and replace our horses.

We buried Father Saeta's remains—little more than ashes and a few charred bones, really—at Cucurpe, with full honors and all possible dignity. He was, we had realized, the Pimería's first martyr.

At the Dolores mission Don Domingo and I visited Father Kino in his quarters, and the two of them talked of ways to find the insurrectos and put an end to the revolt. The padre's adobe room was small, furnished with only a wood bench on which a few Indian blankets had been neatly folded, two chairs, and on the walls, a beautifully-carved crucifix and a painting of a grassy field with vineyards and a stone farmhouse. I wanted to ask him about the painting, but I knew he had more important matters on his mind.

"I see only one way," Kino said after greeting us warmly and pouring chocolate for us in earthen mugs, "that we can learn who the perpetrators were."

"How, Father?" the general said.

"The villagers of Tubutama and Oquitoa know full well who the leaders were. We should offer complete and total amnesty to anyone who comes forward and gives us the names."

"That has not been my policy."

"I know, General. But your policy has not worked." Kino's hair, always a bit disheveled, seemed a little grayer than the last time I had seen him, the lines a little deeper in his narrow sun-weathered face. I believe he had not had a new robe in the two years I had known him.

"I sent Solís back to Tubutama," the general said, "to put pressure on the villagers. Perhaps he will have some good news for us soon."

Kino sighed. "I am afraid to ask how the lieutenant plans to do this."

"He will kill a few Indians. And then a few more. Others will be convinced it is better to talk to our soldiers than to fight them."

Kino was skeptical and insisted that killing innocents only made the problems worse. Don Domingo, as before, favored a harsher approach. I sat quietly, listening and sipping chocolate as the two old friends debated and argued and debated some more. Kino's voice was not a loud one, but it was firm and unwavering and his words, always carefully chosen, carried a sense of deep conviction.

"Then let me do this," the padre said. "I will ride to Magdalena. There

I will ask the villagers to spread out across the desert, as far west as Caborca, and tell every soul they encounter that I will personally stand by their side and protect them from the soldiers if they will do either of two things: bring the instigators and murderers to us, or come in and tell us honestly who they were. Then you can punish the guilty as you wish, but not the innocents. The non-guilty get amnesty. Agreed?"

Don Domingo laughed. "So you would cast the army as the villains, Father?"

"Of course," Kino said, smiling, "if it would save a life or two."

By the end of May it looked as if Kino's plan might work. We had had messages from several chiefs at villages in the western desert stating that they knew who the miscreants were and would bring them to us on the condition that the padre would stand with them and protect them from the army and otherwise certain punishment. Kino and General Jironza selected a place and time for the meeting: La Ciénega, a clearing in a marshy plain with shade trees and a natural spring, near the settlement of El Tupo, a few miles northwest of Magdalena. June ninth.

On the appointed day, more than a hundred Indians from the western villages came in—unarmed, as they had agreed to leave their weapons at a distance—and were met by Kino and a company of cavalry. For reasons I never fully understood, Don Domingo had assigned Solís as commander of the army forces. This worried me, as I suspect it worried the padre, but there was little I could say.

At Solís' command, the soldiers on horseback encircled the Papagos, giving them little room to move. Kino pushed into the milling, nervous crowd of Indios and shouted at Solís, "Give them room to breathe, Lieutenant! They cannot harm you. They have no weapons. Please, order your men back!"

Solís reined his horse to face the padre. "Stay out of this, priest. This is not your business."

"It is very much my business, sir. These people came here because I promised them safety. I beg of you, tell your men to move back!"

Solís pulled his sword. "I warn you, priest, stay out of this!"

"They are a threat to no one, Lieutenant!" Kino argued, "Please! Give them room!"

Unfortunately, one of the chiefs picked that moment to grab a Papago by the hair and shout that he had been one of the instigators and murderers at Tubutama. Solís wheeled his horse around, raised his sword and, before anyone could react, sliced the Papago's head off. The other Indios, confused and suddenly terrified, tried to escape. The soldiers, under orders to stop any exodus, opened fire with muskets and pistols. By some miracle Kino was spared, but within minutes forty-eight Indians were dead, the blood of innocent and guilty alike forming bright puddles and streaming in crimson rivulets over the sand.

La Matanza. The slaughter.

Kino was horrified by this act of savagery. And when they learned of it, so were Don Domingo, the viceroy, the bishop, and the governor of Sonora. It embittered the Indians who escaped and all those who learned of it from them. The ma'makai, of course, lost no time in declaring it as proof of the perfidy of the Spaniards and Black Robes.

The resentment and virulence spread quickly through the settlements of the western desert and, eventually, even to some in the east.

In the next few months many people would die.

La Matanza.

The Pima Revolt of 1695 had fully begun.

CHAPTER 17 Magdalena, Sonora. 1965.

Dirt. That's what had finally done it, in Olvera's hotel room in Magdalena after the drive back from Cocóspera—dirt. At the ruins with the mayor he had noticed the first faint stirrings of...*what*? Whatever it was, it'd nagged him throughout the day, tickled his subconscious mind, teased him with the odd notion that the Cocóspera ruins on that windy hill north of the Sierra Azul somehow held the secret to finding Kino's old bones here in this little village of Magdalena. Olvera had been scrubbing his hands, cleaning grit from under his nails and wondering how he'd gotten so filthy, when he remembered poking his fingers into the soil near the church's foundations. It had been that simple word, *foundations*, that had helped him see it.

So this, Olvera now believed, is how it added up: In 1711 a priest named Campos buried Eusebio Kino under the dirt floor of a small adobe chapel in the Pima village of Magdalena, Sonora. This might be the building now known as the Proctor Chapel, though it probably wasn't—if Mayor Nava and Sánchez de la Vega and the historians in Hermosillo were right. More likely, nothing of Kino's chapel still existed aboveground; any part of it still surviving would be *under*ground. If Olvera and Professor Jiménez were to have any chance of locating Kino's remains, first they had to find the second and third ashlars, the stone footings, on the Gospel side of this chapel. And to recognize the ashlars when they encountered them in their trenching, they had to know how he built them and the materials he used. Simply stated, they had a lot to learn about foundations.

It wasn't much, but it was a start.

That afternoon Olvera telephoned Jiménez to report his arrival in Magdalena. "My hotel room is comfortable and I'm getting settled in, Professor."

"Good. Have you had time to see the church?"

"I'm on my way there now."

"Excellent," Jiménez said, "And Mayor Nava—you've met him?"

"Just this morning. He took me to see the ruins at Cocóspera."

"I've read of them. What did you think?"

"The architecture is very interesting," Olvera told him, "part Jesuit and part Franciscan. I'd love to poke around there a bit more, but I doubt I'll have time for it."

"The Apaches haven't attacked you yet?"

Olvera chuckled. "So far, so good."

"And the ma'makai haven't put a curse on you?"

"The mama-*what*?"

"Pima medicine men," Jiménez said. "Shamans, a type of hechicero. They caused lots of problems for Kino and the others. Particularly in the insurrection of 1695."

Olvera made a note to himself to learn more about shamans. It was embarrassing, his chief, still in Mexico City, knowing more about these things than *he* did, even if his chief was a famous anthropologist and would of course know all about Indians.

"What did you think of the mayor, Jorge?"

Olvera thought about that. "I liked him. He was very generous with his time."

"Where," Jiménez said, "does the mayor believe we'll find Kino?"

"Truthfully? I suspect he believes we won't find him at all. Over the years he's seen lots of people come here looking for the padre. And of course no one's found him yet."

"And you, Jorge? Do you think we'll find him?"

"We'll find him, sir," Olvera said. "It may take a while, but we'll find his old bones."

This much Olvera knew immediately: In Magdalena, the parish church—the church from which the statue of San Xavier had been taken by the soldiers of Presidente Calles—was clearly, unequivocally, of Franciscan origin. Jiménez had said as much, even suggesting it dated from the early 1830's. He was right. In Olvera's search through the archives of the Archdiocese, he had learned that the church was completed in 1832, that its first minister was Father José Pérez Llera.

Forget the archival records, Olvera thought, all you had to do was look at the place. For one thing, it was too modern to be of Jesuit design. For another, it was too large and complex. For yet another, it was built entirely of kiln-dried brick that had been veneered with plaster made from lime and sand. There wasn't an adobe block to be found.

No, this was not the chapel where Campos buried his friend, Eusebio Kino, in 1711. To Olvera's knowledge, no one had suggested it was, but he'd needed to put the matter to rest, at least in his own mind. Nor was this the main Campos church that had been here in 1711. That church was much smaller and had been constructed solely of adobe.

So this church, the 1832 Llera structure, at least, he could set aside.

Which left him three other churches to ponder.

1) The main Campos church, he knew from the archives, had been completed some time around 1705. It was the main church in Magdalena when Kino came to dedicate the new chapel in 1711. As far as anyone knew, this building was no longer in existence.

2) The little adobe chapel itself, the Chapel of San Xavier...It was under this chapel that Campos had supposedly buried Kino. Were remnants of this building still visible in Magdalena? A small mound of crumbling adobe, hidden, perhaps, by bushes or trees or newer buildings, but still somehow accessible? According to Jiménez, the historians in Hermosillo didn't think so. Nor did the mayor, Nava, or his friend, de la Vega.

3) The little chapel in modern Magdalena known variously as the Proctor Chapel, the Chapel of San Miguel, sometimes the Pesquira Chapel. Many of the local citizens, Olvera knew, believed this to be Kino's burial site. On this he had no opinion. He hadn't seen it yet. He thought about walking there now—he knew the general direction—but the hour was already late. Maybe he could go to the library and look through the periodicals. No, it was late for that, too, he realized. So he walked instead to a café near the Palacio Municipal, the City Hall, where he had dinner. From there it was a short, pleasant stroll back to his hotel.

As he walked, questions flitted through his mind. What had happened to the 1705 Campos church? Did the 1832 Llera church, the one in current use, occupy the same site as the 1705 church? If not, where had the old church been? Where would Kino's 1711 chapel have been *in relation to* the Campos church?

Back at the hotel, Olvera retrieved his street map of Magdalena. He sat in his room and studied the map and thought about Jesuit priests and coffins and adobe chapels with footings made of stone.

He even gave some time to thinking about shamans.

CHAPTER 18

The Pimería. Año D. 1695. July.

"There is nothing easy about this land, Juan Mateo," Kino said.

"I know, Father."

"There's nothing soft or dainty about it, or even comfortable. It juts and stabs and trips and bites, and the summer sun is so harsh it sears your eyes and broils your flesh. It rarely rains, but when it does, it often rains too much. And when the wind blows, it always blows too long, or sometimes not long enough."

I had a sip of chocolate and wondered if I could keep it down, with the uneasiness that had been pushing and probing at my stomach. My palms were moist with sweat; I wiped them on my white trousers.

Kino went on with his thoughts. "The animals and insects and reptiles are openly hostile. Even the vegetation is against us. The plants are forever jabbing and sticking and stinging us, as if they wished to discourage all human contact."

The padre was smiling as he said these things.

"Some days," I agreed, "it is hard to appreciate prickly pears."

He was not really complaining; nor was I. He was in a reflective mood, and he had been talking about the events and circumstances that had brought him to this point in his life, speaking honestly of things that had been on his mind in recent months. At the moment I was doing little more than listening, sipping chocolate, and wishing for happier circumstances.

We were in the little room that served as his living quarters at Dolores; we had been here, in fact, since dawn. Waiting for the insurrectos. They would be here soon, we suspected. Kino was wearing faded gray trousers and a pale cotton shirt, and in spite of the July heat I had donned my full dress uniform. My arquebus and pistolas were loaded; my sword was freshly sharpened. We had brought in water, chocolate, and enough food to last a while. We could only guess at what the day would bring, but we had prepared about as well as we could.

"Still, as harsh as the desert is," Kino continued, "I love it here. I can hardly imagine living anywhere else. Can you?"

"I cannot," I told him honestly. He was attempting, I knew, to take my mind off our situation, and I appreciated his efforts.

"You know, Juan Mateo, there was a time when I wanted badly to go to China. To be a missionary there."

"You have no regrets that you came here instead?"

He was silent for a time; weighing it in his mind, I supposed. Then he smiled. "No, I have no regrets. God has blessed me in a thousand ways."

I rose from my chair and stepped over to the door, open now in the growing heat of the day. I could see the mission church and vegetable gardens, the blacksmith shop, and dark-edged thunderheads building on the horizon, as they often did this time of year. I had to shade my eyes against the sun, but I saw no one and heard nothing. I had begun to feel a sort of restlessness, a need to move, to have a look outside. There was nothing to see, but that did little to calm my growing nervousness.

In my chair again, I scanned the room. Like most of the small buildings the padre had built, this one was windowless. For this reason we had no cross-breezes, but with adobe walls four feet in thickness, the room remained surprisingly cool. Kino had few furnishings: a bench that held some folded blankets and a pot of chocolate; the chairs we were sitting in. A cloth bag on the floor held a few clothes and his robe. A beautifully-carved crucifix hung on one wall. On another wall was a painting of a vineyard and a stone house with a grassy field in the foreground and snow-covered mountains behind. I had seen the painting on an earlier visit.

I asked him about it.

"My sister, Caterina, painted that," he said, and I could hear the pride in his voice. "She was twelve at the time. I suspect by now she is quite a good artist."

"So this was your home? Where you were raised?"

He nodded. "In the Italian Alps, near Segno. We called it Moncou and loved every square inch of it. We had cattle and sheep and grapes and vegetables, and there was always plenty to do. The winters were horribly cold, but that seemed to matter little, especially to my sisters and me."

"You had more than one sister?"

"Three," he said. "Caterina was the artistic one. Margherita was the singer, and Ana María was the good-looking one. All the boys liked Ana

María, so there were always plenty of friends around. My mother thought we were very comical."

After a time he shifted in his chair; when he spoke again his voice had a hitch in it and I knew he had been thinking about his family. "After my father died," he said, "my mother had to sell off the house and vineyards to pay our debts. I have always suspected that she used part of that money to pay my school expenses at Ingolstadt and Oettingen. She never said so, though, so I do not know for sure."

"She loved you very much, I think."

He nodded. "Oh, yes. Even if I had a thousand years, I could never repay her for all she did for me." He poured more chocolate for himself from the pot on the bench, and refilled my mug. He took a sip from his cup and said, "Juan Mateo, do you have a life verse?"

I had no idea what a life verse was, and said so.

"It is a Bible verse," Kino said, "that your mother gives you. When you are a small child, usually. Something that fits your personality, a verse your mother believes will have special meaning for you and will guide and protect you during the difficult times she knows will come in your life."

I shook my head. "I have no such verse. Do you?"

"My mother gave one to each of her four children. She gave mine to me when I was eight years old. Psalms, chapter one-thirty-nine, verses nine and ten. Do you know that passage?"

"Give me a minute," I said. In those early years I was never very good at memorizing Scripture, though I routinely tried because it always seemed a thing worth doing. But I usually found my mind so packed with thoughts of weapons and war and hostile Indians, there was little room for anything else.

"Something about...*wings?*" I said.

He smiled. " '*If I rise on the wings of the dawn, if I settle on the far side of the sea, even there Your hand will guide me, Your right hand will hold me fast.*' Beautiful, is it not?"

"Very beautiful," I said. "And interesting. 'If I settle on the far side of the sea...' Do you suppose your mother somehow knew that one day you would leave Italy and come to the New World?"

"I have always suspected so, though she never claimed it."

For a time we listened to the stillness and silence that filled the empty village. Through the doorway I could see a mesquite tree, its dark branches weighted by ripe beans, and in the thin hot breeze I caught the faint scent of creosote bushes still pungent from the last good rain.

I pointed to the open doorway, and in Kino's eyes and the set of his jaw I saw that he knew my next question even before I posed it: "Do you think your mother could have foreseen all these problems, here, in the Pimería?"

"I pray she could not, Juan Mateo," he said. "I fear the pain would be more than she could possibly bear. I can hardly imagine it myself."

It had been difficult for all of us to imagine.

After Lieutenant Solís' massacre of the Pimas at El Tupo in June, the Indians had struck back at us at every opportunity. Their numbers swelled as their anger grew and the ma'makai exhorted them to even greater rebellion. They made more raids on Oquitoa and Tubutama and Caborca, burning more mission buildings and killing all villagers who stood in their way. They ambushed the soldiers who came after them and butchered with impunity any Spaniards, settlers, and miners they encountered. Blood flowed almost daily in the western Pimería. We regularly had news of this in Real San Juan, of course, and with every Pima attack on another settlement or another company of cavalry, Don Domingo regularly dispatched more troops to catch and punish the offenders. But our soldiers could not catch them. Not even Antonio Solís could find them.

So Don Domingo, frustrated in his failure to punish the wayward Pimas and convinced anyway that the trouble would not spread beyond the villages in the western desert, turned his attention elsewhere. He began making plans with General Fuente from Fronteras for a joint expedition against Clavo, an Apache leader who lived far to the northeast of San Juan. Almost as an afterthought, he sent me to Dolores to look after Father Kino.

Which left me, for a time, the only soldier in this part of the Pimería.

Even Coxi, the Pima chief at Dolores, had left. Some of his men had chased Black Skull's band of Jocome-Apaches into the Chiricahua Mountains, and were now trying to root them out. The others, and Coxi himself, had gone after Clavo with Don Domingo and General Fuente.

Later, the generals would admit they had made a colossal mistake, but that would be no help to us now. I had been in Dolores only a few days when Kino and I learned that the insurrectionists were on their way here, intent on total destruction of the Church and complete eradication of all Spanish presence in the Pimería.

I stood and walked to the doorway of Kino's room again, a pistola in my hand. I thought I had heard something—horses, perhaps—but at the door I saw no one and heard no other sounds.

In my chair again I asked the padre about a subject that had been bothering me: Why had Solís not been punished for his massacre of the innocent Indians at El Tupo?

"You need to remember," he said, "there are many who applauded Solís' actions."

"Who?" I said. I did not doubt my own naïvete about some of the ways of the New World, but I could hardly imagine that anyone would actually be *pleased* with the death of innocent people. Forty-eight Indians had died at the hands of Solís' men, and by now we knew with certainty that thirty had been innocent of all charges in the murders at Tubutama and Caborca.

"The miners and ranchers," Kino said. "Many have never liked me or the other frontier priests. They tolerate the army because you protect them from the Apaches, but many resent us because we do not allow them to take pacified Indians as slaves."

"And Don Domingo does not wish to antagonize these people?"

Kino nodded. "That may be a lot of it. To many settlers, Solís is a hero. But do not blame Don Domingo. Remember, he has many responsibilities. And he has to do what he believes is best for Spain."

This time I *knew* I heard something. I walked outside with my arquebus and saw an Indian coming in fast, his horse wheezing and lathered, gray dust kicking up behind him in the heat of the day. I recognized him. His name was Cosme; he was a Yaqui Indian, a friend and servant of Father Campos' at San Ignacio. He dismounted and hurriedly told me that the insurrectos had reached his village.

"They burned the mission buildings there," he added.

By now Kino had joined us. "Everything, Cosme?" he said.

The Indian wiped trail dust from his dark face and took the water gourd Kino handed him. He drank deeply from it. "I saw ramadas and church buildings and kihs on fire." He had another long drink.

"Did they kill anyone?" Kino's voice was calm, but I could see worry in his eyes. He made the sign of the cross. "Where is Father Campos? Did he get away safely?"

The Yaqui closed his eyes and mumbled a prayer. When he looked up again his eyes were wet with grief. His voice broke. "I do not know if he got away. Before the insurrectos came, he sent me into the mountains to watch for smoke from our village. He said if I saw it, I was to ride here as fast as my horse would take me, and tell you of it."

Kino sighed. "They probably hit Magdalena before they attacked San Ignacio."

"I believe so," Cosme said. "And now they are headed this way."

We thanked him, gave him food and a fresh horse, and sent him on to Cucurpe and Arizpe to alert the villagers there.

In Kino's room again I said, "It is not too late, Father. You still have time to get away. If you ride hard you can be in San Juan in two days."

He shook his head. "You know my feelings on that. I will not leave."

"But I cannot protect you! Not from so many of them."

He held up his Bible. "I have this for protection, my friend. But I wish you would go. There is no reason for you to stay."

"We have had this conversation before, Father."

"You are a good man, Juan Mateo. In the two years you have been in the Pimería, you have grown as a soldier and as a Christian. But God does not expect you to die for me."

"I know," I said.

The day before, when we first learned that the insurrectos were preparing an attack on Dolores, Father Kino sang prayers for the villagers, then sent them into the mountains to hide. There were not many: the women and children, and a few men too old and frail to fight with the others against Black Skull and Clavo. When night came, I went with Kino to the mission church. In light from an oil lamp we loaded all the vestments, santos, and chalices into a trunk. We tied the trunk on the back of a mule with ropes and carried it to a cave in the hills outside Dolores. There we buried the trunk.

"Padre?" I said when we had finished and tamped the dirt down with our boots. In the echoes of the cave I had heard my own voice breaking.

"Yes, Juan Mateo."

"Now, in the darkness," I said, "we could ride south and be in Cucurpe by sunrise. If we rode hard, we could be in Real San Juan in two days."

Looking back on it, I am certain Kino knew how frightened I was that night, but he made no mention of it. He had no qualms about speaking of his own fears, in talking about his own demons, but he rarely mentioned the fears he must have easily recognized in others. That night in the cave, in the flickering shadows from the lantern, I could see the steadiness in his strong hands, the serenity in his warm blue eyes. But these had not given me peace or calmed my own fears.

"There is no reason we have to stay, Father," I had insisted. "Nobody expects us to die when there is a way out."

I will never forget his reply.

He took a while to compose it and he looked me straight in the eye when he delivered it.

"I am a priest, Juan Mateo," he said. "God sent me here. He put a Bible in my right hand and a crucifix in my left, and He sent me here to teach the Indians and bring them to His Son, Jesus Christ, for their salvation. Teaching is my job. It is my work. I do not believe my work here is finished, but if it is, God will let me know. He knows we are here, my friend. He knows the insurrectionists are coming; He knows our dilemma. If it is His will that I die—*here, now*, on *this* day—then so be it. If that is not His will, He will tell the insurrectos so, and they will walk away and do me no harm, even though they may not know it is His voice that tells them to do so. Do you see what I am saying, Juan Mateo?"

"...You are saying it is not your decision."

"Exactly. It is God's decision, and I cannot contest His will." He embraced me warmly, then stepped back and smiled. "But you, my friend," he said, "you are another matter entirely. You have the freedom to go. In fact, I insist that you do. I will ride back to the village, get food and water, and bring it to you here. Then you can ride to safety and sometime soon we will see each other again."

"Do you think I should, Father?"

"Yes, my friend, I do."

We walked out of the cave in the darkness. I stood for a few moments in the silence of the night, then tied the shovels onto the mule and pointed my horse back towards the village.

"Juan Mateo!" I heard the padre say, "You are not going to San Juan?"

"No, Father," I had said, "I cannot leave you here alone," and we had ridden back down to the mission and Kino's little room to await the sunrise and whatever the new day would bring.

In the distance now, we heard shouts and the sounds of horses. I glanced out the open door and saw Indios—I guessed their number at more than two hundred—hurrying toward the mission church. They were Papagos and Pimas, as we had expected. A few looked vaguely familiar, though I saw no one I knew by name. All were heavily armed with bows and arrows, knives, and war clubs, and a few carried lighted torches that gave off plumes of oily dark smoke I could smell even here in the room. They stopped before the church, shouting among themselves, gesturing at the church and the buildings around it. Several with torches rushed inside.

"They are here now, Juan Mateo?"

"At the church, Father." I wiped dampness from my face with a cloth even as a cottony dryness seemed to fill my mouth; I felt again the stirrings of nausea.

Kino calmly donned his black robe. He kissed the small bronze cross that hung on a cord from his neck, then knelt in the darkness and began to pray the Pater Noster. When he finished the prayer he stood, made the sign of the cross, and said, "The name of the Lord is a strong tower; the righteous run to it and are safe."

Outside, the sun was boiling, and through the doorway I could see waves of heat coming off the ground. I considered taking off my coat. It was wool, after all, and red, and much too heavy for summer use. For some reason I thought of General Jironza, my uncle, and realized that in the two years I had been in the Pimería I had never seen him without his coat on. Had never seen him, even, with his coat unbuttoned. He had always been the proper soldier, the perfect officer. Strong; capable, professional. I doubted I could ever meet those standards, but in this moment I knew I had to try. I brushed a fleck of lint from my coat sleeve and pulled on my blue bicorn hat.

Kino was waiting at the doorway. "Juan Mateo, if our Lord wills that I should die today and you should live, would you promise something?" If he felt any fear, his voice gave no sign of it.

"Yes, Father, anything." Bile had risen into my throat, and I fought the nausea that seemed to grow in my breast with each passing second.

"Promise that for the rest of your life you will act justly, love mercy, and walk humbly with your God."

"I will, sir."

We heard the Indians coming now, their voices tight and loud with anger.

I pulled my sword and walked out into the brightness and heat of the day with Father Kino.

CHAPTER 19

The concept of death was not new to me. In my mind there was nothing vague or distant or abstract about it, even in those early years. I had killed and seen men killed. I had watched a Piman temastian die of measles, an Ópata vaquero, from rabies caught from a skunk. Once I was with General Jironza when we stumbled onto a campsite just abandoned by Apaches. We found the ropes they had used to suspend a captive mestizo woman above a blazing fire; saw the burned sticks they had used to sear and brand her skin and eyes and genitalia. We found parts of her nude body—a torso, ears, fingers—still smoldering in the coals. The air reeked of charred flesh and for days afterward my uniform was heavy with a poisonous stench, my mind freighted with images I found no way to escape.

No, death was not a new thought for me, even in 1695.

But it was still a frightening one. When Father Kino and I walked out of his quarters at the Dolores mission to face the Piman insurrectos that afternoon in July, my pulse was pounding in my head. My throat felt cankered and raw, as if I had fish bones stuck in it.

The Indio who seemed to be the leader was tall for a Piman, almost my height.

Charcoal tattoos of curved lines and odd geometric shapes covered his forehead and chin. He wore nothing but a faded taparrabo over his loins and, hanging from a rawhide cord around his narrow waist, a beaded bag made from antelope hide. In his right hand he carried a war club; in the other, a bow carved from mulberry. Behind him were at least two hundred Pimas and Papagos, all shouting and gesturing, their dark faces filled with anger.

"See the medicine bag?" Kino whispered.

I nodded.

"Ma'makai," he said.

Thunder rumbled in the distance. Bulbous gray clouds had moved in over the mountains and the air seemed heavy, oppressively hot. I glanced up the hill to Kino's adobe church with its high front façade and the tall tower with seven bells. I could see flitting shadows of golondrinas, the swallows that looked blue in the afternoon light and raised their young in nests of dried mud they built on the tower walls.

The nearness of the church seemed to calm me, though my hands continued to shake and I was aware of the rasping of hot air in my lungs.

The shaman raised his war club. He started to say something, then stopped. He shook the club, and I could hear the *ch-ch-ch* of the snake rattles bound with cord to the handle of the club. The Indians began to dance and chant. I could not make out their words, or guess their meaning, or even hear them, really. But they seemed to be chanting.

Strangely, I could no longer hear *anything*—not the shaman, or his rattles, or the other Pimas. Now everything seemed slightly disjointed, faintly evanescent, as if I were seeing the world through lenses that filtered out all the sound and made everything seem filmy and out of focus. For an instant

I had a sense that I was a character in one of Calderón de la Barca's plays, a tragic figure caught in circumstances that had spun out of control. Then I remembered: No, I was here out of choice, with Father Kino, doing what I believed to be right. I was frightened and my mind was playing tricks, but I was no tragic figure.

I took a breath, eased it out, and took another one. I had made my peace; I had given my confession. I was not *ready* to die, but I was *prepared* to, if that makes any sense. And I knew this: I would not die without a fight. I owed my uncle that much. I owed God and the Compañía and Carlos Segundo that much. I raised my pistol, my hand still shaking, and aimed it at the ma'makai's heart. The July heat carried the acrid scent of the cliffrose that grew on the hillside, and in the breeze I caught the smell of camphorbush sprouting in the moist spill from an acéquia that ferried water down to the gardens and orange groves. I tightened my grip on the pistol's trigger and stole a glance at the padre.

Kino stood in the fading light of the afternoon sun, his Bible in his hand, his face as calm and serene as I had ever seen it. He was waiting patiently, as he had promised, for God's decision on his future. I remembered his words in the cave the night before: "*If it is God's will that I die—here, now, on this day—then so be it. If it is not His will, He will tell the insurrectos so...and they will walk away and do me no harm, even though they may not know it is His voice that told them to do so...*"

I wondered if we would actually hear God's voice or whether we would simply know His will by the unfolding of events.

In that exact moment the mood of the Pimas seemed to change. Some began milling about, talking among themselves, ignoring the ma'makai. Then I saw some of them smiling, and even a few began smoking rolled cigarros of ban vivega, the foul-smelling weed the soldiers called coyote tobacco. One of the Indians came up to Father Kino and held his bow out before him—a gesture that indicated his intentions were peaceful.

The shaman shouted at the men. He chanted and waved his medicine bag. The Pimas, though, seemed almost unaware of him now, as if they, like I, had gone deaf, no longer able to hear his exhortations.

The wind had picked up and I could feel moisture freshening in the hot air. There was a haze in the sky, and if you let your imagination run you could make out the curved outlines of a rainbow over the mountains. To the west the sky was rimmed with pink and gold, and the clouds riding the horizon flickered and flared in shades of red, as if they were backlighted by oil fires.

Fire.

In that instant I realized that I had smelled no smoke and seen no flames. I looked around. There *was* no smoke. Earlier I had seen insurrectos with torches running into the church, but now I saw they had started no fires! I glanced at Father Kino and saw in his eyes that he had realized it, too.

The ma'makai stared at us, his face dark and sullen, but he said nothing more and made no moves against us. Still, I kept my pistol trained on his thin chest, my finger cramped against the trigger.

But that, strangely, was the end of it.

There was no great epiphany, no booming voice from the heavens, no sudden realization of any ultimate truth. One minute the Pimas were gathered before us, chanting and shouting; the next, they were backing away.

We watched them turn and walk silently up the hill to their waiting horses. Once, the shaman looked back. His lips seemed pale, his jaw square and hard, the skin tight over the bones of his face. We watched him climb onto his horse, a big gray mustang. He reined it around and rode slowly out to the trail that would take him and the others back to Tubutama.

I remembered the pistol, finally, and lowered my arm.

My eyes wandered down the hill to the deserted mud huts of the villagers and on down to the San Miguel and the cottonwoods and willows that grew along it. I slipped the pistol under my belt and let the fear and weariness and dread slowly drain from my mind.

Midway up the hill to the church there was a level area, a narrow sort of plateau, grown up with prickly pear and grasses and small clusters of marigolds with bright yellow flowers, where Father Kino had built a bench from half-logs of cottonwood. I strolled up to the bench and sat, my face to the wind, and looked out over the irrigated fields of cabbages and onions and pumpkins and teparies, and at the grapes and squashes and ruler-straight rows of citrus. Now the wind was bending the mesquites and ironwoods that grew near the church; dust filled the air and stung my face. In the past week out in the desert I had seen that the pitahayas, the fruits of the saguaros, were ripening, the pulps already soft and red, the seeds heavy and black like shiny grains of magnetite. Soon the Pimas would begin harvesting the pitahayas to make navait, the sweet wine they would drink at their New Year Ceremony. The villages would come alive with feasting and drinking, with ritual prayers and singing and dancing, and in mid-July, in the first days after the ceremony, the Indians would go into the fields for the year's second planting of beans and corn. And if the prayers had been blessed, the rains would come.

Rains.

The summer monsoons. *Las Aguas*, the settlers called them. The storms would come during July and August, carried on violent winds, with towering thunderheads that piled up over the mountains and ripped the night skies with jolts of lightning that looked like thick white ropes etched across the heavens. The storms would bring rain. The desert would see a new beginning, a rebirth of hope. A renewal of life.

But it was not quite time for the rains, only the humidity and the hard hot winds that blew sand in my eyes and ruffled my tunic and made Father Kino's black robe flap at his legs.

I watched him as he came slowly up the hill. He had been kneeling, praying, and as he drew closer I could see a sheen of wetness in his eyes. I stood when he reached me. He put his arms around me and embraced me. "I was very proud of you today, Juan Mateo. God loves you, you know."

"I know," I said.

He smiled. "He has more work for you here."

"And for you, Father."

"Yes," he said after a time. "For both of us, I think."

Why had the Pimas turned and walked away from us that July day when they had come so many miles with the sole intent of destroying the churches and butchering any missionaries and soldiers they found? Some years after this incident Father Kino allowed me to read his diary, and in it I found the only statement he ever recorded on the insurrectionists and this bizarre episode: *We were all in great straits*, he wrote, *but I sent such quieting messages as I could to all parts, and by Divine Grace the trouble went no further.*

The padre had, I think, a talent for understatement.

But was he right about Divine Grace as the full explanation for the fact of our survival? In the days that followed we learned that the insurrectionists had also spared the missions at Remedios and Cocóspera. These two and Dolores were the missions for which Kino had always had direct responsibility. Many times I had seen Indian children run to him, giggling and squealing as they tugged on his robe and hugged his legs. Many times I had seen adults gathered around him, listening happily as he told them of God's word and His love. He had brought them livestock and horses, vegetables, wheat, and citrus. He had tended them when they were sick, advised and comforted them when they were troubled. Is it possible that he simply underestimated the affection they felt for him? That they would have spared him even if he had not prayed so fervently? Perhaps sometimes that is what Divine Grace is, God's approval of what might have happened anyway. I suspect the padre would say that *everything* happens by God's plan, that *nothing* ever happens *without* His approval. Perhaps he would be right. I recognize that these are questions best left to priests and theologians, not soldiers. Still, I have always wondered.

After the Pimas left us on that strange afternoon in July, Kino and I walked on up to the church, and on the way I asked him if he wanted anything to eat. Some carne asada, perhaps, or tortillas and cheese.

He gave no answer. I had not really expected him to; the light that glowed in his eyes was a private one, between him and God. But I knew him well enough by now to make a few guesses at what he was thinking about: the text for his next sermon, or the ride he would make to the mountains to bring back the villagers still hiding there. Or perhaps he was praying for the souls of the innocents who had died in the revolt, or asking for God's guidance on how he might help end this deplorable war that had so quickly engulfed the Pimería.

I left him there at the door of the church and walked to the carpenter's shop, where I had tethered my horse that morning. In my saddlebags I found enough food to make a meal. Tortillas, sweet grapes, strips of grilled beef and peppers, and a packet of cooked beans. I pulled off my uniform coat and tossed my bicorn on the ground and sat in the shade of an oak tree and ate. This was the first time in a while that I had had an appetite, and it was good to have it back. It was good to sit, too, and relax, and to know that this day was over and could never come back to hurt us again. A thousand thoughts crowded at my mind, a thousand what-ifs and yes-buts. But these were selfish, solemn thoughts, and desperate ones, and for the moment I chose to ignore them. I simply sat and enjoyed my meal and God's grace and the cool shade of that big old oak.

The last time I saw Kino that day he was in the church, kneeling at the first of the stations of the cross. I knew he would not be out again for a while.

That summer, the padre did in fact find a way to stop the war. He rode a lot of miles in doing it, but he managed to get the right people in the right places to agree that the killing had to stop. In August, the month of his fiftieth birthday, he met with representatives of the army, the civil government, and Pimas from the western deserts and eastern rivers. They gathered near El Tupo, at the marshy plain where Lieutenant Antonio Solís had ordered the massacre that had started the bloody rebellion. Kino had insisted that the meeting be held there. To clear the air, he said. To restore the village to its rightful position of respect.

And so it was done. After the signing of the treaty, Kino arranged to change the name of the village from El Tupo to Santa Rosa, as the treaty was signed on the feast day of that saint.

By autumn of that year of 1695, life in the Pimería had mostly returned to normal. Father Agustín Campos and Father Daniel Januske, who had managed to escape the wrath of the insurrectos, returned to their villages of San Ignacio and Tubutama to begin the arduous task of rebuilding. Kino returned to his beloved Dolores and spent the remainder of the summer and fall overseeing the harvests at his missions. That year the rains were plentiful and in the lowlands the second plantings did well.

But the Apaches had not stopped their depredations along the eastern rivers, and I spent much of the rest of the year in the saddle with the Compañía. We lost too many good men to enemy lances and arrows, but we killed some Apaches and Jocomes, and took almost a dozen captives. These we delivered to Real San Juan and turned over to the civil authorities for trial.

Delivered...for trial. I was slowly coming to terms with the meaning of that phrase, though it would be a few months yet before I fully accepted it. Oddly, it would be an Apache warrior who would finally force me to face the truth.

In November Father Kino left for Mexico City on Church business, a roundtrip journey of some three thousand miles. To Don Domingo this must have seemed safe enough, as we knew that Clavo and Mofeta and Oso Azul and their Apaches were raiding regularly along the Terrenate, well north of the route that Kino would take.

But Don Domingo had forgotten Black Skull and his Jocomes, and in May of the following year we would learn that Kino's return route had not been such a safe one at all.

CHAPTER 20 Magdalena, Sonora. 1965.

At first sight of it, about all Olvera could say about the Proctor Chapel was that it was old. It seemed to be flat-roofed. The walls appeared, at least from where he stood in the street, to be of aging adobe. Thick vines and overgrown bushes cast the chapel in shadows and shielded much of it from view, adding to the sense that it had belonged to a far earlier time, a more perilous, primal world.

But could it be old enough to hold the bones of Kino beneath it? Could it date to 1711? To Olvera, there were indications it might.

In the archives, he'd found a scale drawing of the chapel. This revealed that it consisted of several rooms, most arranged end-to-end, as the Jesuits were known to have built the simplest of their hall-style buildings. Ceilings were of mesquite and cane, both commonly used in Kino's time. The walls varied in age. The oldest were adobe; the newer were brick. Floors were brick. The interior walls had an abundance of niches for the placement of santos—religious statues or paintings—as Jesuit churches often did. The exterior doorways were arched. The doors themselves, according to the drawings, were made of pine, with wooden pegs and handmade hinges and nails.

By now Olvera knew that others, both professional and amateur, had been here before him. In the 1920's and '30's, Bolton, Davila, and Lockwood had searched the chapel grounds for Kino's gravesite. In later years, Parodi, Villa, Pesqueira, Colonel Gilbert Proctor, and de la Vega the chemist—all had taken their own brief stabs at it. Some had remained convinced that Kino lay somewhere under the old building. Others, admitting their own failures and aware of the failures of others, had grown skeptical.

The confusion had worsened in the spring of 1963. The citizens of Magdalena, after years of waiting, were anxious to find their beloved padre. The local Lion's Club would wait no more. They obtained permission from the building's owners—by now the old structure served not as a chapel, but as a seldom-occupied private residence—to dig up the brick flooring. Beneath the top layer they found a subterranean floor made of tile. In this they found three holes, all empty except for bits of trash, beer bottles, an old shoe, a cigarette lighter. One hole, though, was large enough to have held a coffin, and this had quickly fired the imagination of Magdalena's citizens. Could this be Kino's gravesite, his bones later removed by Christians persecuted under the regime of Presidente Calles? Many accepted it as fact.

But not everyone. In the summer of 1963, historian Charles Polzer, S.J., from the Arizona State Museum in Tucson, and William Wasley, an archaeologist from the same institution, began their own examination of the site. After a thorough study of the building and grounds, they concluded that this was not Kino's chapel.

There were other reasons, Olvera knew, to doubt that this was Kino's chapel. For one, it was located on Calle Pesqueira, at least three hundred yards from the present church. If the present church occupied the site of the old Campos church, the Proctor Chapel was not likely Kino's, because Kino's would've been *very near* the Campos church.

But again, Olvera thought, forget the other reasons. Forget the adobe, the hall-style design, the flat roof, all you had to do was look at the thing. Like the Llera church he'd examined earlier, this simply was not a Jesuit building. The design—when you pushed aside the bushes and vines and had a good look at the shape of the arches, the proportions of the door openings, the over-all style—was early 19th century neoclassic. It was Franciscan. Polzer and Wasley from Arizona had called it right: This was *not* the burial place of Eusebio Kino.

When Olvera finished at the chapel, he found a telephone and placed a local call to Dolores Vásquez, the woman who claimed, according to Jiménez Moreno, that she had seen Kino's statue of San Francisco Xavier after it was supposedly burned in the brewery in Hermosillo. Olvera introduced himself and told Vásquez his reason for calling.

"Certainly you may come by," she said pleasantly. "Would noon be a good time? I'll fix enchiladas de chorizo and empanadas with pumpkin filling."

"Gracias. I'll be there."

Now he made another call, this one to the mayor, Nava García, at his office in the Palacio. He asked about the local library.

"It's small," the mayor told him, "but quite adequate."

"Do they have historical periodicals? Books on local history?"

"Many, Señor. You're looking for something in particular?"

"Not really," Olvera said. "I just thought if the library were nearby, I might stop in."

The mayor gave him directions. Olvera thanked him again for taking him to view the Cocóspera ruins. He told him of the books and documents he'd found in Hermosillo and Mexico City. He told him about the biography, *Rim*, and mentioned the diary, *Luz*, by Juan Mateo Manje.

"Juan Mateo Manje?" the mayor said. "Who was he?"

"No, young man," Dolores Vásquez said, working at the stove in her small kitchen. "Kino's statue of San Francisco Xavier did not burn in the brewery, as the owner's widow has undoubtedly told you. She's mistaken. I, myself, saw the statue some days later, in the workshop of a painter named Jesus Ortiz. He was repairing defects in the head and one of the feet, as I recall. No, the soldiers of Presidente Calles only *thought* they burned that statue."

"So I've heard, Señora," Olvera said. "But actually I wished to ask about another matter. Do you believe Kino's body was disinterred and removed from Magdalena during the years of persecution?"

Dolores Vásquez was an elderly woman, unmarried still after all the years, with white hair and soft dark eyes. She filled plates with enchiladas and set them on the table with bowls of beans and a pitcher of iced tea.

"I don't believe the padre was moved, no, Señor."

"And your reason?"

She shrugged. "I just don't believe it. Please, sit. Eat."

They ate. "Delicious," Olvera said, and had second helpings.

Dolores Vásquez smiled at this and said, "I understand there is no portrait of Father Kino in existence."

Olvera glanced up from his food. "No portraits *now*," he said, "that's true. There *was* one, though. I've read that it burned in a fire in San Francisco in 1907. I don't know the name of the artist."

She spooned more beans onto his plate and refilled his tea glass. "Do you ever wonder what he looked like?"

"Yes," he said, "I've wondered."

By now Olvera had a picture in his mind. He could see him: a little taller than average, stocky and muscular from the hard work of ranching and farming and running the missions, but still sort of lean and wiry, too, as if sometimes he had too little to eat and spent too many hours on horseback. His hands would have been large and rough, thickened with blisters and scars. He would've been dark-skinned from his Italian blood and from long hours in the sun. Olvera imagined him with a narrow face and high forehead, a strong jaw; an angular nose that had likely been broken a time or two. With his heritage, his eyes were probably brown, but because he was from the Tyrol, so close to Germany, they could've been blue; Olvera hadn't decided about that.

He remembered seeing a sketch of Kino by Frances O'Brien, an artist from Tucson, a composite she'd based on photographs of Chini descendants, including those living even now in the farmhouse in Segno in the Val di Non where Kino had been born. The sketch showed a man very much like the picture in Olvera's mind. He had a shock of dark hair tumbling over his forehead and ears, a few wrinkles, maybe a few scars, and eyes that told you something about who and what he was: calm, but alert; optimistic but maybe a bit cynical, too; gentle, but strong; weary but still going because there was work yet to be done. And the eyes told you this was a man from whom you could not easily hide secrets.

"I think he must've been very handsome," the woman said.

Olvera laughed and had more tea. "Maybe."

"Do you know about the diggings at the ferretería?"

"Diggings? At a hardware store?"

"Workers have uncovered a chamber," she said, "under the floors of the store. Some say it's a secret passageway leading to the church."

"Which church, Señora?"

She spooned more enchiladas onto his plate. "The parish church, of course."

"Who are the diggers?"

"Laborers," the woman said. "They work for some professors from Hermosillo. They, too, are looking for the remains of Father Kino."

"And they believe he's buried under a *hardware* store?"

"It sounded strange to me, too."

Olvera smiled. "Where do *you* believe we'll find Kino's grave?"

"Near the City Hall. Under it, or near it. Empanadas, Señor? The pumpkin is very good."

Why, Olvera wondered, was this woman still single?

The Lockwood document came as a huge surprise. Olvera hadn't expected to find much in the local biblioteca, the library, but he had gone anyway, because the mayor had said it was a fine library and because, in this business, you never knew. He found the document in a dusty stack of old periodicals, issues of the *University of Arizona Bulletin.* Most were from the

'40's and '50's, a few from the '30's. The issue that caught his eye carried the date of February 15, 1934, and featured an article called, "With Padre Kino on the Trail," by Frank Lockwood.

Olvera read English almost as well as he read his native Spanish and he quickly scanned the article for any information on the padre's death. He found it: a short commentary by Father Luis Velarde, who'd followed Kino as minister at Dolores. Olvera sat at a table and added Velarde's statement to his journal notes.

"...Father Kino, mentioned above, died in 1711, having spent twenty-four years in glorious hardships in this Pimería which he explored as thoroughly in the forty trips that he made as two or three fervent workers could have done. He was almost seventy (note to myself: no, he was sixty-five) at the time of his death, and he died as he had lived, in the greatest humility and poverty, not even undressing during his last illness and having for his bed—as he always had—two sheep skins for a mattress and two small blankets of the sort that the Indians use for cover, and for his pillow a pack-saddle. Father Augustin's (note to myself: he must be referring to Father Agustín de Campos) urgings could not persuade him to any other thing.

He died in his Father's house, where he had gone to dedicate a rare chapel that he had finished a short time before in his church of Santa Magdalena, consecrated to San Francisco Xavier, deceased, whose whole body (note to myself: he is writing here of the statue, stolen in 1920's from parish church, possibly burned in brewery) was represented with admirable workmanship on its gilded casket. While singing the Dedication Mass he became sick; and it seems that this Holy Apostle (to whom he was always devoted) called him, so that, being interred in his chapel, he might keep the inanimate effigy company..."

"To discover new lands, and win souls, and to be much in prayer were the virtues of Padre Kino....He never took snuff, nor smoked, nor used white linen, except two coarse shirts, because he gave everything away to the Indians as alms...In the fierce fevers that attacked him, he ate nothing for six days. He would arise only to celebrate the Mass, and then lie down again; so worn out and exhausted nature had its way."

All right, Olvera thought, there wasn't much here he hadn't already known. Still, this was interesting—another account of Kino's death by someone from that era—and he would mention it to Jiménez Moreno when he saw him again.

He closed the *Bulletin*; replaced it on the shelf. He sat again at the table and thought about Velarde's comments. He stared at the wall.

He fidgeted. He cleared his throat. He took a drink of water from the cooler near the checkout desk, came back and sat again. He wiped sweat from his neck with a bandanna. He retrieved the *Bulletin* and re-read Father Velarde's remarks and tried to understand what was bothering him. Was he overlooking something here? Was Velarde teasing him, slipping in clues on Kino's burial site and in his impatience he was missing them?

And what was this about *fierce fevers*?

At the hardware store Olvera found one of the laborers and introduced himself. "I hear you've located a tunnel," he said.

The man nodded and drank water from a canteen. Around them shelves that sagged in their middles held boxes of nails, screws, and bolts, and paint buckets and plumbing supplies.

"Where does the tunnel lead?"

The man wiped his mouth with the back of his hand. He pointed a dirty finger at a trapdoor in the floor. "Be careful not to disturb the earth."

Olvera crawled through the trapdoor and dropped into a narrow underground chamber. In the darkness he fumbled for his flashlight. He saw the rough walls, the flooring of loose planks, and saw that someone had uncovered a few artifacts and left them *in situ*—as they'd been found—but carefully cleansed and dusted. He made a list of the findings: beer and wine bottles, broken cups and dishes, car tires, cardboard boxes containing papers and receipts, bits of newspapers dating to the early 20th century. Trash, all of it; junk.

Outside again he said to the laborer, "This isn't a tunnel; it goes nowhere. It's a cava, a storage room, probably built as a wine cellar or a place to hide guns. Rooms like this were popular among the wealthy in the time of Porfirio Díaz. This has nothing to do with Father Kino."

"Yes," the man said, leaning on his shovel. "That's what my employers say. You found nothing new down there?"

Olvera shook his head. "Only a tarantula and a few scorpions."

CHAPTER 21

The Pimería. Año D. 1696. May.

It was much too nice a day to fight Indians.

We had come down out of the hills east of Arizpe, the mountains thick and green around us, the air clear and mild, the sky a pleasant blue rimmed with clouds that looked like fluffs of cotton—Captain Bernal, Corporal Escalante, nine soldiers, two Pima scouts, and I. At San Juan we had had news of a raid on Remedios—Apaches, probably from Clavo's band. We picked up their tracks east of Bacanuche and followed them southeast into the mountains near Nacosari. But we had lost them on the bouldered slopes of a hard dark canyon and had finally turned our horses back for San Juan.

In the desert the yellow blooms of paloverdes were bright in the morning sun and delicate lilac-hued flowers coated the ironwoods that grew in the arroyos and along the washes. We saw roadrunners and black-throated sparrows, and white winged doves nesting in mesquite stumps, and once we saw antelope grazing on grasses that sprouted in thick green bunches near the bottom of a huge rock wall that had ancient Indian paintings high on its face. The air was balmy, redolent with the scents and sounds of a lingering springtime. Yes, it was definitely too nice a day for fighting.

But the Apaches had turned back too and laid their ambush coming loud and shrill out of the hills, the sun behind them and square in our eyes. Before I could get my arquebus up, an Apache lance caught my blue roan in the neck and he went out from under me and I went spilling over his head onto the ground. Someone shouted, "*Aaiii cuidado!*" and I rolled to my left as an arrow thwonked into the sand just inches from my head. Pain racked my shoulder, but I jumped to my feet—and immediately found an Apache not five varas away. The look on his face told me he fully intended to dispatch me to wherever he thought Spaniards go when they died. I felt a familiar thrumming in my temples. Hair prickled on my arms and I had the same odd sense of revulsion and alarm I had known three years before when I fought Black Skull near Imuris.

War cries and the sounds of gunfire reached me, and I realized that the fight and the soldiers had moved beyond us, farther up a hillside. So here, now, it was just the two of us.

I pulled my sword and pointed it at the Apache.

He was short and strongly built, with massive arms and stubby hands. Streaks of red and yellow paint across his forehead and nose did little to hide the granos, the pimples, that coarsened and pitted his wide dark face. He was bent forward in a crouch, his arms up, his war club at the ready. His eyes were small, his eyelids half closed; he looked as if he might be dozing.

But in my few years in the Pimería I had learned this: Do not let the Indio's eyes fool you. He will be quick and deadly and he will give no quarter.

The Apache grunted and spat insolently on the ground. "You are the pin'dah they call Mon-hay?" His Spanish was near perfect.

"I am Lieutenant Juan Mateo Manje. How do you know my name?"

He wore a tattered white shirt and a cotton loincloth; a water container made from a tanned cow's stomach hung from a leather cord around his waist. "I have seen you before," he grunted, "in the mountains. Black Skull has told me of your cowardice when he fought you near the place you call Imuris. He will be sorry he did not get to kill you himself today."

His words surprised me. "Black Skull is here? With your war party?"

The Indian's voice was thick with contempt. "He is not here. He rode with his men to visit your famous Santo-Jesus-hay, the one called Kee-no."

Madre de Dios, I thought. The November before, Father Kino had left for Mexico City with a few soldiers. I had heard they were expected back this month or next. But could Black Skull— ?

"He went to *visit* Kino?" I said. "How could you possibly know where Kino is? How could Black Skull know?"

"We have people in the mountains along the Bavispe River. They have seen him and his cowardly soldiers. They reported it to us."

The breeze felt hot on my face now and I could smell the Apache's sweat and the wildflowers around us and the fetid mustiness, like unwashed stockings, of the elderberry bushes that grew along the hillsides. "*What*?" I said. "Are you saying Black Skull went to *ambush* Kino?"

"I have told you all you need to know, Spaniard."

But there were other questions I wanted answered. With my left hand I pulled the blue lapis cross from under my shirt. "Have you seen this before?

It was tied to the handle of the knife I took from Black Skull. Where did he get it? Why did he have it?"

"Yes. I have seen it. When I kill you, I will take it from your bloody corpse and return it to him."

I slipped the cross back under my shirt. "Tell me where he got it."

The Indio shrugged. "He killed some miners near the big mountain you call Baboquivari. The blue stone was in a leather bag with other stones of silver and gold. He liked the blue color, so he kept it."

"Who were these miners?"

"He said they had white skin, like you, but they spoke with a strange tongue. They spoke with soft words, like women."

I almost laughed. "They were...*Frenchmen*?"

"We have talked enough, pin'dah. De da jeunee si'ke na."

Even in those early years I knew that si'ke na was their term for the Pimas, pin'dah their word for Spaniard. "You murder Pima farmers," I said, "and you kill settlers and miners and priests who have done you no harm. For this, we have to punish you."

He spat on the ground again. "Your miners have no right to the pesh lickoyee, the silver rocks you call plata. They steal it like cowards from the earth. This land belongs to the Tinneh, the Apache people, and to Ussen, the one true god."

"It belongs," I told him, "to whoever holds legal title."

"Ussen holds title, Spaniard, not you. Or the settlers, or the Pimas, who are little more than trembling bow-legged old women with tattoos of charcoal on their cowardly faces."

"So that is why you murder the Pimas?" I said. "Because they have *tattoos*?" Behind him I could see red flowers on the tall ocotillos that grew from the hard dirt of the desert floor.

"You play word games, Spaniard, but I will tell you why we kill settlers and soldiers. In our battles, sometimes you capture our people. You gag our brave warriors with filthy rags and bind them hand and foot and sell them into slavery to the pesh lickoyee mines far to the south. This we can never forgive."

I became aware of vultures with black wings circling above us, and of an insect buzzing in a clump of sacaton grass that was rooted in the gritty dark soil at the Apache's feet. The blade of my sword glistened in the brightness of the sun.

"No," I said. "We turn all captives over to the civil authorities for trial."

"*Trial*? You have no trials, you sell my people to the miners! And just what is it that you claim the Tinneh are guilty of? This is *our* land; how could we be guilty of *anything* here? No, Spaniard, your trials are a sham. They are an insult to us."

"I do not believe what you say about the mines," I said.

"Then you are a fool."

"You have no more to say than that?"

"De'da ya'ik'tee, pin'dah," he grunted.

"Speak in Spanish, heathen."

"I said, '*You are a dead man, Spaniard.*' " He feinted with his club and before I could bring my sword to bear he came at me low and very fast. I tried to dodge, tried to pound his head with the heavy butt of my sword, but he drove his shoulder into my belly, knocking the air out of me and smashing me to the ground. In an instant he was on his knees at my side, his club high, ready to bash a hole in my head. I slammed his nose with the flat of my hand. This must have surprised him, as he cried out and pulled back just long enough for me to roll away and quickly push up from the ground. My breath came in gasps; I wiped sweat from my neck with the sleeve of my shirt. I reached for the pistol I always kept in my sash. It was gone. All right, I still had my espada of strong Spanish steel, and since that long-ago fight with Black Skull I had learned a few things about using it.

The Apache charged again, this time swinging his war club. I forced him back with quick jabs of my sword, but a wild blow from his club caught my left arm and sent a jolt of bone-rattling pain up to my shoulder. I jabbed at him again, but the pain had dulled my reflexes and I stupidly let him get past my sword. He swung his huge fist and took a layer of skin off my jaw. He swung again; this time his fist slammed into my breastbone. Pain shot through my chest and ribs and grew until I thought my heart would burst.

I stepped back, praying for time to catch my breath and steady myself. The Apache would not allow it. He came at me again, arcing his heavy club—

But God must have seen my plight, because He somehow gave me strength to react. My sword caught the Apache across his chest and split his ribs open. He fell without uttering a sound. My next swing struck his shoulder and severed his arm from his body. Blood soaked his shirt and spurted onto the soil. Red froth oozed from his mouth and gurgled deep in his throat. With the toe of my boot I rolled him onto his back. His half-closed eyes stared vacantly into the sky. I stood over him, my breath coming unevenly and in raspy, painful draughts.

The May sun had grown warm. I wiped sweat from my dust-caked forehead. Slowly the sounds of the desert seeped back into my consciousness;

my mind again registered color and movement around me. A jay called noisily from a mesquite snag. A quail darted from behind a saguaro and a butterfly with silvery wings hovered above a soaptree yucca with dark stalks topped with creamy white flowers.

How did I feel? I cannot describe it precisely, but for a fleeting moment I believed I knew how the victorious gladiator in a Roman arena must have felt. But it was not the victory itself that I savored. It was, I suspect, the growing realization that the enemy I vanquished had lost *his* life but *I still had mine.* So it isn't winning that is important, it is *life* that's important. An elementary point, certainly, but one that I was only then coming to fully understand. I suppose there are those who would disagree—men like Lieutenant Solís, for instance. I can only say how it seemed to me. *Aaiii*, I was very glad to be alive.

I found my blue roan where it had fallen, the Apache lance still skewering its neck. The roan tried to get to his feet when he saw me, but of course he could not. I sliced the veins of his throat. I did not know if horses had souls, but I said a brief prayer for the animal on the chance that they did. He had been a good mount, loyal and strong, and I knew I would miss him. I unbuckled the saddle and worked it off, then retrieved my gourds and had a long drink of the cool water. Eventually I found Captain Bernal and the others up a canyon a quarter mile away. They had suffered three men wounded, but none killed. Nearby I saw the bloody bodies of four dead Apaches. I told the Captain what I had learned about Black Skull's plan to ambush Kino and his party on the Bavispe.

"Good work, Lieutenant," he said. Bernal was a slender man with light skin, thinning blond hair, and a waxed mustache the color of wet straw. You saw few blond Spaniards in the Pimería, but Bernal was one.

"Gracias, sir," I said. As I had expected, he sent two soldados ahead to San Juan to report the news of Kino to General Jironza.

When we had tended our wounded, we knelt and Captain Bernal recited the Pater and offered prayers of thanks to God for keeping us alive. Silently I thanked Him, too, for the sword lessons given to me by Antonio Solís. In a sudden rush of honesty I confessed to Him that I had never really liked Solís. Still, I had learned a lot from him and I had to acknowledge that to God, too.

I chased down one of the Apache paints, got my saddle on it, and we rode down out of the canyon, away from the dead Indians and the buzzing black insects that had already begun to feed on the drying blood. On a sandy ridge above us, I could see gallinazos, turkey vultures, gathering in the angular branches of stunted dark trees that rose into the sky like ghostly skeletons.

It was good to get out of there.

On the ride back to San Juan we saw several burned-out haciendas and a few dead cattle and goats, most of the animals already picked over by vultures and coyotes. But we saw no people. This part of Sonora was deserted. The ranchers—those who had survived the attacks, anyway—had loaded up their families and departed for safer places.

Still, I should have felt good enough about the day's events. I did not, though, and I tried to understand why. I soon discovered that I was finding little satisfaction in my victory over the Apache. Well, that is not entirely true. As I said before, I was still alive and I took a *lot* of satisfaction in *that*. And I confess that in some crazy way, I even enjoyed the fighting. But the dead Apache's words kept buzzing around in my mind, nipping and biting like a hungry mosquito I could not quite swat.

He had been right, I had no doubt, about our selling of captive Apaches into slavery. I had heard rumors of such things since my first months in the Pimería, and had always chosen to ignore them. But the truth was, that is exactly what we did, and deep down in my soul I think I had known it all along. I cannot say I liked it, but there it was: *slavery*. Father Kino, the army, and the civil authorities had always worked to keep the miners and ranchers from taking Pimas and Papagos as slaves. Here we had the proclamation from King Carlos Segundo as our law and guide. In this, we were dealing with civilized Indians. Christianized Indians.

The Apaches and Jocomes and Mansos, though, were an altogether different matter. Everyone knew it. Soldiers, especially, knew it. Which made me suspect that in some strange way, maybe I had already made my peace with the situation. Maybe I had already come to accept the fact of *selective* slavery, the rightness of it. These were Apaches, after all.

So with all this righteous absolution and billowing moral certitude, why did I still feel like I had a lump of coal in my stomach?

I had no good answer for that question. In the long years that followed I would often think about the problem of Indian slavery in Sonora, but I do not believe I ever got any closer to a reasonable premise for our government's policy than the small and private one I had stumbled onto on that bloody spring day in 1696: *They were Apaches, after all.*

But my other source of discontent that day in May was more immediate: the possibility that Kino's party was about to be ambushed—or perhaps already had been—and there was nothing I could do about it.

At noon, thirsty and hungry, we stopped on the banks of a tree-shaded creek with lichen growing on the rocks and silvery pupfish sunning in the shallows. The breeze smelled of wet leaves and humus and the faint sweetness of the lavender flowers coating the desert willows that grew along the bank. We sat in the shade and drank cool water from the creek and ate wheat tortillas and ga'iwesa, roasted corn ground on a metate and mixed with red chilies.

That was when the Pima runner came in, his dark mustang throwing up dust in the warming midday air. He came from the presidio at San Juan under orders from General Jironza, he said, to inform us that a small party of civilians and their cavalry escort had been ambushed near Oputo, on the Río Bavispe. No one, he said, had survived.

I made the sign of the cross and said a silent prayer.

"How many dead?" Captain Bernal asked the Pima.

"General Jironza says eight, Captain."

"Do you know their names?"

"No. No one told me their names."

I could hear wind riffling through the willows now, and quail chattering beneath a sycamore with bark peeling from it in strips that looked like old gray parchment. The air seemed thick and close, almost too heavy to breathe.

"Was a priest among them?" I asked the Pima. "Father Kino?"

The Indio shrugged. "If so," he said sadly, "he is dead now."

CHAPTER 22

San Juan Bautista, Sonora. Año D. 1696. May.

"The officer in charge," General Jironza told me, "was Captain Christóbal de León. His son, Nicolás, was with him. The boy was killed, too. As were the other soldiers and everyone else in the party." The general looked tired, the flesh around his eyes bloated and swollen.

"Jocomes?" I said.

"We suspect so. They have been on a rampage along the Bavispe for months now. But it could have been Apaches. Oso Azul. Or Mofeta or Clavo. Or some new hotheads out to make names for themselves." He shrugged. "Who knows."

Captain Bernal and I had arrived in Real San Juan with our men just an hour before. We had taken our wounded to the surgeon, and from the infirmary I had hurried to the general's quarters to report on our mission against the Apaches, but also to see if he had news of Father Kino. Now I sat across from the general in his spacious office, portraits of governors staring down at us from the whitewashed walls, crossed swords gleaming behind him in sunlight from the windows. He leaned forward in his chair and rested his elbows on his desk. "Did you know de León?"

"Slightly," I said. "I liked him. By all reports he was a good officer."

The general sighed and nodded. "His family lives in Cusiguriache, and we believe he was on his way there when he and his men were ambushed. It would explain why he had his son with him."

His uniform was, as always, clean and neat, but his black hair was matted and he had a haggard look about him, as if he had had too little sleep. He made the sign of the cross and I could see the pain in his dark eyes. He and Captain de León had been friends for many years.

He had already given me everything else he knew: a squad of soldiers on routine patrol along the Bavispe had found the bloody, mutilated corpses of five soldiers—one of them an officer now known to be de León—two Pima Indians, and a young boy now known to be de León's son. They also found the carcasses of the dozen or so horses and pack animals the attackers had killed. The soldiers had immediately dispatched a runner to San Juan with this news, then loaded the stiffening bodies onto their own horses and taken them to the mission at Bazeraca for burial. When Don Domingo learned these things from the runner, he had ordered more cavalry into the field to find and punish the murderers.

"But there is more to the story," he said. "In a burned-out wagon they found a priest's robe. Black. Jesuit."

Mother of God, I thought. I told Don Domingo about the Apache who had claimed that Jocomes had seen Father Kino with soldiers on the Río Bavispe, and planned to ambush them.

He drummed his fingers on the desk. "Yes, Captain Bernal's runners reported that. But are you sure the Apache meant that this happened *recently*?"

"I believe so," I said.

"I suppose it could be true; we have been expecting the padre back from Mexico City any week now. But we have had no word on the progress of his journey. In truth, we have no confirmation that he was with de León's group. He could have been with other soldiers, a unit from Fronteras, perhaps, if he was visiting missions far to the east."

The general was right, I suspected, but this did nothing to lessen my concern. "Perhaps," I suggested, "I should go look for him."

He shook his head and rose from his desk. "For now, I want you to get some rest. Then we will talk about it again."

"Rest," I said, rising from my chair. "That sounds like a fine idea, sir." I gave him a salute, though not a very snappy one. He hardly noticed. When I walked out, he was sitting again, staring tiredly at the swords that hung on the white wall behind his desk.

At the barracks I slept for a few hours, but not well. I dreamed of soldiers in bloody tunics and Indio children with arrows in their bellies, dead young priests and burned-out missions, and dark-haired women in flowing white skirts. None of it made much sense, but there was too much pain and death in it, and I was relieved when finally I awoke.

But even then I found thoughts of Father Kino still tumbling through my mind. Where was he? What had happened to him?

"Maybe he was so badly mutilated the soldiers did not recognize him," Ensign Acuña suggested.

"I refuse to believe that," I said firmly. We were in the officer's wardroom, polishing boots and sharpening our swords.

"Sometimes," Acuna said, "the Jocomes will take the body of an enemy for use in their victory ceremonies."

"No," I said. "They did not kill him."

"But how could he have escaped? If he was even there?"

"He is alive, somewhere," I said, "I know it."

Acuña sighed. "I pray you are right, my friend." He was a short man, stocky, about my age, with dark hair that fell over his forehead and ears.

After a time he said, "I heard that Sergeant Escalante is playing guitar with the old man in the plaza again tonight. It would be good to get out of the barracks for a while."

This was Saturday and we had no other responsibilities.

"All right," I said. "I always enjoy the music."

"We might even have a glass of wine," Acuña said, smiling a little.

The plaza that night was ablaze with light from lanterns strung in the cottonwoods that bordered the square. The place was crowded with revelers, the warm air thick with the smells of grilled meats and sugared breads and festive with the thunderous, pulsating rhythms of vlaminco guitars. In the center of the square I could see women in brightly-colored dresses dancing in hard-soled boots, their small feet pounding out the insistent rhythms of the cantes. Not far from them, Sergeant Escalante and a white-haired old man busily thrummed the strings and woods of their guitars. Sergeant Escalante was good but the old man was better. I had spent enough time in Andalusia to know how the gitanos, the gypsies, played their music. The old man must have been one of them. He wore a black vest over a loose white blouse, dark cotton pants, and a wide-brimmed leather hat with a flat crown. Only his feet told you he was in Sonora rather than some little village near Seville. He wore sandals, and inside them his feet were swathed in strips of baize—cotton flannel dyed a bright red with fluids crushed from the bodies of the cochineal insects that live on the pads of prickly pears. Sonoran stockings, our soldiers called the red baize.

But that night I could not concentrate on the music or the dancing. My mind kept coming back to the soldiers who had died on the Bavispe, and the Apache's claim that Jocomes had seen Kino with soldiers, and had made plans to ambush them. And there was the priest's robe they had found in the burned wagon. Was it Kino's? If he was travelling with Captain de León, where was he now? Had he somehow escaped the attackers? Or had they carried off his body, as Acuña had suggested—a trophy for their ceremonies? That thought had left me feeling adrift, cheerless, almost nauseated, with images of charred bones and mutilated flesh flitting across my mind, and I found I had little interest in the activities of the plaza. After a time I excused myself to Acuña and I walked away from the sounds and bright lights and intensity of the place.

Adobe stores lined the sides of the plaza, and in them you could buy almost anything. Food, furniture, medicinal herbs. Clothing. Horse tack. Papago baskets made from beargrass and devil's claw. Colorful Pima blankets so tightly woven you could carry water in them.

But even in the stores I could not get away from reminders of Father Kino. The Pima blankets took me back to something I had learned from him in my first year in Sonora...

I had been in the church at San Ignacio, having chocolate with Father Campos and the village chief, when we heard Apaches yipping and shouting and we saw Kino come tearing into the village, his little mustang wheezing and lathered, gray dust billowing above the trail behind him. He had lost his hat, but he had a red blanket tied around his neck and flapping at his back. When he reached the church, he jumped from his horse, yanked a pistol from his saddlebag, and prepared himself for a fight if his pursuers came in after him. By then, though, Campos and the chief and I had stepped out with muskets and pistols, and Pimas working in the fields had been alerted by the noise. The Apaches reined around and hastily departed.

But when Kino turned to gentle his horse, I saw two arrows embedded in the folds of the red wool blanket that covered his back. He must have guessed what I was thinking. He brushed dust from his robe and smiled—quite calmly, I thought, for someone who had just been dogged across the desert by Apaches. "Fold it a few times for thickness," he said, "and tie it around your neck."

I chuckled. "I'll remember that."

He pulled the blanket off and looked it over. He winked at me. "Sometimes," he said, "the Lord works His will through a fast horse."

"And sometimes," he added, "He works through a good Pima blanket."

He came inside and had chocolate with us, but he never did say where he had been or what he had been doing when the Apaches took after him. Visiting one of his Pima villages, I guessed, or tending cattle in the foothills or perhaps exploring one of the mountains near the mission. He didn't seem particularly distraught, or even much concerned, by the chase. In fact he never mentioned it again. In the padre's mind, I suppose, being pursued by noxious Indians was simply a part of his job.

But the trick with the blanket was a fine one, and I had filed it away in my mind. That night in a store off the square I bought such a Pima blanket—red, with figures of I'itoi, the Papago's Creator, in black and gray. Back at the plaza I found Acuña still listening to the vlaminco. I had just taken a seat on the bench beside him when I saw General Jironza hurrying towards us, his red tunic bright under the lights of the plaza. From the briskness of his stride, I feared he had news of more soldiers ambushed, or perhaps fresh atrocities along the rivers.

But the Pimería has always been a curious place, full of surprises, and this day was no exception.

"A Pima runner," Don Domingo told us, "has just arrived from Dolores. He came to inform me that Father Kino is at his mission in Dolores and wants to make a full report on his journey to Ciudad de Mexico."

I bowed my head and mouthed a silent prayer of thanks to God.

"Could this be true, Uncle?" I said when I looked up.

"I want you to confirm it, Juan Mateo," he said. "Ride to Dolores at first light tomorrow morning and see the padre, if he is there. Then report back to me."

"Yes, sir," I said, grinning widely now. "Absolutely, sir."

Finally the general permitted himself a smile. "And tell the padre we are very pleased he is back."

The next morning I left San Juan Bautista with Sergeant Escalante and Private DeJulio. We took spare mounts and a few servants and rode at all good speed for the Dolores mission.

If Father Kino was still alive, we would soon know it.

CHAPTER 23

Dolores. Año D. 1696. May.

If you want a long life in New Spain, live south of the Pimería.

In the Pimería, death is always close by. Often it comes at us on a paint pony, or from the bite of a snake, or a fall from a horse. Sometimes it comes with having no water for yourself or your mount in the broiling heat of a summer day. In the mountains it can come in the dust-choked collapse of a mineshaft, or in a bear attack, or in a fall from a rock ledge. Sometimes death comes with the fevers and miasmas that arrive regularly with each wagonload of new settlers and seem almost to rise like fog out of the tidal marshes and insect-clotted waters of the gulf. Sometimes it comes in a form as ancient and elemental as having something that someone else wants—and reaping, in return for it, a steel blade in your back or a musket ball through your heart. From wherever it comes, though, death in the Pimería has always been a stark and private circumstance—often violent, usually painful, always veneered with blood and bile and the rising stink of excrement and rotting flesh.

Still, I knew men—or knew of them—who seemed not to be disturbed by the presence of death. There was a lieutenant of artillery from Fronteras who hanged every Apache he caught, be it man, woman, or child. Nicolás Higuera, a captain from Sinaloa, once rode with his men into the Pima settlement of Mototicachi and slaughtered every Indian there, for no reason that anyone could ever discover. Black Skull liked to hang his captives from a tree by their wrists and burn them alive with a raging fire he set beneath their feet. Clavo, the Apache chief, once ambushed a pack train carrying building supplies to Bazeraca and for years afterward hammered iron nails into the eye sockets of every settler and soldier he took alive. And of course we had our Lieutenant Solís and his sword.

By now I had more-or-less made my adjustments to the ugliness of death. I believed that Father Kino had, too. To me, he always seemed a man who did his grieving privately and expeditiously, then simply got on with his work. What else could he do? Yet I can truthfully say there were times when he was simply unable to conceal the extent of his sorrow over the death of others.

So when Escalante and DeJulio and I reached Dolores that May afternoon and found the padre chopping weeds in his garden, I was not surprised at what I saw. His narrow face looked rigid and tight, like a mask of dark molded clay. His blue eyes seemed veiled, and from the set of his jaw I knew he was seeing things in his memory that he had hoped never to see again. He was singing—in Latin, I think—his voice low and soft and solitary. Nearby, Pima men and women were clearing obstructions from the acéquias that carried water from the San Miguel to fields planted now in beans, squash, and chiles. When Kino saw us, he smiled. For an instant, the tension seemed to leave his face; he looked again like his old self. He made the sign of the cross and embraced us warmly.

"We prayed," I said, "for your safe return from Mexico City, Father, and were pleased when we heard you were home again."

"Thank you, and thanks for coming, Juan Mateo," he said. "I have a lot of questions for you, and I imagine you have a few for me. Come, let's walk over to the church. We can talk there. Do you need water, something to eat?"

"Perhaps later, Father," I said. The air was balmy, the sky so blue and thick it looked as if you could toss a rope around it and pull it to the ground. I saw cattle grazing on the hillsides and on the breeze I could smell peppers and white onions grilling in the cooking ramadas behind the carpenter's shop. I sent the soldiers to tend our mounts and find something to eat for themselves. As Kino and I walked up the hill to the church he said, "You are leaner, my friend. But you have added some muscle, I think."

"Perhaps, Father. We have been in the saddle almost constantly since you left." I shrugged. "Apaches." In the distance I could hear dogs barking and the sounds of Indian children at play.

In the church Kino prayed at the altar, then stepped into a little room he used as an office. When he returned, we went outside again and sat on a wood bench under a mesquite tree. He placed a sheaf of papers in my hand. "My report," he said, "on my visit with Church officials and civil authorities in Mexico City. I wrote it for Father Mora, but I thought the general might like to see it, so I made a copy. Would you deliver it to him for me?"

"Of course, sir," I said.

Mora, I knew, was Francisco Mora, the new rector. He ministered to his own villagers at Arizpe, and though he spent most of his time there, as rector he was actually in charge of all missions in the Pimería, including

Dolores. He wasn't an easy man to work with, I had heard, and I wondered if he had been stirring up toil and moil for Kino during his six-month absence. At the moment, however, I had other matters on my mind and I got right to them.

"Father," I said, "I have to tell you something. Last week, Captain Christóbal de León and a party of soldiers and civilians were ambushed on the Río Bavispe, a few hours ride north of Oputo. As far as we know, no one survived the attack. But our soldiers found a priest's robe in a burned wagon. We feared it was yours, and that you were dead, or maybe carried off by the murderers. If the robe is not yours, we need to know to whom it belonged, so we can notify the authorities and perhaps even try to find the priest's remains. Do you know anything about this?"

Kino sighed. "The robe was mine."

I stared at him. "Jocomes?"

"Probably." When he spoke again, his voice was low and hoarse in his throat. "So it was soldiers who moved the bodies. I wondered. And they took them for burial?"

"Yes," I said. "At Bazeraca, I believe."

"Well, I am glad for that." He puffed his cheeks and exhaled slowly. "It is a sad story, Juan Mateo. And not one I am proud of."

Here is his story, as he told it that day at Dolores:

He had made the ride to Mexico City in seven weeks, arriving there in January, in the middle of winter. He saw the new Provincial, Father Palácios, and renewed his friendship with Juan María Salvatierra, who had once been Visitor but was now teaching at the novitiate at Tepotzotlan. They talked about renewing their efforts to spread God's Word in the Californias and made good progress with plans for it. Kino even had some success in repairing the damaged reputations of the Pimas after the revolt of the past year and after the letters of complaint that had reached Mexico City from troublemakers in Sonora. Kino suspected Lieutenant Solís, he told me, and maybe even some priests who were trying to undermine his work with the Indios. But while he was there, by the Grace of God the Provincial received a communication from Tirso González, the Jesuit General in Rome, who stated in his letter that Kino was to be allowed to conduct his missionary work as he saw fit.

So, his business concluded, full of hope and good cheer, Kino had left Mexico City for the Pimería in February. He had heavy snows in the mountains, and much cold, but had no serious problems with either. He made stops at Guadalajara and Durango, and at Conicari he celebrated Easter.

Though it took him well out of his way, he went from there to Bazeraca—across the mountains near the Chihuahuan border—to see Father Polici, the new Visitor, to talk about more entradas into the lands north and west of the Pimería. But at Bazeraca, they had warned him against riding on to Dolores alone, as the Jocomes had been very troublesome in the area in recent months. By chance, Captain Christóbal de León was there and offered to escort him to Dolores. He and his men were on their way to Cusiguriache, where the captain had his family home. Father Kino, of course, accepted the Captain's generous offer. When their party reached the Bavispe, Kino decided to ride south to see some old Jesuit friends who were then visiting at Oputo. The captain had offered to accompany him.

Kino looked off toward the mountains. When he looked back at me, his breath was loud in his throat; his eyelid twitched. "I told the captain no, Juan Mateo. It was a short ride to Oputo, and I told him I would be back the following afternoon. I assured him I would be safe. Reluctantly, he agreed to let me go alone. He said he and his men would make camp and await my return."

It was a beautiful day, he said, sunny and warm, and he had decided to leave his robe and other belongings with the captain. So, dressed in cotton pants and shirt, he had gone alone to Oputo, seen his friends, had a fine time, and the next day had ridden back to the campsite...

And found blood everywhere.

"I should not have gone to Oputo, Juan Mateo."

"None of this is your fault, Father."

"Or I should have insisted they go on to Cusiguriache. Either way, they would all be alive now."

"But Father—"

"When the Jocomes came," he said, "I was gone; my life was spared. Perhaps God has more work for me in the Pimería, I understand that. Perhaps that is God's will for *me*. But why did the *others* have to die?"

"I do not know, Father," I said. I could see muscles working in his jaw.

He sat quietly for a time, his face damp with sweat. Finally he spoke again. "You know what troubles me most? I am a priest. I am supposed to have the answers. And I have *none*, not even for myself."

"But God has the answers, Father. We just have to trust in Him."

Kino looked away again. "There was blood everywhere, Juan Mateo. On the ground, in the sand, spattered on the trees. All those innocent people, gone..." He squeezed his eyes shut and I knew he was seeing images that would frequent the darker corners of his memory for the remainder of his years. The color had drained from his face; at the tip of his chin a scar I had never noticed was blanched as white as ice.

"Near the campsite," he said softly, "I found a pile of fingers and ears. They had been cut off and hacked into pieces and burned. From their sizes, some had to have been from the boy, Nicolás, Captain de León's son. I buried them. Then I saw a coyote near the river with something in its mouth—a human foot, wet and shiny with blood..."

"...But there were no bodies anywhere," he went on, his voice so low I could barely make out his words, "just blood. Blood everywhere...and those fingers and ears...and that foot."

Madre de Dios, I thought.

He leaned back on the bench, his eyes moist with an ancient knowledge of the evil that men can do to others. "They were fine people, Juan Mateo; the soldiers, the boy, the Pimas. Now they are dead."

I had no words to comfort him, but I tried. "They are in heaven now, Father."

"...And they had a good burial at Bazeraca. Thank God for that."

To the west the sky was streaked with purple, the clouds small and pewter-colored and bunched over the mountains like crumpled sheets of tin. I went into the church and came back with a cup of water for the padre. We sat on the bench under the mesquite for a time, a warm wind blowing through the branches, black-throated sparrows trilling from an oak tree near the church.

Neither the padre nor I could think of anything more to say.

CHAPTER 24 Magdalena, Sonora. 1965.

While Olvera waited for Jiménez's arrival from Mexico City, he methodically worked his way through more of the diaries, yellowed documents, and biographies he'd collected. At first he had wanted only to find some reference, some critical fragment of information, that would lead him to the bones of Eusebio Kino. So far, he hadn't found it. But Kino wasn't turning out to be the sort of man Olvera had expected: contemplative, intellectual, set apart by his spirituality from the people and problems of the frontier. No, Father Kino had paid his dues many times over, and Olvera was finding himself drawn as much to the details of his life as to those of his death.

In his hotel room he went back to his notes.

- ***In March, 1687, Father Eusebio Francisco Kino, now 41 years of age, rode north towards Cucurpe and unknown lands beyond. (Note to myself: I have found no documented description of his mood on this journey, but I suspect he was excited, optimistic. Fate - some would say God—had given him a second chance; this time, he wouldn't fail).***
- ***At last, the Pimería.***
- ***Kino, with Padre Manuel González of Oposura, reached Cucurpe second week of March. There, they met Padre José Aguilar and finished Novena of Grace (a 9-day devotional celebrating canonization of Ignatius Loyola, founder of the Jesuits, & Francisco Xavier). March 13, González, Aguilar, & Kino rode north from Cucurpe up the Río San Miguel 12 difficult miles to Pima village of Cosari, home of Chief Coxi. Kino drawn immediately to the beauty of area and friendliness of Pimas; decided to build 1st mission in Pimería there, on high bluff overlooking Cosari Valley. Called it Mision Nuestra Señora de los Dolores, Our Lady of Sorrows.***

Our Lady of Sorrows...on a high bluff overlooking the Cosari Valley. It must've been a fine place indeed, Olvera thought. Earlier he'd found photographs of the area in *Rim*, the biography, and had at least a vague notion of how it might have looked. Now he searched the book until he found the author's description of the countryside at Cosari:

"Near Cosari, the Río San Miguel breaks through a narrow canyon whose walls rise several hundred feet in height. Above and below the canyon, the river valley broadens out into rich vegas of irrigable bottom lands, half a mile or more in width and several miles in length. On the east, the valley is hemmed in by the Sierra de Santa Teresa, on the west by the more distant Sierra de Torreón. Closing the lower valley and hiding Cucurpe stands the Sierra Prieto, and cutting off the observer's view to the north is the grand and rugged Sierra Azul. At the canyon where the Río San Miguel breaks through, the western mesa juts out and forms a cliff approachable only from the west.

On this promontory, protected on three sides from attack and affording a magnificent view, Kino built his Dolores mission."

Olvera filled a glass with water from the sink faucet, drank deeply from it, and studied the photos. What had Jiménez said about Dolores when he pointed it out on his map? He had said the Pima village and the church, the corrals, orchards, vineyards, everything—all were now gone, crumbled to dust with the passage of time. Nothing remained on the high bluff now, he'd said, but wind and sand and memories.

Wind and sand and memories...

Olvera had another drink of water, a new possibility slowly taking form in his mind. Suppose the Christians of Magdalena had moved Kino's body during the years of persecution. They probably hadn't, because they wouldn't likely have known where it was, either; but just suppose. What better place than Dolores to take it? To a fresh new grave on this peaceful, isolated ridge where the padre had lived and worked for so many years?

Olvera filed the thought away and returned to his notes.

- **Within weeks of first visit to Cosari, Kino had overseen construction of a small adobe chapel on promontory. Nearby, built simple one-room adobe structure for his living quarters. (Note to myself: he probably used Pima craftsmen from Ures, to the south, as Cosari Pimas would not yet have skills for such work). He quickly made Dolores his new home as he introduced the Pimas to new crops, cattle, etc. & celebrated Mass for them, taught them the Salve Regina, Gloria Patri, etc. & the first simple lessons of the catechism. Soon converted Chief Coxi and his family and baptized them, thus adding quickly to Kino's credibility with other Pimas.**

· Between 1687 & '93, Kino rode north and west, established missions at Remedios and Cocóspera on Río Magdalena; at Imuris, San Ignacio, Tubutama, Sáric, and other missions on rivers to the west. Some begun as simple one-room adobe chapels near Pima settlements, some as little more than shaded ramadas for occasional use by visiting priests. In time, newly-trained Pima laborers built larger churches with retablos, sacristies, and casa curals, as well as vineyards, corrals, citrus orchards, wheat and corn fields, etc., to replace original structures and increase production of food and other goods.

· But not all news was good news—

· Apaches from Chiricahua Mts. and from lands around headwaters of Río Gila, in concert with smaller related tribes from Sierra Madres—the Jocomes, Janos, Sumas, and Mansos—all raided regularly in Pimería, stealing cattle and horses, murdering, pillaging, burning. Tribes consistently vicious, predatory toward Pimas, Papagos, and Spanish settlers. All efforts by Kino & others at making non-hostile contact with Apaches proved futile.

Olvera refilled his water glass, drank, and washed sweat from his face. After toweling dry, he returned to his chair and his notes.

· Church hierarchy, ie Rector & Bishop in Sonora, higher officials in Mexico City, Madrid, Vatican, treated Kino no differently than it treated any of its priests on northern frontiers of Nueva España: too much paperwork, too little financial support, too many rules. Other problems harder to document, but probably significant. An example: Rumors persisted that some priests were jealous of Kino's accomplishments and worked at cross-purposes to him when occasion allowed. And consider this: He was Italian (though many believed him to be German) in a land where Spanish blood flowed fiercely and proudly in veins of so many people. Perhaps this created for him, even in these early years, unseen enemies in the Church.

· Some silver miners and cattle ranchers to the south grew increasingly hostile toward frontier Jesuits due to vigorous enforcement by Kino and others of the cédula from King Carlos II banning Indio slavery for 20 years (This of course raised labor costs for owners of mines & ranches). Also, miners and settlers increasingly annoyed with Jesuits for using all their time & energies in the Christianization of Indios. Complained that priests were unwilling to preach or administer sacraments to the settlers & miners. Interesting debate, because most frontier Jesuits saw themselves as missionaries to pagan cultures rather than as parish priests to civilized peoples. Though Spanish law actually forbade Jesuits from ministering to settlers, the settlers and civil authorities often seemed to blame the Jesuits for this.

*· **Not all Pimas and Papagos accepted the Spanish & their black-robed priests. Some, particularly the hechiceros (a generic Spanish term for all varieties of medicine men), actively worked against Kino and others by spreading false rumors about priests and threatening harm to Pimas who did not follow their lead in resisting Spanish colonization. The worst of these hechiceros were the ma'makai—Piman shamans believed by followers to be capable of controlling weather, wars, death, and disease. Stirred up much trouble for Kino, others, sometimes to point of threatening armed revolt.***

*· **These problems would in fact worsen with time. Even in the early years, though, there were troubles enough. And when they seemed almost more than Kino could bear, he always knew where he could go for support and sustenance: his first and favorite mission, Dolores, on the Río San Miguel.***

Olvera closed his journal and set it on the table near his notepad. A warm breeze stirred the curtains at his window. He stared out at a bougainvillea that brimmed with crimson flowers near the hotel office, and thought about Dolores and Kino, and Father Velarde's commentary on his death; and he thought about wind and sand and memories.

CHAPTER 25

San Juan Bautista, Sonora. Año D. 1696. August.

Not long ago I dreamed I rode my blue roan into the little ranching town of Banámichi, summer clouds building on the horizon, hot winds scudding across the desert and kicking up dust that had turned the sky a dark gunmetal gray. In the distance I could see neatly-stacked bags of priming powder, iron balls that formed tall pyramids, and eighteen-pounders firing from a ridge that bristled with artillery, but the cannons made no sound and caused no explosions that I could see. In my dream the village was silent; no one moved. I saw Old Gonzala, the curandera, watching me from beneath a sycamore, her cotton dress whipping in the wind and plastered to her stooped and shriveled body like a pale veneer of whitewash. Then I was in the back of a carreta, a little flat-bed wagon with wheels made from cross-sections of a cottonwood tree, and Wigberto was trundling me away from the old crone—who now had the pretty face and slender body of a young dark-eyed Spanish woman. Perched on her shoulder was Wigberto's macaw, Teodora, her red and blue feathers almost obscene in their flamboyance. I reached for the dark-eyed woman but she stepped away, and in the next instant she was gone.

What could I make of all this? Very little, but I thought of the dream this August night as I stood in the center of a rain-drenched street near the plaza in San Juan Bautista, my head aching, my uniform caked with blood and mud, and stared after the most beautiful woman I had ever seen.

Maybe I should explain.

It had rained that evening, a Las Aguas storm, wind bending the mesquites and cottonwoods along the river and layering our horses with gray dust before the hard rains had begun. Water puddled in the lowlands as rough gray clouds roiled over the desert and lightning webbed the evening sky. Within an hour, rains had filled the washes with frothy dark water that scoured the sand from their bottoms and uprooted trees and bushes that grew along their banks. But by the time my cavalry unit reached San Juan, the storm had passed and we had wandered into the Red Coyote in our muddied uniforms, Captain Bernal and Ensign Acuña and I, wanting nothing but a few tortillas and a bottle of wine to wash the sand and grit from our mouths after a hot wet day on patrol.

We sat at a corner table, the cantina crowded and noisy with miners and rancheros, the air heavy with the smells of mescal and wine and the smoke from cigarros made from ban vivega, weed tobacco, rolled in squares of corn husk and tied with cotton string. Women in cheap clothes stood near the back of the low-roofed adobe room and sipped drinks bought for them by interested men.

I saw few people I recognized, though a big dark-skinned man near the bar looked faintly familiar and across the room I saw Antonio Solís talking to a young woman I took for a prostitute. Solís was off-duty, in black pants and white cotton shirt, but I saw the sword that hung from his leather belt. His hair was oiled and freshly-trimmed; short, as always, and brushed neatly forward. Even from here I could see the glow of alcohol in his dark feral eyes.

The sound of a guitar reached us, and a woman in a red dress jumped onto a table and began to dance. The music wasn't exactly vlaminco, but it was Spanish, heavy with syncopation and a steady twelve-beat rhythm. The guitarro, whoever he was, was good. We listened for a time, enjoying our wine and the thumping beat of the music, but the noise from the drunken crowd and the dancing prostitute finally drowned out the guitar, and we drifted back into idle talk about small matters.

Drunken crowds. Prostitutes.

Perhaps I should explain why I was even *in* such a place as this. I have never claimed that the Red Coyote was a center of prudence and rectitude. But Nueva España was full of cantinas much like this one, and sometimes for soldiers they were the nearest source of nutriments and entertainment, crude as they often were. You may have heard that too many of our soldiers drank too much—mescal and wine were exceedingly cheap on the frontier—and that a few could rightly be called borrachones, stumbling drunkards. This was true. I have no wish to offend anyone, but in Sonora the same charge could be made against some of our government employees and even, I hate to say, the occasional priest. It was not something I was proud of. I can only say that a drink of liquor was often good for the morale of the men, and that I myself rarely took more than two glasses of wine in an evening.

But back to my story of the dark-eyed woman...

After a time the noise and bustle of the place exceeded the bounds of my tolerance, as tired as I was, and I made my excuses to my friends, Bernal and Acuña. Outside, in the darkness and quiet of the street, the hot night air carried the smell of recent rain, and I could hear quail calling from the rooftop of an herb shop across the street.

I suppose it was unwise to walk back to the presidio alone. But it was a short walk and I was armed and I gave no thought to the possibility of robbery. I should have.

He caught me from behind, his arm tight around my throat, his breath hot on the back of my neck. Whoever he was, he smelled of stale sweat and garlic and I could feel his beard against my skin as I struggled, kicking out behind me, trying to reach him with my hands. I felt him pull my flintlock pistol from my sash and heard it *plop* in the mud near my feet. I managed to jab my thumb into his eye; he grunted and cursed. He shoved me hard and I tumbled into the wetness and mud of the street. Before I could react, rough hands lifted me and a fist slammed into my face. I went down again. Blood streamed into my eyes. I pushed myself up and took a hurried swing. In the darkness it went wide. He came at me again and one of his fists caught me over the ear. I staggered backwards, pain lancing through my head. But in a stray shaft of moonlight I had a brief look at him. He was tall and heavy; dark-skinned. I was big, but he was bigger.

I heard my breath rasping in my chest, and felt an odd creaking in my jaw. "I have one peso and three reales, my friend," I said. "If you are actually willing to die for such a small sum, come ahead." I pulled my sword.

By then, though, my eyes had adjusted to the darkness and I could see the shadowy figure of a second man, shorter than the other; thinner. He raised a pistol and pointed it at me. "S'il vous plait, put down the sword, monsieur."

Of course. I should have known. The Frenchman, Henri Pitot.

The big one would be Diego.

"You two," I said wearily. I dropped the sword and massaged my neck where they had tried to crush my windpipe; I wiped blood from the corner of my mouth. "Let me guess, por favor. You are here for the lapis cross again. Right?"

"Oui, monsieur. Give it to us and we will not trouble you again."

I spit out a piece of tooth and a mouthful of blood and winced at the pain that stabbed at my jaw. "I have not seen you in a while. Where have you been?"

"You know where, monsieur."

"No, I do not," I said. "Tell me."

"We will tell you nothing, puta," Diego said.

I spit more blood. "Then why should I give you the cross?"

Henri shrugged. "We have been at Baboquivari Mountain, of course. And every time we came back to see you, we learned you were off chasing the Indios. So now we are out of patience, monsieur. We are tired of waiting. We want the cross. We want it *now*."

"Why do you want the cross, Henri?" I said. "You have never told me."

"And we will not tell you now, monsieur."

"But you have the pistol, sir; you have the advantage of me. What harm could come from telling me now?"

Henri smiled in the darkness. "Diego, take the cord from the lieutenant's neck and get the cross. I will keep the pistol aimed at his heart."

Perhaps I should have just given the cross to them. Father Kino had chastised me for not doing exactly that when I first made the acquaintance of these idiotas. And, I have to admit, the padre had a point. But there are times in a man's life when he has to fight for what belongs to him. When someone tries to take what is rightfully his, he simply has to resist, even if he doesn't fully understand why the miscreant even *wants* his property. Sometimes it becomes a matter of principle. Sometimes a man simply has to challenge a thief.

Besides, sometimes it's just fun to smite a scoundrel.

So I did. When Diego reached for the cord, I balled my fist and hit him square in the face. I felt the bones crumple in his nose, felt warm blood spewing onto my hand; but he stayed on his feet. I hit him in the face again. This time he went down. Before Henri could bring his pistol around, I put my shoulder down, caught him in the belly, and knocked him flat on his back. Behind me I heard Diego bellowing and stomping through the mud after me.

But the sounds of our scuffle must have alerted someone, because I heard shouts and running footsteps—just as Diego bashed me in the back of my head and the night went black and I felt myself spiraling downward into a narrow space that was webbed with heat and streaked with blood.

How long I was unconscious I do not know.

Tiny points of light flashed in the blackness that surged behind my eyes. Dark sounds roared in my ears. The smell of blood reached me. The stench of raw meat seemed to fester in my nasal passages, and I wondered if I had fallen into a matadero, a livestock slaughter yard. The sounds grew louder. In the darkness inside my eyes a harsh light flashed relentlessly. I felt as if I were staked to the ground, spread-eagled, and wondered if someone with a knife was even now preparing to slice off my eyelids so I could not barricade my mind and soul against the pounding malignant pulse of the giant light.

The light was an oil lamp.

And not even a large one, I realized when I came awake, pain racking my head, memories of the fight creeping slowly back into my consciousness. The person holding the lamp was a young woman. She stood over me, her skirts spattered with mud. Her skin was dark and smooth, her face a perfect oval framed by hair that seemed to glow in the shadowed light of the night.

"Are you all right, sir?" she said.

I raised up on an elbow. "I think so, Señora." I could hardly speak for the pain in my head.

"They were trying to rob you?"

I nodded.

"They ran when they saw me coming." She shrugged. "Common street thieves, probably. Most such people are usually cowards. Did they take anything?"

I felt my neck. The cord was gone; my skin felt raw where they had torn the cord away.

"They got nothing, no," I said.

"I am glad to hear it, Señor."

Her words were well-formed and she seemed bright and level-headed, though I judged from her accent that she came from the lower classes.

She was beautiful.

And she had come—*alone, in the darkness*—to help me. Amazing.

"You are staring, sir."

I pushed myself up to a sitting position. "Please accept my apologies," I said, "I meant no harm. My name is Manje. Lieutenant Juan Mateo Manje. If I might ask, por favor, what is yours?"

"You may *not* ask, sir," she said. But she knelt beside me and inspected my wounds. In the light from her lantern now I could see that her eyes were dark, almost black, with flecks of silver near the pupil. On her neck she wore a small gold crucifix on a chain of tiny blue beads. Her hair was long, straight, and black as coal and she tucked a strand of it behind her ear as she checked the cuts on my head and face.

"You are very kind, Señora," I said.

"I will ask you, sir," she said firmly, "to turn your face away from me when you speak. Your breath reeks of alcohol. I can only assume you were drunk and those men decided to take advantage of you in your condition."

"But I only had two glasses of w—"

"Your uniform smells of it, sir. I do not know which odor is more offensive, the wine and mescal or the smoke from those awful cigarros."

While I was trying to think of something witty to say—and who is surprised that I could think of nothing of the sort—she opened a purse that hung from her narrow waist and removed a bag containing something that looked like ground-up red roots. She placed a small portion in her palm and gently smoothed it onto the wounds of my scalp. "Sangre de Drago," she said. "It will stop the bleeding and make the cuts heal faster."

"Gracias," I said.

She stood again and slipped the bag back into her purse. "Next time stay home with your wife, sir, and you will not have to fear street hoodlums and common brigands."

I got slowly to my feet. "But I am not married, Señora."

"Then you *should* be, sir." With that she turned and hurried away, into the darkness of the street. By now my head was pounding with pain. I reached into my boot and popped open the flap that hid a little pocket there, and pulled out the lapis cross. At that instant I remembered the strange dream I had had earlier, of Old Gonzala with her youthful new body and the fresh comely face of a dark-eyed beauty.

The blue stone felt oily and hot to my touch.

My cuts and bruises finally healed and the swellings from my various lumps and bumps eventually subsided. We in the Compañía got on with the challenges that awaited us in the waning months of that year of 1696: chasing Apaches and Jocomes; enforcing the king's laws—most of them just and reasonable and some a little less so; quelling disturbances; keeping peace between the River Pimas and their Tohono brothers in the western desert and trying to minimize the influence of the ma'makai.

And for me, wondering about the dark-haired woman who wore at her neck a little gold crucifix on a chain of blue beads.

Father Kino stayed busy that year, too. With his return from Mexico City in May, the pace of activity in the Pimería had picked up. Summer harvest at the missions had been a good one. Seasonal rains made a good second planting, too, and Kino spent much of the year in his fields and orchards at Dolores and helping Father Campos rebuild his burned-out mission at San Ignacio. In Mexico City, officials had promised Kino he would have new priests for the Pimería, and in the fall, with his vaqueros, he drove cattle northward to the Sobaipuri settlements along the Río Terrenate and the Santa María, preparing the Indios for the missions he planned to build there and staff with the new padres.

And he had been dealing with Father Francisco Mora, the new rector who had come from Puebla and was now minister at Arizpe. Looking back on it, I don't think I ever really believed that Mora was a bad person. But he was young, he had no experience on the frontier, and he was insecure. For these reasons and maybe a few others, too, he made some bad decisions.

I think Father Mora never particularly liked Kino. Why this should be, I was never quite sure. My own opinion is that Mora came to resent Kino's successes, and his own insecurities simply fed fuel to the fire, though there could have been other explanations of which I had no knowledge. One thing I have learned over the years is that it is almost impossible to fully know the motives for another person's behavior. Or even for your *own*, for that matter. At any rate, on his arrival Mora had made it clear that as rector he would be *jefe* and Kino would be *servidor* and you did not have to be much of a genius to see where all this was going. As for me, I just tried to stay out of it.

In October I rode to Dolores to visit Father Kino.

I found him branding cattle with a hot iron, his black robe thick with dust and smelling of smoke from the wood fire that smoldered near a fence made of ocotillo branches that had been rooted in the soil and bound together with rawhide cord. Pima vaqueros were tending the bawling, newly-marked animals and funneling others into the corral to await their turns at the iron. The padre looked tired but contented and he greeted me warmly.

He put me to work with the branding. When we had finished and washed up, we walked to a cooking ramada where Pima women in cotton dresses served us a meal of onions, boiled corn, and green peppers wrapped in warm wheat tortillas.

I told him about the incident with Henri Pitot and Diego in Real San Juan. He remembered that I had had trouble with them earlier. "But you still have no idea why they wanted the cross?" he said.

I shrugged. "It must have something to do with mining. Probably on Baboquivari. But I cannot imagine why a little cross made of lapis lazuli would be important." I told the padre everything Henri had said, and everything the Apache had told me about Black Skull's theft of the cross from the Frenchmen he had killed at Baboquivari.

"Do you have the cross with you? Could I see it?" His gray-flecked hair was damp with sweat, his narrow face burned from the sun.

I pulled the cross from my pocket and handed it to him. He studied it. "Lapis, yes," he said, "I can see flecks of pyrite in it. But I have never heard of lapis discoveries in this part of New Spain. And even if someone has found lapis here, why would this cross be important to the Frenchman and his friend? I have no idea."

I reminded him of Old Gonzala's warning that I should beware of those who speak in strange tongues. Gonzala was a crone, a self-proclaimed mystic and seer. Why should any rational person believe anything she said? Still, I wanted Kino's opinion on this, so I asked for it. "Do you think her warning could have anything to do with the cross?"

He took his time thinking about it. Finally he said, "It is hard to see how it could."

We ate silently for a time, enjoying the sunset and the sights and sounds of the mission and the Indio village. Before we finished our meal, though, I brought up another subject I had wanted to ask him about. "Father," I said, "do you think we will ever get to build our boat and sail the Golfo?"

"I doubt it, Juan Mateo." He sighed. "The Father Visitor is still very much against it." He was quiet for a moment, then said, "But next year I hope to make another trip north to the Río Gila to visit some Indian villages and to have another look at the Casas Grandes. Would you like to go?"

"Absolutely, Father," I said, smiling widely. "Can we leave tomorrow?"

He laughed. "Not quite that soon, I think." He got out his maps and a lantern and we drank chocolate into the night and made plans for our next entrada in the far north.

The critics of Spanish colonization in the New World have made plenty of charges against us over the years; here I am speaking of the Dutch, the Portuguese; the English, the French. A few of their charges have contained a grain of truth. Most have not, but who is surprised at that, considering the source. One of the more frequent complaints is that Spaniards have willfully caused the decimation of Indian populations in New Spain by spreading diseases that were once limited to Europe and Asia: smallpox, measles, typhoid, syphilis, and garrotillo—diphtheria—to name the worst. And I have to admit, there is a tiny bit of truth in that. All right, so there's a *lot* of truth in it, *okay*. But no one could blame us for rabies. Or lightning strikes, either, for that matter.

Here is why I even bring up the subject: In October I heard that the

Frenchman, Pitot, had been bitten by a rabid fox on Baboquivari Mountain. Old Gonzala had come and tried to draw out the poison by rubbing the wound with bezales—stones she had taken from the stomachs of deer—and with her incantations and amulets and hot creosote teas, but she had been unable to save him. Diego was carrying Pitot's body off the mountain when he was caught in a thunderstorm, struck by lightning, and was himself killed. Later I heard that the old curandera had buried them both near the foot of the mountain.

What did I think about their deaths? In a way, I was saddened. They had been inept opponents, maladroit adversaries, but they had been persistent in whatever they were trying to do, and willing to live and die on that big old rough mountain, and that should count for something. Though it did not change the fact that I still had no good idea why they had wanted my lapis cross.

But that autumn I had little time to dwell on memories of Henri and Diego. In late October the Apaches hit Imuris and Remedios and my cavalry unit was in the saddle again. We never caught the main band but we trapped a few stragglers in a box canyon near Magdalena and killed seven of them. We took four alive and sold them directly to representatives of a mining company at Alamos. This time we did not even fake a trial.

And this time it did not bother me. Which means, I suppose, that my views on slavery had changed in some fundamental way. I had adapted, finally, to life in the desert. You might say this was a bad decision, that slavery was unacceptable no matter *who* the slaves were and that I should have resisted a practice that was so inherently evil. But I had come to view this issue as a matter of personal belief rather than judicatory law. I had accepted slavery—for Apaches, anyway—and knew of few settlers, soldiers, or even Pimas who disagreed with that view. After all, the Apaches could have listened to the priests. They could have put down their weapons and joined the Christian family, as the Pimas, Papagos, and Ópatas had. The priests had given them ample opportunities to do just that. So whom can they blame for their fate but themselves?

This year we lost one of our officers: Antonio Solís. The army finally made up its mind to discharge him for his role in the massacre at El Tupo—and probably for a lot of other atrocities, too—and that was fine with me. Some time after that, I heard that he had gotten into a fight in a cantina somewhere to the south and had been killed. I suppose someone shot him in the back; I had always suspected that that was the only way a mere mortal could ever kill him.

That winter was reasonably peaceful, though; none of our men died in battle.

But something happened in San Juan in February of the new year, 1697, that would greatly change my life: a sergeant of artillery was killed in an explosion on the practice range, and Don Domingo ordered all officers and men to attend the services. I had never met the sergeant, though I knew his name was Vásquez. The funeral was held at the post cemetery at the edge of town.

The day was mild, the afternoon air damp with the promise of rain, and I could see gray clouds building in the west. I stood about midway back from the family: a dark-haired woman I took for the wife of Sergeant Vásquez, and two small girls I assumed were his daughters. After the service I joined the line of people who filed past them to pay respects. I could not see the widow's face for the black veil that covered it, but she seemed strong and stoic as she spoke quietly to those who offered condolences. As I came to her in the line I saw in the hollow of her neck a gold crucifix on a short chain of tiny blue beads. I felt a quick flush of heat in my face and prayed that it had not betrayed me. If she recognized me, she gave no sign.

Her name, I later learned, was Adriana, and she smelled of woman's skin and spring flowers and citrus bergamot.

CHAPTER 26  Magdalena, Sonora. 1965.

All in all, Olvera believed his first week in Sonora had been reasonably productive. With Nava García, the mayor, and de la Vega, the amateur arqueólogo, he had seen the Cocóspera ruins and learned that he needed to know more about Kino's construction methods. In Hermosillo the silver-haired widow of the brewery owner had reminded him of the persecution of Christians in Sonora, and from Dolores Vásquez in Magdalena he'd learned that the Christians often hid from the government their most-treasured religious items. These last facts had helped him realize something more: If these same Christians could hide a life-size statue of San Xavier, they could surely hide a skeleton.

In that first week he had read more of *Rim* and *Luz* and other references and added pages to his notes. He learned that Agustín Campos had buried Kino under the floor of the Chapel of San Xavier on the Gospel side between the second and third foundation stones. He found the Lockwood document and in it, Father Velarde's commentaries on Kino's fevers and death. And he examined the parish church and the Proctor Chapel in Magdalena and had come to believe that neither could be Kino's Chapel of San Xavier.

Yes, Olvera would have much to share with Professor Jiménez when he arrived from Mexico City. None of this, unfortunately, altered the fact that he still had no good idea where in Magdalena to dig his first trench.

When Jiménez arrived from Mexico City he said to Olvera, "Jorge, pack a light bag, we're going to Hermosillo."

"Hermosillo? I just came from there."

"I know, but there are people I want you to meet."

"But the trenching—"

"We'll dig our trenches, Jorge. Soon, I promise."

In Hermosillo Jiménez first took him to meet Cruz Acuna, a young priest with the Archdiocese of Sonora. Father Acuña, he learned, had access to the special ecclesiastical archives at the Cathedral of Hermosillo. Jiménez, that crafty old bait-dangler, had somehow managed to persuade the Archbishop to assign the priest as temporary research assistant to Jiménez and Olvera.

Research assistant. Olvera rolled the words around on his tongue, liking the sound of them, especially since Acuña seemed an enthusiastic fellow who clearly knew his way around shadowy old vaults filled with moldy old documents. He appeared to actually *enjoy* such things.

Which could, Olvera realized, free him even sooner to begin his digging.

"Welcome to the team, Padre," Olvera said, smiling widely.

Jiménez then took Olvera to meet the Governor of Sonora, Luís Encinas Johnson. In his office Encinas seated them in comfortable chairs and offered coffee. He spoke briefly of the Presidente's desire for a successful—and speedy—discovery of Kino's gravesite.

"There isn't much money in the federal budget," the Governor explained, "for such projects, and what there is, well, it may not be there long."

"We're fortunate to have what we have, sir," Jiménez said.

"Perhaps, por favor," the governor said, "in some small way I can help, and that's why I asked you to come by. I'm prepared to offer you the use of a car and the services of my personal driver. You may keep them as long as you wish."

"That's a very gracious offer, sir," Jiménez said.

"My driver is good, but he's the curious kind. He'll probably drive you crazy with his questions."

Jiménez smiled. "We'll be glad to have him, Governor."

On the ride back to Magdalena in the governor's car, Olvera told Jiménez what he'd learned about Magdalena. "I've been reading Juan Mateo Manje's diary, too," he said. "The man led a very interesting life."

"Tell me about him," Jiménez said.

The governor's driver, a young vaquero who wore western clothes and a white Stetson hat, said, "Where are you gentlemen from?"

"Mexico City," Olvera said.

"Big place," the driver said. "Much too big for me." He stared at Olvera in the rearview mirror. "Manje? Who was Juan Mateo Manje?"

Soon after their return to Magdalena, Olvera and Jiménez were stopped on the street by a man with dark skin and heavy dark eyes.

"You're the men," the man said, "who are looking for the padre's grave?"

"We are," Olvera said.

The man wore khaki pants and a green shirt with pearl buttons. "Gentlemen, there is a fotografia that you must see. I believe you'll find it very interesting."

Olvera chuckled. He'd heard such gambits before, in unsavory sections of Mexico City and in certain border towns. "Sir, I assure you, we have no interest in your pornographic materials."

"Oh, no, Señor, you don't understand!" The man quickly removed his hat, a gesture of respect. "It's a photograph of Magdalena. It shows the old church you are seeking."

"...You're speaking of the *parish* church?"

"Yes, the parish church, but another church, too."

"A photograph?" Olvera cut in. "Impossible. The other churches were destroyed years ago, probably before cameras were even *invented*."

"But, sir, this is a photograph of a *painting*. And the painting was made in 1864. It says so on the photograph, right on the front of it."

Olvera and Jiménez stared at the man.

"...All right," Jiménez said cautiously, "tell us *exactly* what it shows."

"It shows people walking in the street, and two churches: our parish church and a second church that people say is much older. What church this is, I don't know. Señor, would you like me to get the photograph for you?"

"Por favor, yes! Thank you, sir!"

"Jorge," Jiménez whispered, staring after the man as he hurried away, "do you suppose that man actually has a photograph that shows the old Campos church? Or even more of a miracle, one that shows Kino's Chapel of San Xavier?"

Olvera felt slightly faint. "It would be a miracle," he said, "and I don't even believe in miracles."

CHAPTER 27

"*Extraordinary*," Jiménez said.

"*Amazing*," Olvera said, grinning.

"Dos iglesias." The man who'd brought the photo removed his hat. "It is like I said, no? A photograph of a painting of two churches? Very old churches!" In the street, cars with faded paint lumbered past and children played near small homes that faced the dusty roadway.

"It's exactly as you said," Olvera declared. "Gracias, sir."

For Olvera, it was the battlements along the rooftop and around the espadaña, the tall bell tower, of the larger church that had first drawn his eye: crenellations and merlons like you saw in photos of old castles in Europe. Amazing, you could almost see the Pimas up there, showering the Apache attackers with arrows, then ducking behind the merlons to fit more arrows to their bows.

Olvera squinted in the brightness of the sunlight. Like the man had promised, this was a photo of a painting—a simple sketch, actually—that showed a plaza and, bordering it, two churches. Hills with sharp contours formed the background, and in the foreground were figures representing villagers or perhaps priests. Olvera recognized the larger church as the present parish church, though now it had no battlements. The other, though smaller, was still too sizable to be a chapel. He had no doubts that this was the Campos church of 1705. He saw no other church or chapel, nothing that could be Kino's chapel. Still, having before them a sketch of the old Campos church was a huge step forward. Now they could walk around until they found the same angle on the hills in the background, the same angle on the parish church. They could find the spot where the artist had stood, and from there make a reasonable guess at where the Campos church had been. Of course they might find a newer building in its place now, or perhaps a street, but that wouldn't matter. Because Kino's chapel would have been near the Campos church, the scientists could now make better decisions on where to begin their trenching.

Or so Olvera hoped.

They sat on a bench in the shade of a cottonwood near the Palacio Municipal and examined the markings on the sketch. In one corner it carried the notation, "Magdalena, January 26, 1864." In another corner someone had written, "To Don Francisco González Torrano." The sketch bore the signature, "J. Ross Browne."

González Torrano. Browne. Olvera didn't know these names.

The photograph showed more: The Campos church had a bell tower above the nave, and on the right side, a fortified stairway leading up to the tower. With its thick walls and protective parapet, this was what architectural historians called a "cranked" or "elbowed" staircase, and Olvera knew the design had its origins in the mudejar tradition.

Then Olvera noticed that the corners of the bell tower on the big church were beveled. Chamfered, in the argot of the architects. This feature, too, was often of mudejar origin. He took a closer look at the Campos church and saw that its bell tower, as well, had beveled corners. Built in the Pimería of far northern Mexico by Indian laborers in the first decade of the eighteenth century and it had a cranked staircase and chamfered tower like buildings in North Africa? To Olvera this was very interesting.

The man who'd brought the photo now stood before them again. "Excuse me, por favor," he said. "Would you like to see the painting? Not another picture like this, but the original sketch?"

Olvera and Jiménez stared at him.

"I've just learned from my wife that the original is in Caborca, in the café at the Hotel Amelia."

"Sure, we'd like to see it," Olvera said excitedly. "The *original*? Certainly!"

Olvera found the governor's driver in a café near the plaza. "It would be my honor," the driver said, "to drive you to Caborca."

On the highway the driver said, "Do you think the Apaches ever attacked those two churches in the fotografia?"

"I'm sure they did," Olvera said from the back seat.

"Right here in Magdalena? And the priests and Pimas fought back?"

"No question about it."

"Do you have more stories of this man you call Juan Mateo Manje?"

"I have lots of them," Olvera said, smiling.

"Would you tell another one? About Indians and fighting?"

"Of course," Olvera said, and told him about a young officer, a troublemaker named Solís, who'd ordered the slaughter of innocent Pimas at El Tupo, and how this had led to a revolt by the Pimas. He told him how Manje waited with Kino at his mission for the insurrectionists to come and kill them, and how, in the end, the Indians had spared them.

"Amazing!" the driver said. "Manje must've been a brave man."

"The history books say he was frightened," Olvera said, "but, yes, he was a very brave man."

"If I might say so," Jiménez gently offered, "Father Kino was pretty brave, too."

In Caborca, Olvera and Jiménez stood in the café at the Hotel Amelia and studied the sketch—they saw now that it was actually a watercolor drawing—that hung on a wall near a window. The room, empty of customers at this hour of the afternoon, had tables of mesquite wood with yellow place mats and red flowers in thin glass vases.

The drawing, they guessed, had originally been done in dark bold tones, but by now had faded to a dusky brown; the thick paper had yellowed and cracked from a century of heat and aridity.

"Definitely the same," Olvera said, comparing the photo and sketch. "There's no doubt of it."

The manager nodded. "Of course you can see the details better here, in the sketch."

"Definitely, Señora," Jiménez said. "Could we have coffee, por favor, and perhaps some corn tortillas and beef tamales? We would like to stay a while and study this extraordinary artwork."

On the ride back to Magdalena, Jiménez said, "There's someone I want you to meet, Jorge. Arturo Romano Pacheco. He'll be in Magdalena tonight."

"Romano?" Olvera said, surprised. "The physical anthropologist? He's the best in the country! He's coming to Magdalena?"

Jiménez smiled. "I've convinced him to join our team."

"Madre de Dios! How did you manage such a thing?"

"I think God has decided our Kino team needs help."

Help—certainly they needed *that*, but who could've guessed that Arturo Romano would be joining them! The story had it—jokingly, Olvera had always supposed—that you could hand Doctor Romano a bone and in minutes he could tell you the age, gender, height, body build, ethnic origins, and occupation of the deceased, and occasionally even their favorite flavor of ice cream and the seamier details of their sex life. Olvera didn't believe *all* that, of course. Still, it was a real coup to have the man with them, and Olvera was delighted.

After a time his mind wandered; he found himself thinking about the photo of the old churches with their battlements and bell towers and cranked staircases...

Mudejar. For Olvera, the word conjured up images of dark-skinned Moors in turbans and flowing white robes, scimitars held high, galloping on Barb horses over sandy dunes near the Mediterranean Sea. The word itself referred to a style of art and architecture that arose from a blending of Gothic and Islamic traditions that reached as far back as the Moorish conquest. But the term had, Olvera knew, a broader meaning. Mudejar was a way of life—a way of thinking, of creating—that infused everything from art to irrigation systems, from religion to weaponry, from food to war to carpentry techniques, and it had found its greatest acceptance in the lands most affected by the conquest: the Province of Andalusia, in southern Spain.

A thought came to Olvera: Hadn't Kino lived in Andalusia? At Seville?

He would check his notes again and a map of Europe, but he was certain of it. And what if Kino had studied— ?

"I've been thinking," Jiménez said, cutting into Olvera's thoughts. "Our man once lived in Andalusia, didn't he? While he waited those two years for a ship to take him to the New World?"

Olvera nodded. "I was just thinking the same."

"Perhaps our friend took time from his clerical duties in Seville...and studied the designs and construction techniques of the Moors. Maybe if we knew how the Moors built *their* ashlars, their foundation stones, we would know how Kino built *his*."

"Extraordinary," Olvera said, smiling widely. "I was thinking exactly the same. But how did you know Kino was in Andalusia for two years?"

Jiménez shrugged. "I've been reading."

Arturo Romano Pacheco. Like Jiménez Moreno, he was a dignified man—impeccably dressed now in a dark suit, his white shirt freshly ironed, trousers creased. He'd studied, Olvera knew, under Don Pablo Martínez del Río, himself Oxford-trained, Mexico's greatest anthropologist. Don Pablo had excavated many sites in suit and tie, derby hat and spats, a shiny wooden cane over his arm. He'd taken his field notes in white gloves. Romano wasn't wearing gloves or spats, but Olvera could see the teacher in the student.

"I'm honored to meet you, Professor," he said.

"The honor is mine, Señor Olvera. I know of your work at Copanaguastla in Chiapas. Very well done, sir."

"Thank you," Olvera said, smiling.

Olvera, Romano, and Jiménez had met in Jiménez's hotel room to plan the next day's work. After the introductions, Jiménez said, "First, we have to be certain that Kino's remains aren't under the Proctor Chapel."

Olvera had feared exactly this.

"But Professor," he argued, "many searchers have been over those grounds. They've dug every square inch and found nothing. Besides, that chapel is Franciscan; nineteenth century neoclassic. It isn't Kino's chapel. We would be wasting our time."

Jiménez nodded. "Maybe, but we know there's a possibility that Christians moved the body from its original burial site during the years of persecution. The Proctor Chapel would've been a logical place to take it. Do you disagree with that assessment, Jorge?"

"No, I don't disagree," Olvera said, "but I've just thought of something. Suppose the Christians *did* take the body to that chapel. If they'd re-buried it underground, someone, I still believe, would've discovered it by now. But there's another place they could've buried it that maybe no one has yet examined: in one of the *walls*. I suggest we check out the walls. We could use a simple acoustical method. If that gets us nothing, then maybe we could move on."

"That sounds reasonable," Jiménez said. "Do you agree, Arturo?"

"Certainly," Romano said. "Of course."

"So, it's agreed." Jiménez placed Romano in charge. Olvera, working under him, would test the walls for hollow spots by tapping them with the handle of his trowel and carefully evaluating the sounds. It would be slow, tedious work and Olvera doubted it would produce much useful information. Truthfully, he didn't believe his priest's remains were anywhere near the chapel. This wall-tapping business would be a total waste of time. Still, he supposed, it was better than digging holes in dirt that had been dug a thousand times before.

By mid-morning of the next day, Olvera had tested most of the walls. Some were of adobe, some of fired brick, all of them covered with faded plaster that had cracked and pulled loose in assorted places. So far, he'd found nothing unusual. Now, after a brief rest, he began on the last wall to be examined, the west wall of the nave. He'd been tapping for several minutes when he caught a change in the sound. At first it seemed to be only a slight dullness, a vague echo, perhaps, in the vibration he felt through the handle of the trowel. Or was he just imagining it? He moved his trowel and tapped again and got the same faint dullness. He moved and tapped again. As he inched his way over the wall, the dullness changed to a drumlike tone, almost tympanitic. Now he was sure of it: there was a hollow spot here. He went over the area again, tapping lightly, moving a few centimeters and tapping again, carefully outlining the zone of hyperresonance: chest height...wider than tall...about the size of a coffin...

Olvera's pulse raced in his temples. "Professor Romano!" he called over his shoulder. "I have something!"

CHAPTER 28

"So...what have you found?" Jiménez stood in the doorway to the nave of the Proctor Chapel, staring at the cavities Olvera and Romano had uncovered in the adobe wall.

"Niches," Olvera said, disappointment in his voice. "Two of them."

"Plastered over," Romano said. Dirt and flakes of gritty white paint coated the anthropologist's wingtip shoes and dusted the shoulders of his tailored brown suit.

"Both empty," Olvera said.

Romano scraped loose dirt onto the floor from inside the niches.

"No bones?" Jiménez's suit was neatly pressed, pale blue over a white shirt and dark tie.

"Not even one," Romano said.

When Olvera had found the hollow area in the wall, he and Romano carefully outlined it with chalk, agreeing quickly that it seemed the perfect size and shape to hold a coffin. They'd used a surgeon's knife to cautiously lift the successive layers of paint, whitewash, and crumbling plaster...

...And had found, instead of a coffin, two niches—both empty except for bits of dirt and the hard dark shells of a few dead insects. Olvera had wondered how old the bugs were; he wondered if they had been alive in Kino's time, Madre de Dios, what tales these bugs could tell. No, wait, that was impossible; this was a Franciscan structure, he remembered, built years after his priest had died.

Olvera stared at the niches. "Why would someone plaster up two perfectly-useful niches?"

Romano shrugged patiently.

"It makes no sense," Olvera said.

"In field archaeology," Jiménez said, taking a closer look at the wall, "many things make no sense when you first see them. There's probably an interesting story behind this."

Any other time Olvera might've been interested in whatever story lay behind the plastered-over niches. Now he was interested only in the bones of his long-lost Jesuit, Eusebio Kino.

Olvera chuckled. He'd just realized something: he had begun to think of Kino as *his* priest. Not in a possessive sense, certainly, or even as he might, in some abstract way, lay claim to a rich friend or a famous relative. Still, the priest had become, somehow, *his*. Until a few months ago he'd never heard of Eusebio Kino. Well, maybe he'd heard the name, but he knew nothing of the person *behind* the name. Or even cared, frankly. Now he found himself happily scavenging through centuries-old details of the man's life and chasing his moldy bones across Mexico. *His* bones, Olvera's. Funny what was happening.

Okay, so the bones weren't in the wall of the chapel. But they were *somewhere*, and Olvera would find them.

"So what now?" he said, still grinning.

Jiménez turned to Romano. "I want you to go to San Ignacio. A few days ago I heard rumors there might be some bodies buried under the nave of the old church there. The rumors say one of them might be Kino's. It seems unlikely, Arturo, but we have to look at all the possibilities. Your knowledge of bones would be of great help to us."

Romano nodded. "I can leave today."

"Good," Jiménez said. "And Jorge and I will go to Oquitoa, to learn more about how Kino built his churches. When we finish at Oquitoa, we'll join you."

"But first," Jiménez added, "I want both of you to meet Señor Lopez."

Leandro Lopez was an old man who'd lived in Magdalena all his life. He'd heard that important scientists from Mexico City were looking—yet again—for Kino's grave, and earlier in the day had come by to greet them.

"Because of something my father, Don Ramón Lopez, once told me," he had explained to Jiménez in the shade of a tall cottonwood near the chapel. "About a big stone slab in the ground," he added. Jiménez had listened to the man's story, had thought it interesting enough that he wanted Olvera and Romano to hear it.

Now, in the shade of that same cottonwood, Jiménez made the introductions and Señor Lopez told Olvera and Romano what he knew: Don Ramón Lopez had told him that many years ago, perhaps around 1908, Magdalena's city officials had decided to enlarge and improve the City Hall by adding a clock tower at the front of the building.

"As you have undoubtedly seen," Leandro Lopez said proudly, "it's a fine clock tower, as nice as any in Sonora."

"Very nice, certainly," Jiménez and the others politely agreed.

Lopez went on with his story: The new tower would, of course, require strong footings to support its weight. In the process of excavating for the new footings, the workers had encountered, deep in the ground, a large slab of stone. Roughly square, as nearly as they could discover, and thick. It was, according to the father of Leandro Lopez, very wide.

"How thick and how wide?" Romano wanted to know.

"The width, Señor, oh, perhaps as large as the clock tower itself. As for the thickness of it, I'm sorry." Lopez shrugged. "My father never said. He probably didn't know."

Olvera, who had been listening quietly, said, "It sounds like he's describing a pedraplén."

"A *what*?" Jiménez said.

Olvera explained: A pedraplén—what Norte Americano architects would call a "raft foundation"—was used to stabilize the soil beneath any part of a building that was significantly heavier than the rest of the structure, particularly if the soil was moist or had a high clay content. The builders would create a stone slab in the shape of a flat square or rectangle and bury it in the ground beneath the area that would support the heaviest part of the new structure, then use independent stone footings under the remainder of the building. In Kino's time, they'd made the slabs by embedding river rock in a mortar of mud and clay. Such a structure prevented differential settling of the building—and the consequent racking and contortion that would otherwise follow. These days they use reinforced concrete rather than stones and mortar, but the principle was the same.

Pedrapléns, Olvera went on, had been used in Europe since Roman times. In the days of the Moors they'd been popular in southern Spain, where much of the land was marshy. Not surprisingly, the technique had followed the Spaniards to the New World. And while the Sonoran desert had little problem with overly moist soil, it was known for its rocky substrates and clay.

Olvera said, "Señor Lopez, where, precisely, was this stone slab? In front of the clock tower? To the side of it? Did they build the new tower on top of it?"

Lopez shrugged again and pointed a leathery finger in the direction of the Palacio. "Somewhere over there. I don't know exactly where."

Jiménez turned to Olvera. "Jorge, do you suppose this big stone could be from one of Kino's churches? Could it be from the chapel of San Xavier, where he was buried?"

Olvera stared in the direction of the Palacio. "I suspect it's from one of them, sir. I suspect Kino himself built it." He remembered Dolores Vásquez, who had said as much over her enchiladas and pumpkin empanadas: *You will find his bones, Señor, under, or very near, the Palacio.*

"Kino built it?" Jiménez seemed surprised. "Our priest was also an *architect*?"

"No," Olvera said, "he had no formal training in it. But he was smart, and I'm beginning to think he definitely knew what he was doing."

Jiménez smiled. "Where is that Ross Browne photograph, the sketch showing the parish church and the Campos church? With it, maybe we can find this slab and see for ourselves."

"Ah," Olvera said, his eyes bright. "An excellent idea, sir."

An hour and a half's drive west of Magdalena on Highway 2, past Santa Ana Viejo with its spreading chile farms, sat the village of Altar, at the junction of the Altar and Magdalena Rivers. What remained of the rivers, anyway. In Kino's time, Olvera had learned, they'd run wide and deep, bringing water from the mountains in the northern and eastern parts of the Pimería. Not anymore. Though the area around Altar was still green with bottomlands planted in cotton, wheat, and corn, the rivers had been so depleted by deep wells and modern irrigation projects that they no longer flowed with regularity. A few miles north of the town of Altar, on what remained of the river by the same name, the village of Oquitoa sat quietly in the shade of giant cottonwood trees that grew along the riverbanks.

As Olvera and Jiménez climbed from their car in front of the church on the edge of the village, a hot breeze drove dust devils across the flatlands. Olvera drank deeply from a canvas bag of water. He wiped his mouth with a bandanna, pulled his hat brim low over his eyes, and squinted through the heat at the little church.

San Antonio del Oquitoa sat on a hill dotted with scrub cactus and cemetery headstones. The church, coated on the exterior with plaster that badly needed repairs, was rectangular in shape and had a techo de terrado, a flat roof. Twin bell towers filled most of the façade above the roofline. Olvera guessed the adobe-and-brick walls at four feet in thickness. The heavy wooden doors were scarred, weathered by sun and wind, ancient and venerable, as if they had faithfully protected the little church's congregation since the days of the Apache raiders. Which they probably had, Olvera thought.

"I understand it was built about 1730," Olvera said, "nineteen years after Kino died. But it was built in the same style and using the same techniques he used in his churches."

Jiménez shielded his eyes against the sun. "That's why I wanted us to see it, Jorge. This is probably as close as we'll get to an intact church from Kino's era. Well, there's Cocóspera, of course, at least the adobe core of it, but it's in ruins now, as you know. And Remedios, I hear, but there's little left of it now, either. It seems Kino's other churches have been mostly replaced by Franciscan structures. Anyway, what have you learned about the foundations here?"

"I've found old documents that say these are independent footings made of river stone set in mortar, but with your permission I'll do some digging and see for myself." The wind tugged at Olvera's coat and ruffled his dark tie.

"An excellent idea, Jorge. I've spoken with the priest who visits here, and he's given permission."

Inside, they found a small, well-kept nave with high ceilings made from cross beams of mesquite spanned by shoots of rivercane and split saguaro ribs. Carved oaken corbels set into the adobe walls supported the heavy beams. The sanctuary roof was elevated perhaps three feet above the roof of the nave, and a south-facing transverse clerestory window filled the short drop-off. Light from the window gave a vibrant glow to the altar and the white plastered walls of the sanctuary. Behind the altar a modest wooden retablo contained niches filled with religious objects. A votive candle burned with a yellow flame on a table near the altar and, in a pew at the front, an old man in a faded plaid shirt sat quietly with his wife. The room was surprisingly comfortable, perhaps twenty degrees cooler than the outside air.

"So what do you make of it, Jorge?" Jiménez whispered.

"The interior plaster was added later, I'm sure. But the hall-style design, the high façade with twin bell towers, the clerestory window, the alfarje ceiling—it's typical, all of it."

"*Alfarje*?" Jiménez said. "I don't know this word."

"It's an Arab word for this type of flat roof, one that's anchored with vigas—the thick beams we see here—that are supported at their ends by the corbelling. The spaces between beams are filled with cane or saguaro ribs set at angles to the beams. When ribs and cane are used like this, they're called latillas. They can be laid in a variety of designs, depending on the artistic bent of the builder. In Kino's time they would have covered the exterior surface of the roof with dirt or, if they could find it, a special kind of volcanic ash called pozzuolana that could be made impervious to water. Now, of course, they probably use roofing tar to stop the leaks. It isn't as poetic, but it works better than dirt."

Jiménez smiled, and wiped sweat from his forehead. "Some day, my friend, I will learn something of architectural history, and then you won't have to spend so much of your time educating me."

The elderly Mexican couple rose from their pew and shuffled slowly down the aisle toward the doors. When they were gone, Olvera and Jiménez strolled to the front of the church and stood near the altar. Jiménez motioned toward the clerestory, visible from the sanctuary. "What's the significance of the window?"

"It had two functions, Professor. First, of course, it was a good source of light. Since the window faces south, as they always did in Kino's churches, it puts good light in the sanctuary all day long, all year long. Secondly, it was defensive. Kino learned he couldn't have windows on the ground floor of his churches because the Apaches could force their way in through them. But the clerestory window is high, above the roofline of the nave, as you can see. It's wide, but no more than two or three feet high. Kino built elevated catwalks on the inside walls of his churches so Pima defenders could climb up to the window to fire their arrows at the attackers. If we had ladders to get up there, we could probably still find evidence of old holes in the adobe where they attached the joists that supported the catwalks."

Jiménez stared at the high walls and the ceiling. "So, Jorge, you're convinced the origins of this design are Andalusian?"

"Yes, it's mudejar, sir. Kino's construction methods came out of the Moorish traditions of conquered Spain. His churches look just about like the small churches in the rural areas of Andalusia except that he used local materials—mesquite, adobe, saguaro ribs, cane, things like that—to build them."

"You said earlier that he was a smart man, this Jesuit of ours. I'm definitely coming to believe it."

"He had a number of talents," Olvera said. "Priest, explorer, mathematician. Astronomer. Builder."

Jiménez laughed. "And cartographer. And don't forget, here in the Pimería he was a successful cattle rancher and farmer and vintner."

Outside again, Olvera and Jiménez examined the adobe walls and wooden doors. They made notes and took photographs and enjoyed the views from the hilltop. Before them lay the Altar Valley and through the shimmer of the summer heat they could see cottonwoods and hackberries and stands of grama grass growing near the river.

"He knew a few languages, too," Jiménez said, as if he'd been thinking about the padre's many talents as they worked. "How many languages do you suppose he spoke?"

"Seven, I think, sir."

"Seven?" Jiménez said. "Incredible. As a youngster, of course he would have spoken his native Italian. During his university years in Bavaria, he would've used German. In Seville he learned Español and spoke it the rest of his life. And as a priest, he knew Latin; he said mass in it and wrote many of his letters in it. And, over here, he would've become proficient in Piman. That makes, what, five? Well, okay, six, if you count the language of the Guaicuros in Baja California. Now that I think of it, somewhere I've read that he put together a diccionario of the Guaicuro language while he was there. But *seven*, Jorge? What am I missing?"

"Apache, sir."

"Ah, yes. He would've learned some of that, too."

Olvera chuckled. "A few curse words, at least."

Two days later, Arturo Romano reported on his excavations in the floor of the nave at the San Ignacio church, north of Magdalena. He had found the bones of two individuals: one, an infant; the other, a woman about nineteen years of age. He found no other bones. No priests; no Kino. He also reported that Dr. William Wasley and Dr. James Ayres, archaeologists from Tucson, and Sánchez de la Vega, the pharmacist from Magdalena, had dug up this same floor only a few months before.

"Looking for Kino, I assume?" Jiménez said.

"Not exactly, no," Romano said. "But it's an interesting story. Some years ago someone stumbled onto a metal box that had been buried in an arroyo in the desert near Cananea. The box contained papers and documents, including a confession written by a priest in 1844. The priest wrote that in the year 1820 he took from Magdalena several important documents relating to Kino, and buried them in a trunk under the floor of the church here at San Ignacio. On the back of the confession he had drawn a map showing precisely where he buried the trunk. Somehow Dr. Wasley and his group had come into possession of the map. They were here to look for the trunk."

"They found it?" Olvera said.

"They found no trunk," Romano said. "They found pottery sherds, beads, and pieces of cloth with gold threads embedded in it. They found some human bones, but these were jumbled up, as if treasure hunters had been there ahead of them. A physical anthropologist, Walter Birkby, examined the bones. He reported that none could've been from Kino."

"So," Olvera said, "no trunk, and still no Kino."

"So," Jiménez said. "We're back where we started."

"Except that now," Olvera said, "we know several places his bones are *not*."

"Good point, Jorge."

What had Father Campos written about the site he chose for Kino's burial? "*...And resting in the Lord, he is buried in this chapel of San Xavier on the side of the Gospel where fall the second and third sillas, in a Coffin...*"

Sillas. Campos hadn't meant chairs, they knew that now. He'd meant *sillares.* Ashlars. Foundation stones, footings.

By now Olvera had come to doubt that the Christians had moved Kino's body during the years of persecution. At least he'd found no convincing evidence that they had. And he was confident that nothing of the San Xavier chapel remained aboveground. He was equally sure, after his archival research and his diggings at Oquitoa, that the chapel's foundations would be footings of carved stone block or, more likely, of river rock embedded in a mortar of mud and clay. Perhaps there was a pedraplén under the bell tower, if there'd been such a tower. About that, he didn't yet know. But he would know those ashlars when he saw them.

"I think it's time," Olvera told Jiménez that sweltering afternoon in San Ignacio, "to begin our trenching in Magdalena. That's where we'll find our priest."

"In the past," Jiménez said, "you've mentioned Dolores. You no longer believe he might've been re-buried at the site of his old mission?"

Olvera shrugged. "It's possible. But at Dolores we have no idea at all where to begin a search. In Magdalena, I believe we do."

Jiménez pulled a bottle of water from his hip pocket and drank from it. From another pocket he pulled a map of Magdalena that showed the central plaza and, nearby, the town hall and parish church.

"All right, Jorge," Jiménez said, smoothing the map. "Show me where you would dig your first trench."

CHAPTER 29

Dolores at Cosari, the Pimería.
Año D. 1697. November.

ife is strange, is it not? Sometimes it comes at us at the oddest times, and from directions we least expect. It smacks us right in the eyes. You can be walking along, seemingly thinking of nothing in particular, and *aaiii caramba*, the person who appears before you is the very person whom you suddenly realize you had been thinking about all along. And life is particularly strange in this way when you are young and not quite sure of yourself. About some things, anyway. About *women*, anyway.

I almost dropped my quince candy when I saw her: Adriana Vásquez, from San Juan Bautista. Which explains much of my surprise, because I was in Cosari, at Father Kino's Dolores mission.

Allow me to explain, por favor.

This was the second day of November, after Kino's morning mass celebrating Dia de los Muertos, the Day of the Dead, at the cemetery behind the mission church. The Mass of the Dead, Kino called it. Though the padre regularly admonished us to remember and pray for the dead, the second of November was different, and always very special. On this day the gravesites would be swept, the wooden crosses repaired and coated with fresh whitewash, the dead remembered and celebrated. I never knew the origins of this tradition in Sonora, but they went way back. I have heard that the ancient Egyptians believed the souls of the dead returned to their family homes in what would be our month of November, and that the ancient Celts of Britain believed the dead rose briefly from their graves in this month. Even the Church seemed to encourage the legends: For centuries the first day of November has been celebrated as All Saint's day, the second, as All Soul's Day—a time of prayers for the dead.

But back to Adriana...That November morning was cool but sunny, the air filled with snowy white seeds from the desert broom that grew near the vegetable gardens. The spicy smells of grilling meats and hot tortillas and membrillo candy made from the pulp of quince fruits hovered over the cemetery, where vendors sold wool blankets and food and yellow flowers from carts with wooden wheels. Settlers and Indians and soldiers—all had come with their families for Dia de los Muertos, to hear the mass and visit friends and eat, to clean the graves and tend the grounds and pay their respects to the dead. Colorful ribbons hung from the newly-whitewashed crosses, and the grounds were dotted with earthen pots that brimmed with flowers.

Most of the flowers were cempazuchiles, marigolds, and when I saw Adriana she was holding one in her hand. She stood near the edge of the cemetery with her daughters, both as dark-eyed and pretty as their mother. Her black dress fit her perfectly, and she wore boots that were as dark and shiny as her hair. She wore bracelets of silver on her arms, and even through the crowds I could see the gold crucifix on the necklace of blue beads that nestled in the hollow of her dark slender neck.

Madre de Dios, she was something to make your heart pound! And at the moment mine was doing exactly that, tumbling and bouncing in my chest like a larval moth in a jumping bean.

Should I approach her and say hello? It had been months since I saw her at her husband's funeral and well over a year since she had found me unconscious in that dark street in San Juan. What if she did not remember me? What if she *did*? After all, the first time we met I was covered with blood and mud and I had reeked, she informed me, of cigars and cheap wine. I took a deep breath to calm myself, eased it out, and walked over to bow and greet her, my pulse thudding in my temples.

She remembered me. She smiled faintly—more out of politeness than anything else, probably—but she introduced me to her daughters and got my name right. "These are my children, Lieutenant Manje," she said. "Estafana and Julieta." I bowed and smiled and they greeted me with girlish grins.

Adriana and I talked of small and unimportant matters until her daughters scampered off to play with other children. By then most of my uneasiness had abated and I was able to speak without tripping too badly over my tongue. But at that moment my brain, unaccustomed to such social challenges, I suppose, totally abandoned me. It fled the premises. I know this to be so because I suddenly heard myself saying, "I had not expected to see you in Dolores, Señora Vásquez. I know your husband is buried in San Juan."

And of course the instant I said it I felt like a complete idiot. My face burned with embarrassment. "I beg you, Señora," I blurted, "please accept my apologies for my lapse of manners. Sometimes I say very dumb things."

She stared at me for a moment, her dark eyes unblinking. She sighed wearily and pointed to a nearby grave, where the dirt was neatly mounded and carefully swept. A pot of marigolds rested near the headstone, and on the stone I could see a name and dates: Emiliano Vásquez, 1692-1694.

"...Your son?" I said cautiously.

She nodded, and tossed a pebble onto the mound of dirt.

"I am most sorry," I said, and saw the tears that welled suddenly in her dark eyes. She had lost her husband this year, her son three years before. I had no idea what to say. All the words that rushed to my mind seemed foolish and trite.

She saw my predicament and mercifully saved me from it. "I miss him, of course," she said softly. "But I have come every year to celebrate the fact that he was a good boy and that he is in heaven now."

"Father Kino would surely agree with that."

"I was unsure what to do about my husband's grave. I tended it, of course, but what about this special mass? I suppose one November I will come here and the next I will stay in Real San Juan, and then come back here again the next." She shrugged. "I cannot be in two places at once."

"Señora, I am very sorry—"

She tossed another pebble onto the grave, then turned to me, her eyes still moist. "You are in uniform today, Lieutenant. Are you off on an expedition?"

As you can imagine, I was *very* happy for a change of subject. Maybe on some *other* topic I wouldn't make such a donkey of myself. "Father Kino and I are riding north," I said, "to the Río Gila."

"A long journey, is it not?"

"About a hundred and twenty leagues," I said.

"The desert will be nice this time of year."

"I have no doubt of it, Señora."

"I will pray for your safety, Lieutenant."

I made a slight bow. "Thank you."

She studied me for a time, wetness still glistening in her dark eyes. "Perhaps I should ask," she said, "how is your scalp from your injury that night in San Juan?"

"All healed, thanks to you."

She smiled, finally. "I am pleased to hear that," she said. "And I must say, you surely smell better now than you smelled then."

"Gracias," I said, and grinned, I fear, like a love-struck little boy.

That afternoon we rode out of Dolores headed for the northern lands—Father Kino, I, and ten Pimas from the San Miguel area, with a pack train of Wigberto's mules, all of which were loaded with food and supplies for ourselves plus gifts of ribbons, trinkets, shovels, hoes, and other simple articles of farming equipment that we would give to the Sobaipuri Pimas who lived along the Río Terrenate. On the way we stopped at several visitas and Pima settlements. Kino never traveled without a portable altar, vestments, and the silver chalice and plates he used in offering the unleavened bread for communion. Sometimes he carried a bell wheel, sometimes even a censer—his favorite looked like a lantern and was covered with Papago basket-weaving—for use in blessing the Indios with the sweet smells of incense. In each village he said mass and talked to the Indians about God's love and told them about Jesus and His death on the cross.

At Cocóspera we were welcomed by Father Ruiz Contreras, the new priest, and enjoyed his good and salutary company. We made stops at San Lazaro, Baosuca, and other places where Kino gave lessons on the Holy Faith and God's Commandments. On the 7th of November we arrived at a settlement we named Gaybanipitea. Here we were joined by Captain Bernal, Ensign Acuña, and twenty-one soldados from Fronteras. We stayed the night in an adobe house the Indians had built for visiting clergy. The villagers were happy to see us, and the local chief gave us small presents to make us feel welcome.

Thoughts of Adriana Vásquez helped me pass the boredom of long days in the saddle, though I have to say I was a little uncertain as to what such thoughts represented, or even why I bothered having them. I had made a complete fool of myself with my thoughtless comment about her husband. It seemed quite unlikely that she would have any interest in ever seeing me again. Still, images of her stunning dark face floated before me, and the thoughts came, and I did little to discourage them.

On the ninth we reached Quiburi, a prosperous settlement of Sobaipuris where Coro was chief. Around us we saw good pastureland and large fields of corn and beans and cotton, most under irrigation from the Terrenate. Coro and his people had thirteen fresh Apache scalps hanging from a pole in the village, and we joined the Pimas in celebrating their recent victories. Kino gave talks about God and His Holy Law, and we made many friends among the villagers.

Chief Coro and thirty of his men joined our growing party for our journey on to the north and to the Río Gila and the Casas Grandes.

What kind of man was Coro? He was much like Coxi, chief of the Pimas at Cosari and the villages on the San Miguel, both in appearance and countenance. He was tall, with good posture, bright curious eyes, and charcoal tattoos on his chin and wide dark forehead. He had shiny black hair cut in a ruler-straight line above his brows, and he had narrow shoulders, long, powerful arms, and short legs. Because he was bowlegged, he seemed almost to waddle when he walked. He wore little but a loincloth, though once in the rain I saw him in a handsome coat of antelope hide and he looked every bit a chief. Like Coxi, Coro was a formidable warrior. But he had to be, to survive. One look at a map will tell you why. Quiburi sat on the west bank of the Terrenate. Everything east of the river and north of Fronteras was Apachería—the land of the Apache and Jocome and Manso. Chief Coro's village sat on the very edge of sudden death.

I was always fascinated to see how quietly but quickly Father Kino developed friendships with the Indios. He was very direct in his speech and manners, never shying from the truth. Still, he had a way of energizing them, of somehow giving them comfort and aid in subtle and sometimes unexpected ways. I remember a conversation between Kino and Coro that illustrates this. At noon of our second day north of Quiburi, the two were sitting under a tree, eating tortillas and grilled peppers and drinking cool clean water from the river. Chief Coro's Spanish was primitive and the padre's Piman didn't include much of Coro's northern dialect, so Ensign Acuña translated.

Coro said, "Father, will you send a priest to live with us as we have asked?"

"I have written to the Provincial in Mexico City many times," Kino said. "A year ago I even went to see him about this matter. I asked him to send more priests." The padre laughed softly and rolled his eyes. "The Provincial says some day soon, my friend, some day very soon."

"I understand," Coro said solemnly when he heard Acuna's translation. "My wife gives the same answer when I ask her for another son."

Kino smiled and had another bite of pepper. "I hear that your wife sometimes fights alongside you against the enemies to the east. Is this true?"

"She is very strong, my wife. Yes, she kills many Apaches."

"And your children are well?"

"Yes. Six sons, three daughters. All healthy."

The padre thought about this. Finally he said, "Tending such a strong and vital family, fighting enemies, hunting, preparing the meals for all of you...perhaps your wife is just tired. But I will pray for her, Chief, and I will leave her some canutillo so she can brew a hot tea to take at her evening meal. If it is God's will, she will bear you another good son."

Coro ate in silence for a time, then said simply, "Mucho gracio, Padre."

They loved him.

And the padre, without hesitation, loved them back.

We continued downstream, never far from the rushing, tumbling waters of the Terrenate, moving steadily northward through smaller and even more isolated settlements of Sobaipuri Pimas. Baicatcan, Jiaspi, Muyva, Tutoyda; at each the padre said mass and baptized infants and gave talks on Jesus and the Apostles. Fortunately we saw no Apaches and we could simply enjoy the cool days and the arid beauty of the desert in autumn. Even so, we kept guards out at all times and never relaxed our vigilance.

It did not surprise me that Kino took every opportunity to make additions and corrections to his maps.

I always enjoyed watching him set up his astrolabe, take his altitude sights on the noonday sun or whatever night stars he was using, do the calculations that would give him our latitude, and carefully ink our location onto his much-used maps. To find the star's declination for the day, he used a book of mathematical tables written by Adam Aigenler, a famous cartographer who had been one of his professors in Germany. Kino never left Dolores without his compass, sundial, astrolabe, and *Aigenler's*, and in time I came to think of them as a natural part of his person, almost an extension of himself, much as his robe, vestments, and breviary always seemed to be.

He was good at cartography.

He was born, I had learned, in 1645, seven years after the birth of the man who would be known as Louis XIV, the Sun King of Versailles, and just one year after the Ming dynasty in China fell to the Manchus and Qing. By then, Jesuits born and educated in Europe had been exploring and writing and teaching in Asia and the New World for almost a century. And after riding with Kino for the past four years and watching him draw his maps, I had come to understand at least one of the reasons the Jesuits had been so successful: mathematics.

And one of its practical counterparts, astronomy.

The Black Robes had become experts at using their knowledge of science and mathematics to establish an influence within the governments of the countries in which they evangelized. This was particularly true in the Oriental provinces. Had they gone in without such influence, they might have been executed—beheading was the method of choice for proselytizers in much of China. But the Jesuits had used their skills at computational astronomy to show the superiority of European concepts on the movement of planets, stars, and comets in the heavens and had won the favor of important officials, first among the Ming, and then the Qing. This had given them, over time, enough influence in the imperial courts that they could preach their Christian beliefs with a bit less fear of losing their heads.

And this same body of scientific knowledge had made the Jesuits excellent navigators and mapmakers.

So Eusebio Kino was nothing new. He had been educated in theology, mathematics, and astronomy at the best universities in Germany, and he was simply continuing a way of life begun long ago by the energetic and scholarly followers of Loyola and Xavier.

Still, it was a pleasure to watch him make his maps.

On the sixteenth of November we reached the Gila, a large river that flowed westward, in some areas seemingly deep enough for small ships. We turned west, downstream, along the Gila's southern bank. Two days later we topped a steep hill that gave me my first view of the Casas Grandes. Even from this distance I could see that it had once been a thriving city of adobe buildings, some quite large. A canal from the river fed water to the city. At the city's edge the canal split in two and encircled the entire community, forming an excellent defensive moat and shunting off canals that would have irrigated gardens and neighboring fields. Later, we would measure this canal and find it thirty feet wide, twelve feet deep, almost eight miles in length, and so solidly built that deep water still flowed in it. Amazing.

In the largest building the padre said a mass. Afterward we had a meal of stewed onions and tepary beans prepared for us by our Pima servants. The day was damp from intermittent showers, the wind blustery and keening in the trees, but none of that kept us from enjoying our meal, then having a look around.

Centuries of rain and wind had eroded the roofs and upper parts of the adobe walls on most of the structures, but the lower portions were generally intact. At ground level the walls measured almost six feet in thickness. The inner surfaces were plastered, still as smooth to the touch as brushed wood, still as polished and shiny as the earthenware you can buy at the best mercados in Puebla. The largest building was four stories high, its window openings as square and straight as any I had ever seen.

"So what do you think?" the padre said when he found me studying one of the houses.

"The entire city is extraordinary, Father," I said. "It was large, and obviously a prosperous place—in its time. But now it is empty. The wind blows in the streets and through the windows and makes this eerie sound, as if the people who once lived here are warning us to leave."

Kino nodded, his gray-streaked hair ruffling in the breeze. "Many Pimas refuse to come here. They believe the place is haunted by the ghosts of their ancestors."

"How old do you suppose it is?"

"Coro says his people believe it's been here for hundreds of years. But empty and abandoned for as long as anyone knows."

"Who built it?"

Kino shrugged. "The legends say it was built by a powerful Indian chief called El Siba, which means 'the Cruel and Bitter King.' But nobody knows for sure who he was, or where he and his people came from."

A lot of people, Kino told me, believe El Siba was Aztec. They believed that the Aztecs had originally lived far north of the Gila, that they had been gradually forced southward by the Apaches, in time abandoning even this site to finally settle in the mountains in a place they called Tenochtitlan—until Hernán Cortés came with his horses and cannon and steel swords and took it from them and renamed it Ciudad de Mexico. And some Spaniards, Kino added, believe Casas was one of the Seven Cities of Cibola, thought by many to be filled with treasures of gold and silver and sought in vain for so long by Francisco de Coronado.

"Are you saying, Father, that there might be gold and silver here?"

"I have no reason to believe there is, Juan Mateo." He smiled. "Do not look so disappointed, my young friend. One day you will find a treasure of such value that it will be beyond your wildest dreams. It could be gold. Or perhaps silver, or even a beautiful woman who will become your wife."

I laughed. "You have been talking to Don Domingo again."

But as interesting and curious as the big houses were, a few days later I came across something that was, for me, more intriguing and much more likely to make me a wealthy man: red mud.

I saw it west of the Casas, at a small Pima settlement on the Gila that Kino had named San Andres. A young warrior there had painted his face and chest with the red pigment. I asked him where he had found it.

"Five days journey to the northwest," he told me through our interpreter. "Near a mighty river. We find it in the ground and mix it with dirt to make the mud." He brought some for me to see. It was a heavy liquid, thick and red and oily. With pressure the liquid easily squeezed through the chamois bag in which the Indio carried it. I sliced into it with my knife. The cut surface had the color of a lead musket ball.

My heart was pounding.

Father Kino, who had been watching, asked if I knew what it was.

"Quicksilver, I think," I said.

He nodded. "Probably. If so, it is valuable."

Quicksilver, mercury—whatever you chose to call it—was *extremely* valuable. Miners used it to separate bits of gold and silver from the sands and detritus that clung to them. They could not run their mines without it. To my knowledge there were only three mercury mines in the world: Almaden in Spain, Cuancabelica in Peru, and Carintia in Germany. The miners of Sonora, I knew, had always depended on imported mercury. Anyone who owned such a mine here would find himself a wealthy man indeed.

"Father," I said in my eagerness, "would you object if I were to ride to this big river we have heard about and have a look around?"

"If you want, certainly, go ahead," he said. "But there are Apaches in that area, so take some men with you." Behind him I could see the Gila, and orange sunlight reflecting off its rushing waters. The afternoon breeze, still cool and moist from the earlier rains, rustled the few brown leaves still left on the cottonwoods and sycamores that grew along the muddy banks.

But of course when I had time to think about it, I knew I could not go. We had too few soldiers and already our horses were exhausted. Too, I had promised Don Domingo I would stay at Father Kino's side.

I was disappointed, sure, but what could I do?

The next day we rode out, south along the Santa María, through the Pima villages of San Cosme del Tuk'shon, Bac, Tumacácori, and Guevavi, then to the more familiar Pima settlements of Cocóspera and Remedios, where Kino had already begun construction on good and salutary churches. Finally, we reached Dolores on the Río San Miguel, where I rested briefly before riding on to San Juan and the presidio.

Of course it was good to be home, to sleep again in a comfortable bed and to ease the aches of my saddle-weary body. But some day, I had determined, I would return to those northern lands. I would find the quicksilver.

CHAPTER 30

Sonora. Año D. 1698. January.

"She is very personable, Juan Mateo."

"I have no doubt of it, sir," I said to Don Domingo.

"And she is an appropriate age," he added. "Nineteen, her father tells me." We were in the general's airy quarters at the presidio in San Juan Bautista, where I was feeling the stern, unsmiling presence of the governors who stared down at me from their portraits high on the scrubbed white walls. I was also feeling the stern presence of Don Domingo. He was on yet another crusade, and this time it was not Apaches he was after.

"She plays the violin," he said. "Quite well, I hear." He studied his hands, then looked up at me. "A few years ago," he continued, "her father almost died. Smallpox, I would guess from the scars of his face. Anyway, when he recovered, his wife began having more children. First a girl, then two boys, with less than a year between them. Like a second family." Don Domingo shrugged. "Why did he have more children? Who knows. Perhaps his illness made him more aware of his own mortality. Perhaps, after coming so close to death, he decided he needed more sons to carry on the family name. That would not be unreasonable, I suppose. But my point here is that Zeferina, who was a teenager at the time, has a lot of experience with babies and small children."

I stared at him.

"*Zeferina*?" I said.

"Yes, Zeferina, that is her name. And remember, experience with babies and children is important for a young wife."

In my mind an image appeared, not completely unbidden, of a plump girl with bad skin, a screeching violin in one pudgy hand, a screaming baby in the other.

But personable.

Just as suddenly an image of Adriana Vásquez settled before my eyes, her skin smooth and dark, her black hair shining. I cannot swear to it, but I believe she actually winked at me. I watched her for a moment, then took a drink from the brandy that sat before me on the general's desk. When I tried to find her again she was gone.

"Well," I said finally. "I need to think about this, Uncle."

"What is there to *think* about? How old are you now? Twenty-seven? It is time for you to marry."

"Perhaps, sir. But even with my new promotion—which I am very grateful for, of course—I still have doubts that my salary would be adequate to support a wife and family." In the drafty room I could smell wisps of the general's cologne and smoke from the log fire that crackled in the corner fireplace.

I sipped again at the brandy and studied Don Domingo. His red tunic was freshly cleaned; his white pants, spotless. His coal-black hair, brushed neatly back and curled at the top of his collar, glistened in the afternoon light that streamed in the windows. He looked very professional, as he always did, and earnest, as he almost always did.

Now he leaned over his desk, poured more brandy for us, and smiled knowingly. "Her father has cattle all over southern Sonora. And more land than you can ride in a week. Some day, there could be a sizable inheritance."

"But I am a soldier," I said. "Not a rancher."

His dark eyes gleamed. "I know what you are *really* thinking. You are thinking this Zeferina is probably uglier than a pig in mud."

I sighed. "Not really, sir."

"Truthfully, I have not seen her, but her father assures me she is pretty, and I know him to be an honest and honorable man." The general smiled and leaned back in his chair, and by the look on his weathered face I knew the denouement was already winging its way towards me, like an iron bolt fired from a ship's cannon.

Denouement. I hated it when I used French words. When I used French words, even in fleeting thoughts like this one, something bad always happened to me.

This day was no exception.

"Zeferina's father and I," Don Domingo announced, "have taken the liberty of arranging a proper dinner party in Ures, so the two of you can get acquainted."

I massaged the bridge of my nose. "When would that be, sir?"

"The first week of March," he said earnestly and reached across and filled my brandy glass once again.

The last week of January I rode to Dolores on the San Miguel with two soldiers and three Piman servants to visit Father Kino, whom I had not seen in a while. We arrived at his mission on a pleasant winter day, the air crisp but comfortable, the sky a brilliant blue laced with clouds that gathered over the mountains like lumps of silver ore. I found Kino in his church, busily scrubbing the altar and dusting the paintings and figurines that filled the niches of the tall retablo built from planks of mesquite against the back wall. At first he did not see me, and for a time I quietly watched him as he went about his work. He wore only a white cotton shirt and loose dark pants, but even in the chill air of the empty adobe church a sheen of perspiration coated his narrow face. I heard the faint strains of an old Spanish children's song coming from somewhere nearby, and a moment passed before I realized they came from the padre, who was humming—off-key, as usual—as he toiled at his priestly chores.

He had aged some in the five years I had known him. His hair was noticeably grayer, though it had lost none of its thickness and still tumbled over his forehead and ears as if he had just stepped out of a windstorm. The lines seemed deeper in the flesh around his blue eyes, the wrinkles more obvious in the dark skin of his neck. Yet he had managed to stay slender and strong-looking, and I knew that even now he could ride as far and fast in a day as I could, which had always amazed me, as he was old enough to be my father. I suspect that most women would say he was quite handsome, though I always doubted he had much awareness of how he looked. Here I do not refer to his personal cleanliness. He was always clean—as clean, anyway, as a man can be on the frontier. But I had never seen him with a mirror. I could not imagine that he owned one, or even a hairbrush. His priorities, simply stated, lay elsewhere.

When he finally saw me, he smiled widely and hugged me to his chest. Then he stepped back and looked me over. "It is good to see you, Juan Mateo. I heard you had had a promotion, and I see it is true! Congratulations, *Captain*! And you look even more fit and hearty than the last time I saw you."

"Thank you, sir. And how are you these days?" This close now, I could see beads of sweat on his lip, and shiny streaks of it on his neck. "Are you feeling well, Father?"

"I have no complaints," he said, still smiling. "But tell me, my good friend, what brings you to the fringes of civilization on this fine January day?"

"Nice day for a ride," I said, feigning sincerity. "And I wanted to see for myself that you are staying out of trouble with the rector."

He chuckled. "We have much to talk about, you and I. But first we will get some food for your men and water for your horses." He found a servant and arranged for these things, then the two of us walked down the hill to his adobe quarters where we had a meal of tortillas with beans, onions, and corn. His blue eyes sparkled as we ate. "The Lord is with us in the Pimería," he told me. "We are baptizing more and more children these days, Juan Mateo, and our catechism classes are always full, not only here but at our other missions, too. Father Campos has finally finished rebuilding at San Ignacio. Father Contreras is doing well at Cocóspera, and I now have a new priest at Caborca. Yes, God is with us."

He paused, his eyes suddenly clouding. He made the sign of the cross and whispered a brief prayer. When he had finished, he explained. "Father Saeta. We cannot forget that he made the martyr's sacrifice at Caborca."

"I have not forgotten him, Father." I did not say so, but I had not forgotten, either, that it was just outside the doorway of Kino's quarters—not ten feet from where we now sat—that we had faced the insurrectos and the ma'makai. Those were not the kind of memories that fade just because a few years have slipped by.

"But I have more good news," Kino said, his face brightening again. "The new priest at Caborca has agreed to continue work on the barco we abandoned on the hillside there."

I took another bite of tortilla. "So we will have our boat?"

"If God in His wisdom wills it."

"And if the Father Visitor wills it?"

"Truthfully, I am not sure the Visitor, ah...knows about it...just yet."

I laughed. "He will not learn of it from me, sir."

"Good. But tell me, what have you been doing lately?"

"Looking for Apaches and Jocomes." I shrugged. "But we cannot find them. They seem to have disappeared from the earth. The general thinks they are gathering at one of their rancherias in the mountains, getting drunk on tiswin and planning something big for the first warm days of springtime."

Kino wiped sweat from his forehead with a cotton cloth. "I pray they decide against it. Our Pimas need an end to these horrible wars."

"As we all do, sir," I said, and wondered again why the padre was sweating so much. I wanted to ask him about it, but decided that would be improper.

We talked of other things, too, most of them considerably less somber. He told me the latest news from Campos at San Ignacio, and I told him of the army's latest deeds and misdeeds, and even a few of my own. I thought briefly about telling him of my feelings for Adriana, the widow of Sergeant Vásquez. But finally I decided against it. Why, I was not quite sure, though I knew with certainty why I had not told Don Domingo: he would not approve. Not because Adriana was a poor widow with children, but because she had little education and because she had been the wife of a soldier who had not been an officer. I did not blame the general for his views. That is just the way things were in those days. Still are, usually.

But I did tell Kino about the general's ongoing plot against my bachelorhood with the rich ladies of Sonora.

He chuckled. "Well, what did you expect? You are very eligible, you know. It is not fair to the ladies to forever deprive them of your companionship."

"We are riding to Ures in March," I grumbled, "to meet one of them. Zeferina. I do not even know her last name."

"Don Domingo just wants the best for you."

I sighed. "Yes, Father, I know." I had more tortilla and studied the images of Adriana Vásquez that were winking at me again from the veiled corners of my mind.

But the general and I did not make it to Ures in March. On the 25th of February, an unusually large force of Jocomes and Apaches under Black Skull and Oso Azul attacked and plundered the village of Cocóspera, burning the mission church and outbuildings and killing several Pimas and virtually all the livestock. The resident priest, Father Contreras, valiantly defended his adobe quarters with the help of a few Pima neophytes and miraculously survived. But the size of the enemy force and the extent of the desecration called for a rapid response from our army and substantially changed the general's plans for me, at least for the moment.

Don Domingo quickly mobilized a unit of the Compañía and Kino brought in Pima warriors from villages along the Río San Miguel. With a dozen or so Ópatas from San Juan and another dozen Maricopas who were visiting from the northern rivers, we made a sizable force.

We caught up to the Apaches in the Chiricahuas north of Fronteras, laid an ambush, and killed thirty of them. In the process we took sixteen captives and recovered a number of stolen horses and other booty. Unfortunately we lost several men to arrow wounds, and one of our best corporals died from hemorrhage after a lance wound of his groin. The Lord, though, had smiled on me again. I sustained a knife cut on my neck, but it was small and with His help I had no other injuries. I could not guess how much the mine owners at Alamos paid the civil authorities in San Juan for the Apache captives, but it would have been a lot, as all the Indios were young and looked to be in salutary health.

The newfound peace did not last long.

At daybreak on March 30th, another band of Apaches under a young hothead named Capotcari carried out a raid on the Sobaipuri village of Gaybanipitea, not far from Quiburi, on the Río Terrenate. They sacked and burned the village and killed all the Pimas who chose to stay and fight. Word of these atrocities quickly reached Coro, the chief at Quiburi. He gathered his warriors and rode swiftly for the little village, where the Apaches were still celebrating their victory. Of course we in the Compañía learned of these things too late to be of much help.

Coro, it turned out, had little need of our help. But the events of that day still fascinate and haunt me, because it must have been a scene worthy of the noblest Roman gladiators. For this reason I have included here the relevant portions of the report I filed to the bishop and viceroy on this unusual and glorious incident after I had completed my investigations for Don Domingo:

Capotcari, the young Apache leader, had quickly seen that his forces were outnumbered by Coro's men. He sent a runner to Coro with a novel suggestion: Each leader would choose his ten best fighters, and the ten Apaches would meet Coro's ten Pimas on a field of battle. Coro agreed to these terms and picked nine men, naming himself as the tenth. Capotcari, we later learned, did the same.

It is easy enough to imagine the scene. On an open plain, hundreds of Pimas and Apaches, ancient enemies, forming a boistrous, surging circle, and in the center of the circle, twenty men, facing off, preparing themselves and their weapons for a fight to the death.

I suspect that most settlers and other civilians in Sonora, at a contest like this, would have put their money on the Apaches. Those of us in the Compañía knew better. The Pimas, more skilled than their foes at deflecting arrows with their war shields, managed after a long bloody fight to kill the first nine Apaches. Capotcari, the lone survivor of his chosen ten, then challenged Coro. "We will settle this here and now," he shouted in Spanish, "mano-a-mano!" He should not have. Coro, his charcoal tattoos garish and raw in the afternoon light, quickly threw him to the ground and pounded his skull into bloody shards with a stone.

From what we later learned, this is what happened in the next moments and hours: The other Apaches, stunned by what they had seen and fearing for their lives, fled the area, some on horseback, others afoot. The Pimas, emboldened by their victory, chased them down and killed as many as they could, including the Apache women who had fought alongside the men.

As I have previously stated, I did not personally witness these amazing events, but Sergeant Escalante and I and our soldados arrived at the Terrenate in time to count the

Apache dead for Don Domingo's report: fifty-four at the scene of the fight; and many more who had made it into the hills and nearby mountains before succumbing to the hemorrhage and painful convulsions that followed poisoning by the sap of the yerba de flecha that the Pimas use so effectively on their arrowheads.

Your Excellency can be justly proud of the work of these brave Pimans who, as you can see, represent the highest standards of loyalty so earnestly desired for the Christianized natives of these newly-conquered lands by Our Lord and Christ, by His Majesty, King Carlos Segundo, and by all civil and military authorities who toil for God and King on this desert frontier. Respectfully submitted,

Juan Mateo Manje, Captain
For General Domingo Jironza Petris de Cruzat

On the third day of our investigation, Sergeant Escalante and I were counting enemy bodies in an arroyo when we saw riders approaching. The sky was overcast, the morning air cool and damp and filled with drifting mists that seemed to rise up from the Terrenate like wispy white ghosts and inch their way into the canyons and onto the mountainsides. Appropriate, I supposed, for a place that was slick with blood and littered with corpses that had already begun to bloat and stink. Frankly, I would have preferred a warm, sunny day for such work, but I was not complaining. The chill air probably slowed the putrefaction and made our chore manageable, if not exactly pleasant. In the distance I could see coyotes gathering on a ridge, and vultures with black wings circling low over the mountain.

I found the riders with my telescope.

"Father Kino," I said, surprised. "And some Pimas."

They reached us half an hour later. We welcomed them with a bag of oranges and drew water from the river for their mounts.

"Juan Mateo," Kino said after seeing to his horses. "I had little faith in the reports I heard in Dolores about this great fight. I believed they had to be greatly exaggerated."

"And you came to see for yourself?"

He nodded and looked around, to the dead Apaches and the boulders stained with blood and half-dried vomitus. A rime of sweat veneered the padre's forehead, and his blue eyes seemed pale and wet.

"The reports are true, Father," I said. "The Pimas have won a glorious victory here."

"God was with them," he said solemnly.

"Indeed He was, sir."

"How many dead?"

"We have counted over fifty, so far. Of course some of Coro's men died, too, but only a few."

"And how are you, Juan Mateo? Are you all right?"

"Fine, sir." I touched the lapis stone under my uniform blouse. "I think the cross has brought me good luck."

Finally he smiled. "It is not *luck* that keeps you alive, my friend, it is God's love. He has more work for you in the Pimería, so He is taking good care of you."

"It does seem that way," I said. "And you are all right, yourself?"

"Excellent," he said.

But in spite of his assurances, he looked unwell to me, though I had a hard time saying exactly why. Perhaps it was the sweating. Perhaps his skin was a bit more pale, the flesh around his eyes slightly swollen. I had a sense, too, that he had lost weight. I would have liked to ask him about these things, but knew I should not so I refrained.

After Kino had performed burial sacraments for the Pimas who had died in the fight, he told me he wanted to do his own count of the dead Apaches. "For my report to the Church officials," he explained. "There are some in the provincial's office in Mexico City and even in the offices of the rector in Arizpe who persist in believing the Pimas are in league with the Apaches in their depredations against the settlers and miners. Perhaps this will put an end to such nonsensical thinking."

"I hope so, Padre," I said, and assigned a corporal and four men to accompany him, in the event that some Apache was not quite as dead as he looked.

The last time I saw him that day he was climbing a hill with the soldiers, a wet cloth at his nose in a vain attempt at repelling the rising stench of death.

The next months were busy ones for the Compañía Volante. I was in the saddle almost constantly, though we saw little of the Apaches and Jocomes. Chief Coro's glorious victory over them in April had apparently broken their morale and driven them back to their rancherias high in the eastern mountains. Father Kino stayed occupied, I heard, with teaching and other duties and with the plantings, harvests, and ranching chores that always consumed so much of his time at the missions. I had no reports that he was ill, though, so over time I forgot the fever—if that is what it was—that I had witnessed in January and again in April.

In August I reluctantly rode with General Jironza through the summer heat to a ranch near Ures, where at a lavish party at a great hacienda, I finally met Zeferina.

Actually she was quite attractive and very pleasant, and rumors had it that she found me equally favorable. When we left at the end of the week Don Domingo expressed his fervent hope to her father that Zeferina and I would be seeing much of each other in the coming months.

Perhaps we might have, had it not been for Adriana Vazquez.

CHAPTER 31

Near Banámichi, Sonora. Año D. 1698. September.

For the ceremony the girl's friends had daubed black mud around her eyes. Brightly-colored beads decorated her buckskin skirt and coat and she wore a white cotton blouse and a necklace made from the polished white bones of small animals. Her black hair was cut straight and neatly, just above her brows. In the weeks leading up to the ceremony, her mother had collected the sap of mesquite trees, dried it, pounded it to a dark powder, and mixed it with rich black mud she had scraped from an irrigation canal. The night before the ceremony she would have smeared the mud on the girl's hair and covered her head with a damp cloth. The morning of the first day of the festivities—today—she had rinsed out the mud. Now, with the girl's hair clean and shiny, both daughter and mother were beaming with pride.

Three days from now, on the last day of her puberty ceremony, women of the village would rub charcoal into puncture wounds they would make in her lower eyelids and at the corners of her lower lip with spines from the plant the Pimas call *uhs chewadpad* and we call *corona de Cristo*—the crucifixion thorn. From that moment on, she would be a woman. For now, though, she was free of tattoos and pretty as a painting and still a girl.

Brigida, her name was. Piman, from a small settlement near Banámichi, a cousin of White Leaf, the precocious young muchacha from Dolores who had killed the rattler that day...when, five years ago? Except that White Leaf was no longer precocious and no longer lived at Dolores. Now she was a beautiful young woman who had had her own puberty ceremony a few years before. She and her husband, Antonio, lived in Banámichi, and they had generously invited me to the ceremony. They had been surprised by the early arrival of a new baby, though, and I doubted I would see them this day.

I guessed the number of family, guests, and villagers at two hundred, plus a dozen or so vendors selling flowers and chocolate and quince candy and tortillas with onions and peppers and grilled carne. The place was noisy and crowded, and in the open area around the vah'kih that marked the center of the village, almost everyone was eating or talking or keeping time with their feet to the steady beat of the Piman drums.

The weather was just about perfect. The midday sun was strong but temperatures had already begun to abate as autumn moved slowly down the mountains and the soft yellow hues of early fall stretched from the foothills onto the rolling plain that characterizes this portion of the Sonoran desert. On the ride from San Juan I had seen goldeneyes in full bloom, and asters, and sunflowers six feet tall; lemon-colored meadowlarks and the tiny white flowers of seep willows in thickets near shallow streambeds. I saw red chiltepine peppers growing in the flats and smelled the richness of the earth and the gentle scent of gatuños, the pink blossoms of the mimosas that thrive on the rocky slopes of canyons and draws. Yes, it was quite a magnificent day.

I was watching Brigida as she danced with other Pima youngsters, her dark hair glowing in the afternoon sunlight, when I saw half a dozen women standing together near the edge of the crowd. They were young, dark-skinned, and well-dressed. All were quite pretty. My eyes kept drifting back to them, and finally I realized why: *one of the women was Adriana Vásquez!*

She was as beautiful as I remembered, her black hair even longer, her skin as smooth as any I had ever seen. Her yellow dress was cut low on her bosom and when she turned a little, her dark eyes following Brigida and the Pima dancers, I saw sunlight glinting from the gold crucifix that hung from the chain of tiny blue beads against the dark skin of her neck.

Madre de Dios, I felt my heart thudding in my chest!

Would she talk to me? Or would she turn her back? Who could blame her if she did, after our last conversation? At the cemetery in Dolores, when I made such a dumb and inappropriate comment about her husband, *aaaiiii*, I hated to even *think* about it.

I knew of only one way to find out if she would talk to me: walk up to her and say hello. Then I heard a voice in my ear saying, *But be smart about it, Juan Mateo, take a peace offering. And try not to look too nervous.*

Excellent ideas, both, I thought. I found a vendor, an old Indian with leathery dark skin, and bought a bouquet of blue flowers, then worked my way back through the crowd. I bowed deeply and handed the bouquet to Adriana. "Buenos tardes, Señora. Como esta usted?"

Her eyes widened, but she recovered quickly. "I am doing well, Captain Manje." She hesitated, and made—a bit awkwardly, I thought—a slight curtsy. A flush spread across her lovely face, but was gone in the next instant. She smiled at the flowers. "These are for me?" Her voice sounded scratchy, almost hoarse, but that passed quickly, too. "Thank you! They are so pretty!"

"It is an unexpected pleasure to find you here, Señora."

She introduced me to her friends. One of them, I learned, knew Brigida's family. Adriana and the others had hired a wagon and driver from Wigberto and had come from San Juan to see the girl's puberty ceremony.

"And how are your daughters?" I asked Adriana.

"Fine," she said. "At home, behaving themselves, I hope."

"Would you join me for some chocolate? Something to eat?"

She hesitated, then said, "I suppose that would be all right."

I bought chocolate and sticks of quince candy and we sat on a bench under a towering mesquite, sipping our drinks and nibbling on the candies as we talked of small things and I tried to act as if I were not at all nervous. I doubt I fooled her, but she was pleasant enough that I had at least some hope that she had forgotten my prior offense.

"You look nice today," I said. Yellow, I had decided, was a very good color for her. It brought out the glow in her dark eyes and the beauty of her smooth dark skin.

"Thank you for your kind comment, Captain. The last time I saw you, you were going off to the far north country with Padre Kino. How was your journey?"

"Interesting," I said. I told her about the Río Gila and the giant adobe houses called the Casas Grandes that no one lived in, and about the Indian at San Pedro with face paint made from quicksilver.

"I can tell from the look in your eyes," she said, "that you are going back some day to find that quicksilver."

"If I can," I said.

"Perhaps some day you will be a rich man."

I grinned. "I certainly hope so."

"I wish you luck, Captain."

I believe she enjoyed our conversation, though we talked of nothing of very great importance. After a time she stood and smiled. "Please excuse me, but I must get back to my friends." She laughed softly. "If I stay much longer, they will think you kidnapped me."

"Of course." I stood and bowed. "I would like to see you again, Señora. In San Juan." I cleared my throat, praying that I had not sounded too forward, or too much like a lovelorn schoolboy. "May I call on you?"

Her dark eyes drifted away. "I think it unwise," she said finally.

A lead weight landed in my stomach. Behind her I could see a woodpecker with a red splotch on its head tapping briskly at the thick skin of a saguaro that was plump from the summer rains.

"Por favor," I said, "would you tell me your reason?"

"You know the reason, Captain. You are a good and decent man and, here, it was nice to see you. But back in San Juan, things are different. You know that."

"But Señora—"

"We come from different worlds, Señor. Nothing can change that."

I stood under the tree and watched her start back for the vah'kih and the noisy crowds and her lady friends. A few yards away she stopped and turned. "Thank you for the flowers," she said softly. "They are beautiful." Her eyes were dark and round and completely unreadable.

I bowed again, and gave her the best smile I could manage.

Later that day I rode out of the village and reached the river as the sun slipped behind mountains hidden by a gauzy gray haze in the fading light of dusk. I guess I was thinking about Adriana and not what I was doing, and it almost got me in trouble. I had left my mount below and climbed a low hill to a boulder-strewn ridge that overlooked the river. At the top I found myself looking down on a dozen or so Indians on the opposite bank. I quickly dropped to the ground and slipped behind a boulder. I heard no shouts and had no reason to believe they had seen me. Still, I waited a full five minutes, my pistols and sword at hand, before I risked another look. What I saw amazed me.

The Indians—Apaches—coated head to foot with thick rich mud, were stalking wild ducks that drifted on the surface of the river.

Even with the mud I knew they were Apaches by their horses, ground-tied in a stand of sycamores near the river: paints, rather than the larger, darker mustangs, descendants of Barbs and Andalusians, that the Pimas and Ópatas usually rode.

The Indians were quietly carrying large yellow gourds down to the water and setting them afloat. As I watched, they put out perhaps twenty of these. At first the ducks would flee when a gourd drifted near. But after a time they seemed to lose their natural fear of the gourds and allowed them to come closer. By then, each Apache had pulled over his head a similar gourd, with small cutouts for his eyes and nose. The Indians slipped soundlessly into the water, even imitating the natural bobbing of the gourds on the waves as they approached the unsuspecting ducks. When they were close enough they grabbed the creatures by their feet, pulled them under, drowned them, and stuffed them into deerskin bags tied at their waists. Back on the riverbank they started a fire, cleaned the ducks, and roasted them on sticks over the flames. I must have been hungry, because the smell of roast duck tormented me until I reached my horse and got myself out of there.

They are clever people, the Apaches.

But strange, too, in a lot of ways. For instance, no one knows much about their religion, but the little I have learned has never made sense to me. Of course I am a Christian and, to be truthful, that has colored my attitude.

They are, in their language, Tinneh—The People. They believe they were created first and that all other humans are essentially irrelevant and inherently inferior. Of course the Pimas are The People, too. O'odham, in their language. I have no idea what the Ópatas and Maricopas and all the others call themselves, but it would not surprise me to learn they were The People, as well.

The Apaches, I have learned, have two gods. Ussen is their god of good things. The god of bad things they call Evil Spirit. As Father Kino explained it to me, an Apache cannot approach Ussen directly by way of prayer. He has to go through an intermediary. This might be a medicine man, or possibly the Apache's own spirit guide, which could be an eagle, a bear, a panther, the moon—whatever entity he had accepted as his mentor and guide in his youth. Through this intermediary he can ask Ussen for good things—such as strong children, or a faithful wife, or victory in battle. On the other hand, if he sought *bad* things—to wish upon his enemies, for instance—he could pray directly to Evil Spirit for bad luck in battle, or poor hunting, or serious illness, such things as that.

All Apaches, Kino had told me, believe in the magical powers of pollen. Sometimes their pollen came from corn, but more often from cattails that grew along streambeds. They believe in the holiness of the four cardinal directions—east, south, west, and north—and these figured prominently in their ceremonies, but also in their daily activities. The number four was important to them in other ways, too, according to Kino. Warriors, for instance, often wore four feathers in their headbands, and the youngest warriors, the apprentices, carried four arrows.

When Father Kino told me these things—on a harsh day of my first winter in the Pimería—we were in his mission church at Dolores, a rime of ice weighing on the heavy wood doors, wind whistling through the bare branches of the mesquites outside the adobe walls. In spite of my bravado, in those first months I was very naïve and more than a little frightened, still much in awe of the Apache.

"Is there anything they *fear*?" I had asked the padre. I had considerable interest in this subject, as I had had my own share of fears since coming to the Pimería.

He looked at me for a time, then smiled faintly. "They fear snakes. And owls. And, probably more than anything, they fear witches."

"*Witches*?"

He nodded. "Anything they do not understand and cannot explain by way of their own experience or fit into their own belief system, they generally consider it the work of a witch."

After a time I said, "Tell me about their medicine men."

"They call them di-yins," he said. "Apaches believe they have special powers. Like power over war. Or curing illnesses. Controlling the weather, predicting the future. You know of Mofeta? A lot of people assume he is a chief, but he is not."

"He is a di-yin?"

Kino nodded. "But only for war. No one knows what his real name is. The Pimas call him Skunk—Mofeta—because of the smelly herbs and dead animal parts he carries in his medicine pouch. But he is a smart man, Juan Mateo, and extremely dangerous. Do not underestimate him or any of the others just because they are superstitious."

I remember staring at my sword in the flickering light, and at my pistols, and wondering if I was strong enough and smart enough to survive in such a strange and primitive place as the Pimería.

The padre read my mind—as he always seemed to do in those early years—and said, "Do not worry, Juan Mateo. You will be fine."

"Yes, I will, sir."

He smiled. "Be armed with knowledge and faith," he had said, his blue eyes glowing, "and God will take care of you."

He had taught me the Pimas' pagan beliefs, too. Before the Jesuits came, the Pimas' main deity was one they called Tars, the sun god. They believed that Tars controlled everything that happened during daylight hours. A god they called Night controlled everything between dusk and dawn. But there were lesser gods, too. Tcu'wit Makai controlled the weather. Si'uu, who, like I'itoi of the Papagos, was Elder Brother. Then there were gods like Tcopiny Makai who lived in houses on the far horizon where the sun rose and set, and others like Lightning Magician, that lived along the sun's arc in the sky.

And of course the Pimas had medicine men, too, some of them bad like the ma'makai, believed to have influence with Tars and the other gods that controlled wars and weather, and like the si'atcokam, who diagnosed illness by blowing coyote tobacco smoke over the sick and making their phony diagnoses from images seen in the haze. And the good medicine men, like the hai'itcottam, who used herbs and common sense and simple remedies to treat illness.

Kino said the Pimas, like the Apaches, apparently had no concept of life after death, except for their belief that the souls of the dead sometimes entered the bodies of owls and regularly attempted to torment the living. But before the missionaries came, the Pimas had had no idea of heavenly reward or eternal punishment for their behavior on earth.

"Some of them," Kino had said, a note of irritation creeping into his voice, "are *still* pagan. Of course you would expect that from the ma'makai and their followers, but a lot of Pimas who have accepted Jesus as their Savior still practice the old ways along with the new."

This was, I had since learned, a persistent source of irritation to the priests on the frontier, not just here in the Pimería, but in all of New Spain and even in the Orient. The truth was, many Christianized natives continued to believe in their old gods and to participate in their ancient rituals even as they worshipped their new-found God in the mission churches. In time I came to see that some priests—after lengthy struggles with their consciences, no doubt—accepted this duality of devotion as the best they could do with the Indians, and made their peace with it. I had learned not to raise the subject of such realities around Kino, though. Some days he seemed almost resigned to them, but other days, *aaiiii caramba!*

But after seeing Adriana again, she was still on my mind, and on my ride back to San Juan I thought much more about her than I thought about Apaches or Pimas or medicine men or Father Kino.

I spent much of the next few months on patrol with the Compañia, but little happened. We saw a few hostiles near Nacosari and, later, near Arizpe. But we failed to kill or capture any of them. Which meant that for a time the silver miners at Alamos and the ranchers of Durango had to look elsewhere for laborers. But at least we lost no men and suffered no serious injuries.

In October I saw Adriana Vásquez again, quite by accident, this time in Real San Juan. I had ridden in from the presidio to see a government official about a tract of land I hoped to buy. My business concluded, I stepped out of his office—and there she was, across the street. As I watched her, she went into a store in a row of small flat-roofed adobe buildings that housed businesses selling hardware, herbs, guns, textiles, and other items to the army and the citizens of San Juan. I slipped across the street for a closer look. A sign near the door read, "Alterations; Ladies' Dresses. A. Vásquez, Prop."

Interesting, I thought. So *that* is how she supported herself and her daughters. I had wondered, but I had had no proper way to inquire. Through an open window I could see her girls. Estafana? Julieta? That sounded right. I guessed their ages at five and six, though I could not remember which was which. They were playing a children's game on the floor and I could hear their laughter and loud chatter. They wore white dresses that seemed simple but clean and well-made. Adriana had brushed their hair back in braids that she had tied with ribbons of pink silk.

Aaaiiii, at that moment I wanted to talk to Adriana more than I had ever wanted anything in my life. I remembered her words from our last conversation. *We come from different worlds, Señor. You are a good and decent man and I have enjoyed seeing you here in Banámichi, but things are different back in San Juan, you know that.*

I knew that, yes, but in spite of it I wanted to see her again. I glanced at my timepiece, and it gave me an idea. In one of the markets on the plaza I bought green peppers, goat cheese, tortillas, and four flasks of chocolate. I carried them in a sack to Adriana's store. Estafana and Julieta were still playing on the floor. When I walked in, they looked up, curious. I saw no sign of Adriana. I held my finger to my lips. "Sshhh," I whispered.

The girls giggled.

With an overly dramatic flourish, I set the sack on a table that was littered with scissors and snippets of colored cloth. The adobe walls were bare but there were other tables around, and a few chairs and a rack that held some dresses. I pulled the tortillas from the sack and, with another flourish, placed them on the table.

Adriana picked that moment to walk in from the back room.

Startled probably isn't a strong enough word to describe her reaction. "*Madre de Dios!*" she cried. Her hand flew to her mouth, her eyes wide with surprise. She wore a dark skirt, a white blouse cut low, and a necklace made of red stones that looked like tiny balls of fire against her smooth dark skin.

I smiled. "Señora and Señoritas," I said, and bowed.

The girls giggled again. "You are a soldier," one of them said.

I nodded.

"Our father was a sergeant. What are you?"

"A captain," I said.

"Is that higher than a sergeant?"

"About the same," I said.

They giggled again.

I glanced at my timepiece. "It is time to eat."

And we did. Adriana put a cloth on the table and found some napkins and we had a fine meal—once she got over the shock of it, anyway. We talked about a lot of things and the girls chirped in when they felt like it. I do not know what Adriana thought of our little picnic, or even what her daughters made of the situation, but I enjoyed it. Maybe it was not quite fair for me to use Estafana and Julieta to get my foot in the door with Adriana, if that is what I had done, but–

All right, so that is *exactly* what I had done. Still, I had no regrets.

Well, I had *one* regret. Adriana was still calling me Captain. Not once had she called me Juan Mateo. I vowed to work on that. But she had talked to me, and after our earlier conversations, that was more than I had expected.

I whistled all the way back to the presidio.

The next time I saw Father Kino he had just returned to Dolores from a three-week expedition to the Pima settlements along the Gila. I had ridden over to take his report for the general and found him at his mission church, in the sacristy, a small low-ceilinged adobe room that he used as an office.

He welcomed me with a warm embrace and poured chocolate for me from a pewter pot. We sat in chairs made from planks of mesquite wood and exchanged pleasantries and idle gossip for a while, but he was impatient to tell me about his journey, about the baptisms and masses and the tattooed, dark-skinned Pimas who had happily received his talks on Jesus and salvation, so I listened and made notes for Don Domingo's files. "They were jubilant, Juan Mateo," the padre said, smiling as he always did when he talked about new converts. "They are fine, decent people, and I am convinced they want to know the Lord."

"That is good news, sir." The room's adobe walls were bare except for a single painting that hung behind his pine-planked desk. It was someone's version of the Last Supper, with Jesus seated at a table, the apostles gathered around Him. The painting was done in soft but vibrant colors, and the artist had succeeded nicely in showing the sorrow on the apostles' faces and the details of their clothing.

I laughed. "I had not seen the art work before."

Kino's face gave away nothing. "Is there something wrong with it? Why are you laughing?"

All summer I had been wearing the little lapis cross around my neck—hoping it would bring me good fortune with Adriana, though I knew better than to say such a thing to the padre—and the cord was chafing my skin. I untied it and laid it with the blue cross on the desktop. "I see nothing wrong with the painting," I said, chuckling again, "except that the Apostles are wearing loincloths and they have charcoal tattoos on their faces."

Kino tried to keep his deadpan face, but could not do it. Finally he laughed. "It was painted by one of our Indios here. It is very good, is it not? But you are right, maybe I should think about talking to the Pimas again about the people who lived in the Holy Land in Jesus' time."

We had a good laugh about the painting, then talked about other matters for a while. I asked the padre about the fall harvests and winter plantings.

"I think things have gone well," he said, "though I have to ride out to the fields tomorrow and see for myself. Believe me, I would rather do *that*...than deal with *those* things." He pointed to a stack of papers on the floor.

I leaned over for a closer look. "Letters?"

He nodded, his blue eyes sparkling. "From the Rector."

"How is Father Mora these days?"

"I cannot comment on his general state of mind, but I can tell you he is not happy with *me*. His first letter registered his complaints about our boat project at Caborca. The second was a copy of a letter he wrote to the Provincial in Mexico City. In it, Mora said I was away from Dolores too much, always chasing off after *new* converts when I should be home tending to my *own* Pimas. In the next letter he complained that our wheat crops have been too large in recent years, and *that*, of course, creates too much work for our Pima laborers." Kino laughed and rolled his eyes. "So I tossed the rest of his letters on the floor there. Some day I will read them, but it will probably be a while."

But in spite of his jovial mood, the padre was tired. I could see it in the flesh around his blue eyes, in the pallor of his skin, the slackness of his posture. He had traveled eight hundred miles in the past month and it showed. Though I had never heard him complain, for two or three years I had been aware that he sometimes had pain in his back and hips. I had seen it in his gait, in the way he walked. This day at Dolores I saw it again.

And his fever had returned, I was sure of it. He had lost weight, and I could see a veneer of sweat on his dark forehead and neck.

He pulled out his latest map of the Pimería and with much delight pointed out his route and the Indian villages he had visited. As he talked, though, I found myself paying little attention. Instead I was thinking about his fever, if that is what it was, and wondering if he had tried cinchona.

If you have ever lived in Nueva España, you have probably heard of cinchona. Jesuits' bark, it is often called. In the early years of this century, missionaries in Peru learned from the Indians that an extract from the bark of the cinchona tree sometimes cured intermittent fever. Over the years this knowledge had made its way to Europe and northward even as far as Sonora. By the 1690's the extract could be found in the farmacias of most army surgeons and other frontier doctors. *Intermittent fever*. I have never claimed to know much about illness or prostrations, but I would have bet money the padre had it. Intermittent fever, tropical fever, marsh fever; it went by a variety of names. No one knew its cause, but it seemed to occur in association with the agues and miasmas that often rose like fog from the tidal waters along the oceans and gulfs and, inland, from pools of stagnant water where the air was thick with dampness and dark buzzing insects.

I knew it was improper to ask, but I could contain my curiosity no longer. "Forgive me, Father," I said, "but do you have a fever?"

He shrugged. "A little, perhaps." He stared at me, his blue eyes unblinking, then casually said, "Yes, I have tried cinchona. It helped some."

There he was, reading my mind again. But he had no more interest in the subject of fevers. He retrieved a magnifying lens from his desk and held it over his new map of the Río Gila. For a time he was quiet, studying, busy with his thoughts. After a while he set the lens down and leaned back in his chair. He wiped sweat from his forehead and sighed. "So many new souls, Juan Mateo. And they are so far away. How can we reach them all? How can we assure them of salvation unless we preach to them regularly and hear their confessions and offer them the sacraments?"

"I do not know, Father." In the light from a clerestory window high on the wall, the lapis cross winked at me from where I had set it on the desk. I picked it up, idly flipped it over, and set in on the desk again. A few inches away a tiny black insect was crawling across the desk, slowly working its way toward the little cross. I picked up the padre's hand lens and studied the insect. It had a shiny back and a little round head and lots of short little legs all moving at once. It stopped, and I could imagine it looking up, seeing my big brown eye in the lens, wondering what I was doing. Then it started up again and with the lens I followed its slow progress toward the little blue cross.

"I hope to go back to the Gila soon," Kino said. "Perhaps some day we will have enough priests to keep one in that area on a permanent basis. If we had six more men, we could do a proper job for the Lord here in the Pimería and still be able to expand our ministry west to the Californias and north to—"

But I was not listening to him or even paying much attention to what I was doing with the lens. I was still thinking about the padre's fever and the Peruvian Indians and their cinchona—and maybe even a little about Adriana and her smooth dark skin and ink-black hair—so it might have been a moment before I realized what I was looking at through the lens.

"You are smiling, Juan Mateo. What have you found?"

I glanced up. "A bug."

"A *bug*?"

"Yes, sir, a very interesting bug. And this bug has just led me to something even *more* interesting." By now my heart was pounding in my chest. I handed the lens and the blue lapis cross to the padre. "Have a look."

He took his time, carefully studying both sides of the cross with the lens.

"Strange," he said finally. "Are you thinking what I am thinking?"

"I am," I said, grinning widely, "and if we are right, this explains why Henri the Frenchman wanted the cross so badly."

CHAPTER 32

The Pimería. Año D. 1699. February.

"Go on up, if you want," Father Kino said. "Take some men. Have a look around. You will not be satisfied until you do."

I stared at the blue lapis cross, then up again to the bulging top of Baboquivari Mountain. Clouds with dark cores hung at the peak as if they were tethered to it with invisible ropes. To the west the sky was a hazy gray and I could feel moisture building in the late afternoon air. I pulled the collar of my tunic tighter against the cold, glanced at the little cross again, and thought of a hundred reasons why I should climb the mountain.

In the humidity Kino's gray-streaked hair lay in matted strands against his scalp. His black robe, already smelling of damp wool, flapped at his legs in the brisk wind. His blue eyes sparkled as he studied the rounded knob of gray granite that formed the mountain's peak. "Besides," he said, "how often do you get this close?"

"Not often, sir," I agreed.

He shrugged. "Well, it is your cross, so the decision is yours. But until you go up there and have a look for yourself, you will not know what the inscriptions mean, if they mean anything at all."

I nodded and stared up at the mountain again.

What we had found on the cross with his magnifying lens were engravings—odd, tiny inscriptions, a peculiar arrangement of letters and numbers. Was this some kind of coded map that could lead me to a rich lode of silver or gold? The Frenchman, Henri, and his big-fisted friend, Diego, had apparently spent a lot of time here, and they had wanted the cross badly enough that they tried more than once to take it from me. If they had not found what they were looking for on the mountain, then whatever it was, it was still here. And if the inscriptions on the cross were the clue to finding it, I needed to get up there and find out for myself. Kino was right about the other, too: years could pass before I might be this close to Baboquivari again.

There was just one problem with all this: my orders. I was to stay with Father Kino and Father Gilg at all times so I could protect them from any possible harm. Don Domingo had given me no options on this.

So far we had had no trouble.

We had left Dolores—Father Kino, Father Adamo Gilg, and I—a week before with thirty-six head of cattle, a dozen or so Pima vaqueros, a few soldiers, a rope line of extra horses, and almost a hundred pack mules loaded with provisions and gifts for the Indios we would encounter. Since the mules were Wigberto's, he was with us. He had brought Teodora and a dozen of his loudest and most profane teamsters. But I have to give them credit. When either of the priests was nearby, even the worst of the teamsters delivered his curses in muttered, whispered tones. Whether this novel new form of malediction did much to stir the mules, I could not say. Perhaps it was only Teodora's squawky blasphemies that kept them at their work.

We had moved slowly but steadily along the trail to Tubutama, where we turned north up the Altar River to Sáric and Tucubavia, and then angled northwest to where we were now camped, just south of Baboquivari. In each settlement along the way, the priests had given talks on God's Laws and His love and told stories from the Bible, and I had passed out trinkets and ceremonial canes and given talks on the Indios' responsibilities to their great leader across the ocean, Carlos Segundo.

We were taking the cattle to Sonoita, an Indian village about forty leagues west of Baboquivari. Kino planned to start another mission and ranch there, with the aim of using it as a base for supplying meat and other necessities for further explorations to the northwest. He had told me, too, that he hoped some day to use Sonoita as a source of cattle for the missions that he and his old friend, Father Salvatierra, would one day build in the Californias.

But Sonoita was not our only destination. Kino wanted to preach the Word to more Indians in the western desert, and in the process we hoped to reach the end of the Gila, in the northwest, where this river joined another that was said to be even wider and deeper. We just wanted to *see* it.

But now we had Baboquivari before us, and I wanted to see *it*, too.

Kino chuckled again. "Do not worry about us, Juan Mateo. We will be safe." Behind him I could see cloud shadows hurrying over boulders and across the juniper and piñon pines that gave a green glossiness to the mountainside. By now my heart was pounding in my chest. In my mind I saw a trunk filled with gold and silver coins, a slot canyon with gold nuggets littering the windswept floor; or perhaps a hidden arroyo containing slabs of silver as thick as elephants.

I picked up the cross again. To the bare eye, the numbers and letters were virtually invisible, but under the hand lens they had been clear enough:

V, SAS, and C. 620V-92 and 715V-174. What did any of this mean, if anything? If this was in fact a map to hidden treasure, the numbers could refer to compass headings and distances, and the letters might represent landmarks of some kind. I knew none of this with certainty, though, and I wanted very much to climb the mountain and see what awaited me at the top.

But my conscience-plagued hope of finding riches on this trip came to a quick end. That night, as our servants prepared our evening meal, one of my soldiers raced into camp, his uniform speckled with mud, his horse lathered. He gave me a hurried salute. "Captain," he said, "Apaches, at least thirty of them."

"Where, Corporal?"

He showed me on his map. "To the northeast. Probably ten miles from here."

"What direction are they headed?"

"This way, sir. Straight for Baboquivari."

I conferred with Father Kino. We decided to stay the night but leave for Sonoita before dawn the next morning. I informed Wigberto and his teamsters and the Pima vaqueros and posted extra guards with the livestock and horses and around the perimeter of the camp.

I was disappointed, certainly, as I had been when I could not go after the deposits of mercury on our last journey to the Gila. But things happen for a reason, and God knows what He is doing. If I had stayed to explore the mountain and anything had happened to Kino or Gilg on their ride to Sonoita, I would have felt terrible. Not to mention the fact that my uncle would have stripped me of my rank and sent me back to Spain. I would have been disgraced before the army and before my family. And deserved it, too, for ignoring the direct orders of my commanding officer. Don Domingo would understand my urge to look for silver and gold, but he felt strongly about loyalty and discipline in his officers. Frankly, I could find no fault with that, and at some deeper level of my mind I suppose I was pleased that the Apaches had put my temptations to rest. I made my peace with the situation and promised myself I would come back another day.

It rained that night. Not hard, but with a steady march of heavy drops that made thudding noises on my tarp and splattered in puddles that grew in the mud around us.

I dreamed. Many people I knew wandered through the dream, and a few I did not know. The Apache, I knew, but not from a dream. We had met a few months earlier, near a creek north of San Ignacio. I had been on my way to Imuris with three of my soldiers and Father Campos, who wished to hear confessions and preach to the Indians at the visita there. Because we knew that hostiles had recently been seen in that area, I had offered my services, and the padre seemed pleased to have us along.

That was how it really happened, and in my dream the story began in much the same way. We had camped in a grove of cottonwoods near a creek and the night had passed in peace, the air cool, clear, and bright with starlight.

At dawn I woke to the pleasant smells of chocolate and frying tortillas and something else that I could not identify at first. Then I saw Father Campos at the cook fire using altar bread irons—flat pincers with long iron handles—to bake unleavened bread for communion. I walked down to the creek to wash up.

"Hungry?" the padre said when I returned.

I nodded and reached for the mug of chocolate he held out.

That is what saved me, I believe. The reaching.

The Apache's arrow twanged into a cottonwood where I had just been, and a second arrow smashed the earthenware mug in the padre's hand and sent shards exploding into the air like fragments from a bomb. Someone jumped me from behind, so I sort of lost track of what was happening to Father Campos and the others. I heard gun shots and the groans and grunts of hand to hand combat, but I had all I could manage with the Apache who had me in a vise grip from behind. Fortunately, I had my boots on. I got a boot up and stomped the top of his foot, clad only in deerskin moccasins, as I had suspected. He let out a howl. I spun around, shoved him away, grabbed the padre's altar bread irons, and swung the bread-filled end of it at the Apache's head with all the strength I could muster. It connected. Blood spurted from his nose and seeped from the deep gash I had put in his forehead. He was short and stout, with his dark hair brushed back on his head. Now his eyes were bloody and wide with pain.

Someone—one of the soldiers, or perhaps even the priest; in the dream I could not see who it was—placed a pistol in my hand. I pulled the flintcock back, aimed at the Indio's chest, and fired. I found another pistol and shot him again, this time in the face. He went down. With the toe of my boot I rolled him onto the cook fire. I watched silently as the fire popped and crackled, harsh flames licking at the Indian's skin. The stench of charred flesh rose into my nostrils and drifted on faint breezes across our campsite. All of this, I have to tell you, seemed very real in my mind.

But the dream got a little harder to understand after that. Adriana Vásquez was in it. Father Kino, too. They were at a table in a café. In conversation, though I could hear nothing much of what was said. Adriana seemed to be doing most of the talking. Others I knew came and went in the dream. Don Domingo, my mother, Lieutenant Solís, a Latin teacher from my school days in Aragón; Wigberto, even Teodora the macaw. What they were doing here, I had no idea, but most of them seemed to be mad at me about one thing or another, and the dream lasted far longer than it should have.

I awoke in the darkness and spent a while thinking about this strange dream. As to the fight with the Apaches near San Ignacio, the dream got a lot of it right. But in our real encounter that day, the heathens had killed two of my men; we had killed none of theirs. In the dream Father Campos was unhurt. In reality, he took an arrow in his shoulder and bled all over our camp before I could pull the thing out and get a bandage on him. And the Apache I had introduced to the mysteries of the Eucharist did not die from his head wounds or any lead balls I fired into him. He slipped away, very much alive, in the noise and confusion of the fight.

Before he disappeared, though, blood dripping from his face, he said this to me: "You are Mon-hay. Black Skull knows you. He says he will kill you."

I had thrown a knife at him, but it landed harmlessly in the trees.

Our side had fared a lot better in the dream.

We reached Sonoita three days later without ever seeing the large band of Apaches my corporal had reported. Which was all right with us. We stayed in Sonoita long enough for Kino to preach and baptize infants and talk to the chiefs about the cattle we were leaving. Then, in bright sunlight under clear azure skies, we were once again on the trail.

El Camino del Diablo, it's called. The Devil's Highway.

It stretches from Caborca to Sonoita and then northwest across the desert to the village of San Pedro on the Gila, a distance of almost a hundred leagues. We did not have that far to travel on it—from Sonoita to San Pedro, perhaps fifty leagues—but that was more than enough.

The first European to ride it and survive to write about it was a Spaniard named Melchor Díaz, in 1540. Why he traveled it and where he was going, I cannot recall, but I doubt he had much fun at it. We certainly didn't, and we made the journey in winter. I can only imagine what it is like in summer. Flat, desolate, everything a colorless gray all the way to the horizon, so arid and barren that nothing grows in the hard soil but scraggly cactus and a rare creosote bush. A rattlesnake under every rock; a scorpion under every pebble. There are no trees, so the vultures have to settle for eyeing you from the tops of boulders. Sure, there are a couple of tinajas, water holes, but they are difficult to reach and usually impossible to find anyway because you aren't thinking straight and you have lost your only map and your horse is half-dead and your tongue is so parched and swollen it feels as if it is welded to the back of your throat. Actually, it's like that in winter, too, *Madre de Dios!*

We made it, though, and reached the Indian settlement of San Pedro on the Río Gila on the 21st of February. Indians came from all around to see us and to meet the padres and hear their sermons and talks. We saw Pimas, Papagos, tall Indios we called Yumans, or Quechans, and others from tribes we were never able to identify. We saw hundreds, maybe more than a thousand. Many spoke no language that we could understand, and I doubt they understood much of ours, but still they came and enjoyed our company and the Bible lessons of the padres. They brought gifts of food, and one group from farther west brought a gift of unusual blue seashells. Conchas azules, Father Kino called them. Abalone. He had seen such shells before, he told me.

I had never seen Kino so energized, so enthusiastic in his preaching.

I was pretty energized, myself. Studying the Indians, sketching maps of the area, trying to understand the strange-sounding words of the Yumans.

I found the Yumans interesting. They were tall, many of them six feet or more. The men were naked except for belts they wore around their waists. The belts were made from braided hair and on them they carried small bags filled with pinole and corn. The men shaved their hair down to their ears, like Franciscan friars. The women were clothed only below the waist, in skirts made of deerskin. They wore necklaces of red stones that looked like coral, and earrings made from blue seashells like the ones they had given Kino. The teamsters and soldiers considered the Yuman women to be quite pretty, with trim figures, light skin, and soft pleasant features. Or maybe the men just liked the fact that they wore no tops. Me, I just tried not to stare.

The Yumans, though, did not want us to visit their villages. We knew they lived near the junction of the Gila and the mighty river from the north, no more than a few leagues west of where we were camped, and this was a big disappointment for us. At the first opportunity, I asked Kino about it.

"Are they afraid Wigberto's teamsters will molest their women?"

Kino chuckled. "Probably not, but who knows."

"So we cannot go?"

"They do not want us there now, so, no, we cannot go."

"But why, Father? What is their problem?"

He shrugged. "Does it matter? They do not want us there. That settles it."

At first I was annoyed at this. I wanted to *see* that big river.

I have mentioned before that Kino often seemed to have the ability to read my mind. He could not, of course, but the idea that he could tells you a lot about him. He was one of the most perceptive, insightful men I have ever known. Not that he never made mistakes. Of course he did. But he usually seemed to know what was in a person's heart, and he always respected it. He seemed to hear the words that had not been spoken. This was particularly true in his relationships with the Indios, and probably explains why he always seemed to get along with them even when he had little knowledge of their language. I eventually came to see that there was nothing magical in any of this. He had a gift, simply, and he used it wisely.

So, like I said, I did not stay annoyed for long. Kino had wanted to see that big river as much as I had.

One day, though, I was able to ride to a nearby mountain and climb to its top for a look around. What a sight was spread out before me! I could see the Gila flowing to the west, and I had my first look at the river they call the Colorado as it comes roaring out of the mountainous despoblado far to the north. I saw its twists and turns as it rushed down from the heights, and saw the frothy white water of its tumbling, spilling rapids, and the riparian greenery of the floodplain that stretched away on either side of it. Hours passed before I could make myself leave.

The next day Kino asked me about the rivers.

"The Colorado is larger," I told him. We were drinking chocolate in a ramada at the edge of the village, the skies darkening, rain coming.

"How much larger?" he said.

"Compared to the Colorado," I said, "the Gila is little more than a trickle."

His gaze wandered away to the north for a time. "Perhaps," he said finally, "we can come back later this year and have a closer look."

"I hope so," I told him.

He pulled a map from the folds of his robe and opened it on the wood-planked table. He took a sip of chocolate. "Could you see the gulf from the mountaintop, Juan Mateo?"

I felt a few sprinkles of rain. "Not really," I said.

"...Do you still believe California is an island?"

"The maps say it is," I said. "But I know you have doubts."

He nodded. "I have a suspicion that the body of water we call the Golfo de California reaches no farther north than about thirty-two degrees latitude, maybe a bit higher. But I do not know this for sure. I have no proof."

The evening of our arrival in San Pedro, I had watched him take a star sight and do his calculations with his *Aigenler's Tables*. Here, we were a few minutes north of thirty-two-*and-a-half* degrees latitude. "So you're saying,

Father," I said, "that if we went due west from where we are now, we would *not* encounter the gulf?"

"That is exactly what I am saying. We would have to cross the Colorado somewhere in its course to the gulf, but not the gulf itself."

I waited for him to go on. After a time, he did.

"Think about it, my friend," he said. "If the land we call California is in fact a peninsula extending down from the main land mass that forms the western coast, rather than an island, it means we have the possibility of finding a land route from Santa Fé and San Juan Bautista and El Paso—straight to the ports on the coast—without having to ship goods across an open gulf, with all the perils and obstacles and expenses entailed."

"Which would open all of western New Spain to trade with the Orient."

Kino smiled. "And open it to spread of the Word, too."

"It might make it easier, also," I said, "to keep the Russians out of the Pacific northwest." We had had reports of Russian settlements along the northern coast, and of Russians with muskets and traps taking hides and pelts in the mountains.

I took some chocolate and watched the wind bend the bare branches of the cottonwoods that grew along the river. "There's another reason it would be good to have such a trade route, Father. If the Manila galleons that sail from the Orient each year could put in at the coastal ports of California and then send their goods east on wagons instead of having to sail south around the tip of California at Cabo San Lucas to reach Acapulco, as they do now, they could cut weeks off their sailing time. Which means we could eliminate scurvy. Think how many lives that would save!"

"Russians. Scurvy." Kino beamed. "Spoken like a good military man, Juan Mateo. So, do you want to help me find this trade route?"

"Well, of course," I said, grinning.

He was silent for a moment or so, his face serious now. "Juan Mateo, there is something I want to tell you about. Today, I heard a most interesting story. An Indian told me that we are not the first whites to come to this land. Through our interpreter, he told me he is from north of here, on the Colorado. He said his people have passed down stories of a visitor who came here long ago. This visitor was white and carried a cross and spoke to the Indio's ancestors in a strange and foreign tongue."

"Carried a cross? This was a *missionary*?"

Kino smiled. "It seems so."

"And you believe the Indian was telling the truth?"

"I think so, yes."

"Could the visitor have been a Russian?"

"The visitor was a *woman*, Juan Mateo."

"*What*?"

"The Indio said his ancestors killed her. He said they killed her several times. He said the woman kept coming back to life and preaching again and they had to keep killing her. Have you ever heard such a strange story?"

"Actually, I have, Father." Kino's tale, as crazy as it sounded, was somehow familiar. It took me a minute to remember why, and another minute to remember the woman's name. "María de Jesús de Agreda! Is it *possible*? Could that have been *her*?"

Kino raised an eyebrow. "Tell me about her."

I told him what I knew, memories of the story slowly coming back as I told him of it. In the 1620's a young Spanish nun—she came to be known as María de Jesús de Agreda—lived in a convent in Agreda, Spain. She was said to be quiet and modest and very pious, but one day she made the bizarre claim that she had traveled to Nueva España and preached to Indians who lived along a great river far to the north. In 1630 a Franciscan named Benavides interviewed her, investigated her story, came to believe it, and wrote of it in his book, *Memorial of Fray Alonso de Benavides*. Since she never explained how she got to New Spain and since everyone knew she had not been gone from Agreda since the day she joined the convent, few believed her, even after Benavides' book came out. But none of that stopped her from making her claim, and she continued making it for the rest of her life.

"I have read Benavides' book," I said, "and I can tell you, he was a sound thinker and a reasonable man—and he was convinced of the truth of her story."

Kino stared at me. "You are convinced, too?"

I laughed. "What does a soldier know of such things? But it is interesting."

He had more questions. "According to Benavides' account, what happened in the end? What did the nun say happened when they killed her the *last* time?"

"She told him she came back to life a final time and ascended into the sky and returned to Agreda."

Kino gave me an odd look. "That is what the Indian told me. Close, anyway. He said she went up into the sky, into the clouds, and disappeared." The padre was silent for a moment, then said, "In his book did he give the name of the tribe she preached to on this great river?"

"If he did, Father, I do not remember it."

"How did he say they killed her?"

"With arrows. Each time, they shot her full of arrows."

He nodded. "Yes, that is what the Indian said."

"When did the Indio say this woman came?" I asked the padre. "*When*, exactly, did all of this happen?"

"He said it was in the time of his grandparents."

I did some quick calculations. According to the legend, Sister María came here in the 1620's, which was, what, seventy or so years ago? Yes, the Indio's grandparents might have been alive then and old enough to recall such an event.

Kino rubbed his chin. "But if God transported Sister María here to preach to the Indians and prepare them for the coming of the Christian faith, would He not have given her the gift of tongues? The Indio said she spoke in a strange language his people could not understand."

"Yes, that is odd," I admitted. I would let the theologians argue that one, but I had one more question for the padre. "Did the Indian say what color clothing this woman was wearing?" The nuns of the Agreda convent, I remembered, wore blue habits trimmed in gold.

"Blue," he said. "Definitely blue. The Indios on the Colorado know her as *The Lady in Blue*."

"*Aaaiii caramba*, Father, blue, that is what the book said!"

He nodded, his eyes glowing now in the darkening light of evening.

It began to rain, and we had no time that night to continue our conversation. Nor did we the next day. Actually, in all the years that followed we rarely talked of these matters again. Kino, I think, was simply too practical to waste time in idle talk about things we could never know for sure. Not me. I was intrigued by the story. Still, as much time as I would later spend thinking about Sister María and the Indios who lived along the Colorado and their Lady in Blue, I would never learn the truth of the matter. Were the women one and the same? Was this one of God's miracles? If not, how else could we explain it?

"Do not worry about it, Juan Mateo," Kino always said when I brought up the subject. "When you get to heaven, God will answer all your questions."

The next morning before sunrise, as we loaded the pack animals and readied ourselves for departure in the dank cold of a late winter day, Teodora swooped down and landed on Kino's saddle. She preened herself, then turned her attention to the rest of us.

"*Get moving,*" she squawked, "*you ugly stinking mules, let's go home.*"

We headed for home.

We did go west again that year of 1699. In the fall, Padre Kino and I, with Father Leal, the new Visitor, and Father Gonzalvo, rode to Bac, on the Santa María, expecting to be joined there by Captain Bernal and his troops. We had hoped this time to reach the junction of the Gila and the mighty Colorado. But at the last moment Don Domingo sent Bernal's forces to help Coro in a campaign against the Jocomes, and we were forced once again to alter our plans.

We rode hard and visited a lot of Pima villages on the Altar and Magdalena rivers and their tributaries, and other places, too, so that Father Leal and Father Gonzalvo could see the missions and visitas that Kino had established. It was a tiring trip, and I for one was pleased when I finally got back to San Juan.

On this latest expedition, like the one before, I had no opportunity to explore Baboquivari. No chance to look for quicksilver or other riches along the Gila and in the mountains farther north. I did what I could to mask my disappointment and told myself I already had everything a young man could want: a steady salary, the respect of my peers, a life packed with excitement, good friends, and travel. But truthfully I cannot say I managed to convince myself.

On that cold February day in San Pedro on the banks of the Gila, though, we had received something from the Yumans that would turn out to be far more important than quicksilver or gold—the blue abalone shells, the conchas azules.

You find this hard to believe? So did I when Father Kino first told me.

CHAPTER 33 Magdalena, Sonora. 1965.

"I wonder," Olvera said, "about malaria."

He pulled a dusty bandanna from his pocket and wiped sweat from the handle of the soft-bristled brush he had been using to clean the ribs of the skeleton that lay partially exposed in trench #22. He glanced at Wasley, then removed his fedora and swabbed at the dampness inside it. He put the hat back on, pulling the brim low over his eyes against the glare and heat of the sun.

Wasley, a short, stocky man with rimless glasses and a smooth, nearly-bald head, drank from his canteen and stared at Olvera. Both men were soaked with sweat, their khaki shirts limp in the heat of the afternoon.

"There would've been plenty of mosquitoes," Olvera said. Closer to the City Hall and parish church, workmen paid by the government stood chest-high in trenches and shoveled dirt onto mounds that dotted the open areas.

Wasley took another drink of water. "*One* mosquito," he said, "is plenty. But what's this about malaria?"

The Kino team had grown. The old bait-dangler, Professor Jiménez, had once again used his connections in Hermosillo and Mexico City to bring in more people with special skills. Conrado Gallegos, a topographical engineer, had come to make drawings of the town and the trenches. Kieran McCarty—a Franciscan priest from Tucson, an historian with solid knowledge of the frontier missions—had offered his help. In Hermosillo, Cruz Acuña, the young diocesan, continued his search through the archives of the Archdiocese, continued to forward bits of information on Kino and his Chapel of San Xavier. Arturo Romano, the physical anthropologist, was still on the team. Charles Polzer, the historian from Tucson, was in Spain that summer but offered to act as an advisor to the project, as did Ernest Burrus, a Jesuit historian from Rome, and Sánchez de la Vega, the pharmacist.

And now they had William W. Wasley, too, another stroke of good fortune. And another testament, Olvera knew, to the negotiating skills of Professor Jiménez. Wasley, chief archaeologist with the Arizona State Museum in Tucson, knew much about the frontier missions and was an excellent teacher. He was generous and pleasant, with a ready smile, and Olvera had liked him immediately.

They'd retrieved the Ross Browne photograph of the sketch from 1864 that showed the parish church, which was still here, and the church of Father Campos, which had disappeared years before. With the help of the topographical engineer, they measured angles and elevations from landmarks in the photo, paced off the distances, and made their best guess as to where the Campos church had stood—somewhere near the front of the present City Hall. As for Kino's chapel, they had even less information on which to venture a guess. They were certain, though, that it would've been very near the Campos church because they'd learned that in the Jesuit era chapels were always built close to a larger church. But in what direction it would be from it, and *how* close, they had no good idea.

Professor Jiménez, on the other hand, believed they would find the foundations of the Campos church nearer the present parish church, perhaps in the vacant lot that lay behind it, or somewhere under Calle Madero, the street which fronted the church on the north and separated it from the City Hall. If Jiménez turned out to be right, then the Chapel of San Xavier, under which they expected to find Kino's remains, would be much nearer the parish church, too. Who was right? Where should they site their first trench?

In the end, they'd compromised. They opened *two* trenches: one near the vacant lot, one near the front of the parish church not far from the City Hall. In August they dug their first trench.

And turned up nothing.

So they'd kept at it. Trenches now crossed the plaza at odd angles, turned at even odder angles, and headed off in other directions. They had trenches in front of the parish church, trenches around the City Hall, and trenches in the streets that fronted the plaza. If you could put them end-to-end, they would have extended a kilometer or more. But they had found little of importance until, in trench #22, a workman had stumbled onto this skeleton...

An adult; probably male. They'd found no artifacts that would date the burial and no remnants of a coffin. The skeleton lay on its back, legs straight, the arms crossed over the abdominal area. To Olvera, this suggested a Christian burial.

The teeth had been interesting, too. Most were gone, but a few incisors remained and Olvera had studied them at length. Photographed them. Sketched them on clean white paper in the afternoon heat—

"What's this about malaria?" Wasley said again, intruding on Olvera's thoughts. "And mosquitoes. What are you talking about?"

They found a bench under a cottonwood tree at the edge of the plaza and Olvera told him about the Lockwood document. "There was a commentary in it by a priest named Luis Velarde. I think he was the priest who followed Kino as minister at Dolores after Kino died. Anyway, Velarde wrote that Kino had 'fierce fevers' that kept him in bed for days at a time."

"You're thinking of the years he spent on the Baja coast before he came to the Pimería?"

"The coast, yes," Olvera said, wiping sweat from his eyes. "He would've been exposed to mosquitoes. Apparently his fever was intermittent, which suggests he was all right between episodes, and that the problem lasted for some long period of time. To me this sounds like malaria."

"Could've been, I suppose."

"Of course it would be hard to know for sure. If he got malaria during his years on the gulf coast, but still had it when he died, that suggests he had it for at least twenty-four years. Is that possible, Bill?"

Wasley shrugged. "There are doctors in Tucson who would know. When I get back, I'll ask around."

Olvera watched the workmen digging steadily in the plaza. Since late morning the buildings around them had begun to gather the sun's heat, intensify it, and shoot it back at the workers in sweltering bursts. The little shade they'd enjoyed from the trees in the plaza had been transient, slipping silently from them as the sun inched across the gray-hot sky.

Of course even in the heat the townspeople had wanted to see the skeleton, had crowded around #22, each hoping to be the first from the village to view the bones of their beloved priest. The policía had come and kept them back, and this had annoyed a few of them. Still, the people had been good to the scientists and laborers. Several times a day a boy from a café near the plaza brought them water and lemonade, and a vendor sometimes gave them tacos and carne asada, always refusing payment, from his pushcart with squeaky wooden wheels. Olvera and the others had smiled at the rickety old cart when the old man came by.

Now they could see him across the plaza, wisps of gray smoke curling above the small cookstove on his cart. Wasley said, "There was a time when a squeaky wheel around here could cost you your life. I've read that in Kino's day, settlers and soldiers used the pulp of prickly pears to grease the axles of their wagons so Apaches couldn't hear them in the desert."

"Interesting." Olvera leaned back on the bench and closed his eyes. After a time he said, "Do you think the Apaches wanted to kill Kino?"

"No doubt about it. But he rode the desert for twenty-four years and they never laid a hand on him. Amazing, isn't it?"

"Very," Olvera said. "How do you think he managed to survive so long?"

Wasley smiled. "Most people around here would say it's because God was looking after him; God wanted the padre to complete his work. Maybe they're right. What do you think, Jorge?"

"I don't know." Olvera shrugged. "I've never been much of a believer in such sentiments, but it's an interesting hypothesis."

They sat silently for a time, sipping water, resting.

"You hungry?" Wasley said finally. "Want something to eat?"

Olvera watched the old man across the plaza, saw him remove a piece of meat from his grill and wrap it in wax paper, saw him hand it to a boy on a bicycle, take the coins offered, and slip them into the pocket of his grease-stained apron.

Olvera said. "Not now. In another hour or two, maybe."

Carne asada. Chunks of beef cooked outdoors on a grill, usually with onions or hot peppers. Sometimes the meat was tough and stringy and caught in Olvera's teeth when he chewed. In a few weeks there would be many vendors of such meat in the plaza, at the Festival of San Francisco Xavier. Olvera was looking forward to it. The days would be cooler then, and the town would be alive with dancing and music and vendors selling food and religious items and trinkets and balloons. The festival would give him a few days to rest and enjoy himself and be a tourist again. He would eat the carne then. Afterwards he might need antacids and some of de la Vega's stomach powders, but that would be all right, too.

Olvera rose from the bench. "Actually, I like carne the way they fix it here. I didn't think I would. In Mexico City the food is much different. It's more refined. Gentler on one's stomach."

"Sure," Wasley said. "But they're very practical here in Sonora. Their cooking fits the way they live."

Olvera was rested now, ready to return to his skeleton in trench #22. He laughed. "In Mexico City," he said, "they say that Sonora is where civilization ends and carne asada begins."

Later that day Olvera telephoned Jiménez, now back in Mexico City, to tell him of the skeleton the laborers had unearthed in trench 22.

"That's good," Jiménez said, sounding, Olvera thought, more solemn than usual.

"Believe me, Professor," Olvera assured him, "this is a good skeleton. It's well-preserved, with several intact teeth. You'll be pleased with it."

"Forgive me, my friend, for my foul mood, but I have bad news. The Minister of Education has just notified me that he's cutting off all our funds."

"*What*? Cutting off all—"

"It's true. You know about the big festival next month, the Festival of San Xavier? Officials are estimating there'll be close to ten thousand people in attendance. The Minister says we have to stop digging so laborers can fill the trenches. The government wants to be certain that during the festival no one falls into an open trench and gets hurt."

"You're saying we have to quit *now*?" Olvera said.

"By tomorrow," Jiménez replied.

"But the skeleton! We—"

"Doctor Romano will examine it, but he can't do it in Magdalena. I want you to pack it carefully and send it to Mexico City. I'm sorry, Jorge, but after tomorrow there just won't be any more funds to pay the laborers or our salaries or anything else."

"And after the festival...our generous and benevolent government will allow us to come back?"

"Jorge—"

"But we have an intact *skeleton* now, sir. It could be *Kino!*"

"...My friend," Jiménez said after a pause, "do you really think it's Kino? I doubt it or you would've told me so before now."

Olvera sighed into the telephone. "The incisors are definitely shovel-shaped, sir, which tells me it's an Indio. But we're close, I *know* it. He's here somewhere, maybe within a few feet of one of our trenches. Professor, por favor, could you talk to the Minister just once more? Ask him to continue our funding for another week? A few more *days*?"

"Jorge, I can't work miracles. We just don't have any more time."

Time.

Up to that day, Olvera and the others had dug a lot of trenches. They'd found numerous foundations and some interesting artifacts, but nothing that could have been from a footing or pedraplén of a 17th or 18th century Jesuit chapel.

In trench #4 they uncovered a stone footing, but it turned out to be from a once-thriving seminary built in 1921 by a priest named Navarette. The building, they learned, had been razed some years earlier.

Trench #1, near the parish church, yielded an olla, an earthenware jug, that contained dirt and the bones of small birds, probably from some pagan ceremony intended to bring good luck to the inhabitants of whatever structure had occupied the site. What structure that had been—a Piman mud hut, the adobe casa of a settler, or something more recent—the scientists had been unable to determine.

In trench #5 they found the wall of a septic tank that'd probably served Father Navarette's seminary. They'd found bottles of liniment; a bottle of tequila. Bones from dogs. Bones from horses. Part of an old aqueduct. Incomplete skeletons of more humans; mostly Indians, a few Mexicans. Buttons made from seashells and buttons made from bone. But not much else.

Time. Now they were out of it, and still the dry dark earth of Sonora refused to yield up its long-dead Tyrolean priest, Eusebio Kino.

CHAPTER 34

Sonora. Año D. 1700. March.

"What I fear most, I suppose," I told Adriana, "is the Apache I do *not* see."

"They say that about rattlesnakes."

I chuckled. "And lawyers."

She was silent for a time, then said, "You do not fear the *other* Apaches, the ones you *do* see?"

"Not as much as I once did, no." I had a sip of chocolate and wondered if my comment had sounded boastful. I hoped not. "But I respect them," I added.

Adriana raised an eyebrow. "*Respect* them, Captain Manje?"

"Definitely. I respect their abilities as warriors, as fighters."

We were at a small table on the patio of a café not far from the plaza in San Juan, enjoying the cool late-morning air and the cloudless azure sky. We weren't the only patrons but we were early enough to miss the worst of the midday crowd and that was fine with me. Until that moment we were talking mostly of small things, but she had suddenly turned serious and asked me this: *What, as a soldier, did I fear most?* I was certain the question had grown out of her worries for her husband in the time of her own marriage, and now for her daughters and even herself after her husband's untimely death. She had known her share of troubles, and there had been times when I could see the pain that lingered in her dark eyes. Still, I had never heard her complain, and I admired her for that.

"In Spain," I said, hoping to lighten the mood, "the generals taught us that the fiercest fighters in the world are old Moors on horseback and any Englishman on a ship."

She laughed. "The generals were wrong?"

"The generals," I said, smiling, "had never met an Apache."

In the past few months I had seen her several times, though always during the day, never around her children; never with the two of us alone. That seemed to be the way she wanted it and of course I had honored her wishes, though I cannot say I understood them. There had been times when I ached to...well, no, I will not go into that. This narrative is not the proper place for recording such intimate thoughts, and my intent has been to keep this document as free of pruriency and chatter as possible. I will just say this: Happily for my sanity, there had been *other* times, like today, when I found a degree of contentment in simply being with her. At least she was now willing to see me, here, in Real San Juan. She still called me Captain Manje—never Juan Mateo—and that continued to frustrate me, but as always she was pleasant company and on this fine spring day I was enjoying my time with her, chaste though I remained.

She looked good. Her dark eyes were full of light and health; her black hair framed her oval face and shimmered in the brightness of the sun. Her smile, though seldom offered, seemed magnificent to me, and I never failed to be amazed at the smooth clean softness of her skin. Today she wore a vest of black leather over a wine-red dress that managed to define her slender figure in a way that was both sensual and dignified. She was, I can tell you, a beautiful woman.

"Well, there's always *something* to fear," I said, getting back to her question. "But I suppose the nature of what I fear has changed. I used to worry that I would do something stupid in battle and get myself killed, or get lost in the desert, or I would be so frightened of the Apaches that I would freeze and not be able to fight. Or I would fall off my horse in front of the men and look like an idiot, or I would do something that would get some of my men killed or injured." I shrugged. "I worry less about such matters these days."

"Because you are more experienced now?"

I considered it. "Yes. I think I have learned a few things."

I was not boasting, por favor. I had enjoyed my share of victories on the battlefield, but I had known losses, too, and learned from all of them. That very day I was sporting a deep cut on my shoulder that an Apache had given me in a fight near Remedios the week before. I had chased him down, broken his nose, and put a .60 caliber lead ball through his foot, but before he slipped away he managed to kill my horse with his lance and carve me up nicely with his knife, and I was still unsure whether that little brawl should count as a victory or a loss. My point, though, is that I no longer suffered an unreasonable fear of the Apaches. They no longer crowded my waking thoughts as they once had.

"Maybe you have grown up," Adriana said.

"I pray I have," I said.

Her dark eyes glowed with something I could not quite read. "But you love it, I think," she said. "The fighting."

"Yes. Even when I was so scared I feared I would turn and run, I loved it."

" '*Loved* it,' you said. That means you no longer do?" she said.

I shrugged. "Honestly, these days I would rather use my time to poke around the mountains, looking for gold and silver, or exploring with Father Kino."

"How is the padre? Have you seen him lately?"

"The last I saw him, he was fine. Well, he had some fever, but except for that he seemed all right. I just had a letter from him. He says he wants to talk to me about some shells."

"Shells?"

I told her about the blue shells the Indians had given Kino at our last visit to the Gila. Neither of us could imagine why the padre was suddenly interested in such shells, but we played a little guessing game until we grew bored with it. For a time we just sat in the sun, enjoying our chocolate and the cool breeze. Finally I said, "So, Adriana, how are your daughters?"

"Fine. They ask about you sometimes. They still giggle about the day you brought tortillas and chocolate to the dress shop and put the food on the table with such a theatrical flourish."

I grinned, a little sheepishly, I think. "I felt sort of silly doing it."

She reached across, almost touching my hand.

"I am glad you came that day, Juan Mateo," she said.

I stared at her, my heart thumping in my chest. "You just called me Juan Mateo."

Her laugh was soft and tinkling and surprisingly warm in my mind. "Is that all right?" she said.

"Sure. Certainly it is all right," I said. "Oh, *absolutely*!"

The blue shells. *Conchas azules*, Kino had called them. Abalone. Bright and shiny and silvery-blue. They had been a gift to Kino from the Yumans, a tribe that lived a few leagues west of the village of San Pedro on the Gila, near the mighty river that Kino had called the Río Colorado. The shells were pretty, their coloring highly unusual, but I had thought little of them beyond that. I had not supposed that Kino had made much of them, either.

But he had, and when I rode to Dolores to see him a few days later, I learned why. I found him in the mission carpenter's shop, making repairs to a saddle. It was good to see him again, and I was particularly pleased to observe that he had no evidence of fever. In fact he seemed as vigorous and filled with good cheer as I had ever seen him. We walked down to the river and strolled along the bank. The village had been loud with the sounds of busy people and barking dogs, but here at the river the silence was broken only by the burble of rushing waters and the peaceful stir of the warm wind in the cottonwoods and sycamores that shaded the banks.

"So how is the Rector these days?" I asked him.

He laughed. "You are trying to ruin my good mood, Juan Mateo?"

"Just making a small joke, Father."

"I see," he said. "Well, Father Mora is...Father Mora."

It was my turn to laugh. "You are answering all his letters promptly, I assume?"

His blue eyes twinkled. "The very moment I receive them."

For a time we talked about minor matters, and as always I took delight in the sharpness of his wit and the warmth of his company. He gave me the latest news from the western missions and I told him of the cavalry's latest forays against the Apaches and of Don Domingo's latest forays among the wealthy families of Sonora in his tireless quest for a proper wife for me. Again I considered telling Kino about Adriana and my growing affection for her. As on previous occasions when I had had such an opportunity, I decided against it, and as before, I was not quite sure why. Was I worried that Kino, like Don Domingo, would not approve of her? If not that, then what was it?

"In your letter," I said, putting my thoughts of Adriana away, "you mentioned the blue shells."

"Ah, yes, the shells." We stopped in the shade of a massive sycamore, its brown bark scaling away, its leaves new and green and fresh. From high in the branches I could hear the trilling of a warbler, and I saw hummingbirds with black chins taking nectar from the red flowers of penstemons that grew near the water.

"On our ride back to Dolores from our last trip to the Gila," Kino explained, "I did some thinking about those shells. They had stirred up something in my memory. I never figured out what it was, but somehow I had a feeling that those shells were important. Back here again, well, truthfully, in time I simply forgot them. But not long ago I was at Remedios and I had a visitor—a Pima from a settlement on the Gila. He brought a gift for me from a Maricopa chief who lives near him. The gift was a cross, decorated with shells."

"...*Blue* shells?"

His eyes glowed with excitement. "Abalone. Blue, exactly like the ones the Yumans gave me at San Pedro."

"And that started you thinking again?"

"Yes, and remembering," he said. Behind him I saw a family of javelinas rooting in a stand of prickly pears that were bright with yellow flowers. On the breeze I could smell the blooms of copa de oro, the goldpoppies that formed a vivid orange carpet over the wet rich earth of the floodplain.

"I finally remembered," the padre went on, "where I had seen such shells before. But not where you might think, not at the gulf. Do you remember I told you that before I came to the Pimería I spent several years with Admiral Atondo? We were trying to establish colonies on the gulf coast of California. First at La Paz, then at San Bruno. Eventually we had to abandon both."

"Yes," I said. "You told me about that."

"In December of 'eighty-four, we left our ships and our little log fort at San Bruno and rode our horses over the mountains and across to the Pacific coast."

"That is where you saw the blue shells, on the *Pacific* coast?"

"On the Pacific side, yes," he said. "We reached the ocean at a large bay—an estuary, actually—on the last day of December. We called it Bahía de Año Nuevo. New Year's Bay. That is where I saw the blue shells."

"But you never saw such shells on the *gulf* coast?"

"Never," he said. "Never on the gulf, in all the years I was there, on either the California side of it or this side."

"Interesting." I stared out at the river. In the shallows an egret flapped its long white wings and rose silently into the air. "So," I said, "the obvious question is: if the abalone shells occur only on the Pacific coast, and if California is indeed an island, and if the Indians of that area have no boats large enough to carry them across the gulf, how did the shells get to *this* side of the gulf?"

"You have stated the problem very well, Juan Mateo. And I am almost certain that no Indians there have boats large enough to sail the gulf."

"So you are thinking...what? There must be some kind of land bridge between California and the Pimería? This could be proof that California is a peninsula and not an island?"

"Do you not think this is possible?"

"But all the maps show—"

"I know what the maps show, my young friend." He smiled. "I am just not sure I believe them, and I know of only one way to find out. So, do you want to go?"

"Go?" I said. "Where?"

"Back to the Gila. Next month, if I can get a pack train organized by then. I want to talk to the Maricopas and Yumans about the blue shells. I hope to find someone who can tell me how the shells got here." He smiled again. "I also want to explore the Gila and maybe even ride far enough west to see the Río Colorado."

"And you believe Father Mora will approve such a journey?"

"I will happily tell him about it...after we return."

I chuckled. "That seems reasonable."

"So," he said, "you will go?"

"To explore the Gila again and see the Colorado? Of course!"

But General Jironza soon had other plans for me, and in this year of Año D. 1700, I would find no time to explore the northern lands with Kino. Shortly after my visit to Dolores we had word in San Juan that hostile Indians were murdering innocents and burning villages in the western desert, the land of the Sobas, the Hia C'ed O'odham. The general sent me with two other officers and a unit of horse cavalry to find the culprits and put an end to their depredations.

The culprits turned out to be Jocomes and we did finally halt their carnage, though not without committing a little of our own. In the next three months we killed or captured over seventy enemies. The dead we left for the coyotes. The prisoners we bound with stout rope; we stuffed rags in their mouths and sold them at auction to representatives of mining companies in Alamos and other towns far to the south. The miners, I have no doubt, beat them unmercifully, but by then we cared little about what happened to them. Maybe it is not very Christian to feel that way, but that is how we felt. I am not trying to justify it or make excuses for myself, I am just telling you how it was.

Once during the campaign, I saw Black Skull. Not that I would have recognized his face, even if I had had a good look at him, which I did not. It had been too many years since I fought him near Imuris in my first year in the Pimería; his dark face had grown hazy in my mind. Still, this Indio was the right size and about the right age, and he had the same bearing, the same insolent swagger, that I remembered so well. Too, he had the same ability to make my pulse thrum in my temples and the hair bristle on the backs of my arms. Oh, yes, it was Black Skull.

I saw him after a particularly bloody battle near Unuicut, after we had lost four soldiers and a young lieutenant to the Jocomes and I had ordered my men up onto a mesa for defensive purposes while we evaluated our wounded and planned our next move.

I was studying a map when I heard a sentry's shout and looked up. There he was, the Jocome, thirty varas from us, a grim and solitary figure dark against the slate gray sky. In that moment of cognizance, that first instant of recognition, a cottony dryness filled my mouth and I could hear blood thrumping in my ears. Before I could react he raised his bow. I felt a sting of hot air against my neck and knew his arrow had missed me by a fraction of an inch. I got off a shot with my musket, but I was too shaken to have any accuracy and my ball kicked up dirt behind him. A few of my soldiers shot at him, too, but they had no better luck than I. By then, he was gone.

I sat in the shade of a tree until my pulse slowed and my breathing returned to normal. I remembered Kino's warning that day near Imuris. *You will have to kill him, Juan Mateo, because he will not forget. His anger will grow, and he will try to kill you.*

But had he recognized me? I doubted it. Not that it mattered, really. He was an Jocome and I was a Spaniard and under any circumstances our duties required that we kill each other. This day, it seems, he had come very close to doing just that. *Madre de Dios.*

When I felt a little better, I washed the sweat from my face. I retrieved a bottle of wine from my saddlebag and had a long swallow. And another. Then I ordered my men onto their horses and we went looking for more Jocomes. We found some. We killed them. But for the remainder of the campaign we saw no more of Black Skull.

In September we rode high into the Chiricahuas after Mofeta and Clavo and their bands, and engaged them on several occasions. In October we chased Oso Azul and his men into the Guachucas and set up a successful ambush. In each of these encounters we killed a few Apaches and took a few more prisoners. On one occasion I had my horse shot out from under me. Luckily I landed in soft soil; the damage to my shoulder and ribs was minimal. I found the Apache who had killed my mount and I put a musket ball through his heart.

But the Compañía Volante lost men, too. During that year, nineteen good and loyal soldiers died in the service of King Carlos Segundo. Another thirty sustained injuries severe enough to land them in the hands of the post surgeon, who did his usual competent job of patching the wounds, draining pus from the abscesses, and amputating the ruined limbs.

Me, I was blessed by the Lord with a lack of serious injuries that year. Oh, I had the usual litany of knife cuts and bruises and aching bones and close calls, but the enemy never got his hands on me for more than a few seconds at a time.

Not everyone in the Compañía was so fortunate. Once, in the Chiricahuas, the Apaches took two of our soldiers who were standing watch. For the rest of the night we heard their screams. At dawn we found them hanging by their wrists from a tree limb over a smoldering fire that still popped and flared when melting bits of fatty flesh dripped onto the embers. The Apaches had stripped them naked and slowly roasted them as they pushed burning sticks through their eyes and up their rectums. We cut them down and gave them Christian burials and got out of there as soon as we could. Still, the stink of burnt flesh followed us for days.

But even with this and all the rest of it, by year's end we had done the enemy some damage. We had done all right.

Father Kino did all right that year, too, from all accounts. I saw little of him in those busy months, and most of what follows I learned long after the fact, some of it from the padre himself, some from others who saw him more often:

In mid-April he left on his journey to the Gila and Colorado Rivers, as he had planned, but with no military escort and only a few Pima servants. When word reached him of the Jocomes' atrocities in the west, he wisely altered his plans and stopped at the Pima settlement of Bac on the Santa María. But being who he was, he wasted no time cursing the darkness. He lit, in his own unique way, some important candles. First, he sent out runners in all directions with instructions to find and bring back anyone with reliable information on the blue shells. Then he organized a work crew of Indians and on the 28th of April, 1700, they dug the first trench for the foundations of a permanent church at Bac, which he had named San Xavier del Bac in honor of his patron saint. When they had the heavy foundation blocks in place, Kino felled a tall tree and sawed it into planks and built the forms they would use in shaping the adobe blocks for the walls.

On the 28th, the day they started the trenching, runners began coming in with western Pimas and Maricopas and even Yumans from the far northwest, all with knowledge of the blue shells. From the 28th to the 30th Kino met with them, at what he would later call his Blue Shell Conference, and from them he learned these things: 1. The Indios, as he had suspected, had no boats that could cross the gulf. 2. The shells had come from a distant sea, ten to twelve day's journey west of San Pedro. 3. The shells had reached the Pimería along regularly-used trade-routes, by hand-to-hand trading.

"But did the shells have to be carried across a wide body of water to get here?" Kino asked the Indians.

"Wide water, yes," everyone agreed.

"How wide?"

"Oh, very wide, Father," they all said.

"As wide as the gulf?"

"Not that wide," they said. "But as wide as a big river."

"As wide as *what* big river?"

"The Colorado," they told him.

"Ah," he said. "...And that's the *only* water the shells had to cross to get from the distant sea to the Pimería?"

"The only water, Father," they all agreed.

"There was no *small* sea, like the gulf, between the *big* sea and the Pimería?"

"No small sea, Father," they assured him. "Only the river."

"The *Colorado* River."

"Yes," they said. "Only the Colorado River, Father."

Can you imagine the look on Kino's face when he heard these words? If he'd had a table, he would have jumped on it and danced a vlaminco!

Because of the ongoing problems with the Jocomes in the west, though, the padre could not ride on to the Colorado, as he must have desperately wanted. He remained at San Xavier del Bac long enough to instruct the Pimas in how to mix mud for the adobe blocks for the new church, and to teach the catechism, then made the long ride back to his mission at Dolores. I have no knowledge of what his mood was on the ride home, but if he was depressed because he could not go on to the Colorado, I doubt his melancholy lasted long. By now he had become convinced that Bac would make a good staging area for farther explorations of the northwest, and at Dolores he quickly rounded up several hundred head of livestock and sent them with Pima vaqueros back up the long dusty trail to Bac—a small first step in establishing the little Indian village on the Santa María as an important working ranch. The padre, I had long ago learned, wasted no time.

And he wrote to his old friend, Salvatierra, the hatchet-faced Jesuit who by now had been re-assigned to a mission in California. Kino told him of the Blue Shell Conference at Bac and wrote that he was now sure that California was not an island, that there was a land route between California and the Pimería, and that if he could find it they would have a way to supply the struggling California missions with the bounty of the Pimería's missions. I can easily imagine the enthusiasm Kino poured into that letter, and Father Salvatierra's joy when he read it.

Our padre, his appetite whetted, spent the summer months as he usually did: tending to his clerical duties, teaching his beloved Pimas, overseeing the harvests, looking after the livestock—and happily making travel plans for the cooler months of autumn.

In late September, Kino rode out of Dolores with ten servants and sixty pack animals and did what he had not been able to do in April or before: he reached the junction of the Gila and the Colorado Rivers. The Yumans had a village there, and Kino named it San Dionysio, after the saint whose feast day occurred during his visit. Because he was short of time he made no attempt at crossing the tumbling rough waters of the Colorado, but he climbed a mountain and from its peak he saw to the west, beyond the river, a vast rolling land of hills and desert and stubby green mountains. *California*, now he had no doubt of it. He could not see the gulf, but he believed it had to be to the south, hidden by other mountains, just beyond the reach of his telescope. So, he thought, California was indeed a peninsula, not an island! There were trade routes out there! And innocents who needed to hear God's word and to know the salvation of Christ!

Well, perhaps he still had not *proved* there was an overland route to California, but he was becoming more and more sure of it.

The end of the year saw Eusebio Kino a very happy man.

The year did not end quite so well for me.

In November, back from the Jocome and Apache wars, I rested for a time and then rode west to Tubutama and on north to Baboquivari Mountain. I found a way onto the mountain from the east and followed a dry wash as far as my horse could take me. I found a few springs with ample fresh water. I saw red foxes, javelinas, bighorn sheep, even an oso negro, a black bear. But I never saw any gold or silver. I never saw I'itoi. I never saw the graves of Henri Pitot, the Frenchman, or Diego, and I saw nothing even to suggest that they or anyone else had ever been on the mountain. I found nothing that offered even the smallest clue to the meaning of the letters and numbers engraved on my little blue lapis cross. I found nothing at all.

Carlos Segundo died this year, 1700, and Spain fell into turmoil, even more than normal. Carlos had willed the throne to his grandnephew, Duke d'Anjou of France, a grandson of Louis XIV. Austria, we heard, had protested, wanting the crown to pass to Archduke Charles, an Austrian with some minor claim to it. We heard the Austrians were threatening to form an alliance with the Netherlands and England to fight d'Anjou and Spain. Whether there was anything to the rumors, we had no idea. Perhaps the Austrians and their friends worried that d'Anjou would bring Spain under France's influence and that the two powers would attempt to conquer the world, who knows what those puffed-up thieving Austrians were thinking. Frankly, I could hardly imagine decent Spaniards joining forces with Frenchmen to do *any*thing, but in this modern age I suppose it could happen. Anyway, I had a feeling Spain would soon be at war again.

Adriana.

The general's plots to marry me off.

The lapis cross with its engravings that whispered of great treasures.

The soldiering. The fighting and fear and blood and death.

My year ended, well, just...*wrong*. I felt unsettled in some vague way, a little disoriented, not quite sure who I was and where I was going. I was thirty years old, a good enough soldier, a decent enough man. But what was out there for me, and did I really want it?

CHAPTER 35

The Pimería. Año D. 1701. February.

This month, Father Juan María Salvatierra came back to the Pimería.

By now the padre had started a mission in Baja California at a place he called Loreto, and he and Kino had become even more committed to finding an overland route from the rich pastures of the Pimería to the struggling missions of California—*if* such a route existed. Kino believed it did, and Salvatierra wanted desperately to believe it, too. Me, I would have been pleased to have such a route, for reasons I have already stated, but I still had some doubts. On the occasions when I voiced my skepticism, Kino would only smile and say, "Be patient, my friend. God will give us our answers soon enough."

"But Father," I always argued, "the maps show—"

"Have you forgotten King David's words in Psalms? Chapter sixty-five, verses twelve and thirteen? *'The grasslands of the desert overflow; the hills are clothed with gladness. The meadows are covered with flocks and the valleys are mantled with grain; they shout for joy and sing.'* "

"I doubt David was talking about *our* desert, Father."

He shrugged grandly. "Maybe so, maybe no."

"You sound like Wigberto."

The padre's grin widened; his blue eyes sparkled. "A wise man, Wigberto."

I should have guessed he had another expedition planned.

At Kino's urging Salvatierra had sailed back across the gulf to the mainland and made the long ride from Sinaloa to Kino's mission, Dolores, and in late February the three of us left Dolores with pack animals and enough soldiers and Pimas to keep us safe from attack by Apaches, who had been raiding regularly in the Pimería in recent months. We were bound for the far northwest and the Río Colorado.

We made stops in Magdalena and Caborca, and then at the settlements of Bacapa and Sonoita. Bacapa, we believed, was one of the villages visited by Francisco Coronado in 1540 in his search for the Cities of Gold on the plains of Cibola. The Indians had no gold for us, but they welcomed us with singing and dancing and gifts of food. The priests gave talks on God and His mysteries, celebrated mass, taught the catechism, and baptized sick infants and adults. We found little time to rest from our trip, but Kino was happy to be among his Indian friends again and Father Salvatierra, who spoke Piman as well as our translators, clearly enjoyed it, too. At Sonoita, which Father Kino had named San Marcelo de Sonoita, we re-supplied our group with meat and grains from the cattle and stores that Kino had brought up from Dolores on an earlier visit.

In all this time we saw no Apaches or Jocomes, and in the saddle I had ample time to reflect on other matters, some of which had begun to trouble me greatly over the past year. Adriana, for one. I had come to see that I had to do something about her soon, and I could identify only two choices: declare my love for her and ask her to be my wife and suffer the consequences to my career, or remove myself from her situation and betroth myself to one of the rich women that Don Domingo was always pushing me after. And what was I to do about Don Domingo? Ask him not to labor so hard on my behalf? How could I? He was family, and he was only doing what he thought best for me.

"As the son-in-law of a wealthy man, Juan Mateo," the general had reminded me yet again, "you would have much more control over your life than you will ever have as a soldier."

"I know that, Uncle," I had said for the hundredth time.

As for Adriana, I had doubts, frankly, that she would even marry me. She had given me little encouragement for a proper courtship.

And the army? That question lingered, too. Austria, with the Netherlands and England, had declared war on Spain and France in protest over Spain's choice of the successor to Carlos Segundo, and everyone in Nueva España felt the war could go on for years. Should I remain in the service of the new king—Duke d'Anjou, or Felipe V as he was now called—or resign and find something else to do? But what else did I *want* to do? What else *could* I do? On that long journey to Sonoita I had plenty of time to ponder these matters as the desert scrolled slowly past.

Mostly, though, I thought about Adriana. I had no problem bringing up an image of her pretty face, her smile, the brightness of her dark eyes. Most of the time, in fact, I had more trouble getting her *out* of my mind. Which was fine with me. Such thoughts kept me warm on our many long nights in the desert.

Often on our journey Kino rode at my side, though sometimes hours passed in which he said little or nothing. At these times he seemed almost unaware of my presence, as if in some arid corner of his mind he was wandering alone, struggling with some unseen problem or searching for a solution to some dilemma that had been presented only to him. At other times I sensed that he felt a need to be part of the group, to connect in some fundamental way with anyone nearby, friend or stranger, to listen and talk and even laugh a little. I never learned to predict his moods, but that was all right. When he pulled his horse alongside mine, I usually waited for a cue. If he wanted to talk, we talked, and if he wanted quiet I tried to see that he had it.

Some of his stories I found quite interesting, and some, disturbing. One afternoon I had worked up a sweat walking my horse up a steep hill, and the padre pulled a cotton cloth from his saddlebag and handed it to me. I wiped my face, thanked him for his kindness, and gave it back. Before he returned it to his bag, though, he hesitated briefly, staring at the damp cloth. When we were mounted again and underway on level ground, he asked me if I had ever been to Alicante, on the southern coast of Spain.

Which allowed me to make a good guess at what he had been thinking as he stared at that cloth.

"I have not been to Alicante," I told him

"Our ship," he said, "pulled in there for a few days on our sail from Genoa to Cádiz. There were nineteen of us—Jesuits, just out of school, all excited because we were bound for the New World, but all of us already tired of being seasick. We were ready for solid land under us and the captain put into the harbor there not a moment too soon for us."

I chuckled and waited for him to go on. Finally he did.

"There is a church on the edge of town where they keep the Veil of Santa Veronica on display. Do you know of this veil?"

"The priests in Aragón," I said, " taught us that it was the cloth used by the compassionate woman to wipe Christ's brow on His way to Calvary. They said the cloth now has an image of Christ's face on it. Did you see it? Is it true?"

Kino smiled. "It is true."

"Is it really *His* face?"

"I suspect it is," he said, "though I cannot prove it."

"They say sick people have been cured by touching the veil. Is that true?"

He shrugged. "I saw no such thing myself, but one night we saw monks with lighted torches carrying the veil through the streets. They were praying and chanting. Plague had reached some neighboring villages and the monks thought the veil might keep the Black Death away from Alicante."

"And did it?"

The padre laughed softly. "You are full of metaphysical questions today, my friend."

"I guess we are blessed here in the Pimería, Father. We have other problems, but at least we have no plague to worry about."

The smile faded from the padre's dark face. "We saw a plague ship off the Spanish coast, not far from Alicante. No harbor pilots would go out to it and no port authorities would let it come in. What a horrible way to die—no food or fresh water left, the ship adrift at sea, everyone on board sick or dead, no priests to offer last rites..." His voice trailed off. He made the sign of the cross and whispered a brief prayer.

I knew him well enough to know he would have wanted badly to go to the ship to offer sacraments. I can guess that he and the other young Jesuits set up a fuss and howl about it, but I also knew their ship's captain would never allow them to go. It must have been an awful scene for the padres to witness. There was nothing I could say that would not sound trite and stupid, so I kept my thoughts to myself.

For the rest of the day Kino, too, kept his thoughts to himself. He was off in a corner of his mind again, I supposed, probably thinking about the irony of the veil with its healing powers and the drifting plague ship that was so close to it and yet so far. I talked some with Father Salvatierra and my soldiers, but mostly we rode in silence, all of us absorbed in our own thoughts. I could not speak for the others, but I was feeling blessed that we had had no illness and very few troubles on this first leg of our journey. When we made camp that night I said a prayer of thanks.

But our expedition could not go forever without problems, and they began a few days out of Sonoita. On the advice of an Indian guide, we had decided to try a new route—new for us, anyway—to the Colorado, in hopes of finding more water and pasture for our animals than we would see on the trail we called El Camino del Diablo. On leaving Sonoita we turned southwest on a route that took us south of Pinacate Mountain, which Kino called Cerro de Santa Clara, and into the shifting sun-seared dunes that filled the empty miles between the mountain and the gulf. Our plan was to reach the gulf and turn northward, following the coastline as far as it would take us.

Pinacate was interesting but bleak. We had no doubt that it had taken its origins in a massive volcanic eruption, as it had the shape of a cone at its top and it sat on a mesa composed of liga—black lava rocks—that extended for miles in every direction and gave the land a scorched and desolate appearance. Near the base of the mountain we found a settlement of Indians so poor that they had no clothes, not even loincloths, and sustained themselves on little more than locusts, roots, and lizards. Few plants could survive in this harsh country and we saw that the Indians had no possibility of growing crops. Still, it was here that I learned of incienso, the white brittlebush, that the priests happily collected for its sweet-smelling resins. They gave some to the Indians, who chewed it and used it as a poultice, and kept the rest to burn as incense in their censers. The priests also gave sacks of corn and beans and sugar to the Indians and taught them to make pinole.

On an earlier visit Kino had climbed Pinacate and from its peak had seen, he assured us, the gulf—and across it, the mountains of California. Frankly, I think the padre had seen no such waters. I believe the waves he described were ridges of sand created by the blustery winds that blew almost constantly in the area. We had some good debates on the subject, and on the blue shells and their origins. Who won the debates, I could not say. Kino was, as always, quite persuasive in his arguments, but I had seen old documents from early Spanish explorers which stated clearly that California was an island and that the gulf extended much farther north than latitude thirty-two degrees. Anyway, we had some fun with it, and we always managed to stay on good terms even in the heat of our disagreements.

But in the sands west of Pinacate, we bogged down. We ran out of water, and found little that was drinkable in the undulating white dunes near the shore. After a few days we were forced to turn back for Sonoita. There we rested and watered our animals and talked about other routes that might get us to the Colorado in the little time we had remaining. Finally we decided to try a route that would take us north of Pinacate but south of the Devil's Highway, hoping to reach the river—or the gulf, whichever we might find—somewhere around latitude thirty-two degrees.

That did not work, either.

Again we bogged down in sand. We found little water for our horses and pack animals. Our Papago guides refused to go farther because they feared an attack by the Yumans. Worst of all, we were running out of time; Father Kino had been away from his responsibilities at Dolores for more than a month. That was too long, he told us. We would have to turn back.

But there was one thing we could do before we turned back. We found a tall mountain—the closest was near a little Indian village called Pitaqui, six leagues north of Pinacate—and climbed it. We scrabbled over boulders, dodged thorny cactuses and annoyed cascabels, and finally worked our way to the peak. It was one of those fine spring days in the desert, the sky a gentle blue, the clouds soft and white and close, the air sparkly and crisp and so amazingly clear you could see every ridge and cut and canyon in the stubby green mountains that rose in the distance.

"What do you think, Juan María?" Kino said to Salvatierra after we had had a look at the horizon with our telescopes.

"I see the mountains of California," Salvatierra said, his big face stretched by a grin, "and I see where the gulf ends—almost due west of us. North of that, I see more desert and mountains. Nothing else."

"And you, Juan Mateo?"

I shrugged. "The gulf curves off to the west. I am not sure I see where it ends."

Kino chuckled. "You are outvoted. I agree with Juan María. I think we have our proof."

"Ninety-five percent of it, Father," I argued, "not one hundred percent. To prove it, we have to actually ride our horses into California, no ships."

He considered my words. "You are right. We still have not proved it, have we? Not completely."

"Not yet," I said, and saw a sparkle come into his blue eyes.

"Then in November we will come back," he said. "We will find proof so convincing that even you, Juan Mateo, will believe it."

We shared a good laugh at that, then worked our way back down the mountain, retrieved our horses, and pointed them towards Dolores and the Río San Miguel.

CHAPTER 36

San Juan Bautista, Sonora. Año D. 1701. May.

In his office at the presidio Don Domingo told me there was a young lady he wanted me to meet. Teresa, her name was. Her father was Don Calixto Badilla, a prosperous businessman who owned ranches near Ures and Oposura. A good and honorable man, the general assured me.

"I hear Teresa is very pretty," he added.

I was staring out the open window of his office to the parade ground, watching soldiers as they marched in formation. I heard the shouts of sergeants and I could smell mimosa and horse droppings and the faint, sweet blooms of the ironwood trees that grew near the general's quarters.

"Nephew. Have you fallen asleep?"

I stirred. "Sorry, sir."

Don Domingo stared at me, his eyes bright, his coal-black hair brushed neatly back on his scalp. His uniform was, as always, carefully tailored and immaculate. "Is there someone else," he said, "I should know about?"

"Someone *else*, sir?"

"Juan Mateo, in many ways San Juan is still a small town. I have heard rumors."

"What rumors, sir?"

His dark eyes bored straight through me.

I sighed and leaned back in my chair and told him about Adriana. What choice did I have? The general was not a man from whom you could withhold information, not when he knew you had it. So I told him how we had met and about her dressmaking shop and her children; I told him how I felt about her. I told him everything.

While I talked, Don Domingo's eyes never left mine. I think he never even blinked. When I finished, he sat quietly for a time, picking at the skin around his fingernails with a small knife. Finally he spoke. "I knew her husband, Sergeant Vásquez. He was a good soldier, a loyal servant of the king."

"Adriana said as much, sir."

"And how does this woman, Adriana, feel about you?"

"I do not know," I told him honestly. "She has given me little encouragement."

He picked at his nails again, then looked up at me. "Do you know of a man named Jacinto Fuensaldaña? He is the military governor of Sinaloa. He is also a wealthy silver miner."

"I have heard of him, yes. *He* has a daughter, too?"

For the first time in our conversation Don Domingo laughed. "Actually, I know nothing of the man's offspring."

"Then why— ?"

His laughter faded and he turned serious again. "Fuensaldaña has been telling lies about me to the viceroy and other representatives of the new king."

"Why would he do that, sir?"

"He wants my job."

"He wants to be military governor of Sonora? Commander of the Compañía Volante?" I could hardly believe this. It was preposterous. No man could take Don Domingo's job. How could anyone do such a thing?

"That is what he wants, yes. My job."

"*Aaiiii*...can he actually *take* it from you?"

The general stared out the window, sweat shiny on his brow. "Possibly. He has a lot of influence with the viceroy and the top generals in Mexico City."

"Sir, if there is anything I can do to help— "

"There is," he said. "Don Calixto and I have arranged a visit for you to meet his daughter, Teresa, at their hacienda in Oposura. They are expecting us next week."

"Next week, sir? I am scheduled to lead a patrol up the Bavispe next—"

"Your orders have been changed, Captain."

On the appointed day the general and I met Don Calixto and his family at their hacienda near Oposura and stayed three days with them. Teresa was, like her German-born mother, fair-skinned and blonde and very pretty. Each day we rode with a chaperone to the river and had picnics on blankets we spread in the shade of sycamores and each evening after dinner Teresa played a harpsichord and sang for us in the large, airy parlor of their home. I greatly enjoyed our time with the Badillas and found Teresa to be a pleasant young woman. I told Don Calixto as much, and saw Don Domingo smile at my words. Still, on the ride back to Real San Juan, I reminded the general that I was making no promises.

He rummaged in his saddlebags, found a cigarro of coyote tobacco, lit it, and blew out a plume of smoke thick enough to alert every Apache in Sonora.

"No promises, Juan Mateo," he said, smiling behind the smoke. "I understand, certainly. Of course. Absolutely."

In early June we rode against the Apaches again, as they had returned to their old habits of raiding the small ranches and Pima settlements along the Bavispe and Terrenate and Santa María. After Chief Coro's great victory over Capotcari's Apaches, the chief had moved his people from their village of Quiburi on the Terrenate to a fertile green valley west of the Guachuca Mountains, where they would be safer from revenge attacks. At the time Don Domingo had approved of such a strategy, but we now realized that this had left much of the northeastern Pimería with too few Pima warriors to defend the other villages and had, in time, actually emboldened the heathens.

For two weeks we followed the tracks of a group led by Clavo and Oso Azul and saw the settlements they had burned and the mutilated bodies they left behind. We followed their tracks up into the Chiricahuas and back down again, but saw no hostiles. We never caught sight of a single one.

But a week after our less-than-victorious return to San Juan, I did see two Apaches. Both tried to kill me.

To explain, first I must tell you about Esmeralda.

Esmeralda was Wigberto's hinnie. If you have been around horses and mules much, you know that mules come from breeding jack burros with mare horses. But Esmeralda was not a mule, she was a hinnie, which is what you get when you mate a jenny, a female burro, with a stallion horse. I know the terms are a little confusing and it is hard to imagine the actual mechanics of it, but sometimes it happens and hinnies are the result. Not that anyone but Wigberto would actually *want* such an animal. Hinnies are generally smaller than mules, but the ones I have been around were three times as smart as a mule and six times as stubborn and they ate everything they could get their ravenous slobbery lips around. In these ways they differed little from Wigberto himself.

Wigberto loved his hinnie, and he never made a pack train expedition without her. But Esmeralda, in some odd way that only animals comprehend, had made friends with Teodora, Wigberto's colorful macaw, and these days any time you saw Esmeralda you also saw Teodora, usually perched on the hinnie's back or strutting on her rounded gray rump.

Why am I telling you all this? Because it was Esmeralda who delivered me to the two Apaches—and Teodora who saved me from them. This incident was so bizarre and unlikely that it forced me to stop and have a good long laugh at myself, and I suppose that alone did as much as anything to pull me out of my recent doldrums.

An interesting word, doldrums. In the sense that I use it, it means a state of depression or dejection, but it is actually a naval term that refers to a part of the ocean near the equator where little wind blows and ships can barely move. Which describes pretty well how I had been feeling lately. Fretting about my courtship—or lack of one—of Adriana Vásquez; my annoyance with Don Domingo for persisting in his search for a bride for me, and now my new worries about his position with the Compañía; my growing weariness with fighting and blood and death. Frankly, that is exactly where I had been: in the doldrums.

But about Esmeralda and Teodora, this is what happened:

We were a large group. Father Campos, myself, eight soldiers and nine Pima servants, plus Wigberto and ten of his teamsters tending the wagons, the remuda of spare horses, and the fifty or so pack animals. We were on our way from Real San Juan to San Ignacio with a load of building supplies and poultry for Father Campos' mission. We had seen no hostile Indios and were glad for that. The first evening we made camp on the bank of a pebbly creek about six leagues north of San Juan. Cottonwoods and willows lined the creek, and a flat plain dotted with sacaton stretched for a quarter of a mile on either side of it to the foothills of the rough, granite-capped mountains that rose into the pale skies around us.

The day had been pleasant, not yet burning with the heat of summer, and the men asked permission to have a chicken pull before their evening meal. I had been thinking about Adriana and Don Domingo and slipping deeper into my doldrums, and I thought, well, why not. If it would be good for the men's morale, perhaps it would be good for mine, too. Maybe I would even take part.

In case you have never seen a chicken pull, I will explain how it is done. First you take the meanest rooster you can find and bury it up to its neck in the ground, with only its head sticking out. Then the men take runs at it on horseback and the winner is the first man to pluck it from the earth at full gallop with his bare hand. By then, of course, a few bets have been made, a few wine bottles opened; some blood has been shed, and there have been a few friendly fistfights. Soldiers have been enjoying the sport for centuries, though it has always had its critics and detractors, I suppose, among the genteel.

Someone suggested we ride mules instead of horses. Campos, I think.

I asked Wigberto about the mules.

"Certainly," he said. "There is a small rental fee, of course, but the soldiers have recently been paid and—"

"How much?" I said.

He grinned, and I could see a sliver of onion stuck in his teeth. "Five reales for ten mules."

"Including Esmeralda?" I suppose it was the mood I was in.

Wigberto shrugged. "If you wish."

"She has experience with chicken pulls?"

He belched, and the odor of raw onion wafted over our campsite. "Maybe so, maybe no. You take your chances, Señor, like everyone else."

Father Campos, as pastor, went first. He came up with a few feathers and not much else, but I had never seen him with such a grin. I suppose, like me, he was just in a mood for something like this.

As commander, I went next. On Esmeralda.

Perhaps something frightened her. Perhaps it was stubbornness, perhaps it was simply a general lack of interest in roosters, I do not know, but here is what she did: She bolted, taking me with her, bounding straight across the grassy flats in the direction of a low granite-bouldered hill dotted with prickly pear and cholla.

Straight to where, I soon saw, two Apaches sat on paint ponies, watching.

Whether this was a chance encounter or they had been stalking us all day in hopes of picking off a straggler, I had no clue. But there they were. Two of them.

And there I was, arms flailing, coattails flapping, struggling to stay in the saddle and trying to get Esmeralda stopped before we reached the hill and the waiting Apaches. But I could not stop her, or even slow her. And clinging to her hairy rump, of course, was Teodora, bouncing and tossing, squawking and screeching at this indignity so rudely foisted upon her.

What the Apaches thought of all this, I can hardly imagine.

Finally, though, Esmeralda saw the Indians, made her own assessment of things, and decided to stop. And when she straightened her forelegs and dug her hooves into the dirt and skidded to a halt, of course I went tumbling over her head and landed belly down in a cloud of dust not thirty yards from the hill.

The Apaches raised their lances and started their horses towards me.

For the first time, I had some idea how the rooster felt.

Blood dripped from my chin and I had sharp pains in my ribs. Otherwise, I was all right—if you discount the gut-puckering fright I felt at being dumped without a flintlock or sword before two hostile Indios. From a distance I heard shouts and horses and knew my men were coming. I knew, too, that they would not reach me in time.

I pushed myself up and stood and watched the Apaches, their faces painted with ochre and vermilion, their horses coming at a slow trot. I had no wish to die, but I had no wish to die a coward, either, and I had decided I would make a run at one of the Indians and try to pull him off his horse and take his knife from him. I was deciding which one to go for and how to do it when the most amazing thing happened. I heard a flapping sound and felt a rush of air on my face as Teodora swooped in, her red and blue feathers glistening in the sunlight. She landed on the ground a few feet in front of me. The Apaches stopped. They stared at her.

Teodora looked them over, spread her wings and preened, then squawked in perfect Spanish, "*Get going, you stupid whores! Get moving, you shiftless bastardos, before I take a whip to your lazy, hairy asses!*"

Who knows, perhaps these two had never seen a macaw before. I am certain, though, that they had never *heard* one, because they cried out and reined their horses around and dashed flat-out for the mountains, their eyes the size of doubloons.

I was still laughing when Father Campos and the soldiers reached me. I told them what had happened.

"They are afraid of witches," Campos said. "They thought the bird was a witch."

"A witch." I took a drink from a gourd of water Campos handed me. "Father Kino told me about Apaches and witches. I had forgotten."

"It is good that Teodora learned to talk from a teamster," he said, grinning, "instead of a priest."

After I had cleaned the blood from my face I said, "Father, I feel the need for a strong relaxant. Would you care to join me for a few cups of wine?"

He chuckled. "I would be delighted, Captain."

I climbed onto Esmeralda and we rode back to our campsite for a meal of tortillas and goat cheese and a tall bottle of wine.

I told the soldiers to let the rooster go.

I had seen little of Father Kino since our expedition to Pinacate earlier in the year, so at the first opportunity I rode to Dolores in the summer heat to visit him. He had been busy at his mission, working in the fields, getting in the harvests. He showed me a new adobe storage building he had just completed, and showed me some remodeling work he was doing in the carpenter's shop and in the sacristy of the church.

The padre seemed well. I saw no sign of fever and he looked as if he had regained any weight he might have lost. He was in a fine mood. "I am planning another trip to the Colorado for this autumn, Juan Mateo," he told me. "Do you want to go?"

"Of course," I said. "As always."

That evening after dinner we walked down to the San Miguel and I told him about Adriana. Don Domingo knew about her now, so I supposed it could not hurt to tell the padre. Besides, I really wanted to know what he thought I should do. So I told him

He sat on a tree stump, his feet dangling in the water. "I knew about it, of course." He shrugged. "Rumors. I was wondering if you would ever tell me yourself."

I sighed. "It seems like everyone knows. But what should I do, Father? Pursue Adriana, or marry a rich man's daughter as my uncle would have me do?"

He thought about it for a time, then said, "I cannot advise you on such a thing, Juan Mateo. This is a matter of the heart, and I have learned that such decisions are best left to those involved, not their priest. But I know what I would do if I were you. I would pray. I would ask God for the wisdom to know what is right for me and for the women involved and for my family. I would pray."

I had hoped for more from him, but had not expected more, I suppose. I had never known him to be shy about voicing his opinion, but he had never imposed his judgment on my personal life and it seemed he had no desire to start now. But his suggestion was a good one. I would pray for wisdom; I would look to God for advice. I have no idea why I had not thought of that before, but I had not.

Kino and I sat quietly, watching javelina and then antelope drink at the river. Birds chittered in the trees and to the west the horizon was streaked with clouds that glowed in shades of lavender and pink and orange. After a time I told the padre about the general's worries over his job.

"Yes, I have heard," he said. "If Don Domingo is replaced, I suppose you could lose your job, too, for political reasons."

"It is possible," I said.

"If that happens, what would you do?"

I shrugged and tossed a pebble into the river.

"I have no idea," I said. "I cannot imagine what I would do."

CHAPTER 37 Mexico City. Winter of 1965-66.

The pictures were driving Olvera crazy.

First, there'd been that Ross Browne photo of the sketch of the two churches from 1864. That hadn't panned out; at least it hadn't led them to the foundations of the Campos church. But more sketches had turned up in recent months and now the scientists had several that showed both the present church, built in 1832, and the Campos church, dating to 1705. None, predictably, included the Chapel of San Xavier. All were confusing because no two were drawn from quite the same perspective. Worse, no two were drawn with the same attention to detail. Which made it difficult to calculate angles and distances from common landmarks, made it *impossible* to know precisely where the Campos church had stood *in relation to* the present church. This in turn was all the more annoying to Olvera because he had come to believe that the final piece of the puzzle was right in front of him. It would be something simple, he suspected. But whatever it was, he hadn't found it. He would, though, he was sure of that. He'd promised himself this: When he returned to Magdalena, he would again study the parish church and the other landmarks—for as long as it took. He would make sense of it. He would find Kino's grave.

If he returned to Magdalena.

The wait, too, was driving him crazy.

Not that he wasn't enjoying his stay at home. It was good to see his friends again and his family and to be back in the mountains where he felt at home. Still, he was a scientist and he couldn't quite chase away thoughts of the unfinished project in Magdalena in the northern desert.

They had stayed in touch, of course, during the months after the government cut off their funds: Father Acuña and Conrado Gallegos, the engineer, in Hermosillo. Wasley, back in Tucson. Olvera, Jiménez, and Romano in Mexico City. All busy but waiting patiently, hoping for a call from the Minister with news that their funds had been restored and they could return to Sonora.

Not long after Olvera's return to Mexico City he had a call from Bill Wasley. "I spoke with some friends at the medical school here," Wasley said. "I told them about Kino's fevers and asked if he could've had malaria."

"What did they say?"

"They said, sure, malaria was common back then. I told them about Kino's travels—from Italy to Spain, across the Atlantic to Veracruz, and across Mexico to the Gulf of California and the Baja area, then on up to Sonora. They said, sure, he could've picked it up several places along that route. Especially if he made other trips to the gulf—which we know he did—even after he left California and moved to the Pimería. The doctors tell me it's the Anopheles mosquito that carries the malarial parasite, and they're all over the African coast and the tropical areas of Central America and Mexico. They said some kinds of malaria are worse than others, and he could've had a fairly benign type for ten or twenty years, or a real bad kind for just a short time."

"So it's a possibility, then."

"Definitely a possibility."

"Gracias, my friend. Are you keeping busy these days?"

"I am, but I'm ready to get back to Magdalena."

"Me, too," Olvera told him.

To keep himself occupied, Olvera went back to the national archives and found even more documents on Kino and his missions. He read everything he could find on the Apaches and on the defensive battlements of the Spaniards. He studied the histories of the missions at San Xavier del Bac and Tumacácori and of the presidio at Tubac. He read monographs on the culture of the Pimas and Papagos, on the operation of an astrolabe, on flintlock firearms, and on methods used in making adobe block and kiln-fired brick. He read every journal in the library with articles on the architectural history of Sonora.

And he thought about traza.

He wasn't sure why he'd thought of it—traza. It had just popped into his mind.

He'd been thinking about the ruins at Cocóspera and the church at Oquitoa and the fact that Kino's churches always seemed to face south; wondering about that and, he supposed, a dozen other things. Traza was an old Spanish word that had no good modern equivalent. In its simplest form, it referred to the general design of a village or city, to the layout of streets and buildings.

The concept, he knew, went back to Greco-Roman times. In the first century B.C., Rome's most famous architect, Marcus Vitruvius Pollio, wrote a treatise he called *Ten Books of Architecture*. In it he set forth his ideas on the design of the perfect city. He advocated development on the chessboard pattern, with the city's most important buildings—its temples, government buildings, and markets—in the center. The major north-south road he called the *cardo;* the major east-west route, the *decumanus.* The center of the city was the point where these met, and it was here that he would place the *forum*—what Spaniards call the plaza.

Vitruvius Pollio's ideas caught on quickly in Europe. In the sixteenth century, King Felipe II of Spain liked them so much he adapted them into Spanish law as the *Ordenanzes Reales*, the Royal Decrees. But traza wasn't just a way to decide where to put your finest buildings. For anyone who led an entrada in a foreign land under the Spanish flag, it had a far broader meaning. This was because Felipe II made the decrees part of his *Leyes de Indias*, the Law of the Indies, that governed development of all new communities in the New World. It'd always been a source of amazement to Olvera that the villages of Sonora, Mexico, owed their designs to a Roman who'd lived two thousand years before.

Olvera had to go back to his old textbooks to remind himself of the details of Felipe's *Leyes.* As he read he made notes and added them to his journal.

For Kino himself, perhaps the most important ordinance was #1: "No person, *without our authorization*, can make a new discovery or entrada, or establish a new settlement, hamlet, or camp...*under penalty of death...*"

There were others that caught Olvera's eye, laws that governed everything from how to choose a site to how to protect the area from attack by hostile forces.

Ordinance #40: "Very high places shall not be chosen [for settlements], as they are disturbed by the winds and are difficult to access. Choose intermediate sites, provided with free breezes, especially from the north and south. And if it should be next to a mountain range, it should be seen that this will be on its east side or to the west. If for any reason a high place should be built, it should be seen that there is no fog. And if a site should be founded on a riverside, see that it is laid out on the east side."

#128: "Once the traza of the settlement has been laid out and plots divided among the inhabitants, each one shall put up his hut, tent, or corral, and together all of them shall build a trench around the village in order to defend themselves from Indian attack."

#29: "The discoveries should not be called conquests, for they have to be made in peace and charity."

#14: "The discoverers with the officials will name all the land discovered, including each province and the mountains and most important rivers."

All interesting enough, sure, but what did traza have to do with finding his long-lost padre? Just this: Eusebio Kino had settled a foreign land under the Spanish flag, and he was a trained cartographer. He would've known of Philip's decrees and that they were still the law of the land. He would have situated his church and chapel in the village of Magdalena in such a way that they would be at the center of the village, at the point where his cardo and decumanus crossed. He would have built his churches in a strictly north-south or east-west orientation. Which meant that the footings, and the pedrapléns under the bell towers, for those that had them, would've been oriented the same way. Olvera already knew what Kino's footings would *look* like: river rocks in a mortar of mud and clay. Now, with the concept of traza fresh in his mind, he had yet another means—the *orientation* of the footings—to help him recognize them when he saw them. When he returned to Magdalena he would take his best compass, because he had no doubt that Kino's foundations would run straight and true.

If he returned to Magdalena.

He tried not to let his hopes get too high. It was possible, even likely, that the Ministry would not grant them more funds. In Mexico City there were always many worthy projects begging for the small amounts of research money.

So he read and studied, enjoyed his family and friends, and passed the time.

Finally the call came. It brought good news: their team would have funding—for a few weeks, at least.

Olvera left Mexico City on April 16, 1966, by train, and arrived in Hermosillo on the 19th. He visited briefly with Encinas Johnson, Governor of Sonora, who again promised materials and support for their project. When Professor Jiménez arrived, they returned to the state archives to look at some old documents known to be from the burial register of the Chapel of San Xavier. After brief stops in Tubutama and Altar, they arrived in Magdalena the last week of April. They were excited and optimistic, and with good reason: They had funds to pay the laborers, at least for a while; Dr. Romano and Dr. Wasley would soon join them; they had more information on Kino and his missions; the Governor had again offered his assistance, as had Fathers Kieran McCarty and Cruz Acuña. No question, things were looking up. With all this support, they would quickly find Kino's grave.

Well, maybe *quickly* wasn't precisely the right word.

And, as they soon learned, they would also be getting help from an unexpected source—a zahurino. A dowser.

Maybe *help* wasn't quite the right word, either.

CHAPTER 38

Magdalena, Sonora. April 29, 1966.

In the months since the original trenches had been refilled for the Festival of San Xavier, winter rains had smoothed the grounds. Soft new grass now grew in the plaza and along the sidewalks. Bougainvilleas with crimson blossoms and verbena with flowers of purple and pink formed colorful hedges against the whitewashed plaster of the small stores and municipal buildings that fronted the plaza. On this cool pleasant Friday, the sun was still low on the horizon when Olvera and Wasley dug their first new trench near the front of the parish church. Avoiding areas they had excavated the year before, they worked with the solemn intensity of men who harbored no doubts of their eventual success.

In this first trench they found no underground walls or foundations—nothing at all, actually—that could have been from the Jesuit period. Disappointed but still optimistic, they started more trenches, some nearer the Palacio, some extending into the street that separated the Palacio from the church. In the open area northeast of the church they unearthed a single porcelain sherd—Chinese, from the mid- or late-eighteenth century. Interesting, but what could they do with one pottery sherd in an area of nineteenth century liniment bottles? With the help of laborers paid by the government they found a few stone foundations, but these were made of fired brick with lime mortar and were clearly of Franciscan origin. The Jesuits, the scientists knew, had used neither lime nor brick. So Olvera and the others kept at it, enlarging their trenches and opening new ones, digging, searching, digging again, into the next day and the day after.

But these trenches, like the others, yielded no trace of Kino's presence; the few beads and other artifacts they found dated to the Franciscan period, or later. Had they miscalculated? Completely missed the oldest portion of the village, the Jesuit area? Where, they wondered, was the Campos church? The Chapel of San Xavier? Where were the bones of their priest?

The zahurino came with his divining rods the first Sunday in May. He was a small man, thin, with a heavy mustache and stringy dark hair that grew long over his ears. His faded khaki trousers and white shirt hung loosely on him in the tepid breeze that blew across the plaza. From the steps of the parish church he looked out on the trenches and mounds of loose dark dirt that littered the area. "I see you haven't yet found your padre," he said to Olvera and Santos Saenz, the parish priest.

"We'll find him," Olvera said.

"My rods can find him," the man said. "And I will charge nothing for my services. I wish only to be of help." He smiled amiably and made a slight bow.

"We have God's help," Saenz said, "we don't need yours. Go away, you fraud." The priest, Olvera saw, was a man who dealt firmly with those who passed themselves off as seers and sorcerers.

But word of the man's offer quickly reached Jiménez, who arranged a meeting with him at the church and asked that Olvera, de la Vega, and Father Saenz be there, too. At the meeting Jiménez said, "We must give the man an opportunity to prove himself." He turned to the zahurino. "So, Señor, how do you do it? Tell us, por favor."

The man showed them two metal rods. "It's very simple, Señor. I hold the rods in my hands, loosely, like so, then ask questions of them. They give their answers by pointing in one direction or another. For one who is highly skilled, like myself, it's not difficult to read the answers in the movement of the rods."

"All right," Jiménez said politely, "then have your rods tell us where we can find the body of Father Kino."

Olvera and Saenz protested, but Jiménez stopped them. "No, we have to give him a chance."

"But Professor," Olvera countered, "this is nothing but superstition. His rods are fakery. He's probably being paid by treasure hunters."

"It doesn't matter. We're going to see what he can do."

"Gracias, Señor Jiménez," the man said, smiling faintly. "You are most kind. Please, follow me." He walked slowly through the church, following the rods, talking softly to them. Down hallways, in and out of rooms; out onto the patio, then back inside. Finally he stopped in the church office, where the priest and his secretary had their desks. The rods, twitching slightly, pointed to the south wall.

"The rods see something," the dowser said solemnly. "What's on the other side of this wall?"

"The bautisterio," Father Saenz grumbled. The baptistry.

"Please take me there, sir."

"Since your amazing rods know so much," the priest snorted, "have *them* take you."

The man smiled confidently and followed his rods down a hallway, around a corner, and into another corridor, Olvera, Saenz, de la Vega, and Jiménez following close behind. He stopped near a doorway, the rods pointing to the wall a few feet from the closed door.

"Here?" the priest said.

The dowser nodded.

"You're sure?"

"The rods are sure, sir."

"Incredible." Saenz arched an eyebrow. "The rods are sure that Father Kino is buried in the *women's restroom*?"

The man's face flared with embarrassment. "But you have no sign on the door!"

"Our women need no sign! They *know* where their facilities are located."

"Perhaps, sir," the man said, smiling, his composure back, "the rods made a very slight error. Sometimes this happens when they sense that unsympathetic observers like yourself are giving off distorted energy fields. If you would take me to the baptistry now and promise no more tricks, the rods are willing to try again to find your buried priest."

Saenz hesitated, frowning, then shrugged and walked the group down the corridor to another doorway that led into the baptistry. The room was cramped and spare, with tile flooring and walls of white plaster, the space empty except for the elevated concrete basin in its center. The priest nodded toward the north wall. "The office is on the other side."

"The rods are pulling very hard, sir. There's no question, they're telling us that Padre Kino is in that wall."

"So *now*," the priest retorted, "you're saying Kino was buried inside *this* wall? Not the other, in the women's facilities? You're changing your mind?"

"The rods have new information, sir, and now they're saying he's here, yes."

"This church," the priest said, "was built in 1832, more than a hundred years after Kino died. Do you think we're fools? You want us to destroy the walls of my church because your *rods* say so? That's ridiculous!"

"It isn't ridiculous, sir. It's very scientific."

Olvera, who'd been watching quietly, chuckled and whispered to de la Vega, "Scientific? The man's even more of a fraud than I thought. I suspect Kino and his friend, Juan Mateo Manje, would have a good laugh out of this."

"They'd probably kick the dowser's butt," de la Vega said under his breath, "all the way to Texas."

The man turned to Jiménez. "So, Professor," he said solemnly, "you will excavate the wall in the baptistry as the rods have suggested?"

"Father?" Jiménez said. "It's your call."

The priest stared at Jiménez, then at the dowser, and finally back at the wall. He sighed. "If you're convinced it must be done, Professor...go ahead, excavate the wall."

The zahurino smiled widely, then turned to Olvera.

"So, Señor Olvera, my new friend," he said cheerfully, "tell me, who was Juan Mateo Manje?"

They excavated the wall. Roughly four feet thick, it was built in three layers. Brick formed the outer layers, while the inner core consisted of stones embedded in concrete. Olvera and the laborers dug a tunnel about two feet into it but found no evidence of a burial. Fearing permanent damage to the wall, they continued their search by boring carefully spaced holes into it with an electric auger drill. It was hard, sweaty work and the drill bit filled the air with a gritty dust that choked the workers and burned their lungs. Still, they kept at it.

While Olvera and the others tunneled reluctantly into the wall of the baptistry and worked in the trenches in the street, documents with new information were arriving almost daily by mail. Some came from Father Acuña, still sifting through the archives of the Archdiocese in Hermosillo. Others came from Father McCarty in Tucson. Some would turn out to be important in the search for Kino; others wouldn't. The trick, as always, lay in figuring out which were and which weren't.

For example, in a document called *Archives of the Archbishopric of Hermosillo*, Acuña found this obituary and forwarded it to the scientists in Magdalena:

> **Manuel González...Año D. 1702**
>
> Jesuit missionary. Entered the Missions of the Province of Sonora before 1687; evangelized the region of Oposura, and accompanied Father Kino on one of his expeditions to Californa which took place in 1702, becoming gravely ill on account of the hardships suffered on the journey, and on his way back he died in Tubutama in April of the same year.

At first this seemed like old news, of no real importance to them. Olvera and the others already knew that González had been the Father Visitor in Oposura in 1687 and that he rode north with Kino on his first venture into the Pimería. They knew he was there when Kino chose Dolores as the location for his first mission, that he became a good friend and advisor to Kino, and that he died in 1702 after a long horseback journey with him to the western Pimería.

But they hadn't known what happened to Manuel González *after* he died. Hadn't known, in fact, that *anything* happened to him after he died.

Sometimes, they were about to learn, *after* can be very important.

Jiménez Moreno found the first hint that there was more to the story. He'd been thumbing through the libro de entierros of the parish church in Magdalena, looking for anything that might help them in their search for Kino, when he came across a curious note from the year 1712: "According to the burial register which corresponds to this year, Father Agustín de Campos brought from Tubutama the remains of Jesuit Fathers Manuel González and Ignacio Iturmendi."

Brought the remains of these Jesuit Fathers from Tubutama...to Magdalena? Now what was *that* all about?

Sánchez de la Vega found the rest of the story in a collection of documents he traced, finally, to the Bancroft Library in Berkeley, California. The collection was called *Santa María Magdalena Misión.* In its English translation:

> Año D. 1712. I have brought from Tubutama the bones of Father Manuel González, who during many years was missionary at Oposura and who died in Tubutama on his return from a trip that in 1702 he made to the Colorado River in the company of Father Kino; and the remains of Father Ignacio Iturmendi, missionary of Tubutama, who died there the 4th of June of 1702. At the end of January I buried them solemnly in this Chapel of St. Francis Xavier; those of Father Manuel in a small box on the Side of the Gospel and those of Father Ignacio in another little box on the Side of the Epistle. (Signed by Father Agustín de Campos in Santa María Magdalena)

This was big. Because now the scientists knew that under the chapel they would find not one, but *three*, sets of bones: 1) Eusebio Kino's fully-articulated skeleton between the 2nd and 3rd ashlars on the left side of the nave, and 2) a jumbled pile of bones (González), also on the left side, and

3) a jumbled pile of bones (Iturmendi) on the right side. And finding *all* of them, exactly where they were said to be in church documents, would be immensely helpful in knowing they had found the real Kino chapel—*when* they found it.

Olvera and Wasley now dug with renewed energy. They opened new trenches in the plaza and in front of the Palacio and, at Jiménez's urging, even dug up the floor beneath the choir loft in the parish church. They found a few artifacts from the Franciscan period but, as before, nothing from earlier times.

Sometimes, though, progress comes in unexpected forms.

Like, for instance, rain.

On the night of May 2nd clouds filled the sky and rains came and cleansed the air and formed rivulets down the muddied slopes of the trenches and tall mounds of earth beside them. Early the next morning, Olvera finished his breakfast of eggs, chorizo, and coffee and went out to inspect his trenches. The rain had stopped; the air was cool and pleasant.

The rain had come steadily but not hard, and Olvera expected to find little damage to his trenches. He found little. But as he examined the complex of diggings near the front of the Palacio, a flash of white caught his eye. Something small—on top of a muddy mound of earth near trench #4. A shell? Whatever it was, it'd been exposed and washed clean by the rain. He took a closer look.

A seashell, yes, but it had a conical perforation at one end; the other end had been sanded flat. Interesting. Probably from a pendant or necklace, he guessed, and probably pre-Spanish. He would ask his friend, Wasley. Wasley would know. But the location of the shell was interesting, too: at the very top of the mound of dirt. *Inverted stratigraphy*, archaeologists would call this. Simply stated, its basic premise was this: As a general rule, where something turns up in a pile of dirt is inversely related to its original depth in the trench. For example, a bead or sherd that turns up in the *highest* part of a pile probably came from the *deepest* part of the trench—because it was in the *last* shovelful of dirt tossed onto the pile.

And in this case, the deepest part of the trench was...*what*?

Curious now, Olvera climbed into the trench. He poked his finger into the soft earth at the bottom. He found an inch or so of mud, and immediately beneath that, hardpan—a thick layer, he knew, of archaeologically sterile calcium carbonate. So, the afternoon before, the workman had scooped his last shovelful of dirt from the top of the hardpan in the deepest part of the trench; the shell pendant had been in that last scoop of dirt. Interesting.

And the shell was old. The oldest object Olvera had found so far, he was sure of it.

As he inspected the bottom of the trench, something else, at first barely visible in the mud, caught his attention. He pulled it from the soft muck: an oval piece of flint, with sharp edges all around. A scraper? For use on deer or antelope skins? Yes, he was sure of it. And this was old, too. Older, probably, than the seashell.

Wasley was having lunch—carne asada from the old man with the squeaky cart in the plaza—when Olvera found him on a bench in front of a small store that sold religious items to tourists. Olvera dropped onto the bench beside him.

"How are you, Bill?"

"Tired, but good," Wasley said. A dark crescent of sweat flared out from the armpits of his khaki shirt. "Find anything under the choir loft?"

"Nothing."

"In the baptistry?"

Olvera rolled his eyes. "We drilled a lot of holes. And found nothing. I hope you've had better luck than I've had."

"I feel like I've turned a couple of tons of dirt in the last twenty-four hours. I don't have a lot to show for it." Wasley took a bite of carne, chewed it slowly, and grinned at Olvera. "So where is the dowser now?"

"He's vanished," Olvera said, laughing, "like a puff of smoke. Father Saenz is not real happy, all the holes everywhere. I told him we would have our men repair the damages. That seemed to satisfy him. A little, anyway."

Wasley nodded. "Can't say I blame him for being upset. But I don't fault Jiménez, either. He's not the kind of man who leaves a stone unturned."

"He's thorough, no question." When Wasley finished his lunch, Olvera took him to trench 4 and showed him the shell and scraper.

"Yes," Wasley said after studying them, "definitely pre-Spanish."

"I've been thinking," Olvera said. "Near the front of the church, and back to the northwest of it, everything we've found has been of fairly recent origin—tequila bottles, liniment bottles, things like that. But as we moved east and northeast of the church—into the open area here—the artifacts are older: buttons made from bone, the porcelain sherd. Now, here, in trench 4, much closer to the front of the City Hall, we have the scraper and seashell pendant, both *very* old."

"You're saying that the farther northeast we get from the front façade of the church, the older the artifacts."

"Exactly. What do you make of it?"

Wasley took a long look at the buildings and trenches around them. "Well," he said finally, "I suspect your trench #4 is giving us the oldest settled area. I think you've found Kino's *forum*. Which convinces me that we've been right all along in believing his chapel is very near where we now stand. We're at the center of the old village."

"I think so, too." Olvera smiled. "This is good news."

"Oh, yeah, it's *great* news. But we need to dig faster now. We have to start earlier each morning and work later each evening."

"Sure, especially now that we know we're close, but why— ?"

Wasley motioned toward the City Hall. "About an hour ago Jiménez had a call from the Minister in Mexico City. I don't know what the Minister said to him, but it sure put Jiménez in a rotten mood."

Olvera wearily rubbed the bridge of his nose. "I don't like the sound of that." He sighed. "They're cutting off our funds again?"

"Maybe," Wasley said. "But let's not give up. We've been getting some great stuff from Acuña and the others in the archives. Maybe this week the postman will bring us something that'll lead us straight to Kino's grave."

Oddly enough, the postman did.

That evening at his hotel, Olvera found in his mail a manila envelope with a return address in Tucson. Inside it, protected by layers of clean white cardboard, was a pencil sketch of Magdalena. According to the scribblings on the back, it'd been drawn in 1851 by an artist named Henry Pratt. Olvera and Wasley had seen other drawings and paintings of the village from the nineteenth century, but none had been much help. This one, though, seemed different. At first, Olvera wasn't quite sure how. In his room he placed the sketch on the table near his bed, taking care not to soil or bend it. He sat at the narrow table, adjusted the reading lamp, and quietly studied the sketch.

CHAPTER 39

San Juan Bautista, Sonora. Año D. 1701. September.

At Don Domingo's urging, I saw Teresa Badilla, Don Calixto's daughter, a second time at Oposura in that summer of 1701. I enjoyed my time with her, though on occasion I found my mind wandering, my thoughts returning to Adriana Vásquez. As I had feared, by summer's end I still had no notion of what to do about marriage and Adriana. I had prayed for wisdom, as Father Kino suggested, but clear and concise answers still eluded me.

Don Domingo's opinions on my marital status were well known to me, of course, and lately he had become even more insistent. Still, he had made no threats and I appreciated that. The simple truth was this: if I were still in Spain, already my family would have chosen a mate for me and I would have had little choice in the matter. In Europe, and now even in much of the New World, a man of good breeding was expected to marry into a family that had wealth and power and to ally himself with his bride's family in ways that would bring even more wealth and power to his own family. I had been able to escape such a fate only because I was on the Sonoran frontier, where the rules were thankfully a bit less rigorous.

In September I saw Adriana again.

She lived with her two daughters and her late husband's mother near the presidio in a casita that she rented from a shopkeeper who lived next door and sold herbal concoctions and amulets and powders. I called for her in a one-horse carriage on a warm but pleasant Sunday morning after mass.

It was the first time she had allowed me to see where she lived, a modest adobe structure, quite plain, but cleanly kept. She introduced me to Señora Vásquez and I enjoyed a short conversation with Estafana and Julieta, the daughters. The girls giggled a lot, and teased me some. They seemed to expect me to tease them back, so I did. What Adriana thought of these little exchanges, I could only guess. There had been times when I believed she purposefully kept me at a distance from her daughters, and other times, like this, when—well, I just did not know.

At a small park near the river Adriana and I found a table in a shaded area where breezes stirred the hackberries and willows that grew near the water. The park was owned by the army, and in the early years of the presidio Don Domingo had sent his carpenters out to build tables and benches. Most Sundays the park was filled with soldiers and their families. This day, though, we had it to ourselves, at least so far. We set out a meal of wine, cheese, grilled peppers, and bizcochos—dark wheat biscuits—with honey and quince jelly.

On the ride out, I had told Adriana the story of Esmeralda and Teodora and the wide-eyed Apaches, and we were still smiling about that when we sat at the table. Her laugh was deep and throaty, her smile as bright and warm as I had ever seen it.

"You look nice," I told her. Her yellow dress gave a glow to her dark eyes, and she had her shiny black hair pulled back in a braid, fastened with a comb made of silver and decorated with pale green stones. Even from across the table I could smell the freshness of her skin and the rose-scented water she had daubed behind her ears.

"You smell nice, too," I said.

She gave me the smile again. "You are most generous with your compliments today, Juan Mateo. Gracias."

She had unpacked the goblets and plates, and now we drank wine and ate and talked comfortably about her dress shop and her daughters and about people we knew. I told her the latest news of the army and the latest on the maraudings of the Apaches and Jocomes. Serious subjects, every one, but we managed to find a bit of humor in all of them. We had a fine time.

Fall had begun to inch its way down the mountains, and around us we could see the blue flowers of asters and the waving yellow blooms of sunflowers that grew in tall stands near the road. Hummingbirds with black chins darted and ricocheted through the bushes; meadowlarks the color of cream flitted among the cottonwoods and sycamores. Above us a red-tailed hawk circled in an azure sky.

"It is beautiful here," Adriana said. "Thank you for bringing me."

"Yes," I said, "it is always pleasant." Plump gray quail with black plumes on their heads studied us from the shade of a palo verde, and in the distance I could see deer drinking at the river's edge. In a few weeks the male deer would begin to lose the soft velvety coating on their antlers, and on the mountainsides they would begin polishing the newly-exposed horns on the trunks of rough-barked trees in preparation for the winter's rut. For the moment, though, they were amiably drinking together from the burbling waters of the river.

Thoughts of deer and mountainsides somehow reminded me of Baboquivari, and of course that reminded me of the little lapis cross. These had been on my mind lately and that probably explains it. Anyway, I realized I had never mentioned the blue cross to Adriana, even though we had first met the night Henri Pitot and his friend, Diego, tried to take it from me on a muddy street in San Juan Bautista. So I told her about it, and about the near-invisible etchings Father Kino and I had found on it. "I think it has something to do with the location of a mine," I told her. "Silver. Possibly gold. Probably on Baboquivari Mountain."

"Do you plan to look for this...hidden treasure?" she asked me.

I took a bite of cheese and nodded.

"...And if you find it," she said after a moment, "and become rich, what would you do then?"

I thought about her question, then shrugged. "I suppose I would buy a hacienda somewhere south of here, maybe around Ures or Conicari. General Jironza thinks I should learn the business of cattle ranching." I smoothed honey on a biscuit and had a bite of it. When I glanced up, Adriana was studying me.

She looked away. Her eyes seemed almost moist in the morning light. Around us, other tables had begun to fill with families here for a picnic.

"And what *else*," she said, "does the general think you should do?"

"What do you mean?" I said.

"You know what I mean."

I stared at her. "...Are you all right?"

"I am fine, Juan Mateo."

"If I did something, or said something I should not have, I apologize."

She sighed. "No. It is nothing, please."

I sliced more cheese and placed it on her plate.

She was staring at me again, her eyes dark and wet.

"When you go to Baboquivari?" she said.

"Yes—"

"I will be praying for your safety, Juan Mateo."

"Thank you," I said. "...Are you sure you are all right?"

She touched my face, then quickly drew her hand back. Where her fingers had been, my skin felt prickly, moist, layered with heat, and I realized this was the first time she had ever touched me. My heart thumped in my chest.

"Adriana—"

"Forgive me, por favor," she said softly, looking away again, "for taking such a liberty. I am just feeling a little sad. And perhaps a little hurt. I have enjoyed this day, and all our times together—"

"Adriana, I—"

"Please, Juan Mateo, do not say any more."

On the ride back to San Juan, I tried to understand what had happened here, tried to see what I had done wrong. I had no success.

The first week of October I rode out of San Juan for Baboquivari with Francisco Acuña, the young lieutenant who was one of the army's best translators. I took Francisco because he was a good friend as well as a brave soldier, because he was trustworthy, and because in Sonora it never hurt to have someone around who spoke several languages. We had a rope line of spare horses and half a dozen mules loaded with food, water, and digging implements, and enough time off from our army duties to have a good look around. Too, we had my lapis cross with its faint, strange engravings that still made no sense to me.

We worked our way northwest to Dolores and on across the flat dry desert to Tubutama, up the Altar River to Tucubavia, then turned northwest again towards the domed peak of hard brown granite that beckoned in the distance: Baboquivari. Wah Kiwulk, the Papagos call it. According to my maps, it was part of a mountain range that measured maybe two leagues in east-west dimensions and fifteen or so leagues from its southern tip to its northernmost reaches. We saw no hostile Indios and rode steadily towards the tall peak under pale cloudless skies in the cool of early autumn.

We could find no way up from the mountain's south side, so we went in from the east, up a rough canyon, as I had done on my earlier visit. We slowly worked our way uphill, past stands of mesquite and palo verde, past tall saguaros, scrub cactus, and ocotillo, past chollas covered with thorns that glistened in the sunlight like new-fallen snow. Higher still, we got into piñons and juniper and scrabbled up rocky draws and over boulders of dark granite through stands of bushes we called manzanitas, their trunks coated with bark that resembled thick reddish-brown varnish, their branches laden with berries that looked like tiny apples.

We stayed on the mountain a week. We found springs of fresh water, a cave containing animal bones, and a bear's skull, polished and whitened with time, half buried in the rocks. We saw coyotes and bighorn sheep and once we spotted a mountain lion eyeing us lazily from its perch on the limb of a piñon pine.

We saw deer, and dark droppings that were probably from a black bear but could have been a grizzly's, and in a meadow we saw a solitary palm tree—how it got there we had no idea. We found an open field of chiltepines, the little red peppers that grow wild, and in the same clearing we found a stone corral that looked as if it had been there a hundred years. As to who built the corral and why, we had no clue.

"For *horses*?" Acuña asked me. "A hundred years ago there *were* no horses in the Pimería. The Papagos had no horses. Most of them still do not." Acuña was a short man, thickly built, with strong hands and a quick mind. Physically, he reminded me a little of Father Campos, though the lieutenant was darker-skinned, mestizo rather than Spanish.

"Perhaps Coronado's men passed through here," I said.

"Do you really think so?"

"No," I said, "but I suppose it is possible."

We sat in the shade of a juniper and rested. I found my magnifying lens and took a long look at the blue lapis cross and its odd, faint inscriptions: the letters V, SAS, and C, and the numbers and letters 715v-174 and 620v-92. Even with all the discussions we had had about this on our ride from San Juan, we still knew little about what any of it meant. Did the numbers followed by v's represent distances, perhaps measured in Spanish *varas*, each about thirty-three inches by the English standard? And the smaller numbers, were they compass headings? And what about the letters? Did they represent landmarks that might lead to the treasure? All of these things seemed likely, but suspecting it was not the same as knowing it.

"Maybe this treasure, whatever it is, is on the *west* side of the mountain," Acuña suggested, grinning. "Over where I'itoi lives."

I shrugged. "It could be anywhere."

Finally we did find something, though what it had to do with our search I had no idea: at the bottom of a rocky drainage, a small dam made of stones and packed earth, as if someone had tried to obstruct a natural watercourse in order to make a tank for collecting rain water. The tank was empty, the rocks and silt dry at the bottom of it. Near the dam we saw the track of a large snake, curling and looping over the sand. Windblown and faded already; an old track.

"Someone killed it," Acuña said solemnly. "Which explains why there is no water in the tank anymore."

"What are you talking about?"

He chuckled. "*La corua.* Have you not heard of that legend?"

I had never heard of it, so Acuña explained. "Manuel González, the priest at Oposura, told me about it when I first came to the Pimería. The Papagos say la corua is a large serpent that lives near water sources like natural springs and tanks, and guards them. The serpent has a gold-colored cross on its forehead and a big mouth but no teeth. The Indios say the creature is harmless. Still, I have heard that if someone claims to have seen such a thing near a water hole, no one will go near the place."

"And Father González told you if someone killed la corua, the water would dry up?"

Acuña nodded.

"And where exactly," I asked him, "did Father González say we would find our treasure of gold and silver *in relation to* this water source and this dead serpent?"

He chuckled again. "The padre neglected to tell me that."

How old was the dam? It was hard to be sure, but judging from the condition of the dried mud between the stones, I doubted it was more than five or six years old. Except for the dam itself, we found no sign of human presence in the area. So was the dam important for our search? I had no idea.

We found a few other things on the mountain: a three-legged skunk; vultures feeding on a deer carcass; a rattlesnake skeleton wrapped like a coil of rope around the trunk of a juniper; a boulder, maybe twenty feet in height, that had weathered in such a way that from a certain angle it resembled the face of an old man, with ears and nose and large sad eyes and a droopy mustache that had been stained a pale greenish-brown by the lichen that grew in coarse plaques over its surface.

But we found nothing we could correlate with the letters and numbers on the lapis cross. We found no gold or silver or anything at all that suggested anyone had ever dug for ore or anything else on this mountain. Or that anyone had even *been* here, really, except for the dam and the stone corral. We found, truthfully, nothing at all. We were disappointed, of course, but for now there was little else we could do. We had run out of time. That last day it occurred to me that Adriana's prayer for my safety had been answered, as neither Acuña nor I had sustained any serious injuries. I wondered, as I had every day and night of our journey, how she was.

The next morning we broke camp and headed back for San Juan and the predictable and routine lives that awaited us at the presidio.

Predictable and routine lives? If that had ever been true, such a life was about to end—for me, anyway.

In that early autumn of 1701, two things happened that would change my life greatly. The first: My uncle, Don Domingo Jironza, was unceremoniously removed from his position as Military Commander of Sonora and General of the Compañía Volante, and replaced by General Jacinto Fuensaldaña, a rich miner from Sinaloa who had never suffered, to anyone's knowledge, from an excess of ethics or an overabundance of good reputation.

Another was that I myself was appointed to a two-year term as Alcalde Mayor of Sonora. This was a civilian position—an important and influential one, surely, but one that put me behind a desk and covered me in paperwork, not a prospect I particularly relished. Still, the post had been offered by the viceroy himself, so how could I refuse? And, truthfully, the timing was right for a change of vocation. I doubted Fuensaldaña wanted me around the presidio; he would know that my loyalties still lay with my uncle. Too, the military authorities in Mexico City had promised that I could keep my officer's commission for the duration of my service as Alcalde Mayor. And since my office would be in Real San Juan, I might even be able to see more of Adriana—if she would allow it. For all these reasons, I deemed it wise to accept the viceroy's generous offer.

I immediately dispatched a letter to Kino at Dolores to explain why I would be unable to accompany him on his next expedition, scheduled for early November. He sent his congratulations on my new appointment and promised a full report when he returned from the Colorado.

He kept his promise. When he returned, he sent word, and in December I rode to Dolores to take his report. With a pack train of mules and a few Pima servants, he had followed the Camino del Diablo northwest across the desert to the Gila, then rode west on the river's south bank to San Dionysio at the junction of the Gila and Colorado Rivers. Two days' ride south of the junction, some Yumans and members of a tribe he called Quiquimas ferried him on a little log raft across the fast-moving waters to the west bank of the Colorado.

He told me he had actually *set foot in California.* His eyes glowed as he said it.

"You are sure of this, Father?" We were in his quarters, drinking chocolate and sitting on chairs under his sister's painting of the Chini family home at Segno.

He was still beaming. "I am certain. I was in California! Now I know we can move cattle and supplies to Father Salvatierra at Loreto without having to transport them across the gulf by ship."

I had a sip of chocolate. "You are certain the gulf was *south* of you? Not *west*?"

"Many leagues to the south," he said firmly. "It does not reach as far north as San Dionysio."

"So, Father," I said, teasing him a little, "how many cattle can you get on that log raft?"

Now he laughed. "You make a good point, mi amigo. I still do not know *how* we will get the cattle across."

"But God will show us a way," he added.

That winter Kino re-drew his official map of the Pimería, revising the western parts and showing Baja California as a peninsula with the gulf ending at roughly thirty-two degrees latitude, and San Dionysio about twenty leagues north of that at just below thirty-three degrees. He called his new map *Paso por Tierra*—Passage by Land. The map was happily received by Spanish officials, and within months of publication it found great fame in Europe as well as New Spain.

Me, I remained unconvinced.

CHAPTER 40 Magdalena, Sonora. May, 1966.

Bill Wasley tapped the brakes, eased the van off the graveled road, and brought it to a stop near an ironwood tree that grew in a clearing just off the roadway. He and his passenger, Jorge Olvera, climbed from the van, steaming mugs of coffee in their hands. On a strap over his shoulder Wasley carried a canvas water bag; Olvera carried a leather briefcase. A light breeze blew out of the south and riffled the leaves of the ironwood and the slender green branches of the paloverdes near the clearing. Behind the men, a mile or so to the east, lay the river and the town of Magdalena. To the west, a short walk from the car, a steep hill stood between them and the harsh flat desert that stretched all the way to the Gulf of California. Thin clouds on the horizon glowed with a faintly orange tint. It was a few minutes past dawn.

The scientists stared up to the jagged rocks at the top of the hill.

Wasley took a last sip of coffee.

"Ready?" he said.

Olvera nodded. They started up, slowly at first, wary of rattlesnakes and the sharp spines of the cholla and prickly pear that dotted the rocky slope. A quarter mile up the hill, they stopped in a clearing. Breathing heavily already, Olvera opened his briefcase and removed the sketch of Magdalena he'd received in the mail at his hotel the evening before. It showed a panoramic view of the village and the countryside around it, and had clearly been drawn from the hill on which they now stood. Saguaros and organ pipes and small bushes filled the foreground of the sketch. Beyond these were the hill that sloped steeply to the river and the cottonwoods and hackberries that grew along it. Beyond the river, the village in the sketch looked spare and angular in a broad valley cuffed by saw-toothed mountains that formed the far horizon. The sketch differed little from what they saw when they looked down the slope to the real river and the real town. But it differed in a few important details.

Olvera looked around, studying the vegetation on the hillside.

"No," he said. "Not here."

They started up again, working their way past scrub cactus and giant saguaros and organ pipes, over boulders and past outcroppings of gray granite and crumbly dark sandstone. The sun had moved higher; the air had warmed. From somewhere in the distance they heard coyotes yipping; a red-tailed hawk circled in thermals at the top of the hill. Again Olvera and Wasley stopped to scan the vegetation around them. "Nope," Wasley said. "Not here, either."

They moved on, stopping occasionally to drink water and review the sketch. Twice they saw coyotes on a distant ridge and, once, a rattler coiled on a flat rock. They kept going, steadily gaining altitude. By now they were damp with sweat; their legs had begun to ache. Finally they stopped again for water and another look at the sketch. Again they studied the vegetation around them.

"Yeah," Wasley said emphatically as he swigged from the water bag. "Right here. This is it."

Olvera nodded his agreement. "This is where Pratt stood when he made the sketch. I'm sure of it, too."

The sketch, actually a reproduction of the original, had come from Olvera's friends, Byron and Jane Ivancovich, in Tucson. They'd obtained it, Olvera had learned, from a library at Brown University in Providence, Rhode Island. The sketch came from a collection of writings by an explorer named John Bartlett. It had been drawn in 1851 by Henry Pratt, an artist who traveled with Bartlett.

Why was the sketch important? Because it was *old*—over a hundred years old; because it showed things that interested Olvera and Wasley greatly. Things like the parish church, still in existence, and the Campos church, now gone. Things like the high adobe wall that surrounded the churches and other buildings in the center of the village. The scientists knew that saguaros and organ pipes often lived for hundreds of years. They'd been confident that with patience—and a large canteen of water—they could find the actual cacti Pratt had drawn and they could stand where he'd stood. And, finally, they had.

Olvera glanced at the sketch again and wiped sweat from his neck. "I'd guess the adobe wall was primarily for defensive purposes."

"Sure, Apaches," Wasley said. He glanced at the sketch in Olvera's hand. "The Campos church is interesting, too."

"And it's the Campos church, no question. It's much too large to be Kino's chapel." Olvera drank again from the canteen. "The more I look at the drawing," he said, "the happier I am that we decided to climb up here. It's given me a better perspective on the place."

"Definitely," Wasley said. "And the artist drew it long before the City Hall was built, which gives us a little different view of things."

"Right, and look at the Campos church and the angles of its walls compared to the walls of the parish church." Olvera smiled. "Now, my friend, I'm convinced. I'd suspected it from the first time I saw the sketch, but I wasn't sure. Now I am. Are you thinking what I'm thinking?"

Wasley stared out across the valley to the town. He nodded. "I thought so, too, but I didn't want to commit myself until I saw the town from up here. Now I believe it. The sketch is telling us that the Campos church was definitely located to the *northeast* of the parish church."

"Exactly."

"Which would put it almost smack in front of the City Hall."

"And very near where I found the shell and the flint scraper!"

"Right there, yeah."

"And if the Campos church is *there*," Olvera declared, "the Kino chapel can't be far away. Ah, it's all starting to come together, isn't it?"

"At last."

Olvera slipped the sketch back into his briefcase and closed and locked the lid. "One day soon, amigo, we'll drink wine and sing and celebrate over the bones of our priest."

"...If our luck holds. That's a big if."

Olvera's face changed. "Will the Minister stop our funds again?"

Wasley shrugged. "Jiménez says he's threatened it. Probably within the next week. For what reason, no one knows."

"So we'll need to hurry." Olvera smiled at a new thought. "What will the mayor say if we have to dig up his office?"

"I asked him that question just yesterday. He said we could dig up the floor under his own desk if it would help us find the padre's grave."

Olvera drank again from the canteen and stared out at the town. "Then we're in agreement," he said finally. "We'll concentrate our efforts at the front of the City Hall."

In Magdalena, Olvera and Wasley and the hired laborers resumed their search.

They began new trenches near the front of the City Hall, and extended trenches already started in that area. They began a few trenches in other areas, too, but they continued to put their energy and expectations into the area at the front of the City Hall. They found a few artifacts, but none from the Jesuit era. And they found a lot of bones—so many bones, in fact, that they figured they'd stumbled into a cemetery. But the bones were Mexican and Indian. None could have been from a European.

Near the City Hall they found more foundations, too. But these were made of fired brick with a lime-based mortar. They were Franciscan, not Jesuit. Over the next few days the men continued to dig, opening more trenches and enlarging the ones already begun. For Olvera and Wasley it was hard, hot, sweaty work.

But others were laboring, too, and finding perhaps a bit more success.

Jiménez, studying the libro de entierros of the parish church, came across two obituaries with implications for their search. One reported the death of a man named Salvador de Noriega, a Spaniard. It stated simply that in the year 1739, he "was buried in front of the door of the Chapel of San Francisco in Magdalena."

The second was equally brief. "El 27 de Junio de 1837: José Gabriel Vega, 90 years of age...his body was buried in front of the niche of Señor San Francisco in the Old Chapel."

Olvera smiled wryly at all this. The more questions they answered, it seemed, the more questions they raised. For instance: the Spaniard, Noriega, was said to be buried under the door of the chapel. Where was this door? What direction had it faced? South, as they usually did in Kino's churches? Or some other direction? And what of Noriega's ancestry? He was a western European? Well, so was Kino. Would he and Wasley—or the anthropologists who examined the bones—confuse them? Would they find one...and think they had the other?

As for Vega, he'd been buried beneath a niche named for San Xavier. Where, precisely, was this niche? On which wall of the chapel, and where on that wall? And, most importantly, *where was the chapel*?

Even Olvera himself had added to the confusion when he found in the archives the death notices of three children who'd died in 1740. All buried by a priest named Gaspar Stiger. All buried, simply, "under the chapel."

Jiménez said, "Gentlemen, we have a lot of bodies under that chapel. Has anyone counted them?"

"We have Kino," Wasley said, "between the 2nd and 3rd footings on the left side. And we have the priests González and Iturmendi on the left and right sides."

"And Vega under the niche," Olvera added, "and Noriega under the doorway. And now the three children. I count eight, altogether."

"That makes a lot of bones, gentlemen."

"Many bones," Olvera agreed.

"Lotsa, lotsa bones," Wasley said.

"The Minister phoned again today," Jiménez told them.

Olvera rolled his eyes. "He's stopping our funds?"

"He says he can promise us four days. Can we find Kino in four days?"

"Yes," Olvera said, "we can find him."

"Lotsa, lotsa bones," Wasley said again.

Olvera wondered if the stress was affecting Wasley's mind.

Kieran McCarty, the Franciscan, had been busy, too. In the archives at San Xavier del Bac, the old mission in Tucson, he had just found some of the answers the men sought. They came in a document written by Fernando Grande, who'd been sent to Sonora by the viceroy in the late 1820's to inspect the frontier missions and report on their economic viability. He filed his report in 1828 in a paper he called *Cartas de Sonora*, or Letters From Sonora. In the *Cartas*, McCarty found this passage referring to the Chapel of San Xavier in Magdalena:

> The chapel of this town is moderate. It is of adobe material. The entrance portal faces south. There is a moderate little tower in which are located three bells and another smaller one. It has nothing that draws particular attention. The only altar is in the sanctuary. On it are set an image of the crucified Christ and another of the Virgin of Dolores; at the feet of the larger carving is the smaller one, which is of ordinary quality. And in some niches which form a retablo along the wall of the altar are set a statue of St. Magdalene, the patron of the pueblo (this is small but well-carved), a statue of St. Francis Xavier, and one of Blessed Joseph Oriol; the latter is imperfectly carved. Midway in the nave of the chapel is a niche where there is located in a case a large carving of St. Francis Xavier, an object of devotion everywhere in northwest Mexico. It is a beautiful and solemn sculpture.

Now this was big, Olvera knew. *Very* big, because this was the first detailed description of the chapel anyone had found. Grande confirmed for them that the chapel faced south; confirmed that it had a niche large enough to hold a sizable statue of Francis Xavier "midway in the nave;" and that the chapel indeed had a bell tower. The tower meant that the men might find a pedraplén as well as stone footings.

And the next day they found such a structure—a few yards from the southeast corner of the City Hall and several feet beneath the surface: river rock in a mortar of hard clay and mud, resembling a single great slab of cobblestone, large enough to support a bell tower. Of course the question arose: Assuming this was indeed a pedraplén, had it been under Kino's chapel, or under the Campos church?

Questions, sure, there were still a lot of them. But they were making progress; they were *moving*. They were learning things; *finding* things. Kino was out there and they were close and they *knew* it. So now they had...how many days? Three? All right, sure, Olvera thought, they could find Kino in three days.

CHAPTER 41

San Juan Bautista, Sonora. Año D. 1702.

We have now reached the end of the period that I recorded in detail in the diary I kept of my early years in Sonora. For the remainder of this narrative I will largely be forced to depend on a few long-forgotten notes—which I trust very little because I do not recall the context in which most were written—and my memory, which these days I trust even less. I will do the best I can.

I can tell you that in my new position as Alcalde Mayor, I spent much of 1702 and the following year giving speeches, signing documents, chairing meetings attended by venal, self-important bureaucrats, hosting boring parties for government officials and their wives, presiding over noisy festivals, and smiling my way through banquets given in honor of people I scarcely knew. Well, perhaps I exaggerate my discontent, but do not ask me for details. Fortunately for me, the two years I served as head of the government of Sonora remain little more than a faintly-disagreeable blur in my mind.

But a few things happened in that first year that I recall vividly.

In April, I managed to slip away from my entourage of servants, secretaries, and sycophants long enough to visit Father Kino. He had just returned from yet another expedition to the Colorado. According to rumors reaching San Juan, he had endured many hardships on his journey, and even lost his good friend, Father Manuel González, the priest at Oposura, who had accompanied him. As you can imagine, I was anxious to see Kino and to learn the facts of the situation.

We met in Magdalena on a warm cloudless spring day, a light breeze nudging the leaves of the cottonwoods near the ramada that sat in the center of the little Pima settlement and served as the church when visiting priests, most often Father Campos, came for services. Kino and I sat in the shade of the ramada and tried with little success to talk while Indio children giggled and hugged the padre's legs and tugged at the frayed hem of his robe as their mothers watched patiently from a distance. Fortunately, the youngsters soon lost interest in us and went off to run foot races along the river.

"Finally," Kino said, watching the last of them scurry away, "we can talk."

He looked tired. I could see it in the languor of his movements, in the flatness of his smile and the dark flesh around his blue eyes, in the patient but deliberate way in which he had played with the children. Still, I was pleased that he had agreed to meet me. It was good to see him again.

"We were in California, Juan Mateo," he said.

I chuckled. "I *knew* you would say that. I want to hear all about it."

"Of course, but first I want to know about you. How are you? Are you enjoying your work as gobernador? I hardly recognized you in your civilian clothes."

"I am well, Father." I told him of my new duties and responsibilities.

"But you liked being an army officer more, I think."

"It was an honor to be chosen for this position," I said, "but truthfully, yes, I liked being a soldier more."

"Do you see much of the new general, Fuensaldaña? What kind of man is he?"

"Not a particularly likeable one. I avoid him when I can."

"I hear he has a nephew at the presidio."

"Gregorio Tuñón," I said. "A captain. He is even worse."

Kino laughed. "Perhaps you are a little biased, Juan Mateo."

I shrugged. "Yes, probably." Around us Indian women worked steadily in the cooking ramadas, and beyond them on the hillsides I could see the mud-and-twig huts of the villagers, and the irrigation canals that spread out from the river, and men and women working in the fields and tending the sheep and goats and the fat brown cattle that grazed in the river's grassy floodplain.

"And Don Domingo," Kino said, "I am almost afraid to ask—how is he?"

"Still depressed, but not as much as a few months ago. I think he will be all right. He will find something to do."

"Nothing lasts, you know," he said after a time. "Times change. Lives change. We lose people we love." He had turned serious now, his dark face lined with grief. "I have to tell you about Manuel Gonzalez. I suppose you heard what happened?"

"Some of the rumors said he was sick, others said he was killed by

Apaches. In San Juan we did not know what to believe."

"No, not Apaches." Kino shook his head and sighed. When he spoke again his voice was low, almost hoarse. "Manuel made no complaints. Not at first, anyway. He tried to keep it to himself, but by the time we reached the Gila, I knew something was wrong. He refused to eat, and when he tried to, he threw his food up. Finally he admitted that he had severe pains in his abdomen. Soon after that, he was so weak he could hardly stay in the saddle."

The padre made the sign of the cross, then continued: "We had gone downstream on the Colorado, hoping to find a place where the river widened and was shallow enough that we could get the horses across. By the time we had gone five or six leagues, though, Manuel was too sick to continue. And now he was running a fever. I knew I had to get him to medical help as fast as possible. I decided to go straight east, across the dunes of the Gran Desierto, to save time. That turned out to be a horrible decision, Juan Mateo. We bogged down. The wind was fierce out there and we could find no water for our animals. We had to turn back. When we reached the Colorado again, we turned north, up to the Gila, then retraced our route to Sonoita on the Camino del Diablo."

His eyes were moist now, his voice scratchy, so low I could barely hear him. "There was little we could do for Manuel. Poor man. At Sonoita we made a litter and the Indios carried him on their shoulders to Tubutama. He died there, and Father Iturmendi buried him there."

"...I am sorry, Father," I said.

"I miss him very much. He was a good friend and a loyal companion for all the years I have been here. Did you know it was Manuel who brought me to the Pimería? He was with me the day I first rode into this land."

"This *spacious place*," I said, "that the Lord set your feet in."

Kino nodded and tried to smile. "You remember David's words. Good. Psalms, chapter thirty-one, verses nine and ten. *'I will be glad and rejoice in your love, for You saw my affliction and knew the anguish of my soul. You have not handed me over to the enemy, but have set my feet in a spacious place.'* "

"Seven and eight," I said.

"What?"

"Verses seven and eight," I said. "Not nine and ten."

He glanced at me, hesitating. I knew he was running the words through his mind again. Then he laughed softly; his blue eyes brightened. "My old brain is getting tired and forgetful, isn't it? But you are a good student, Juan Mateo. You always were."

We sat for a time, neither of us saying much, both of us thinking, I suppose, about Father González. Finally Kino rose from his bench, walked to his horse, a dark mustang tethered near the ramada, and retrieved a gourd of water. I watched him as he turned the gourd up and took a long drink. No question, the padre was growing old. He moved less quickly now, and his back was not quite so straight, and at the joints of his fingers I had seen knots of hard flesh like those the post surgeon called huesos ancianos, *old man's bones*, in the old army veterans. Still, I had never heard the padre complain. I had watched him ride into Magdalena earlier this day and he had handled his horse as well as any soldier or vaquero I had ever known. I worried about him, though, worried about the hard pace he always seemed to set for himself.

In the ramada again he smiled and said, "Cheer up, my friend. Not *all* the news I bring is bad." He offered me a drink from his gourd. I had a small sip and thanked him.

"Our missions in the western desert are growing," he explained, his eyes bright again. "The ranching operations at Sonoita and Bac are doing even better than we had dared to hope. The Yumas and Quiquimas along the Colorado and the Maricopas on the Gila have been friendly to us and seem to be receptive to the Word. Iturmendi is doing well at Tubutama and Campos is working hard at San Ignacio. We have a good priest now at Caborca. The Rector, Father Mora, seems to have forgotten most of his quarrels with me. And we have large new churches under construction at Cocóspera and Remedios."

He was not through. He pointed around at the village. "Magdalena is growing, too, Juan Mateo. We see more Indios coming in every month. Father Campos and I have been drawing up plans for a new church here. We will put it in the exact center of the village, as Spanish law requires. It will be a beautiful church, a proper place for the Pimas to worship, an excellent place for us to teach and perform the sacraments, so all the Indians can know the gift of salvation."

It must have been the word "sacraments" that reminded him. He glanced at me, his eyes curious. "Have you decided what to do about Adriana...and marriage?"

I blew out a mouthful of air. "Well, I prayed for wisdom, as you suggested, Father."

"And received it?"

"Some," I said. "Not nearly enough."

"Don Domingo has not given up his campaign to find a wife for you?"

"Even in retirement," I told the padre, "Don Domingo is still Don Domingo."

For the remainder of 1702 and the year following, I stayed busy with my governmental duties and saw little of the padre. I heard that he spent much of those two years working on his new churches at Remedios and Cocóspera and improving farming operations at some of his newer missions such as Sáric, Busanic, and Bac. And of course he preached and taught the Gospel at every mission he could reach. But he had no opportunity to return to the Colorado.

Kino had drawn some criticism for taking Father González with him on his long expedition of 1702, of course, not surprising when you considered who his critics were: miners unable to take Pimas as slaves because of his vigilance, disgruntled settlers who resented the time he gave to the Indians, malcontents in the clergy who were jealous of his successes. What Mora, the Rector, thought of it, I never knew, or cared, really. Father Kino had no way of knowing before the expedition that Manuel González would take sick and die. As far as I was concerned, that was the end of the matter. Others disagreed, though, and Kino suffered for it, as he often did when misfortunes hit our frontier world.

In Europe the war against Austria, England, and the Netherlands went on—the War of Spanish Succession, they were now calling it—with Archduke Charles of Austria still trying to depose our new king, Felipe V. You know my feelings about the French. I can hardly imagine my countrymen fighting alongside them against anyone, but apparently they were—with some notable successes, we heard. By now Portugal had sided with us, too, and that helped. Particularly on the seas, as the Portuguese had a very fine navy. I must admit, though, none of this inclined me toward any greater fondness for the French.

We heard that the English had sacked and burned the Spanish settlement of San Agustín in a place they called Florida on the east coast of Nueva España, and we wondered if the war would extend even to our little part of the world. English coming from the east, Russians coming down the California coast from the Pacific northwest. It would not have surprised me to learn that Vikings in steel helmets with horns were even now sailing up the Golfo looking for women to molest and villages to pillage, maybe *they* could find a land route to California.

Rumors and gossip spread quickly across Sonora. There was nothing I could do about the English, Russians, or even the French, though, so I lost little sleep over the news that came with each wagonload of new immigrants from Europe. For now, worrying about such matters was General Jacinto Fuensaldaña's responsibility; worrying about speeches and boring banquets seemed to be mine.

In those years I had no opportunity to return to Baboquivari. I saw Acuña in San Juan on several occasions, and gave him permission to go back with the lapis cross to look for gold and silver, should he wish to. He thanked me, but I later learned that he never got back, either. The cavalry stayed after the Apaches, and Acuña, like me, simply had no time for Baboquivari's offerings, whatever they might be.

There was another conversation from my time in the governor's office, though, that I recall in detail. This was 1703, a warm September day, silver clouds pressing against the mountains, the sky a deep ocean blue. I had taken an agriculture official to Remedios to show him a new irrigation system Father Kino had engineered, and on our return to San Juan we were riding quietly, enjoying the scenery, making little conversation. Much of the time, actually, I had been thinking about Adriana. I had come to a decision about her, finally, a decision about marriage, and I wanted to see her as soon as possible to make my feelings known to her. I was still thinking about her, her warm dark face and shiny hair still fresh in my mind, when we met Old Gonzala. We had just topped a hill and there she was on her mouse-colored stallion, her silver bracelets jangling in the still air. She wore a cotton dress of no particular color. A faded shawl kept her wrinkled face in shadows, her gray eyes dark and secret.

"Señora," I said. She was as bony and stooped as I remembered.

"You used to be a soldier," she said, her voice low and raspy.

"And?"

"And nothing." She glanced at the man riding with me, then turned her odd gray eyes on me again. "We will not see you around here anymore, soldier."

"You are a fake," I said. "A fraud, a nosy old harridan who snoops and hears a few things and uses the information to make the settlers and Indians believe you have magical powers. You have no powers. You have no ability to see the future."

"I know many things," she scoffed. "I knew about the O'odham uprising before it happened in 'ninety-five. You of all people should remember that!"

I shook my head. "A lucky guess. Anyone could have predicted it."

"Here is something I know, soldier. Soon you will be gone."

"*Gone?*"

She cackled, a screeching sound that almost split my ears. She nudged her horse forward. "*Gone from the presidio,*" she droned as she passed us on the trail, "*gone from the government. Gone from San Juan. Gone even from the Pimería.*"

Gone from San Juan? From the Pimería?

But the old crone, I have to admit, turned out to be right.

Chapter 42

San Juan, Sonora. Año D. 1703.

Adriana...

On a Sunday morning in mid-October, I rose early and breakfasted on grilled beef, tortillas, chocolate in cow's milk, and boiled chicken eggs prepared by my kitchen servants. I dressed in cotton trousers and a fresh white camisa, and at mid-morning saddled my favorite Andalusian and rode down to the river. Well, to be truthful, I ate little of the meal my cooks had prepared, as my appetite, usually hearty, had totally abandoned me this day.

Though the day was indeed a beautiful one.

The clouds were streaks of silver in a sky that made me think of finely-ground blue powder, the breeze a cool and pleasant reminder that summer was past. On my ride I saw hawks perched on saguaros, coyotes loping along a ridge, and chiltepines growing wild, their branches heavy with chiles. Near the river, walnuts were ripening on the nogales, their leaves, like those of the cottonwoods, already showing the first hint of autumn color. Beneath the oaks, the ground was thick with acorns. I saw white-crowned sparrows in the trees and foxes patrolling the foothills and, in the distance, antelope drinking at the river. High on the mountains the nights would already be cold, the animals silent, the aspens already turning a glorious gold; the maples, their vivid red. But here in the desert the weather was still mild, the fruits and berries plentiful, and we were in that fine season the Pimas call Wi'ihanig Mashath, the Month of the Harvest Moon.

Adriana met me at the river.

I helped her down from her horse. "Thank you for coming," I said.

Earlier in the week I had gone to her dress shop and asked her to meet me here, though I had offered no reason for my request. Now here she was, and my heart was thumping wildly in my chest.

Her dark eyes darted over me. "Why am I here, Juan Mateo?"

Today she had her shiny black hair pulled back and held with a silver comb. Her dress, the color of aged wine, accented the narrowness of her waist and gave her dark skin the look of soft, smooth silk. At her neck she wore the gold crucifix on the necklace of blue beads that I had seen so often. *Aaiiii*, she was beautiful.

"I need to talk to you," I said.

She nodded. "All right."

"Adriana—"

She waited.

"...Adriana, there is something I have to say."

"This is something you could not say in the dress shop?"

I blew out a deep breath. "No. No, I could not. Would you like to walk, or have something to eat? I brought some cheese."

She shook her head, then looked away, her eyes restless now. "I have a feeling this is something I do not want to hear, Juan Mateo. Perhaps you should go ahead and say it."

I willed the words out of my mouth. "...Adriana, I cannot see you again."

"You—"

I sighed. "Early next year I am marrying someone else."

Her eyes glistened with moisture now. "Who is she?"

"...It does not matter. Her people are a long ways from here."

"She is rich?"

"Her father is quite wealthy," I said honestly.

She was crying now, tears inching down the dark skin of her face.

"Are you angry with me, Adriana?"

She sobbed and shook her head.

I wanted to reach out and touch her, to feel the warmth of her skin.

"Do not worry about me, Juan Mateo. I am all right, just very sad. In my heart I have always known it would not work for us. Still, I always hoped that somehow it might. I prayed it would. Was I wrong to do that?"

"No," I said softly.

"The truth is, we come from different worlds...with different rules. And I have to accept that."

"There is something I want you to know," I said.

She looked up at me, her eyes still wet. "What?"

We talked for a while longer, but none of what we said is the concern of anyone but the two of us. Forgive me, por favor, for electing to omit it from this narrative.

When Adriana rode out she stopped once and looked back at me, her eyes dark and moist, but she said nothing more. What more was there to say?

In December I finished my term of service with the civil government of Sonora and moved out of the governor's casa and out of Real San Juan.

CHAPTER 43 Magdalena, Sonora. May, 1966.

Olvera opened his leather briefcase, pulled out a photograph, and placed it on the table in the little café where he, Wasley, and Romano were having a breakfast of sausages and eggs, toasted tortillas, and coffee. Through the window they could see clouds gathering. Outside, the air had smelled of rain.

The photograph was black-and-white, faded with age. Olvera tapped it with his finger.

"Have a look," he said, taking a bite of egg.

Wasley studied the photo, then handed it to Romano. It showed a vaquero on horseback pausing to light a cigarette as he flirted with two young women standing near his horse in a wide dusty street. The parish church and the City Hall filled the background. The day had been sunny and bright; it was a pleasant scene that spoke of an earlier, less complicated time. The photographer, probably unnoticed by the cowboy and his lady friends, had taken his shot from the middle of the street, perhaps twenty yards northeast of the City Hall's clock tower, a prominent structure that rose above the building along its front and formed a covered portal for the main door to the building.

"The photograph," Olvera said, "was taken in 1938." He sipped his coffee and had a bite of tortilla.

"Now, por favor," he said, "look at this." He handed the men a pencil sketch of a scene very similar to the one depicted in the photograph they'd just examined. The sketch, like the photo, included the parish church. But there was no City Hall. Instead, it showed a second church, smaller than the parish church and clearly made of adobe. Little remained of the smaller church: a double-tiered bell tower at one corner and a battered, half-crumbled adobe wall that angled away from the tower; nothing else. The back of the sketch bore the name of the artist, Alphonse Pinart, and the date, Año D. 1879.

"It showed up in the mail yesterday," Olvera said.

"Interesting," Wasley said. "It shows the parish church, of course. And the ruins would be the Campos church, I presume. It was drawn before the City Hall was built, so we wouldn't expect to see that. Unfortunately for us, it doesn't show the Kino chapel, but I suppose by 1879 the chapel was already completely gone." He shrugged. "I can't make much more of it than that."

Romano held up the sketch and photo and examined them. "I agree with your assessment, Bill. But what's surprising to me is that the sketch was made from almost *exactly* the same site from which the photographer took his shot of the cowboy. I find that to be incredible."

"Amazing, isn't it?" Olvera poured refills of coffee around. "The artist and the photographer seem to have stood in virtually the same spot to record their views of Magdalena. A coincidence, sure, but that's why the two views are interesting...and probably very valuable to us."

They waited for Olvera's explanation. It wasn't long in coming.

"I don't believe the smaller building, the adobe ruins," Olvera said, "is the Campos church."

Wasley glanced up from his eggs.

Olvera smiled. "It's the Chapel of San Francisco Xavier. Kino's chapel."

"Jorge, are you sure? How can you know this?"

"Three reasons. One, the bell tower on the ruins is too small to be from the Campos church. If you compare it to the other elements of the sketch, I believe you'll agree. Secondly, you recall the sketch of Magdalena by J. Ross Browne. From 1864, I think it was. Hold on, I have it here someplace." Olvera thumbed through the contents of his briefcase, found the sketch, and handed it to Wasley.

"Now, in Browne's sketch," Olvera went on, "you can see that the bell tower of the Campos church had an external staircase—what they call a *cranked* staircase—that led up to the roof. It was mudejar in design and part of a defensive parapet built to protect the defenders. See it? All right, now look again at Pinart's sketch. The bell tower in his sketch has no such external staircase. To get to the roof, a person presumably climbed a spiral staircase *inside* the tower."

"...And the third reason?"

"Look again at the Browne sketch. See how the Campos church faces the plaza? It faces east. But the smaller building in the Pinart drawing faces *south*, toward the *parish church*. Even though most of its adobe walls are gone, I became convinced that it faced south when I studied the angles of the walls that remained, and the way Pinart shaded them in his sketch. I believe he drew this church from its backside. He was standing behind it, looking into the apse."

Romano let out a low whistle. "Bill, he's right."

Wasley nodded. "So, Jorge," he said. "What do you make of all this? How does it help us?"

From his briefcase Olvera pulled two sheets of thin, transparent paper.

"Tracing paper." He held both sheets up so Wasley and Romano could see through them. "On one," he said, "I traced the buildings and other structures in the old photograph from 1938. On the second, I traced the buildings and other structures on Pinart's sketch. It took a while to get them matched up, but I think I finally have. It worked because the photographer and the artist stood in the same spot with the same angles and distances, the same perspective, on the buildings they saw before them."

"And," Wasley said, seeing it now, grinning, "you *laid one tracing atop the other* and got—"

"I got a composite view that tells me where Kino's chapel stood in relation to our modern City Hall." Olvera placed the tracing of the photograph on the table and covered it with the tracing of the Pinart sketch, carefully aligning the dome and other parts of the parish church in the two. By now Wasley and Romano were at Olvera's side, carefully studying the tracings.

"Incredible," Wasley said.

"Amazing," Romano said.

"Jorge," Wasley declared, "you're a genius."

Olvera smiled. "I'm no genius, but I'm a very happy man."

In the overlay, Kino's chapel sat squarely in front of the City Hall, within a few feet of its clock tower and portal and doorway.

"Amazing," Romano said again.

"Somehow I've managed to forget," Olvera said. "How much time do we have before the Minister cuts off our funds again?"

"Jiménez says two days."

Olvera took a last sip of coffee. "All right, gentlemen, I believe we have some digging to do."

They did some digging. They did a *lot* of digging. With the hired laborers they formed teams and started new trenches in front of the City Hall, and extended old ones. They dug up the street immediately in front of the clock tower, extending the trenches to the edge of the concrete sidewalk under the portal. Working with little rest, Wasley's team soon found their first Jesuit foundation. *Zoquete*, the Sonorans called the hard, lumpy material: river rocks bonded with a mortar of mud and clay. They found it under the street at the southeast corner of the City Hall. As pleased as they were to find it, they still had no way of knowing whether it was part of Kino's chapel or the Campos church. So they made careful notes and drew detailed diagrams. They photographed it and took samples for chemical testing. And they kept digging.

In trench #17, very near the clock tower, Olvera's team found a second zoquete foundation. They dug alongside it for a few yards, scooping dirt away, exposing it. It seemed to run straight, but in exactly what direction? Olvera stood at the end of it with his compass, sighted down the length of it, locked the needle, and checked the reading: *ninety degrees.*. To confirm, he took another sight from the other end: *two hundred and seventy degrees*. So the foundation ran east-and-west, precisely as Vitruvius Pollio's traza and King Felipe's *Leyes* demanded; exactly as Kino would have built it. Olvera, coated with sweat and grime, stood in the trench and grinned.

While Olvera and the other scientists labored in their trenches, Father Acuña and Father McCarty continued their searches through the microfilm libraries of Hermosillo and Tucson. Almost daily they mailed to Olvera and Jiménez bundles of documents, maps, letters—anything that could possibly aid in finding Kino and his chapel. Professor Jiménez had remained in Magdalena to study the records of the libro de entierros. He was also searching desperately for a way to convince the Minister to extend their funding for a few more weeks. Not that he believed they needed that much time. Olvera and Wasley were making important finds now, big finds, and Jiménez believed it was only a matter of days, maybe *hours*, before they would unearth their long-lost padre. But Jiménez was a solemn and careful man and again he would telephone the Minister in Ciudad de Mexico and plead his case. Still, he was confident.

Olvera and Wasley were careful men, too, and confident. They were confident they knew how the Jesuits built their foundations; confident they could recognize these foundations when they saw them. But they were careful, too, and concerned that too few of their laborers knew these things. It was all too easy, for instance, to confuse a zoquete foundation with the earth and stones that formed the ancient riverbed known to lie beneath this part of the village. Could the workmen always tell an underground Jesuit wall or foundation from a Franciscan one made of fired brick or quarry stone and lime-and-sand mortar? Or from hardened earth with a few smooth rocks in it? Could *they*, the scientists, *always* know with certainty?

"We can *almost* always know the difference," Romano insisted.

"Even so," Wasley said, "I think we ought to take a look at Remedios."

"Remedios? The old ruins? What's there for us?"

"Not much, anymore," Wasley said. "But that's the beauty of it. No one has rebuilt it or added anything to it. What you see at Remedios...is exactly how Kino built it. When Charlie Polzer and I were excavating in the Proctor Chapel last year, we learned a lot by taking a good look at Remedios."

"We'll need to convince Professor Jiménez," someone said.

"Then let's go find him."

Jiménez immediately agreed: Olvera and Romano and Wasley would visit the ruins at Remedios, make careful notes on the foundations, and take two of their best workmen with them for instruction.

"But make it a quick trip," Jiménez added. "The Minister is not in a generous mood. He says he can finance our project only through tomorrow. He says if we haven't found Kino by then, we'll have to return to Mexico City."

Eusebio Kino had built his Nuestra Señora de los Remedios at the site of a Pima village called Coagibubig on the Río San Miguel, about twenty miles northeast of Magdalena and almost directly north of his own home mission of Dolores. Olvera and the others knew that Kino's church at Remedios was virtually a carbon copy of his mission at Cocóspera. And like a lot of his missions, it sat on a high bluff that sloped steeply down to a wide, deep river and offered spectacular views of the valley. The Pima village, of course, had disappeared long ago, and by the middle of the twentieth century little remained of the church but a few scattered mounds of brown adobe that had melted back into the earth. But because it sat on a hill and there were areas around it in which the soil had eroded, they quickly found foundations they could expose for study.

They found what they'd expected: the foundations at Remedios were identical to the zoquete they'd found in front of the City Hall. When they were certain the workmen could recognize a Jesuit foundation, they hurried back to Magdalena.

There, they found that Professor Jiménez had been busy. He'd abandoned his work in the archives and put on his field boots. With a team of laborers in trench #17, he'd found yet another Jesuit foundation. Oriented north-and-south, it was north of the foundation Olvera had found. Following it still farther north, Jiménez had discovered that the wall made a sharp ninety-degree turn to the west, toward the City Hall. Olvera and the others crowded around for a look. Could this be part of Kino's chapel, perhaps its north wall? It seemed possible. Working quickly, the laborers found more footings. Gradually the outlines of a rectangular building took shape; incomplete, but still a building. But was it the right size?

Olvera took the measurements: roughly five by sixteen meters. Sixteen by fifty-two feet. He felt his heart thumping in his chest.

"Perfect for a chapel," he whispered. "Too small for a church."

"I think we're here," Wasley said, staring at the footings. "I think this is it."

"No question, this is it." When Olvera's heart had slowed he said, "The laborers are working better now. With more confidence. They recognize Kino's work when they see it."

Wasley nodded. "We've been lucky today."

Their luck was still running. Later that day, working in a new trench near the clock tower, a workman found what looked like part of a human bone. Without disturbing it, he called for help. Romano, the physical anthropologist, carefully cleaned the bone, then slowly and methodically exposed what turned out to be a complete skeleton: from the length of the long bones and the articulated height, most likely an adult. From the shape of the pelvis, a male.

Olvera stood beside the trench staring down at Romano as he worked on the skull with a soft-bristled brush. In the trench the ribs and spine and pelvis and most of the large leg bones were exposed. Much of the skull was still encased in hard dirt, and Romano worked slowly around the eye sockets with his brush.

Olvera removed his hat and wiped his brow with a dirty bandanna. His hand trembled slightly as he slipped his hat back on.

"Is it an Indian, Arturo? Or a mestizo?"

In the trench Romano shook his head. "Probably neither."

Olvera's eyes glowed. "A European, then?"

"I think so, yes."

"Madre de Dios, man, tell me, is it Kino?"

Romano chuckled at Olvera's impatience. "I don't know yet, Jorge. The man wasn't carrying any ID."

CHAPTER 44

Banámichi, Sonora. Año D. 1704.

arly this year, I married.

My new father-in-law gave us two thousand acres in the grasslands south of Banámichi and I purchased another thousand with money from my own savings and with funds advanced to me by Don Domingo. There, near a winding, pebbly creek, my wife and I built a home and a fine ranch. Within a year we had cattle, sheep, and goats, and more than twenty servants and vaqueros on our payroll.

I also had a host of new relatives: Granillos, Vivars, Peraltas, they were everywhere. If you have ever lived in Sonora, you will recognize the names. Most were ranchers, though many were in other businesses, too: mining, mercantile, land development; even the army. All had prospered. But they treated me well and accepted me as I was, and for that I was grateful.

I set about learning the ranching business.

And trying to forget Adriana.

In January, though, before I married, I rode to Remedios, the Pima village a few leagues north of Dolores. Padre Kino had finally finished his new church there and an identical one at Cocóspera, and he had invited friends and officials from all over Sonora and New Spain for the solemn Mass of Dedication at each church and for the festivities that would follow. I have no idea how many officials he knew but I know how many friends he had, and people came by the thousands to help him celebrate, despite the fact that in that year, 1704, January was a wet and bitterly cold month.

It was at this great celebration at Remedios that I met Johann Steinhoffer. He was a Jesuit, originally from Bohemia, and had only recently come to the Pimería, sent by the Provincial in Mexico City for the purpose of teaching herbal medicine to the Pimas. Brother Juan, as he was known to the Spanish-speaking settlers. In time I came to call him Juanito, as he was a small man, though not surprisingly, a hardy and resilient one. For years he rode the deserts of northern Sonora, usually alone, sharing his knowledge of herbs with anyone who cared to learn. He often stopped at our ranch at Banámichi, and we always enjoyed seeing him.

The Apaches tried many times to kill him, of course. They never succeeded. Whether this was simple luck or the Lord's will, I never knew, though I have always suspected the latter. Like Kino and Campos, Juanito Steinhoffer seemed to live under God's cloak of protection.

It was from Brother Juanito that I learned about the little white-flowered shrub he called quina-quina. The Pimas and Papagos would come to call it copalquina, the settlers, copalchi. By whatever name it went, though, it cured intermittent fevers, according to Juanito. And it grew in Sonora, he said, unlike cinchona, which you had to get from Peru. Father Kino, of course, would never admit to even *having* fevers, at least ones of any seriousness, so I convinced Juanito to prepare a quantity of the copalchi bark for me and I sent it to Kino at Dolores with instructions for steeping the tea. "To help you sleep soundly, mi amigo," I wrote in my note. Whether it worked—or even whether he actually ever used it—I never knew, but I can say that in the next few years I never saw the padre when he had signs of fever.

General Fuensaldaña, to no one's surprise, was too much of a thief to stay out of trouble for long. Whatever irregularities he had involved himself in at the presidio, the officials caught him at them. They arrested him and took him to Mexico City. We later heard he was put on trial and went to jail. Whether any of this was true, I never knew with certainty, but I do know that no one around here saw him for the next few years. I thought the generals in Mexico City might ask Don Domingo to take command again at the presidio, but they didn't. They allowed Fuensaldaña to name his own successor, and of course he chose his nephew, Gregorio Tuñón y Quiros, a captain of cavalry. Though Tuñón accepted the position, he had always been more interested in mining than soldiering, and for the next few years military protection for the padre's missions was minimal to non-existent. The Apaches, of course, took advantage of this. Many settlers and innocent Indians died. None of this seemed to trouble Tuñón. He was rarely seen at the presidio.

I worried about Father Kino. Though I had kept my commission in the army, for practical purposes I was a civilian now. I had little authority because I had no command, no soldiers. If Kino or anyone else needed help against the Apaches, there would be little I could do. I worried about that, too.

And Kino? Not surprisingly, he had been busy.

A new port facility had recently been built at Guaymas on the gulf coast, and Kino and Salvatierra had decided to try a new way of moving cattle and supplies to the missions of California. They had not abandoned their idea of finding a land route to the north, but the Baja missions were in desperate need. They needed immediate help, even if it had to come the expensive way—across the gulf by ship. Francisco Piccolo, a Jesuit, had been assigned to Guaymas as the Church's shipping agent, and after Easter Kino rode out of Dolores with a pack train and servants to test a new route that would take him south to Opodepe and Pitic, then on to the new port for talks with Father Piccolo.

It was some months after his journey to Guaymas that I next saw him.

I took my wife's uncle, Captain Simón Romo de Vivar, with me, and we arrived at Dolores on a Sunday morning in September, the skies clear, the breeze gentle and cooling. Father Kino met us at the door of the church and greeted us warmly. Captain de Vivar was a pleasant if quiet man, a successful rancher as well as an able soldier, and he and Kino seemed to get along well.

After mass, the church crowded with Pimas and Ópatas, we rode to a quiet place on the San Miguel and sat in the shade of a sycamore. After I had answered the padre's questions about everything new in my life—and there was much to tell him, of course—he gave us news from the other missions. The Apaches had been vicious and persistent in their attacks. Many Pimas had died. But Apaches died, too, he told us, and that had given the Pimas some satisfaction.

"But you are all right here, Father?" I asked him.

He nodded and smiled. "The Lord is looking after us."

"And at San Ignacio, Father Campos is all right?"

"He worries, as we all do, but he is well."

"That is good to hear, sir," I said.

His smile grew. "Agustín and I plan to begin trenching for the foundations of our new church at Magdalena sometime soon, Juan Mateo. Within a few months, if the Lord wills it."

"So," I said, "new churches at Remedios and Cocóspera, and now Magdalena, too."

"Yes, the Lord has blessed us with churches. Now if He would just bless us with more priests to staff them." He shrugged. "Nothing has changed. I write the authorities in Mexico City and request more priests. They write back and say they have none to send. I get cramps in my fingers from all the letters I write."

We talked about other things, too. In Europe, the war against the Austrians that seemed to go on and on. The new port at Guaymas. Gregorio Tuñón and the problems at the presidio. The fall harvests, and the prospects for the next crop of winter wheat. The Apaches, again.

"You heard Clavo died, Juan Mateo? Measles. The rumor is, he got it from a Mexican child he took from a wagon full of campesinos that he and his men attacked."

"So, he will not be driving nails through the eyes of any more settlers."

"We thank God for that," the padre said. "But we still need you back in the Compañía, my friend."

I shrugged. "As long as Tuñón is in charge, I would not be welcome at the presidio, Father. And anyway, I am married now. I have other responsibilities."

"Do you still miss the army?"

"Yes," I said. "More than I expected."

We sat quietly for a time, until Kino broke the silence. "Have you seen Black Skull in recent months, or heard anything about him?"

"Black Skull?" The padre's question surprised me. "No, I have not seen him in a long while. And I have heard nothing about him recently. Why?"

The wrinkles deepened in Kino's brow. "Rumors. They say Black Skull plans to kill you. They say he knows about your wife and ranch. You have heard nothing of this?"

"No, nothing." I thought about it a little, and said, "I see no reason to worry. He has been trying to kill me for years and has not succeeded. But if he tries to hurt my new wife or her family, I suppose I will find his rancheria in the mountains and do to his family whatever he has done to mine."

Kino sighed. "There seems to be no end to it, does there? We have tried to make peace, but they refuse to talk to us. We send emissaries to them, but what do the heathens do? They hang our people over a fire and burn them to death."

I glanced at Kino. "At the ranch now, it is no longer just my wife and me."

"What do you mean?"

I smiled. "She tells me I am going to be a father."

The padre's blue eyes sparkled. "The Lord has blessed you, mi amigo."

I did not see Father Kino again in that year of 1704. I did, though, see Apaches at my ranch. Usually they were trying to steal our horses and kill the cattle. Once, a dozen of them, whooping and shouting, came with torches and flaming arrows and tried to burn us out of our new casa. By God's grace, Captain de Vivar was visiting and most of my vaqueros were there; we killed two of the heathens and ran the others off before they could do much damage. If Black Skull was among them, I did not recognize him.

In that year we killed enough of them that they must have learned we had every intention of defending the ranch. Still, we knew they would return, and we fortified the place as well as we could.

In 1705 and the year following, I saw Father Kino a few times, but usually only briefly. I heard he had some problems, but that he had plenty of successes, too. With Father Minutuli, now priest at Tubutama, he rode west to the gulf on another journey of exploration. They saw the island called Tiburón and renamed it Santa Inéz, after a beloved saint whose feast day fell during their visit. Knowing Kino, I have no doubt that he spent many hours pondering how the island might be used as a port in supplying Salvatierra's California missions.

At the missions of the Pimería, the harvests went well. The new churches at Remedios and Cocóspera were always full for each mass, their catechism classes well attended. Kino and Campos, working with Pima craftsmen, finally finished their new church at Magdalena and Campos began regular services there. Kino made more trips to the western desert, even climbing Pinacate again for another look at the gulf and the massive mountains far to the north. More adobe buildings went up at Busanic and Bac, even as far west as Caborca. If the new priests Kino had requested ever came, the missions would be ready for them.

By all appearances, the padre from the little village of Segno in the Italian Alps still had not slowed his pace.

I had been busy, too. At the ranch we had more troubles with the Apaches, of course, but I was learning the cattle business, making money for the first time in my life, and enjoying my new role as a father. These should have been good times for me. But problems were brewing in Sonora, and I would soon find myself in the middle of them. Most arose from the old dilemma: How do you allow for colonial expansion and growth of commerce in a newly-conquered land and still protect the rights of the natives? The twenty-year proclamation from King Carlos Segundo prohibiting repartimiento—the use of Christianized Indians as slaves by miners and ranchers—was about to expire. But Carlos Segundo was dead and unable to issue a new one, and no one in Sonora knew what Felipe V thought of all this, if he thought of it at all, which I doubted.

Repartimiento. I knew what Father Kino thought of it. He detested it. He had enforced the old proclamation with relentless vigor and would continue to do so until forced by the law to stop. And believe me, I had no interest in owning Pima slaves. Still, laborers were hard to find on the frontier of Sonora, and many of my new friends and relatives in the mining and ranching businesses viewed slavery as necessary for their economic survival. For the first time in my life I could see their point. I had been out of the army for...what, four years? Including the two I spent as Alcalde Mayor? Somehow by 1707 the world looked different to me.

But there were other sources of conflict with the Church, too. For one, the Jesuits still refused to preach to the settlers, or even to offer the sacraments to them. They persisted in seeing themselves as frontier ministers, responsible only for the Indians. Which might have been fine except there were no *other* priests—no *secular* priests, as they were called—north or west of San Juan. Simply stated, there was no one else to do it. And what the Jesuits sometimes seemed to forget, or just to ignore, was that most settlers—whether Spanish or anything else—were Católicos, too.

For another, the Church considered much of the Pimería, if not all of it, to be Indian land. But here is the problem with that: the Pimas had no legal standing. They had never purchased the land. They had no deeds, they held no titles or grants. So how could anyone say they owned it? We had no doubts that gold and silver were out there. Why should we not be allowed to mine them? And the grazing lands and water rights, why should they not be ours, too, if we were willing to survey the land, pay for it, and bring it into production?

Understand, por favor, I had no quarrel with Padre Kino on these matters. He was still my friend, my teacher. Truthfully I can say he had been almost a father to me. But the voices for change were growing louder in Sonora, and everyone seemed to hear them but the Church.

So I joined with my new friends and relatives and wrote a letter of complaint about the stubbornness of the Jesuits and posted it to the viceroy, the Duque of Albuquerque, in Mexico City. The Duke referred my letter to Francisco Piccolo, who by then was back in the capital and serving as the Father Visitor for Sonora. I have no idea what the duke thought of my missive, but I soon learned how Father Piccolo received it. He flew into a rage and reported me in the most unflattering terms to the Governor, Juan Fernández de Córdoba.

That was when they threw me in jail.

CHAPTER 45

Parral, Nueva Vizcaya. 1708.

I will not plague you with a lengthy description of what it was like to be in jail in this place called Parral, but I will say this: you do not want to be there. Scorpions, roaches, centipedes as long as my foot, and you can just about imagine the kind of rot they served for food. No, amigo, you do not want to be there.

I asked the guard, Corporal Dominguez, if he knew I was a general.

Which by now I was, if you can believe it—General Juan Mateo Manje. The army authorities in Mexico City had finally seen the error of putting Don Gregorio in charge of the presidio and they had asked me to take command of a unit of the Compañía Volante. They said I could still live at home and manage my ranch, it is close enough to San Juan, they said, and I could use my own judgment on when to soldier and when to ranch. So I had accepted their offer. I had a good foreman and so far he had managed to keep things running well enough when I was away fighting Apaches and Jocomes in the mountains. Which is where I had just been, thank you, when the Jesuit authorities convinced our surly and dull-witted Governor Córdoba to have me arrested, have all my property and possessions impounded, and have me placed in handcuffs and set on a mule and escorted across the Sierra Madres to Parral and this filthy stinking jail cell.

"I do not want to hear your problems, General," the corporal said, his eyes red and watery from mescal. "I have enough of my own."

I will not even complain about how long they kept me. Just know that it was long enough that I had come to believe I would *never* get out. What had happened to my wife and children? My land, my livestock? My home? No one would tell me!

But finally I did get out, and here is what was so bizarre: It was the *Jesuits* that got me out. The Jesuits, whose wrath had *put* me there! I never knew how much Kino had to do with my release, though I suspect it was plenty, because I heard he was furious when he learned I had been arrested. Anyway, the Jesuit potentates got together in Guadalajara or Durango or someplace a lot more pleasant than the jail at Parral and decided perhaps they had taken things a mite too far. Perhaps they could find a compromise here, maybe work things out so no one got their precious little reputations soiled because of some ridiculous backlash from the citizenry here. This Manje is a general, after all, a law-abiding fellow with influential family and friends, the sort of people who give generously to the Church, maybe we had better back off here and rethink this thing.

If you are beginning to suspect that I resented being in jail hundreds of miles from my family for doing nothing but writing my beliefs in a letter to the viceroy, you are right.

Not that anything really changed after I got out. The Church would continue to hold that the Pimería was Indian land and not available for development. The Jesuits would still minister only to the Indians, and we found no reason to believe that secular priests would be coming any time soon to minister to us and all the other settlers. There still would not be enough low-wage workers to keep the ranches and mines operating as economically as the owners wanted, and some would continue to take Pimas as slaves when they thought they could get away with it.

The jail incident did not go unnoticed, though, in Sonora and across much of Nueva España. A lot of people, myself included, had begun to believe the Jesuits were taking for themselves far too much power. I do not believe I had ever given much credence to such a thought before, but from that year forward I would. So would a lot of others.

But these insights would come later. For now, I was out of jail and on my way home!

Aaaiiii caramba, it was good to see my family again. We had a glorious reunion and I gave great thanks to God when I saw that my wife and children had suffered no physical harm during my absence. I learned that my land and possessions had been legally returned to me and that my taxes for this year and the next had been officially waived. I even had a note from Padre Kino apologizing for the trouble and pain I had endured and inviting me to Dolores for a visit. He had no need to apologize, as he had had nothing to do with putting me in jail. Still, it was good to hear from him, and I wrote immediately to thank him and let him know I would ride to Dolores at the first opportunity, which I did.

I went back to ranching and soldiering and tending my family. My sons were old enough now to sit on my lap in the saddle, and many times they rode with me when I went out on inspections of our property. Domingo, almost three when I got back from Parral, took to horses from the beginning, but in a deliberate and careful way, as if one day he might be a breeder of fine horses, or a gentleman rancher himself. Eusebio, barely two, was the more rambunctious one. He took to horses as if one day he would win every rooster pull in Sonora. On their fourth birthdays I gave each a pony and assigned a loyal servant the job of teaching them everything they needed to know about horses. They were fine boys, solid and strong and filled with spirit. Our daughter, Isabela, still an infant when I returned from the ordeal at Parral, was as loving and pretty as her mother. They were a pleasure, all of them.

But mine were not the only youngsters I would tend that year. Another came to our ranch the following autumn, and that visit would have a profound effect on my life. Allow me to tell you about it, por favor.

Do you remember White Leaf, the Pima girl who killed the cascabel in the arroyo in my first year in the Pimería? By this year of 1709 she and Antonio, her husband, had four children of their own and were working for me at the ranch. Antonio was one of my best vaqueros. White Leaf was even more proficient now with her bow and arrows than when she saved my life. She had become an Apache-killer, as she had vowed. I seem to recollect it was to avenge her father's death. At any rate, she had succeeded. By now she had seven Apache and Jocome kills to her credit.

Anyway, this day Antonio and White Leaf were with me. We had ridden into the foothills a few leagues south of the casa, looking for some calves that had strayed from their mothers and wandered onto a mountainside, into bear and coyote and mountain lion country.

It was a gray morning in late November, rain threatening, clouds moving in low and dark from the southwest. We had slowly worked our way up the mountain, looking for the calves, listening for their bawling cries, spurring our wary mounts over sandstone ledges and around granite boulders, coming slowly out of a landscape of scrub cactus and saguaros and up into a zone of piñon pines and juniper where the chill of winter had already settled in. I could smell moisture on the wind, and the strong odors of damp wool and horse sweat. By noon we still had seen no sign of the calves. We found a clearing and stopped to rest. We sat on a rock and enjoyed a light meal of wheat tortillas with quince jelly.

I was reaching for a gourd of water when the first arrow tore through the sleeve of my coat and thunked into a nearby pine tree. We ducked low and scurried for the protection of a boulder a few yards away as a second arrow burned skin off my thigh and another caught Antonio's chestnut gelding and knocked it off its feet. We huddled behind the boulder, unable to see our attackers.

"Are you all right, Don Juan Mateo?" Antonio asked me.

I nodded, my heart thumping in my chest, and checked the priming powder in my musket. My leg was bleeding and had started to ache, but the wound seemed small and I had no time to worry with it anyway.

"I hear them," White Leaf whispered. She pointed beyond the boulder, to a tumble of large gray rocks partially hidden by juniper trees and a thick stand of manzanita. She had her bow ready, an arrow fitted in the string. Antonio had two flintlock pistols and I had the musket and my sword. We would fight.

White Leaf risked a quick look over the top of the boulder. "They are coming," she said as she ducked and an arrow careened off the boulder where her head had just been.

"Apaches?"

"Jocomes, I think," she said. "Seven, maybe eight of them."

A light rain was falling now and moisture had begun to bead on the Pimas' dark faces; the charcoal tattoos on Antonio's chin looked like smudges of blue mud. In the distance, thunder rumbled, but was soon drowned out by the cries and war whoops of the Jocomes as they came at us over the rocks.

"On my count of three," I shouted, "rise and fire, then spread out. White Leaf to the right, Antonio to the left. Let's see if we can confuse them."

In our first volley of fire I saw one go down with a lead ball in his chest and another stumble with White Leaf's arrow in his thigh. After that I sort of lost track of things. I remember an Indio coming over a boulder, his lance arcing through the air. I dodged the lance, then caught him square in the knee with my sword and saw him go down, blood spurting, his dark face contorted in pain. Another came at me from behind and got his arms around me. I stomped his foot, got loose from him, hit him hard enough in the face to stagger him, and ran him through with my sword.

I turned, bracing myself for the next attack. But I was alone. The mountain had gone silent and still, the rain coming softly, the wind light but chilled through the pines and juniper that ringed the clearing. Except for the dull ache in my leg and the bodies around me, I would not have believed there had even been a fight. I sat on a rock and reloaded my arquebus. Half a minute later, Antonio and White Leaf loped into the clearing. Both were unharmed except for a few scratches and bruises.

I whispered a brief prayer of thanks to the Almighty.

We counted four dead. That left...what, three or four more still alive? And what about the Indio that White Leaf had hit in the thigh? We found him hiding in a stand of manzanita no more than thirty yards from the clearing, his leg bloody and already swollen from the arrow that still protruded from it.

I had guessed that the others had left the area, and as far as we could tell, they had. This was not cowardice, believe me. The Apaches and Jocomes were among the smallest of the Indian tribes, and I had learned years before that when they lost the advantage of numbers and surprise, they usually withdrew from a fight. As a tribe, they could hardly afford the loss of even one man, much less seven or eight. As I said, this was not cowardice; it was simply a wise husbanding of resources.

White Leaf fitted an arrow to her bowstring and drew it back, aiming square at the wounded Jocome's chest. "I will kill him now, Señor."

The Indio tried to push himself away from her, tried to crawl, his eyes wide with pain and fear. But of course he could go nowhere with the arrow in his leg.

I shook my head. "No. Do not kill him."

White Leaf glanced at me. "But Don Juan Mateo—"

"No," I said. "Not like this. Not with him lying here in the dirt unable to fight. Anyway, he is only a teenager." He was thin, still young enough to have pimples spread across his face. I guessed his age at sixteen.

Antonio protested. "He was old enough to try to kill us, Señor."

"But he cannot kill us *now*," I said.

I suspected he had a knife strapped to his leg inside his moccasin. He did. I slipped it out and threw it into the bushes, then tied his wrists behind him and lifted him onto the back of my horse. Of course he struggled and fought me when I took hold of him, but he quieted some when I got him up behind the saddle and wrapped a blanket around his injured leg. We headed home, riding as fast as we could, the Pimas behind me on White Leaf's gray mare. The rain had turned to a fine mist now, and the darkest of the clouds had moved on to the east, giving us hope that we had seen the worst of it. The boy kept his silence on the ride, but I could see the pain that showed in his dark eyes and in the set of his jaw.

We saw no sign of the other Jocomes.

At my casa I carried the boy in and put him on a bed in an otherwise-empty and windowless room at the rear of the house. My wife took one look at him, nodded, and without a word began cleaning the blood from his leg.

I scribbled a note detailing the boy's injury but omitting any mention of his tribe or who had shot him. "Ride to the presidio at San Juan as fast as you can," I told one of the servants, handing him the note. "Find the post surgeon and tell him to come as soon as possible. If he asks, tell him the boy is Spanish, a relative of mine."

"And if he will not come, Señor?"

"Remind him," I said firmly, "that I am a general."

The surgeon arrived the next afternoon. His eyes widened when he saw the boy, but he said nothing and went to work as if the victim were another Spaniard no different from himself. He removed the arrow, dusted the wound with flor de membres—powdered roots and flowers from the desert willow—to protect against festering, and put a bandage on it. He did not think the thigh bone was broken, but said we would know soon enough.

The boy stayed with us three weeks. By then he could stand without help for short periods of time, could walk a dozen yards with the use of a cane, and had even begun to put on some weight. I gave him a bay gelding from our remuda and rode with him as far east as the Río Bavispe. At the river's edge I could see three riders high on a ledge on the other side, watching us. The Jocomes who had been with him, I had no doubt. They had been watching the casa and waiting, unwilling to abandon him, for all this time.

When the boy reached the other side, he raised his fist, let out a war whoop, and spurred his horse up the slope to his waiting friends. He never looked back. That was all right, I had not expected him to.

Why had I helped the boy? It likely had something to do with the fact that I now had children of my own. Perhaps for the first time in my life I could imagine how it would feel to know your child was injured and suffering out in the desert. Would I do it again? Probably. I had no idea who the boy's parents were, or even if they were alive, but I knew I would want them to do the same for any child of mine. Had my actions been naïve? Even foolish? I admit the possibility of it. The boy was, after all, an Jocome. But I did what I did, and I felt no remorse for having done it.

I reined my mount around and headed back for my ranch and my waiting family.

In early December I had a letter from Father Kino saying he had had a fall from his horse and he knew rumors were going around and he just wanted me to know he was all right. He had landed on a granite rock that had far too little bounce to it, he wrote, and he had broken his nose and lost two of his lower front teeth. Aside from the fact that he looked a little demented when he laughed—which by now he could actually do again, he said—he was fine.

At the first opportunity I rode to Dolores to see him, and made it in time for Sunday mass the week before Christmas. After services we sat on a bench near his quarters and had a meal of toasted corn, wheat bizcochos sprinkled with cane sugar, and grilled beef with peppers, and we drank chocolate from clay mugs with paintings of angels on them. The day was cold but bright with sunlight, the skies a smooth blue, completely cloudless. The padre looked fine, though his lip was still swollen, his nose still discolored.

"I try not to frighten the horses," he said, grinning.

I laughed. "You look pretty scary, Father."

Of course he wanted to know about my family and I told him how my children were growing and told him about the private tutor we had contracted for teaching them, and the padre gave me the latest on his western missions and Salvatierra's missions in California. He told me about new buildings he was constructing at Remedios and Cocóspera and the cattle he had recently moved to Tubutama. The Indios had a good crop of winter wheat growing now at Tumacácori and Bac, and at Sonoita, too, he told me.

"God has been good to us, Juan Mateo," he said.

"Very good, Father."

"But you know something?" he said. "It saddens me that I have been unable to make any more journeys of exploration to the Colorado."

I wondered if it were lack of time or lack of money or simply the infirmities of age that had kept him from making the long rides.

"I would say it is more a lack of time than anything else," he said. "I have just been too busy here and at the other missions."

See? Even now, after all these years, the man could still read my mind.

"We had some fun on those trips, Father."

He nodded and had a bite of grilled beef, chewing it slowly, gingerly, as if his jaw were still tender from loss of the two teeth. "We saw some beautiful country, some unusual sights."

After a time he said, "But times change, of course. And I suppose we change, too, in our own way."

"True." I spread honey on a sugared biscuit, ate it, and licked my fingers.

Kino was staring at me, his blue eyes curious.

I had a feeling I knew what he was going to ask.

You might have noticed that in the latter parts of this narrative, I have made little mention of Adriana Vásquez. I had had some difficulty putting her out of my mind, particularly in that first year of my marriage. But enough time had passed that I had made my peace with the situation. In fact, I had learned quite by accident that two years ago she had married a sergeant of cavalry who resigned from the army and took his new wife to Guadalajara, where he went into the mercantile business with his father. Adriana and her husband were doing well, I had heard, and recently increased the size of their family by one husky healthy baby boy.

But if Father Kino had questions, well, I would try to find him some answers.

He did. "So, Juan Mateo," he said, chewing a pepper, his eyes growing bright with the heat of it, "you are happy with your decision not to marry Adriana?"

"Yes," I told him that day at Dolores, "I have a family now, a wife and children. They are my priority now and they always will be."

"I am glad of that, Juan Mateo."

I had another sip of chocolate. "Me, too," I said

CHAPTER 46

Magdalena, Sonora. May, 1966.

By sunrise on the morning of Thursday, May 19, Olvera and the others were at work in the trenches near the clock tower of the City Hall. The guard, an off-duty policeman, was already warning away early-bird citizens curious to see the skeleton that lay partially exposed near the footings now believed to be part of the south wall of Kino's chapel. Romano resumed his work on the bones while Olvera, Wasley, and the laborers started new trenches and enlarged some of the more-promising old ones. They worked quickly and without rest. This was, they suspected, their last chance to locate and identify with certainty the remains of Padre Kino. Professor Jiménez had been unable to change the Minister's mind. Tomorrow there would be no more funds.

At ten minutes after nine o'clock, Olvera, already thirsty and damp with sweat, found Romano working at the bottom of his trench.

"Definitely a European?" Olvera had grown restless, vaguely dissatisfied with the direction his digging had taken him, needing something more productive to fill this last day but not knowing quite where to find it. So he had come to Romano's trench.

"A European, yes," Romano said. "I'm more and more sure of it."

"Well," Olvera said after a drink from his canteen, "I don't think it's Kino."

Romano looked up from the skeleton. "I agree," he said. "If we can believe what Fernando Grande wrote in his report to the viceroy, the doorway of Kino's chapel faced south." He gestured toward the stone-and-mortar footings a few feet away. "And if this is really Kino's chapel, these bones are on the *south* side of it, where the doorway would have been. Which means—if we can also believe the burial register—this is Salvador de Noriega, the Spaniard. It isn't Kino."

"My thinking, exactly." Olvera glanced at the trenches along the north end of the chapel and the mounds of dirt that grew steadily higher. Dust tickled his nose and made him sneeze, and he could hear the muffled *thunk* and *clink* of picks and shovels as the workmen probed the dry rocky soil in the depths of the trenches. "I believe the men will find Kino over there," he said. "But until they find *something*, there isn't much I can do there. You need any help here?"

Romano shook his head. "There's barely room for me and the bones down here. But thanks anyway, Jorge."

"If you need me, I'll be in the parish church. In the archives."

In the archives, a few minutes after ten o'clock, Olvera found something that caught his eye: a passage in a document from 1844 called *Apuntes Sobre los Acontecimientos Acaccidos*, written by José Llera. Llera, he remembered, was the priest who built the parish church in 1832. Translated from Spanish, the passage read:

> "Among the necessities these pueblos were suffering, one of the major ones was that the chapel of Magdalena where an image of San Francisco Xavier is venerated was menaced with ruin. With all the bountiful benefits that it pours upon the inhabitants of Sonora, the image has won the greatest veneration. I immediately thought of preventing the chapel's collapse which could probably have a tragic ending. But as I did not count on anything but some alms from the bishopric, and some fringe benefits paid by the neighbors and from where my subsistence came, with other expenses for indispensable things and for those involved with the devotion I could only add a buttress which would support the wall that was already leaning over…"

"*...Could only add a buttress...*" A buttress was a thick wedge-shaped layer of stone masonry added to a wall to give lateral support. Actually, Llera had used the word *estribo*. Literally, this meant "stirrup." Like many Spanish words, though, estribo had several meanings. And Olvera knew that in this context Llera could only have meant a buttress.

He almost wished he hadn't seen the document.

He hurried back to the trenches and asked the laborers if they'd seen anything that could've been a footing for a buttress. No one had seen such a thing. For the next hour Olvera searched doggedly along the north and west sides of the chapel's foundations. He stopped only rarely to drink from his canteen. His shirt grew dark with sweat, but he, like the others, found nothing that could've been a buttress.

At noon he found Wasley on a bench near the plaza eating a sandwich of fried eggs and avocado.

"Bill," he said wearily, "I think we have a problem. I've just learned that Kino's chapel had a buttress. Father Llera built it because a wall was starting to sag." He pointed across the plaza to the tall mounds of dirt near the Palacio.

"But we've found no footings," he added, "for such a buttress."

Wasley frowned. "Are you saying it isn't Kino's chapel?"

"I'm saying that until I find a buttress, I won't be sure of it."

"So what do we do now?"

Olvera shrugged. "We keep looking."

He continued his work in the church archives, but returned to the trenches at three o'clock to talk with the laborers. The trenches had grown deeper and wider, but the workmen had found nothing more. No Kino, no buttress.

He returned at four o'clock. Still nothing.

But for the team of scientists, things were about to change.

They changed first for Wasley.

At 4:30 that Thursday afternoon, two workmen using their picks at the bottom of trench #17B—just inside the northwest corner of the small rectangle of Jesuit foundations—struck a fragment of bone, knocking it loose from the soil. They saw what seemed to be part of a skull. They called Dr. Wasley, who'd been working nearby. He examined the bone and the site and quickly saw enough to suspect that he had before him not only a complete skull—intact except for the hole in the calverium, the skull cap, from the workman's pick—but possibly a complete, fully-articulated skeleton. He climbed out of the trench and looked around. He was standing, he realized, between the 2nd and 3rd of several footings that formed the west wall of the foundation. The left side, if the door had indeed faced south. The Gospel side, if this was indeed Kino's chapel.

Second and third footings. Left side.

Wasley sucked air past his teeth; let it slowly out. He closed his eyes and said a quick prayer. Within minutes he was in the City Hall in the room that Professor Jiménez had been using for an office. Jiménez looked up from the stack of papers on his desk and gestured toward a chair. "Please, have a seat," he said, smiling. "What happened? You look like a little boy who just fell into a vat of ice cream."

Wasley dropped into the chair. As calmly as he could, he reported what he'd just seen in the trench.

"What do you suggest we do now?" Jiménez said.

"I suggest we telephone the Minister and tell him we have a second European, probably Kino."

Jiménez checked his wristwatch. "We have a second *skeleton*, yes, but are you sure we have a second *European* skeleton?"

"I don't know for sure. Romano will have to make that determination. But the location of the skull tells me—"

Jiménez glanced at his watch again. If Wasley was right, he knew, they had to act quickly. This was their last day of funding; every minute counted. "All right," he said hurriedly. "Find Olvera and Romano. Take them to the trench and show them the skull. Then all of you meet me in the lab at a quarter past five. If you hurry, you can make it. Oh, and get a policeman to guard the trench. No, better, get *two* policemen."

At fifteen after five Olvera, Wasley, and Romano were waiting in the City Hall in a room the mayor had turned over to the team for use as a field laboratory. White sheets covered desks and file cabinets, now pushed out of the way along the walls of the room. Steel-topped tables filled the center of the room. Bones of every size and shape covered the tables, and Olvera saw calipers and soft-bristled brushes and osteometric boards; hand lenses; chemicals in glass bottles; small picks and probes that looked to Olvera like dentists' instruments. The pungent odor of acetone filled the warm air and mingled with the darker smells of cleaning agents and other substances Olvera didn't recognize.

"Bill Wasley has shown you part of a skull in trench Seventeen-B," Jiménez said as he stepped into the room. "And Jorge has found documentary evidence of a buttress on Kino's chapel. So far, no one has located such a buttress." He took a chair at the head of the empty table where the others were already seated.

"We'll worry about the buttress later," Jiménez added. "Now, I need to know what each of you thinks about the two skeletons: one at the south end of what may or may not be the Kino chapel, the other near the north end." He glanced at his watch. "I suspect the Minister is still in his office. He'll want to know if we believe either of these is Kino. *Really* believe it. Arturo, do you?"

Romano nodded. "This latest, the one between the 2nd and 3rd ashlars, yes, I believe that will turn out to be Kino. I can't be certain of it, of course, until I've examined all the bones in detail. You know the process. First I have to expose the entire skeleton and look for remnants of a coffin or any other artifacts that could help in identification. Then I have to remove the skull, clean it, and take a lot of measurements. The same goes for the long bones and pelvis. All this takes time. As for the buttress, I don't know what to make of that."

"I understand," Jiménez said. "But now I'm concerned only with the bones. The skeleton you found along the south wall...you're sure this is a European...but *not* Kino?"

"I believe that's Noriega, the Spaniard, sir. We have documentary evidence that he was buried under the doorway of Kino's chapel...and that the doorway was on the south side. And my preliminary measurements suggest it's most likely the skull of a western European."

Jiménez continued around the table. "And you, Bill?"

"The one on the south side, that's Noriega, I agree," Wasley said. "The most recent one—to the north, on the left side of the nave between the 2nd and 3rd footings—from the location alone, that's Kino. I'm sure of it, even without the buttress. I'm not worried about the buttress."

"And you, Jorge? The one on the north?"

Olvera nodded. "If we've found Kino's chapel, we've found Kino."

"And you'll continue your search for the buttress?"

"Of course, sir."

"All right, gentlemen," Jiménez said, rising from the table. "I'll place the call to the Minister. Let's pray he'll give us another day or two."

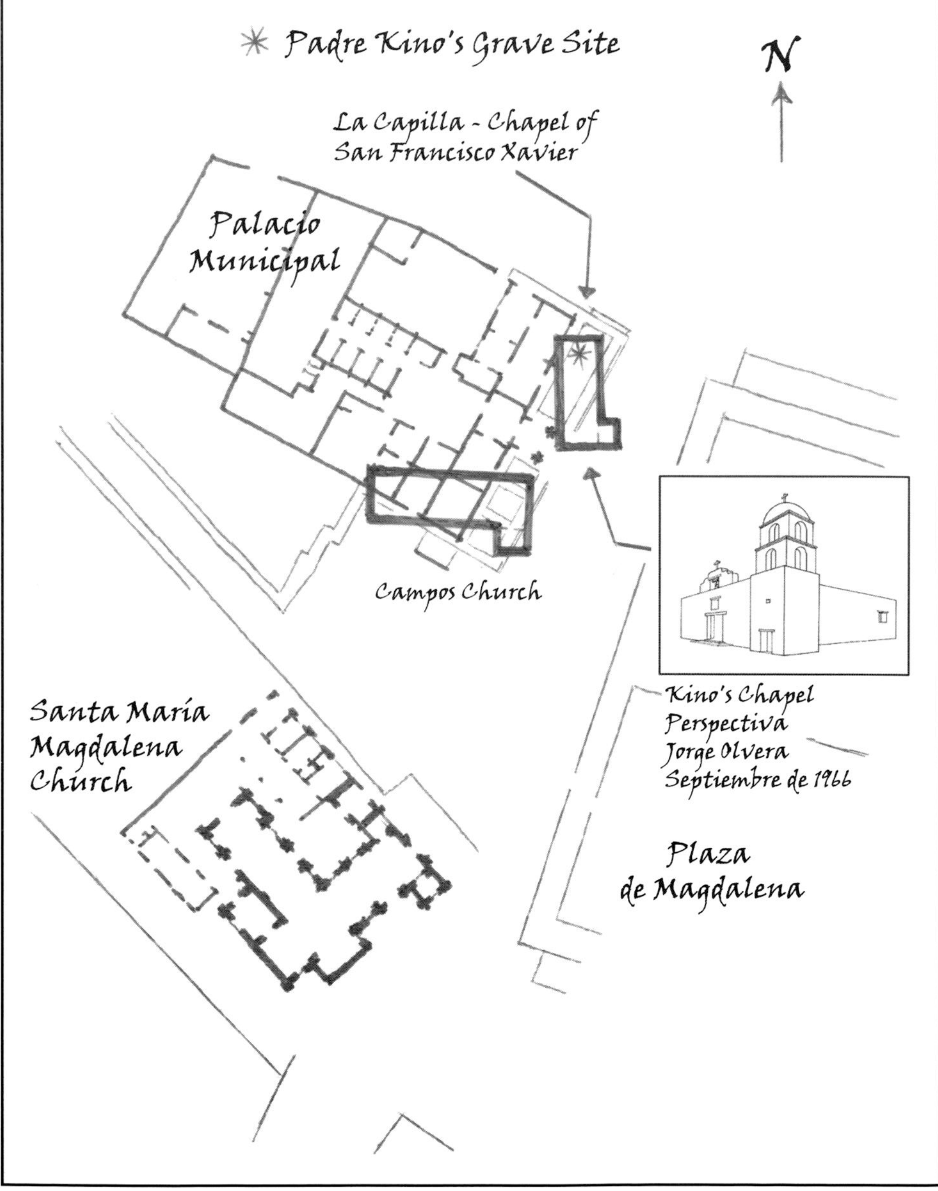
Location of Padre Kino's Grave
Plaza de Magdalena, Sonora, Mexico
1966
Padre Kino's Grave Site
N
La Capilla - Chapel of
San Francisco Xavier
Palacio
Municipal
Campos Church
Santa Maria
Magdalena
Church
Kino's Chapel
Perspectiva
Jorge Olvera
Septiembre de 1966
Plaza
de Magdalena

CHAPTER 47

The Pimería. Año D. 1710. May.

"I had forgotten how large it is," Francisco Acuña said.

"As had I, my friend," I said as we reined our horses to a stop a few leagues from the base of Baboquivari. "And how steep."

Acuña drank from his water gourd and squinted at the mountain in the brightness of the afternoon sun. He wiped his chin with the back of his hand. "You are still convinced that we will find gold or silver up there?"

"*Something* is up there," I said. "Whatever it is, I do not believe Henri Pitot ever found it." I had made a large-print drawing—my eyes were not as good as they had once been—of the strange letters and numbers Father Kino and I had found, years before, on the little lapis cross. Now I pulled the drawing from my saddlebag and looked it over again. No simple explanations, no easy-to-follow directions, had suddenly and magically appeared on the paper. I had not expected any, so I suppose I was not too disappointed.

"When were we here before?" Acuña asked me. "Five years ago? Six?"

"Almost nine, my friend." Madre de Dios, the time had slipped by.

"So perhaps in nine years someone *else* has found this treasure."

I shrugged. "Anything is possible."

The sun was strong out of the west now, bright in our eyes, but tempered by cool breezes that seemed to drift down from the mountain. Around us the land was ablaze with color: ocotillos with green branches topped with red flowers that grew in neat rows like tiny bursts of fire; white blossoms riding atop the arms of saguaros; creamy-white flowers that looked like miniature church bells rising from the stalks of soaptree yuccas. In the distance I saw prickle poppies with large white blooms, palo verdes dotted with yellow, and ironwoods splashed with lavender. Near the base of the mountain I saw antelopes grazing and coyotes loping along a ridge of hard brown granite.

Acuña grinned. "But if the treasure is still here and we find it, we can claim it as ours, right? And we are rich?"

"That is possible, too," I said.

"Then what are we waiting for?"

We spurred our horses toward the boulder-strewn canyon on the east side that we knew would get us to the top of the mountain.

One last try, I had promised myself.

Over the past few years I had been so busy with family and the ranch that I had almost forgotten the little cross and its strange engravings. But two weeks before, my wife had taken the children to visit some of her family in Guadalajara for a month and I found myself bored and restless without them. Acuña, I learned, had some spare time, so I left the ranch to my servants and vaqueros and took some mules loaded with food, water, and digging tools, and met Acuña in Arizpe. We had made good time to Tubutama and on up the Río Altar to the mountain that now rose before us into the cerulean sky: Baboquivari, home to I'itoi—the Papago's Elder Brother and Creator—and home, possibly, to hidden riches of gold and silver. One last try, I had told myself.

Why had I come? Truthfully, not for the promise of gold or silver. My ranch had blessed me with all the income I could want, but even without it my father-in-law would see that my family and I never lacked for a thing. I had come, I supposed, for the challenge. For the chance to find something that no one else had been able to find. To do something for myself without the help of uncles or fathers-in-law or anyone else. Or perhaps, to be truthful about it, I had come just to add some excitement to my life.

And Acuña, why had he come? He was a captain now, with all the privileges of the rank, but he was still chasing Apaches, still serving as translator for the army, on a salary still barely adequate to support a family. Perhaps Acuña really needed the money that could come from finding whatever might be up here. On the other hand, perhaps he had come for reasons not much different from my own. Neither explanation would have surprised me.

We followed the main canyon to its end, then turned our horses and mules southwest, into a narrower drainage covered with volcanic rocks that looked as if they had formed from granite that had been spewed into the air as a liquid and then hardened when it came to rest and cooled. Here, they were coated with plaques of soft green lichen and on the horizon they formed bizarre spectral shapes, like ghostly soldiers marching in formation. When the slope became too steep for our animals, we left them in a draw and climbed on foot over boulders and onto ledges, past forests of hackberry and oak and juniper and walnut, until we reached the base of the mountain's lumpy dark peak. Why we had come here, I could not say. Perhaps we just wanted to see the peak from close up, this bulbous knob of hard granite that so dominated the landscape in this part of the Pimería.

We found a ledge to sit on and ate peppers in wheat tortillas and enjoyed the views. At this elevation we could see for what seemed like a hundred leagues, the low desert cut by meandering washes and undulating foothills that rose and fell to the horizon, and everywhere more mountains, purple and sharp-edged against the pale blue of the sky. But here in this area we saw nothing we could correlate with the numbers and letters from the lapis cross, and after a time we worked our way back down to the canyon and our horses and pack animals, and made camp for the night.

The next morning after a meal of stewed tepary beans and squash we turned north, following the spine of the mountain range though a ways below it, riding our mounts when we could, but more often walking them. The terrain was rocky and treacherous, the mountainside steep, our progress slow. Still, the weather was pleasant and we saw deer, and a mountain lion watching us from high on a ledge, and a black bear with cubs, and hawks that dove on us and tried to drive us away. But for three days we saw nothing that looked even vaguely familiar from our visit nine years before.

On the fourth day, though, near sundown, we saw something we knew we had seen before: a boulder, at least twenty feet tall, that had weathered in such a way that it looked like the head and face of an old man, with eyes and ears and a bulbous nose and a droopy mustache stained greenish-brown from the lichen that grew on it in thick patches.

"Reminds me of a campesino I once knew," Acuña said, smiling.

"I knew an old cavalry sergeant in Spain," I said, "with a nose like that."

Since it was almost dark, we picketed the animals and made camp for the night. While we were gathering firewood Acuña said, "Do you think this boulder could be one of the landmarks we are looking for?"

"The last time we were here, we did not think so," I said. "But we could have been wrong. Tomorrow we will look around and see what else we can find."

At the campfire we had a meal of dried beef and wheat tortillas and made a pot of chocolate. "Francisco," I said, taking a sip of the warm drink, "I am more and more convinced that the numbers followed by small v's represent distances, and that the v's tell us they used Spanish varas as the unit of measurement."

"You mean, C, whatever *that* is, is 620 varas from SAS, whatever *that* is."

I nodded. "And probably on a compass heading of 92 degrees from it. I think the second number, the smaller one, represents the compass heading."

"So SAS would be 715 varas from V, whatever *that* is, on a compass heading of 174 degrees."

"Exactly," I said. In the darkness I could hear coyotes yipping somewhere above us, and closer, the rustle of leaves from the chill breeze that blew through the oak and walnut trees ringing our campsite. Even this late in the spring, nights in the mountains were often cold. I had a Pima blanket—red, with images of I'itoi woven into the dense wool with heavy gray and black thread—that I always carried on long rides, and now I wrapped it around my shoulders for warmth.

"But that still leaves us with unanswered questions," Acuña said. "Whoever made the etchings gave us three landmarks, if that is what they are—V, SAS, and C. So which of the three is the treasure, and which two are just landmarks to help us find the one that really matters, the one that marks the location of the treasure, whatever *that* is?"

I chuckled. "There are a lot of *whatevers* in this project, Francisco."

Acuña had changed little in the years I had known him. His skin was darker, perhaps, and more roughened by the sun, but he was still solid and strong. His dark wool pants fit him loosely, and he wore a yellow-and-blue striped sarape over a cotton camisa that had faded to the color of rust. His thick black hair hung over his forehead as he stared into the campfire.

"So," he said, "if we can identify any one of the three landmarks, we can use the distances and compass headings to find the other two. And one of the three will be the site of the treasure, whatever it is."

"That is how I see it, yes."

"...Do you think it will be a silver mine?"

I shrugged. "A vein of gold, perhaps."

He poured more chocolate for his cup and added some to mine. "I suppose it could even be a buried trunk full of treasure," he said, "hidden by Coronado's men more than a century and a half ago."

"Anything is possible," I said.

In the darkness Acuña's eyes reflected the glow of the flickering fire. "I have a feeling about this," he said softly. "Tomorrow we will find the treasure."

I smiled. "How do you know this?"

"Because," he said, "this time I brought a secret weapon."

"A *secret weapon*?"

"If we had had it when we were here nine years ago..." His voice trailed off as he stared into the fire.

"Was it really that long ago?" he said finally. "Nine years?"

"Sadly, my friend, it was. Now tell me, what is this secret weapon?"

He took a drink of chocolate and eyed me over the top of his cup.

"Tomorrow, Juan Mateo," he said mischievously, "I will tell you tomorrow."

CHAPTER 48

"*Visage!*" Acuña shouted, loud enough, I feared, to stir every Apache north of the San Miguel.

We had risen at dawn, the sun inching up like a pale ball of gold to spread its warming light over the east slopes of Baboquivari, and I was heating biscuits and strips of chicken meat on a griddle over the campfire. Acuña sat cross-legged on the ground, reading from a book, his yellow-and-blue sarape bright against the bark of the oak trees behind him.

"Vee-zosj?" I said, glancing in his direction. "What is *that*?"

He pushed himself up and hurried to the campfire. "A French word, *visage*," he said, grinning widely. "And your accent needs improvement."

I stared at him. In the cold morning air I heard ravens calling from the slopes and I could smell dew on the grasses that grew in tufts between the oak and walnut trees around our campsite. "Francisco," I said, "what are you talking about?"

He grabbed a twig from the ground and drew a large cross in the dirt, then filled in the letters and numbers he had memorized from my drawing of the lapis cross. "There!" he said, gesturing excitedly, "at the top of the cross! The V, my friend, the V. It stands for *visage!*"

"...And you know this because—"

He handed me the book he had been studying. It was bound in dark leather, with the title, *Diccionario,* on the cover in large gilt letters. Below were the words, *Español-Francés y Francés-Español.*

He was beaming. "My secret weapon. I ordered it from Mexico City. Last year I convinced the general that there were more Frenchmen in Sonora every year and that I needed such a volume for my translating duties. At the time I had no idea I would need it for another search of Baboquivari!"

I chuckled. I had never seen him so excited. "But *visage,*" I said, "what does the word mean?"

"It is the French word for *face*!" He pointed behind me, at the huge boulder that had reminded me of the old cavalry sergeant I had known in Aragon. I stared at the granite formation, at the ears, eyes, and nose, and at the thick mustache discolored by plaques of greenish-brown lichen.

"And you really believe this, Francisco?"

He was beaming again. "We have no *better* ideas, do we?"

On our earlier search of the mountain, nine years before, we had assumed the letters represented Spanish words. But thinking about it, why had we? Pitot, after all, was a Frenchman! Had we been *that* easy to fool?

Smiling, I handed Acuña hot biscuits and strips of meat on a plate. "You are saying, then," I said, "that we are now at V, and that SAS, whatever *that* is, is 715 varas south of where we now stand. If you are right, mi amigo, we are close!"

"*Very* close," he said. "So now we have work to do, eh?"

Acuña sighted the compass and I ran the rope.

We had corrected our compass readings to compensate for the magnetic effects of iron deposits in the earth. Then, sighting down the compass needle, we had lined up a course of 174 degrees, almost due south from our campsite and the boulder face—the *visage,* according to Acuña. The V on our map, he had assured me. Did I believe him? Did it *matter* if I believed him? As he had said, we had no better ideas. And anyway it was exciting to think we *might* be onto something.

Our longest rope was a little less than thirty varas in length. With a measuring rod we had marked it in one-vara increments so we could lay it out on the ground for marking off distances. If you are not fairly familiar with the Spanish language, you might not know about the vara. In our culture, it is a standard unit of measurement. A vara equals thirty-three of what the English call *inches,* so it is a bit less than what the English would call a *yard.*

It took us all day to lay off the 715 varas on a course of 174 degrees. It took so long because we had to lay the rope around trees, over boulders, across and down the sides of rock ledges, across crevices and washes and over and around a hundred other obstacles, all the while watching for rattlesnakes and hostile Indios and every other problem you can imagine. But we were having a great time, stretching the rope out, making our measurements and stretching it out once again, and the day passed quickly.

We finished the 715 varas about sundown, and found ourselves on a flat shelf of granite that extended out at least twenty varas in every direction. There was no way anything could be buried here, or hidden in any other way. Disappointed, we searched around the edges of the shelf, at the rocky ground and dirt and trees, but we saw nothing that looked helpful.

"Could this shelf itself be the SAS? What is the French word for granite?"

Acuña thumbed through the dictionary. "*Granit.*"

"So we are not at SAS," I said. "Whatever that is."

He sighed. "Somehow," he said, "we have missed it."

We made camp close by, and during our evening meal of beef and onions and wheat tortillas I said, "Something has been bothering me, Francisco, and I think I know what it is."

"Allow me to take a guess, por favor," he said. "If whoever made the etchings in the cross used *French* words for the landmarks, why would he use a *Spanish* word for his unit of distance? Yes, that has been bothering me, too."

"Exactly," I said. "So we have two possibilities. Either the small v stands for something other than vara, or the large V is something besides the boulder face. Is there any French word referring to a unit of distance that begins with the letter v?"

He retrieved the dictionary from his saddlebag and lit an oil lamp for more light. "The only thing I know to do," he said, "is to go through the French section and look at every word that begins with a v."

When I went to sleep that night, he was still working at it, low flames from the campfire casting light that flickered in the shadows of his dark face.

"*Verge,*" Acuña said the next morning as I climbed out of my bedroll.

"Vair-sj?"

"The French word for yard," he said. "Same as the English yard. Thirty-six inches. I found it last night after you went to sleep. You were snoring so loudly I could hardly concentrate, but with diligence I found it."

I laughed and reached for my boots. "All right, so, if we multiply—"

"Already done," he said. "Since a verge is three inches longer than a vara, we multiply three inches times 715, which gives us 2145 inches, or 178.7 feet, or 59.6 yards. Or more importantly for us, 65 varas. That is how much farther we have to go."

"And that should take us straight to SAS, whatever that is."

He was beaming again. "If God wills it," he said.

I scanned the slope to the south, where I saw little but granite rocks and ocotillos and a small clearing ringed by piñons and junipers.

"Down there?" I said.

"By the end of the day, my friend, we shall both be rich!"

Sixty-five varas on a course of 174 degrees put us at the edge of the clearing we had seen from our campsite. "I see lots of junipers and pines and small bushes," I said. "Not much else."

"Juan Mateo, look." He pointed to a small tree a few varas from the clearing. He already had his dictionary out.

"*Madre de Dios*," I whispered. We had seen it nine years ago, too, and ignored it: a rattlesnake skeleton, coiled like a length of rope around the trunk of a juniper, the snake's bare white ribs now dug tightly into the bark.

I wasted no time. "What is the French word for snake?"

He had already found it. "*Serpent*," he said, pronouncing it something like zair-pohn.

"And the word for skeleton?"

He thumbed pages. "Squelette."

"Could that be it? SS, for serpent skeleton?"

"...Perhaps, but let me try something else here—"

"Try *rattle*snake," I said.

By then, he already had it.

"*Serpent a sonnettes*," he said.

I stared at him. "SAS. Can you believe it?"

"*Madre de Dios*," he said, his eyes wide with excitement.

We searched the clearing but found no mine openings or caves or unusual mounds of earth or anything else, really. But by now neither of us believed this was where we would find anything, anyway. We had become convinced that the treasure was located where the map indicated the letter C, 620 yards from where we now stood. So we started off on a compass course of 92 degrees. It was slow going and difficult, as it had been the day before, but we were excited and worked without rest until we had run the measuring rope the entire 620 yards. At the end we were in a flat clearing surrounded on two sides by granite boulders and on the others by a forest of pines, junipers, and oaks. The place was secluded, silent, scarcely visible from anywhere else on the mountain.

"A perfect place to hide something," I said.

Acuña had his dictionary out again. "The French word for box or trunk is *coffre*," he said, glancing up at me. "That would explain the C. And it probably means they buried something in the ground." He looked around, at the boulders and trees, and then at the rocky soil at his feet. "Somewhere right around here, probably," he said.

"We are going to be rich, Juan Mateo," he added, smiling widely.

"Over there, look!" I pointed towards a low rock near one of the boulders. Here the granite was mottled grayish brown, and beyond it I could see something protruding into the air, dark and roughened, like a strip of leather.

We hurried to it.

It was, we discovered, an old trunk made of wood planks and leather, its lid rusted shut, its planks warped, its padlock moldered and broken, its dark exterior savaged by years of exposure to hot sun and wind and pelting rains. A few yards away we found the hole it had come out of—probably four feet deep before the years had partially refilled it with dirt and drifting granite sands and dead leaves and the pale white skeleton of a small rodent that had probably fallen in and been unable to climb out again.

I sighed. "Someone got here ahead of us, Francisco. A long time ago."

I could hear him breathing heavily beside me. "Yes," he said after a time, "but we have not seen what is *inside* the trunk."

"Whatever was here is now gone," I said. We pried the hasps and padlock away and slowly raised the lid, straining against the rusted hinges. Finally they gave, and with a loud *crack* the lid jerked open.

Inside we found spider webs and dead insects, an old crucifix, and a few specks of what was probably gold dust. I pulled the crucifix from the trunk and carefully wiped the dirt and oxides from it with a cotton rag. Bronze, maybe two inches in length, it had a hole at the top with a rawhide cord still attached. It was designed in the baroque style and I recognized it as a Jesuit crucifix, the kind that Fathers Kino and Campos and the others always wore on a cord around their neck.

We looked around, but saw nothing else of value. No gold, no silver. Nothing at all.

We retrieved our horses and mules and readied them for the journey home.

"Are you all right, Francisco?" I asked him as we mounted up.

He sighed. "I am all right. A little disappointed. And you?"

"A little disappointed," I said.

How did I really feel about losing out on whatever the trunk had once held? I did not know then, and I still do not. I had no idea who had buried it, or where they had stolen it, or even what it was, really. I did not know if Henri Pitot and Diego had found the trunk before they died and cached its contents elsewhere, or if they had died still searching, or if they even knew themselves what was in the trunk. But this I did know: I had been carrying the little lapis cross with its hidden map for a lot of years—since I took it from Black Skull that hot summer day near Imuris where Father Kino and I had encountered him with his wife and his little son in my first month as an eager young ensign in the Pimería—and in that time the cross had surely spiced up my life. It had given me some excitement, had it not?

But the excitement of this day was not quite done. Our presence here had been noted by a small band of Jocomes, and they would be waiting for us when we rode down off the mountain.

CHAPTER 49

They came at us out of the foothills east of Baboquivari. Jocomes, screaming their war whoops, lances raised high in their fists, their paint ponies kicking up dust in thick gray clouds. I thought I counted five of them, though it was hard to be certain in all the noise and confusion. I shouted at Acuña and pointed to the southeast, thinking we might be able to reach the trees on one of the creeks that fed the Altar a few miles away. He nodded and dropped the rope line to the pack mules and we spurred our horses, lashing them hard as we searched the horizon for cottonwoods, or some kind of cover, *any* kind of cover.

All this happened in the space of about four seconds. Madre de Dios, how had we stumbled into such a mess!

Fired from a bouncing saddle, an arquebus is almost useless, but I turned and fired mine anyway. Acuña had two pistols in his belt and managed to squeeze off shots with both. I glanced back to see if we had hit anyone. We had not, it seemed, and the Indios had gained some ground on us. The two in front had their bows up and were taking aim, their ponies pounding after us over the harsh desert terrain.

I heard an arrow zing past my ear and saw another as it thudded into the ground ahead of me. We ducked low and spurred our mounts even harder. I could hear the Jocomes shouting and whooping behind us as our horses sprinted over desert dotted with scrub cactus and cholla with thorns that looked shiny and white in the sunlight. We jumped a draw, landed roughly on the other side, scrabbled up a rocky hill thick with saguaros and prickly pear, then sprinted hard when we reached level ground again. Already I could see sweat foaming in the dark hair of my horse's back. An arrow ripped at my pants and furrowed the skin of my calf, drawing blood and burning like a sliver of hot iron. In that moment I remembered the red Pima blanket I kept in a roll behind my saddle. I tore the cords off it, dogged it around my shoulders, and tied the ends around my neck so the bulk of it hung across my back.

And not a second too soon. I had just finished tying the blanket when I felt a hard blow to my back and knew I had been hit by an arrow. Then a second arrow thunked into my back. Both areas stung and ached as if someone had struck me with a miner's pick, but neither felt as if an arrow had pierced the blanket. Mother of God, can you believe such a thing? Ahead of us now we could see a creek and a line of tall green cottonwoods.

We almost made it.

The reason we did not: an Jocome arrow caught my horse in the hip, knocked his legs out from under him, and sent me tumbling over his head into the dirt and sliding into a clump of chollas bristling with sharp thorns. My fall broke no bones, but it must have stunned me, because I have no memory of pain and even now I can barely remember Acuña's turning back, lifting me onto his horse behind him, and tearing off again for the string of trees that by then must have looked to us like a small stretch of heaven.

But God, I suspect, did not want us to reach those trees. Acuña's big horse stumbled—maybe in a gopher hole, maybe it took an arrow, I never knew—and went down hard, spilling us, almost crushing us as it rolled and skidded through the dirt. When I had my breath back, I pushed myself up from the ground and wiped grit and blood from my eyes. I helped Acuña to his feet. His face was cut and bruised, his shirt torn and soaked with blood. He checked his horse, then looked at me and shrugged. He had lost his sword and knife. Like me, he had lost his flintlocks, too. I pulled my sword from my belt and cut the veins in his horse's neck so it could die peacefully. Then we stood in the desert under the hot May sun and waited for the Jocomes.

"Are you ready for death, Francisco?" I asked him. The Indios had slowed their horses and were taking their time, confident now, enjoying their victory as they leisurely closed the distance, dust trailing in the air behind them.

"I am ready, yes," Acuña said.

I became aware of the pain that gnawed at my back and hips and the cactus thorns that chafed and burned in my skin. Blood ran from my nose, trickled onto my chin, dripped onto my shirt. I glanced at Acuña. He looked even worse, and from the way he held his arm I wondered if the fall had broken a bone in his shoulder.

He smiled faintly. "Take the red blanket off, por favor. You look silly."

I laughed, but my ribs hurt too much to do a lot of it. I slipped the blanket off my back and found two arrows dangling from it with their heads buried in the tightly-woven wool. I made the sign of the cross and whispered a quick prayer. I thanked the Lord for all the years He had given me. I asked His forgiveness for my sins, asked Him to keep watch over my wife and children, and asked Him to let me die as a brave man and not a cowardly one.

When I finished my prayer, the Jocomes were less than twenty yards from us. They were clothed in little more than taparrabos and tall moccasins and all carried large bags of arrows across their backs; stripes of red and yellow coated their wide, dark faces. But I saw only four of them now.

"I thought there were five Indios," I whispered to Acuña.

"Now there are four." Blood oozed from the corner of his mouth, and I saw that he had lost a tooth in the fall. "Perhaps we killed one of the bastardos, after all," he added.

I shrugged. "Perhaps." I did not think so, but I let it go. At the moment I had more important things to think about. Like death, and perhaps even torture. Was this how we would die? Out here in the desert, butchered and bleeding, alone, without even our wives and children to comfort us? This was not a new thought. I had had it many times in my career. Still, it was not a pleasant thought, and I chose at that moment to put such morbid things from my mind. I would deal with the situation as it existed, in the present, and not worry about how it might end.

Acuña wiped blood from his face. "I will see you in heaven, Juan Mateo."

"We missed the treasure on Baboquivari, my friend."

"The treasure was of little importance," he said.

"Scriptures say that wisdom and understanding are more valuable than gold and silver. Do you believe that?"

"Yes, I believe it," he said. Oddly, he was smiling. Silently I prayed that I would be as brave and unfaltering as I knew he would be.

Dust drifted up and stung my eyes as the Jocomes reined their mounts to a stop in front of us. They looked impassive, their faces giving away nothing, but I could sense their excitement in the snorting and prancing of their horses. I could smell blood and dirt and horse sweat and, oddly, the yellow blooms of sunflowers that grew in the sand not far from where we stood.

"Spaniards," the leader said from his horse. "Today you die." His Spanish was good. He had a wide face, thick arms, and he seemed tall for an Jocome. He had some gray in his hair and I guessed him to be about my age.

From somewhere behind him I heard another horse coming in. Maybe the fifth Indio, but I could not see him for the four horses that blocked my view.

It took all the strength I had to raise my sword. I pointed it at the leader. "We will not die alone. You will die first."

"You will die alone, pin'dah, and in much pain." He raised his bow and without another word, shot me. The arrow caught me in the flesh of my right leg and went deep. I clenched my teeth against the pain that lanced through my thigh. I reached behind my knee and felt the arrow point poking through the skin. When I brought my hand up, it was covered with blood. I tried to lunge forward and swing my sword at the Indio who had shot me, but I could scarcely move and my blade sliced harmlessly through the air. He watched me from the back of his horse, his dark face stoic and grim.

I gestured to Acuña. "Break the tip off," I said, my voice raspy from pain. "I will pull it through from the front."

He did, and I cannot begin to tell you how it hurt. But this I had vowed: I would not scream or beg for mercy. If the heathens were going to kill me, I would make them work for every minute of their glorious little victory.

I tossed the broken, bloody shaft onto the ground in front of the leader's horse.

"Take it," I said. "Our army will track you down and you will need all the arrows you can find."

"I know you," he said.

By now I could see the fifth Indio, coming slow on his horse. The leader turned to watch him for a moment, then raised his bow and gave a war whoop. The rider gave a whoop and raised his lance high in his dark hand.

The leader turned back to me. "I know you," he said again.

I could hardly bear weight on my wounded leg and I was already feeling weak from loss of blood. I braced myself against Acuña and said, "I am General Juan Mateo Manje of the Army of Spain. This is Captain Francisco Acuña. Yes, I suspect you know of us. I suspect you have run from us and hidden from us many times like the cowards you are."

"I know of you," the Jocome said. "And I have seen you."

He fitted another arrow to his bowstring and fought to steady his horse, which by now was excited by the smell of blood, snorting and trying to rear.

The fifth rider had reached us now. He was slender but strong-looking, with big hands and wide shoulders. Young. I guessed his age at seventeen or eighteen.

Madre de Dios! He had painted his face with vermilion and ocher like the others, and he had put on some weight, but now I recognized him! Actually I did not know his name, because he never spoke in the weeks my wife and I tended him in our home, but this was the boy White Leaf wounded at my ranch the year before! When he recovered, I gave him one of my best horses and escorted him to the Río Bavispe and watched as he joined his friends on a ridge overlooking the river. Now, his horse—*my* horse at one time—had blood stains spreading over a foreleg. So Acuña and I had not missed, after all.

"Hola, muchacho," I said to the boy. *Hello, young man.*

He nodded but said nothing, his face as dark and blank as granite.

The leader said something. The boy nodded. The leader aimed his arrow at me. At my *other* leg, this time. Before he killed me he would give me the pain he had promised. All right; if this was God's will, so be it. The arrow ripped my clothes and took skin and gristle off my left leg. It burned like fire and blood soaked my pants, but I made no sound. I gave him no satisfaction.

He loaded another arrow.

But now the boy held up his hand and said something. The leader answered him and the two talked quietly for a moment. Then the older man shook his head angrily and spat out a string of words that had to be curses. He raised his bow, brought the arrow to bear on my chest. He pulled back on the string; I could see the muscles flexing in his brawny shoulders. The boy spoke again, louder now. Then he lowered his voice and said something more. What he said, I had no idea, but the older man's eyes widened. He looked at the boy, then back at me.

He slowly lowered his bow.

He studied me from the back of his horse, his dark eyes moving calmly over me. Finally he said, "Do you know who I am, Spaniard?"

I shook my head. "I know you are an Jocome and you kill defenseless people. That is all I need to know about you." I felt dizzy; the pain had grown almost unbearable in my legs.

"We fought once, many years ago. Near Imuris. You were with the Santo-Jesus-hay you call Keeno."

I stared at him. "Are you Bl— ?"

"I am Black Skull."

"*Madre de Dios*," I said softly.

He pointed at the boy. "My son," he said. "I will not kill you today because of the kindness you showed him last year. Without the care you gave him, he would have died. I knew about the kindness; I did not know it was you who gave it."

I glanced at the boy. Somewhere in a back corner of my mind I remembered a toddler playing in the grass in a clearing the day I fought Black Skull. Ish-kay-nay, was that his name? Maybe a year old at the time.

I nodded. "I did not know the boy I helped was your son."

"...Would you have helped him if you had known?"

I thought about that. "Yes, I think I would have."

Black Skull stared at me, but made no reply. Finally he reined his pony around, motioning for his men to follow. We watched as they rode slowly away. They stopped once and looked back at us, then headed for the mountains at a gallop, dust rising like wisps of gray smoke behind them.

Acuña made the sign of the cross and grinned through the blood on his face. "God has smiled on us today."

"He usually does," I said.

"Let's go find that creek, amigo, and get ourselves cleaned up."

"That, my friend," I said, "is an excellent idea."

We hobbled to the creek and drank cool clean water and bathed our wounds in the shade of the cottonwoods. That evening, some Pimas we knew from Tucubavia stopped at the creek to water their horses. They were surprised to find us there, of course; they gave us pinole and wheat biscuits to eat and retrieved our saddles and tack from our dead horses. They looked for our mules, but found no trace of them. When we were rested, they took us to San Juan.

I had plenty of time that summer to think about Black Skull and his son, as I spent almost a month in the presidio infirmary under the care of the post surgeon and my wife, who came from Banamichi to tend my wounds.

Though I had ample time to think about the Jocomes, I confess I thought about them very little. I had other priorities.

In those long weeks at the infirmary my wife and I talked of many things—the ranch, our children, our hopes for the future. We read good books together, and prayed, and occasionally we went out to eat in one of the fine cafés that San Juan was known for. I wrote letters to Father Kino, to Father Campos, to my in-laws in Sonora, even to my mother in Aragón—and received many letters wishing me well. When I was mended enough, my wife took me home in a carriage to our hacienda. The summer passed quickly. My duties at the ranch kept me busy and helped me gain strength. By autumn I knew I was back to normal. Well, as close to normal as I would ever be again. My right leg would bother me for the rest of my life and my back, probably broken in one of my falls, would never be completely free from pain. Still, by October I was riding every day, tending my livestock and supervising my vaqueros.

In late autumn I rode to Dolores to visit Father Kino.

I arrived there on November 2nd, the day known as Dia de los Muertos across Sonora. In my early years in the Pimería there had been little at Dolores but a scattering of mud-and-twig huts, a few irrigated fields of beans and corn and squash, Kino's adobe church, a few workshops and corrals, a small vineyard, and a few cooking ramadas. Now as I rode through the village I saw all of these, but I also saw small homes made of adobe, and more fields under cultivation, more livestock grazing on the hills, larger citrus orchards, a livery, gardens, more vineyards, a winery, and adobe shops that sold blankets and clothing and anything you could think of that was made from cotton or wool. I saw open air shops that offered meats and fresh vegetables, a small inn and café, and a shop that sold flintlock firearms.

Now, on the Day of the Dead, the cemetery grounds behind the church had been neatly groomed, the graves swept, the crosses freshly-painted and draped with ribbons of blue and red and yellow. Marigolds in painted earthen pots added their festive colors to the grounds. Even this early in the morning the place was crowded with people who had come to see old friends, to eat, to talk in low voices and pay their respects to the dead.

I reached the mission church in time for the first mass.

Father Kino took his sermon from the Book of Genesis. He told the Pimas about the great flood and Noah's boat and all the animals on the boat. He told them that we all came from Noah and his three sons and their wives, that we were all related in God's eyes, and that He expected the Pimas to treat everyone as if they were members of their own family. He gave his lesson first in Piman, then in Spanish, and the Indians seemed to enjoy it. Because this was a day for honoring the dead, the padre talked about death and how they should not fear it. The Lord, he told the Pimas, is preparing a place for them in His home in heaven and wants to welcome them there. Kino spoke with his usual passion and humor, and though he sang the liturgy a bit off-key, as he always did, no one seemed to care.

Later that day he took time from his clerical duties to visit with me. At his quarters—still the same one-room adobe in which he had lived when I first came to the Pimería—he warmed a pot of chocolate and poured cups for us. We sat on a bench outside the door in the warm sunlight.

"It is good to see you again, Juan Mateo," he said. "These days it seems our paths rarely cross. I hear you have had much success with your ranch."

"God has blessed me," I said.

"And how is your family?"

"They are well, Father. They send their best wishes."

He chuckled. "I hear you are still tormenting the Jocomes."

"You heard about my little altercation with Black Skull and his son?"

Kino nodded. "You did the boy a kindness, and the father recognized that. That is how it should be."

I took a sip of chocolate and watched a family of Pimas—father, mother, and two girls—walking to the cemetery, the mother carrying a wreath of marigolds. Possibly for the grave of a stillborn, or maybe a child who died from measles or pneumonia. Or here, in this part of the world, a friend or family member dead at the hands of Apaches.

"Do you think we will ever have peace with the hostiles, Father?"

He glanced at me, then looked out at the cultivated fields and at cattle grazing lazily on the hillsides. "Not for many years, I fear," he said.

"Is there *anything* we can do to stop the killing?"

"At this point, I know of nothing," he said, a sigh in his voice.

The padre had changed in the years I had known him. His hair still tumbled over his forehead and curled over his ears, but it was no longer just slightly gray; now it was entirely white. He still had a look of strength and determination about him, but now his dark face was creased and roughened from long years in the sun and wind. His voice seemed softer, his manner a bit more subdued. Though he never complained about pain, he moved slower now and he seemed more stooped than the last time I had seen him. *Old man's bones*, the post surgeon would call it.

He had grown older in these years, definitely. Still, his blue eyes were clear and alert and I had no doubt that he could ride as many miles in a week as I, that he could still brand cattle all morning, hoe weeds out of the canals all afternoon, and preach into the night. Frankly, I could not imagine that he would ever slow his pace. Not until death took him, anyway.

"Do you have any journeys planned?" I asked him.

"Tomorrow," he said, smiling, "I have plans to ride up to San Ignacio to see Agustín Campos, and on up to Guevavi and Tumacácori to look at some new irrigation canals the Pimas are building along the Santa María. Would you like to come?"

"I wish I had the time, Father."

"Perhaps next year then." A breeze nudged the mesquites that grew nearby and brought the rich smells of grilling meats from vendors selling near the cemetery.

"I hear that you and Father Campos are building a new chapel at Magdalena," I said.

Now he smiled widely, and in his face I saw the Kino I had known in earlier times. "God has given us the resources to build it," he said, his eyes sparkling, "and we praise Him for that. Agustín has done much of the planning and supervised most of the construction and, as always, he has done an excellent job. He tells me the new chapel will be completed by next spring. Probably March, he says, if all goes well. He plans to call it the Chapel of San Xavier, and he has asked me to sing the Mass of Dedication."

"I hope you will, Father."

"Of course I will," he said.

I stayed that night at the inn. Sometime in the early morning hours clouds came in and gave rain that made puddles in front of my casita and pattered and plonked on the window shutters and narrow wooden door. It was a sound rarely heard this time of year, and when it first awoke me, I lay for a time in my bed, enjoying it, not wanting to return to sleep. But finally I drifted off and slept until the first rays of morning light slipped into my room.

I dressed quickly and went to the church to help Kino load his pack animals and ready his horse for his trip to San Ignacio and the northern lands. The clouds had moved to the east and the sky looked like pale blue cream, the rising sun like a ball of molten gold. A cold breeze stirred the damp air. Mid-day, I knew, would bring warmer temperatures, but for now I was glad I had worn a coat.

When we had the mules loaded and tethered in a rope line I said, "I hope you plan on taking servants and soldiers, Father."

"A few," he said. Today he was wearing dark pants, a faded cotton shirt, and a wide-brimmed hat made of yellow straw. He did not look much like a priest, though I did not suppose it mattered a lot. I could think of no one over the age of two in the Pimería who did not know who he was.

"Please give Father Campos my regards," I said.

"I will. He will be sorry he missed you."

Down at the river the leaves of the cottonwoods and sycamores were turning to copper and gold. I saw ravens circling high above the trees, their *quoking* calls audible even from that distance in the thin, clear air. I could see dew sparkling on the willows near the river, and I could smell the dampness of the earth, the strong odors of the mules, and the wet planks of pine and oak that we had loaded. Around us the mountains seemed patched in shades of green and purple, all muted and veiled now by the lingering morning mist.

I began to saddle the padre's horse for him. When I had the strap cinched I said, "It is a beautiful morning. A fine morning for a ride."

"A fine day to carry God's Word, Juan Mateo."

I hung his astrolabe on a cord over the pommel. "Father, do you think we will be able to hold on to this land?" I cannot say what prompted my question. Perhaps I was feeling patriotic, or philosophical, or perhaps just worried, I do not know.

Kino looked around, taking in the mountains, the desert, the river. "Yes, I think we can hold it," he said, finally, "at least for a time. Civilization is coming, Juan Mateo. More people, more villages; more everything. North to the Colorado and up into the despoblado, as far west as the Pacific and as far east as the Atlantic—settlers will fill these areas in numbers that we can hardly imagine, and God will bless them richly. The Apaches cannot stop that. The ma'makai cannot stop it."

"But I do not know," he added, "that this land will always belong to Spain."

"Who could take it from us? Russia, France? England?"

"Any of them could try."

Madre de Dios, I thought. "Who among them could succeed, Father?"

He chuckled. "You should know such things better than I."

I handed him the rope line for the mules.

"But what about Spain's claim to it?" I said.

Smile lines crinkled at the corners of his eyes. "You are full of questions for which I have no answers, my friend." He made the sign of the cross. "But God has the answers. We just have to wait and trust Him to tell us. And He will, when He is ready."

"Oh, wait," I told him. "I almost forgot something." From my saddlebag I took the baroque crucifix of bronze that I had found in the old trunk on Baboquivari. I handed it up to him. "I cleaned it as well as I could."

"This is for me? Thank you, Juan Mateo. It is beautiful!"

The cross seemed to almost glow in the morning sunlight. I had given it a new rawhide cord, and now the padre slipped it over his head and snugged it around his neck so the crucifix lay on the front of his faded cotton shirt.

He was beaming. "How did you know? The one I have worn for years I lost not two weeks ago." He laughed. "My horse stepped on it and broke it. And now God has brought me another, even more beautiful. Can you believe it?"

He stared at me for a moment, his face serious now. "I know you worry, Juan Mateo. About the Apaches, the Jocomes. The English, the French. Por favor, do not fret about such things. Your responsibilities now are for your wife and family. Do you remember what the Lord requires of us?"

I remembered. "Micah, chapter six, verse eight. He requires us to act justly, love mercy, and walk humbly with our God."

Kino was smiling as he reined his horse around. He turned in his saddle, his white hair glistening in the sunlight, his blue eyes shining.

I wondered if he would have any last words for me.

As usual, he did. "God is in control, my friend," he said. "That is all we really need to know."

This was the last time I would see Father Kino. He would die in March of the following year, 1711, with his old friend, Campos, at his side in Magdalena only a few hours after singing the Mass of Dedication for the new Chapel of San Xavier. And that beautiful chapel is where he would be buried.

In the years since, I have missed him greatly, of course, but I have never been alone in my grief. He is mourned by all who knew him. I have often found myself wishing I had had more time with him. More time to know his thoughts, to absorb his energy, to take from his store of wisdom; more time simply to enjoy his company. Still, I recognize that God had blessed me with many good hours and days in the company of this fine man, and for that I have always been grateful.

What he died of, I never heard, but it pleases me to know the Apaches never stopped him. Nor did the Jocomes or the ma'makai; or illness or accident. No, when God was ready for the padre, He simply came for him.

To me, all of this seemed fitting and proper.

It was fitting and proper, too, I believe, that the last time I saw Kino he had his Bible in one hand, his astrolabe in the other, and a beautiful crucifix at his breast. And he was riding out to visit his Pimas, the people he loved.

God is in control, mi amigo, and that is all our padre really needed to know.

CHAPTER 50 Magdalena, Sonora. May, 1966.

"Like peeling away layers of an onion," Olvera said.

Romano chuckled. He leaned closer to the partially-exposed skeleton in trench 17B and brushed dirt from one of the ribs.

"But *slower* than peeling an onion," he said.

"Slow is good," Wasley said, grinning. "Except that we want the answers *now*."

"You'll have them," Romano said, "in due time."

Since discovery of the skull in 17B between the 2nd and 3rd footings on the west side of the chapel nave, Romano had been carefully exposing the general outlines of the skeleton. Now, with layers of the arid dark soil peeled away, the scientists were getting their first glimpses of solid gray bone: the pelvis and a proximal femur, an elbow, a few metatarsals, parts of the rib cage. *An adult*, Romano assured them. A *male*. Olvera and Wasley pressed him, of course: Was it a European? Was it *Kino*?

"Mother of God!" Romano had said with mock exasperation. "These things take time!"

And now, in fact, they had more time, because the Minister had extended their funding. Professor Jiménez had telephoned him with news of their latest find, had asked for additional time. At first the Minister refused, claiming the pesos were obligated to other worthy projects. But Jiménez reminded him that the citizens of Sonora loved their padre, that many of these citizens were of voting age, and that discovery of Kino's remains would put many favorable articles about the Minister—and of course his favorite official photograph—on the front pages of every major newspaper in Sonora. Maybe even a few in Mexico City. The Minister's voice lost most of its edge. "You really have reason to think this is Kino?"

"We believe it's him, sir," Jiménez said pleasantly. "If we had another week or so, we could know for sure."

"Of course, then! Now that I realize you simply need more time to continue the excellent work you've been doing, I'm honored to put the resources of our humble government at your disposal. For one more week."

And Jiménez had said, "Thank you, Minister, you're most generous."

By the end of that day, though, they still hadn't proved the remains were Kino's. Nor had they the next. Romano cautioned them: *The man wasn't carrying any ID.* And he'd reminded them that the only proof they would ever have would be largely circumstantial. "Small proofs," he had said. "We look for many of them and hope they all somehow add up to one big, irrefutable proof. In physical anthropology, that's how we do it. That's the best we can ever do."

Over the next few days, though, they added nicely to their growing assortment of small proofs. They found: the cobblestone pedraplén of the chapel's bell tower, deep in the earth near its east wall; the jumbled bones of Fathers González and Iturmendi precisely where Campos said he'd buried them—on the left and right sides of the nave, at its north end; the bones of José Vega, the Indio, near the middle of the west wall. They already had the skeleton of Noriega, the Spaniard, beneath the doorway along the south wall. Olvera even found the footings of the buttress, deep in the earth just outside the chapel's east wall.

When the scientists had met again in Romano's field lab, Jiménez wasted no time. "Gentlemen," he said, "we've made certain assumptions about the skeleton in 17B based on the fact that we believe the foundations are those of Kino's chapel. I understand Jorge has found a buttress. Are we now in agreement that we have Kino's chapel? Jorge? Are you satisfied?"

"Absolutely, sir."

"Arturo?" Jiménez said.

"I'm convinced of it," Romano said.

"And you, Bill?"

"You bet," Wasley said. "The building is too small for a church. It's the right size for a chapel. The footings are identical to those of the churches at Remedios and Cocóspera—and we know Kino built those. And we have all those bones and a buttress that are exactly where they're supposed to be. Yes, this has to be Kino's Chapel of San Xavier."

"All right," Jiménez said. "Arturo has already assured us that the bones in 17B are those of an adult male, and we know that Kino was sixty-five years old when he died. So we come to the biggest question of all: Arturo, are you now convinced that these are the bones of a *western European* adult male of the *right age*?"

Romano nodded. "I'm sure of it."

"Small proofs, but important ones," Jiménez said, and smiled.

But the biggest proof that they'd found Kino would come the next day.

"What is that?" Olvera said, pointing at a vague area of thickening over the rib cage of the skeleton in 17B. The workmen had enlarged the trench, making more space at the bottom. Now the scientists were huddled around the bones, Romano closest, Romano carefully brushing sand and grit from the sternum and ribs in the warm sunlight that streamed in from above.

"Jorge is right," Wasley whispered. "There, on top of the clavicle. Left side. At the proximal end."

Romano cautiously teased more dirt from the sternum and left collarbone. At first the scientists could make out only an ill-defined something, a vague shape that lent an odd lumpiness to the veneer of detritus still covering the clavicle. With gentle strokes Romano worked dirt and sand from its surface. Slowly, gradually, it came into view. Across the left clavicle, corroded but definite and undeniable: a crucifix, maybe two inches in length, the sculpted figure of Jesus still recognizable.

"Madre de Dios," Olvera whispered. His pulse raced in his temples and he felt an odd prickling on the skin of his face.

"Praise be to God," Romano said softly.

"Bronze," Wasley murmured. "Baroque style, seventeenth century—"

"The size is right, too," Olvera said, his voice low. "The Jesuits wore such crosses on a cord around their neck." He wondered why he was whispering, why all of them were whispering. His legs felt weak, his mouth so dry he could hardly swallow.

Wasley said, "It's him, isn't it. It's really him. Eusebio Kino."

Olvera nodded. "Madre de Dios," he whispered again. "Yes, it's him."

That evening, Olvera met Wasley and Romano in the plaza. The air was cool and pleasant and Olvera could hear the faint chinging of wind chimes from the doorway of the store that sold books and religious items to tourists from Arizona. He grinned. "Well, my friends," he said, "we did it."

Romano said, "What's next for you, Jorge? Back to Mexico City?"

"Soon, yes," Olvera told him.

"And you, Bill? Back to Tucson?"

"As soon as I can pack my bags."

"I'll stay," Romano said, "and finish my examination of the bones and prepare my written reports. With luck, it won't take long." The warm scent of orange blossoms drifted in from trees that grew along the street.

"It's a funny thing," Wasley said. "We go to interesting places and play in the dirt and have a fine time of it, yet we're always happiest when we're heading home."

"Anyone hungry?" someone said.

They walked to a café on Calle Madero and had iced tea and carne asada with tortillas. They talked of their families, of their careers, of digs they'd been on and strange things they'd seen. For dessert they had empanadas drenched in chocolate, and, later, coffee.

The evening passed in pleasant conversation.

After a time, though, they didn't say a lot. There didn't seem to be much more that needed saying. They'd come to find the padre, and they had found him.

AUTHOR'S AFTERWORD

If this story is too long, Kino himself is to blame, so many and so continued were his activities.

These aren't my words. They're the words of Herbert E. Bolton in the closing pages of *Rim of Christendom*, his detailed and masterful biography of Kino. Bolton was right: the padre's activities were indeed many and continued, and today in the borderlands of northern Sonora and southern Arizona we can still see the salutary effects of his ministry. He rode into the Pimería to change the O'odham, to make their lives better. At this he was immensely successful.

But Bolton's choice of the word "continued" is informative. It reminds us that the process of change, once begun, is often unstoppable.

After Kino's death in 1711, the Spanish army often left the missions of the Pimería unprotected. Whether this was due to a shortage of soldiers or a change in priorities, the result was the same: a frontier mission system increasingly at the mercy of its enemies. Father Campos and the other priests did what they could to protect the Indians and keep the churches going, but in time many of the missions became little more than visitas, some even abandoned. The Apaches grew bolder, their attacks more destructive. This forced the Pimas and Papagos to spend more time fighting and less time tending to their families, their crops, and their faith.

Some Pimas held firm to their Catholic religion, some returned to their native beliefs, and some managed to blend the two into traditions that barely resembled either. There was little the priests could do about it. But the problems facing the fathers were even greater than they knew: In Mexico City and Madrid, government and Church authorities had come, over the years, to distrust the Jesuits. *They're taking too much authority for themselves, these Jesuits,* they said. *They won't listen to us. They think they know what's best for the Indios. They won't even allow us to collect taxes from the Indios on the food and textiles they produce at the missions.* The voices of discontent grew louder. By 1767, Carlos III could no longer ignore the complaints; he ordered all Jesuits arrested, put in chains, and brought back to Europe. The following year he requested that the Church send priests of other orders as well as secular, diocesan priests to replace the Jesuits he'd expelled throughout the Empire. Franciscans took over most of the missions in Northwestern New Spain; other missions fell to the limited care of the secular bishops.

In time the missions were rebuilt, many of them in the form we see today. The Indians, some of them, came back to the faith. Others chose to keep their native beliefs or some combination of native and Catholic traditions. Some, especially in the twentieth century, became Protestants.

The routes by which goods and people moved between California and the vast lands of the Pimería and the busy commercial centers to the east changed, too. Though Kino never found a way to get his cattle across the Colorado River, others who followed him did. First by ferries, later by bridges. The padre had been right all along: California isn't an island.

The native villages changed, as well. They grew, of course, and the farmlands around them expanded with improved techniques for irrigation and well-drilling. But over the centuries many of the Indians moved away or intermarried with the Mexicans who came to the villages in increasing numbers, and many settlements gradually lost their Indian identity.

Perhaps Magdalena, the little village where Kino died, changed even more than most. Not long after the discovery of Kino's gravesite, citizens of the town formed a committee and charged it with the task of planning and building a monument to the padre. They brought in Francisco Artigas and Gustavo Aguilar, architects from Mexico City and Hermosillo, to design it, and hired a company, Constructa Federal de Escuelas Publicas, to build it.

The monument was dedicated on May 2, 1971—a beautiful park-like plaza in the center of the little town. Kino's skeleton, resting in precisely the spot where it was found, had been enclosed under a thick transparent plastic cover for viewing by the public and covered with an attractive gazebo-like roof. The citizens of Magdalena, as you might expect, are justifiably proud of their town and their monument and, especially, their padre. As part of their dedication ceremonies, they renamed their town Magdalena de Kino.

Today you can go there and see the padre's bones.

And what of Jorge Olvera, the archaeologist? His life, too, changed in major ways. After discovery of Father Kino's remains, he returned to Mexico City and finished his graduate studies. He and his wife, María Luisa, had a daughter. They named her Maricarmen and Olvera set about learning to be a good father as he settled into his busy new career. From that time on, he would work primarily in the fields of architectural and art history, in projects that would take him all over the world.

In a long, rambling, and highly enjoyable phone conversation I had with Dr. Olvera in October, 2001, he told me this story: His wife died, he said, when their daughter, Maricarmen, was still quite young. Not long after this, he had to go to Spain on business, and elected to take his daughter with him. He reminded me that he had never been a Christian, not in any real sense, and that he'd always thought of himself as an agnostic. Certainly he had never been a churchgoer.

In Madrid he fell at an excavation site and broke four ribs. The doctors, he told me, put him in a hospital and kept him there for several weeks. When they finally let him go, they advised him against flying back to Mexico until he was completely recovered. Since he had little else to do, he decided to drive to the old Spanish port city of Alicante on the Mediterranean. He wanted to visit the place, he said, because he knew Kino had stopped there on his sail from Genoa to Cádiz in 1678, and he just wanted to see it. Olvera reminded me that Kino had celebrated mass at the old church at Alicante, the church famous because it's where the Veil of Santa Veronica is kept on display. This was the cloth used by the compassionate woman to wipe Christ's brow on His way to Calvary. The cloth, Olvera, told me, was reputed to have a powerful effect on anyone who saw it. Of course he took his daughter, Maricarmen, with him to the coast.

In the church Maricarmen asked if she could pray for her mother. Olvera told me he was still feeling pain in his ribs. In fact the pain hadn't eased much at all and he was still having trouble bending. Even so, he knelt with his daughter, not out of any belief in prayer, but because at the time it just seemed like the right thing to do. When she finished her prayer, he rose from kneeling, he told me, and at that moment a very strange thing happened: the pain disappeared from his chest. It was gone.

"*Gone*?" I said.

"Completely. All of it. And it never came back."

"Maybe it was just coincidence," I suggested.

"It wasn't coincidence," he said firmly. "It wasn't my imagination, either."

"You're telling me that you were suddenly *healed*?"

"That's what I'm telling you," he said. "It was a miracle."

He went back to Madrid, he told me, and related the story to his doctors there. They took x-rays and did other tests and finally agreed with him: yes, it was a miracle. Later he sent copies of his medical records to someone at the Vatican, he couldn't remember whom. So they would know about this miracle, he said. I asked him if anything ever came of it. He said no, he'd never heard back from them.

We talked about other things for a while. Before we finished our conversation, though, I asked the question that had been hanging in the air:

"Did the miracle at Alicante make you a believer?"

"Oh, yes," he said. "Definitely. I'm a Christian now."

Did Olvera experience a real miracle? I don't know. Manje might have believed it. And Kino? It's hard to know what he would've thought. My readings have led me to believe that Kino had little time or energy for this sort of speculation. On the other hand, maybe it doesn't much matter what anyone else thinks. Maybe it only matters that Jorge Olvera believed it.

But it's an interesting story, isn't it? And it shows us yet another way in which Eusebio Kino changed the lives of those who followed him, even briefly, to his little chapel in Magdalena. He'd come many miles from the Tyrol of Italy to his beloved Sonoran desert, and we can only guess at how many other lives he has touched through the centuries in all of this great land he called the Pimería—on the Far Side of The Sea.

Ben Clevenger

GLOSSARY

acéquia – irrigation canal

adobe – bricks made from mud and straw, shaped in wood molds, and (in Kino's time) sun-dried

agua – water

alamillo – aspen tree; literally, little alamo

alamo – cottonwood tree

alférez – ensign, 2nd lieutenant; the lowest officer rank in the Spanish Army

ak chin – Pima term for the mouth of an arroyo; also, a term for summer flood-farming along desert washes

Akimel O'odham – see O'odham; the River People; proper name for the Indians known to Kino as Sobaipuris; lived along the San Pedro, Santa Cruz, and Gila Rivers

amigo – friend

año – year

Apache – probably from the Zuni word *Apachú*, meaning "enemy." Called themselves the Tinneh or Dine. In Kino's time, most lived north of the Gila River and east of the San Pedro River; they raided frequently in the Pimería, sometimes with Jocomes, Mansos, Sumas and other related tribes from the Sierra Madres in what is now the Mexican state of Chihuahua.

Apacheria – lands inhabited by Apaches

arquebus – early flintlock rifle; a musket

asalto – attack, assault

azul – blue

ba'bawi – Pima word for tepary beans

Bahia de Año Nuevo – the bay on the Pacific coast of Baja California where Father Kino first saw the blue abalone shells; now known as Laguna de San Gregorio

bajada – sloping alluvial fan of rock and gravel extending down the side of a mountain; from centuries of wear by rain and wind

barco – boat

botas – boots; also, leather or deerskin leg coverings comparable to modern gaiters

breviary – small book carried by priests on frontier; contained prayers, psalms, hymns, readings, quotations from Scripture and other teachings

bulto – statue

cabacera – mission that served as headquarters for other missions and visitas in the area; usually had a full-time priest; Dolores was a cabacera

caballo – horse

calabaza – squash, pumpkin; gourd with edible pulp, often used as water bottle

camino – road; trail

Camino del Diablo – the Devil's Highway, a rough trail from Caborca, Sonora, to the town now known as Yuma, Arizona; famous for heat and lack of water; many travelers have died on this route

camisa – shirt, blouse

campesino – farmer or settler, poor, usually mestizo

cantina – bar, saloon

capilla – chapel, small church; in Kino's time, these were made of adobe and roofed with mesquite or pine logs and saguaro ribs caulked with earth and twigs

cascabel – rattlesnake

Ce'dagi Mashath – Pima term for the month of March

cerro – hill

Cerro de Santa Clara – now known as Pinacate Peak; in northwestern Sonora

cerveceria – brewery

chumbera – prickly pear cactus

ciudad – town, city

Ciudad de Mexico – Mexico City; in Kino's time, the largest city in New Spain; built from the ruins of Tenochtitlan, the Aztec capital

Compañia Volante – a highly mobile cavalry unit used for fighting Apaches; originally commanded by Juan Mateo Manje's uncle, General Domingo Jironza Petris de Cruzat; Manje spent many years as an officer in this unit

cordillero – mountain range

Cosari – Pima village on the San Miguel River in present-day Sonora where Kino built his first mission in the Pimería, Nuestra Señora de los Dolores; this was his home base and headquarters for twenty-four years.

curandera – a woman, usually mestizo, who practiced herbal folk medicine

desierto – desert

diablo – devil

di-yin – Apache term for their medicine man; believed to have special powers over specific entities such as rain, war, sickness, animals, etc. In the 19th century, Geronimo, for instance, was considered by the Apaches to be a di-yin for war.

entrada – opening, entrance; term used by Spanish explorers to describe initial attempt at colonization of an area

epazote – from the Nahuatl (Aztec) word, epazotl; an herb used for the Rx of intestinal worms

escudo – Spanish gold coin; minted in several sizes, largest was the doubloon

espada – sword, usually long with narrow blade

espada ancha – sword with short, wide blade; favored by experienced Spanish cavalry officers

espadaña – bell tower; beam from which church bells hang

estómago – stomach

flecha – arrow (saeta, Latin)

gallinazo – turkey vulture

Gaybanipitea – small village of Sobaipuri Pimas on the San Pedro River (called the Río Terrenate in Kino's time), two miles south of Quiburi, a larger Pima village which was the home of Chief Coro; at site of present-day Fairbank, Arizona

Ghost Pony – in Apache belief system, a symbol representing death; to die was to ride the Ghost Pony

golfo – gulf

Golfo de California – now often called the Sea of Cortez

hai'itcottam – type of Pima medicine man; used herbs and simple therapies to treat illness and injury; did not rely on "magic" or threats of harm

hediondilla – creosote bush, sometimes called greasewood

Hia C'ed O'odham – proper name for some of the Pimas of the western desert called Sobas in Kino's time; hunter-gatherers; now often called Sand Papagos

hombre – man

iglesia – church

ihkow – Pima term for small edible root-potatoes that grow wild in the Pimería

IHS – in the Greek alphabet, the first three letters of the word, "Jesus." Used by Jesuits as symbol of their Order, the Society of Jesus

Indio – Spanish term for Indian of any tribe

ixtle – Nahuatl word for the fibers teased from agave leaves and used in making of slings in which water gourds were carried

jabali – javelina, the collared peccary

jefe – boss, supervisor

Jocome – small tribe related to Apaches; lived in the Sierra Madres in what is now the Mexican state of Chihuahua; often joined Apaches of Chiricahua, Nednhi, and Bedonkohe bands for raids in the Pimería; related to the Manso-, Jano-, and Sumo- Apaches of Chihuahua

ka'wyu – Pima word for horse

kih – Pima word for their small domed huts made of mud, twigs, and straw

lanza – lance

league – in Kino's time, about 2.5 miles

Libro de Entierros – a church's burial register, kept by priests

lickoyee – Apache word for white (the color)

llano – grassy plain

madre – mother

ma'makai – type of Pima medicine man; believed able to control weather, crops, and war, and able to cause disease and death; much feared by the Pimas

mayordomo de recua – pack-train master

mestizo – person of mixed Indian-Spanish blood

milgan – Pima term for any person of Spanish, Anglo, or European background *mofeta* – skunk

molino – mill

mosca – fly

muchacha – girl; young woman

muchacho – boy; young man

muerto – dead

mujer – woman

Nahuatl – the Aztec language

nogal – walnut or walnut tree; the modern city of Nogales on the Arizona-Mexico border takes its name from these trees, which grew wild in that area in Kino's time

nopal – the leaf (pad) of a prickly pear plant

Nuestra Señora de los Dolores – Kino's first mission in the Pimería; at the Pima village of Cosari on the Río San Miguel; Dolores remained his major mission base during his twenty-four years in the Pimería

Nueva España – New Spain

Ohb – in Kino's time, the Pima word for Apache

olla – an earthen jug used for storing water

O'odham – proper name for the Pima groups that occupied the Pimería Alta in Kino's time. The Papagos (Tohono O'odham) lived in the desert northwest of Dolores; the Sobaipuris (Akimel O'odham) lived north of Dolores along the Santa Cruz, San Pedro, and Gila Rivers; the Sobas (Hia C'ed O'odham) lived to the west, near the Gulf of California; other O'odham not clearly identified with these groups were simply called Pimas or Upper Pimas

Ópata – small tribe that occupied lands southeast of the Pimería; had villages at Cucurpe, Opodepe, Tuape, and San Juan Bautista; because they had been under Spanish rule longer, they were often placed in positions of authority over Pimas and Papagos in the newer missions of the Pimería

oso negro – black bear

oso plateado – grizzly bear

padre – father

Palacio Municipal – City Hall

Papabota – Manje's term for the Papagos

Papago – the Pima group that occupied the vast desert northwest of Dolores; from "bean eaters," so-called by Spanish because they were highly successful at cultivating tepary beans; now called Tohono O'odham

Papagueria – desert lands inhabited by the Papagos

Pater Noster – The Lord's Prayer; literally, Latin for Our Father

perezoso – lazy, slothful

pesh lickoyee – Apache term for silver; literally, white iron

peso – coin, usually silver, valued at eight reales

piedra – stone, rock

piedra de molino – millstone

Pimería Alta – literally, the "land of the Upper Pimas"; Kino's term for what is now much of northern Sonora and southern Arizona; it was bounded roughly by the Magdalena River on the south, the Gila River on the north, the San Pedro River on the east, and the Gulf of California on the west. More than 32,000 square miles.

pin'dah – Apache word for any person of Spanish, Anglo, or European ancestry; sometimes written as in'dah

pinole – powder or paste made of toasted corn, sometimes with added sugar, ground beans, or squash; eaten dry or mixed with water or other liquid to make a nourishing drink

pitahaya – Pima word for the fruit of the saguaro; ripens in early summer; eaten raw, also used in making jams and wine

plata - silver

poco – a little bit; slightly

por favor – please

pozole – soup or mush made of hominy, beans, spices; a porridge made of corn meal; sometimes written as posole

presidio – frontier outpost of the Spanish Army

Quechans – in Kino's time, a small Indian tribe with homeland near the junction of the Gila and Colorado Rivers; sometimes called Yumans

Quiburi – Sobaipuri Pima village on the San Pedro River; home of Chief Coro; two miles north of present-day Fairbank, Arizona

quince – a hard apple-like fruit used by Spanish for making jams, jellies, candy

rabia – rabies; common in the Pimería in Kino's time

ramada – covered shelter with corner posts of mesquite branches, roofed with rivercane, yucca leaves, twigs, etc.

rancheria – any Indio village

reata – rope, usually braided rawhide; lariat takes its origin from la reata

remuda – horses kept as spare mounts

retablo – on wall behind altar in a church, with niches for religious paintings and statues; in Kino's time, usually made of mesquite or pine

rio – river

sala – main room of a house; the living room

San – a male saint

San Dionysio – Quechan village located at junction of Gila and Colorado Rivers; now the modern city of Yuma, Arizona

San Juan Bautista – in Kino's time, a silver mining town that was the capital of the province of Sonora; headquarters of military and civil authorities of Sonora; about sixty miles southeast of Dolores

Santa – a female saint

Santa María River – now known as the Santa Cruz

si'atcokam – a type of Piman medicine man; diagnosed and treated illness with "magic" powers; shaman

sierra – mountain

Sierra Azul – mountain range north of Cosari and Kino's Dolores mission

Sierra Guachucas – now known as the Huachuca Mountains; near present-day town of Sierra Vista, Arizona

Sierra Madres – large mountain range in what is now north-central Mexico

Sierra Prieto – mountain range south of Cosari and Kino's Dolores mission

silla – Spanish word for chair

si'l – Pima word for saddle

Soba – see O'odham; smallest and most nomadic of the Pima groups, they lived in the western desert near the Gulf and survived primarily by hunting and gathering; now sometimes called Sand Papagos or Hia C'ed O'odham

Sobaipuri – see O'odham; Kino's term for the River Pimas (now known as the Akimel O'odham), one of the major Pima groups; lived along the Santa Cruz, San Pedro, and Gila Rivers in what is now Arizona; under their chief, Coro, they were fierce fighters against the Apache in Kino's time

soldado – soldier

taparrabo – loincloth; usually of undyed cotton

tepary beans – small white, tan, or brown beans that are native to the Pimería; rich in nutrients, resistant to drought and heat; cultivated by the O'odham

teniente – lieutenant

Terrenate River – now known as the San Pedro

tiburón – shark

tohono – Pima word for desert

Tohono O'odham – see O'odham; the Desert People; proper name for the Indians known to Kino as Papagos or Papabotas

Ussen – the main Apache god; sometimes written as Yusn; creator of White-Painted Woman and Child of the Water, the first Apaches

vaca – cow

vaquero – Spanish term for a man on horseback who tends cattle; origin of the word buckaroo

vara – unit of measurement, equals thirty-three inches

visita – small mission station with few facilities, often only a small ramada; used by visiting priests; located in smaller Pima rancherias

watto – Pima word for ramada, an open-air shelter roofed with branches, twigs, yucca leaves, etc.

zancudo – mosquito

REFERENCES & SUGGESTED READINGS

Bleser, Nicholas J. *Tumacácori; From Rancheria to National Monument.* Southwest Parks and Monuments Association

Bolton, Herbert E. *Kino's Historical Memoir of the Pimería Alta* (Bolton's English translation of Eusebio Kino's diary, *Favores Celestiales*). Berkeley and Los Angeles: University of California Press, 1948

Bolton, Herbert E. *Rim of Christendom; A Biography of Eusebio Francisco Kino.* Tucson: University of Arizona Press, 1936

Bolton, Herbert E. *The Padre on Horseback.* Chicago: Loyola University Press, 1932

Burrus, Ernest, S.J. *Kino and Manje; Explorers of Sonora and Arizona. St. Louis, Mo.*: Jesuit Historical Institute, 1971

Connolly, Sean. *Encyclopedia of Rifles & Handguns.* Edison, New Jersey: Chartwell Books, 1995

Dines, Glen. *Sun, Sand, and Steel; Costumes and Equipment of the Spanish/Mexican Southwest.* New York: G.P. Putnam's Sons, 1972

Fontana, Bernard L. *Of Earth & Little Rain.* Tucson: University of Arizona Press, 1989

Griffith, James S. *Beliefs and Holy Places; A Spiritual Geography of the Pimería Alta.* Tucson: University of Arizona Press, 1992

Haley, James L. *Apaches: A History and Culture Portrait.* Norman: University of Oklahoma Press, 1981

Hanson, Roseann Beggy; Hanson, Jonathan. *Southern Arizona Nature Almanac.* Boulder: Pruett Publishing Company, 1996

Hartmann, William K. *Desert Heart; Chronicles of the Sonoran Desert.* Tucson: Fisher Books, 1989

Karns, Harry J. *Luz de Tierra Incognita.* (Karns' English translation of Juan Mateo Manje's diary by the same name). Tucson: Arizona Silhouettes, 1954

Kessell, John L. *Spain in the Southwest.* Norman: University of Oklahoma Press, 2002

Lockwood, Frank C. *The Apache Indians.* Lincoln and London: University of Nebraska Press, 1938

Moore, Michael. *Medicinal Plants of the Desert and Canyon West.* Santa Fe: Museum of New Mexico Press, 1989

Morgan, Richard. *A Guide to Historic Missions and Churches of the Arizona-Sonora Borderlands.* Tucson: Adventures in Education, Inc., 1995

Officer, James E.; Schuetz-Miller, Mardith; Fontana, Bernard L. *The Pimería Alta; Missions & More.* Tucson: The Southwestern Mission Research Center, 1996

Olvera, Jorge. *Finding Father Kino.* Tucson: Southwestern Mission Research Center, 1998

Pickens, Buford. *The Missions of Northern Sonora; A 1935 Field Documentation.* Tucson: University of Arizona Press, 1993

Polzer, Charles W., S.J. *A Kino Guide; His Missions, His Monuments.* Tucson: Southwestern Mission Research Center, 1968

Polzer, Charles W., S.J. *Kino, A Legacy.* Tucson: Jesuit Fathers of Southern Arizona, 1998

Roca, Paul. *Paths of the Padres Through Sonora.* Tucson: Arizona Pioneers' Historical Society, 1967

Russell, Frank. *The Pima Indians.* Tucson: University of Arizona Press, 1975

Shaw, Anna Moore. *A Pima Past.* Tucson: University of Arizona Press, 1974

Smith, FayJackson; Kessell, John L.; Fox, Francis J. *Father Kino in Arizona.* Phoenix: Arizona Historical Foundation, 1966

Trimble, Marshall. *Arizona; A Panoramic History of a Frontier State.* Garden City, New York: Doubleday & Company, Inc., 1977

Walker, Kathleen. *San Xavier; The Spirit Endures.* Phoenix: Arizona Highways, 1998

Webb, George. *A Pima Remembers.* Tucson: University of Arizona Press, 1959

Wills, John E. *1688; A Global History.* New York: W.W. Norton & Co., 2001

Worcester, Donald E. *The Apaches – Eagles of the Southwest.* Norman: University of Oklahoma Press, 1979

Ben Clevenger was born and raised in the Southwest. He received the MD degree from the University of Oklahoma and specialized in pathology at George Washington University. Dr. Clevenger served as a medical officer in the USAF before moving to North Carolina, where he practiced medicine. Retired now, he lives with his wife in Arizona, where he enjoys hiking, writing, sailing, Southwestern history, and poking around old Spanish missions. His interest in Father Kino dates to the late eighties, when he first visited Mission San Xavier del Bac near Tucson.